THE RIBBON SKIRT

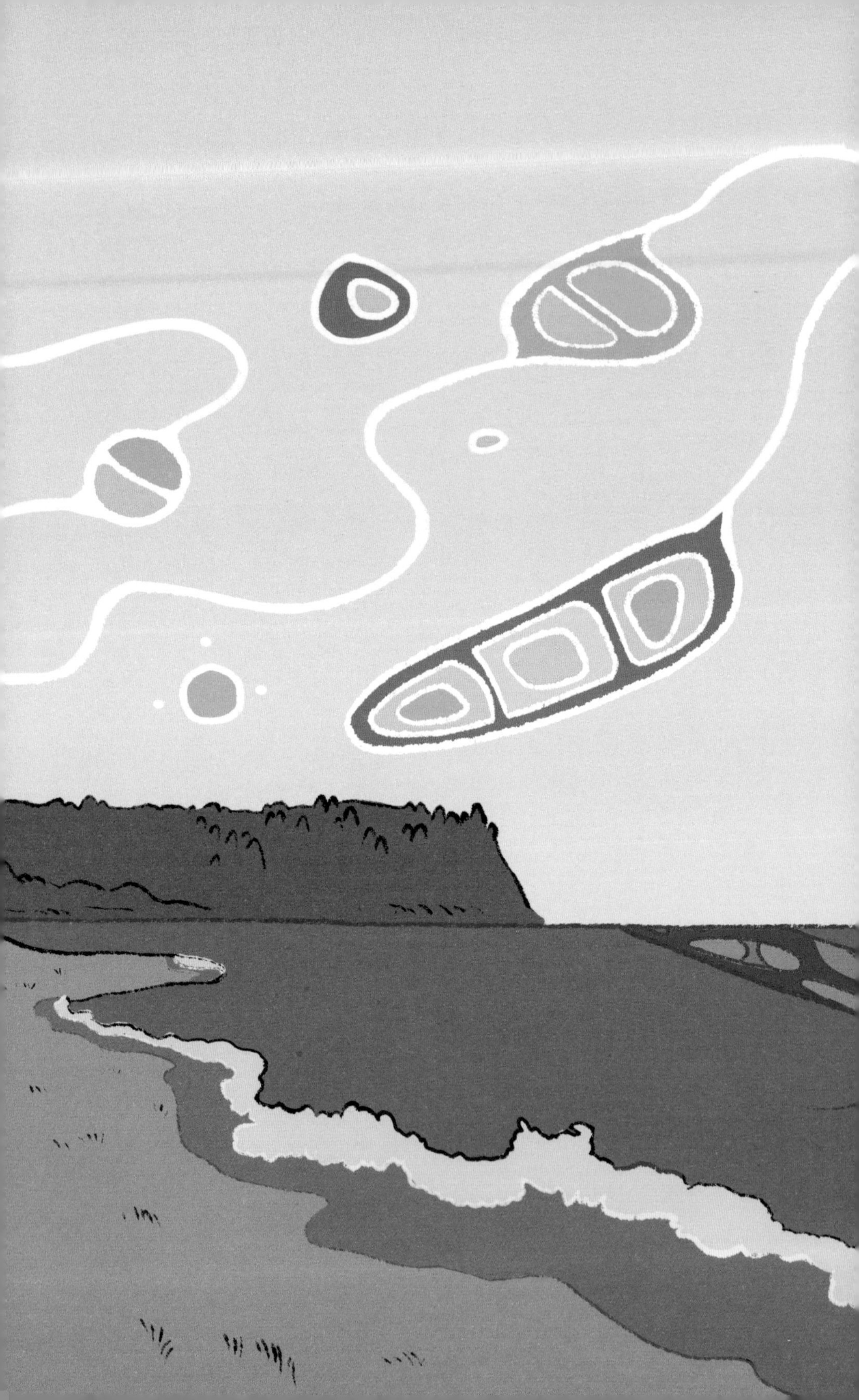

THE RIBBON SKIRT

CAMERON MUKWA

graphix

An Imprint of

SCHOLASTIC

Anang and their community speak Southwestern Ojibwe, also known as Minnesota Dialect of Anishinaabemowin. Anishinaabemowin is the name of the language spoken by the Ojibwe, Odawa, and Potawatomi peoples.

The author thanks Awanigiizhik Bruce for their help in checking the accuracy of the Anishinaabe language that appears throughout the book.

Copyright © 2024 by Cameron Mukwa

Library of Congress Control Number: 2023947646

ISBN 978-1-338-84326-2 (hardcover)
ISBN 978-1-338-84325-5 (paperback)

10 9 8 7 6 5 4 3 2 1   24 25 26 27 28

Printed in China   62
First edition, November 2024

Edited by Cassandra Pelham Fulton
Book design by Carina Taylor
Creative Director: Phil Falco
Publisher: David Saylor

Dedicated to two-spirit
kids of all shapes and sizes.
Your ancestors believe in you!

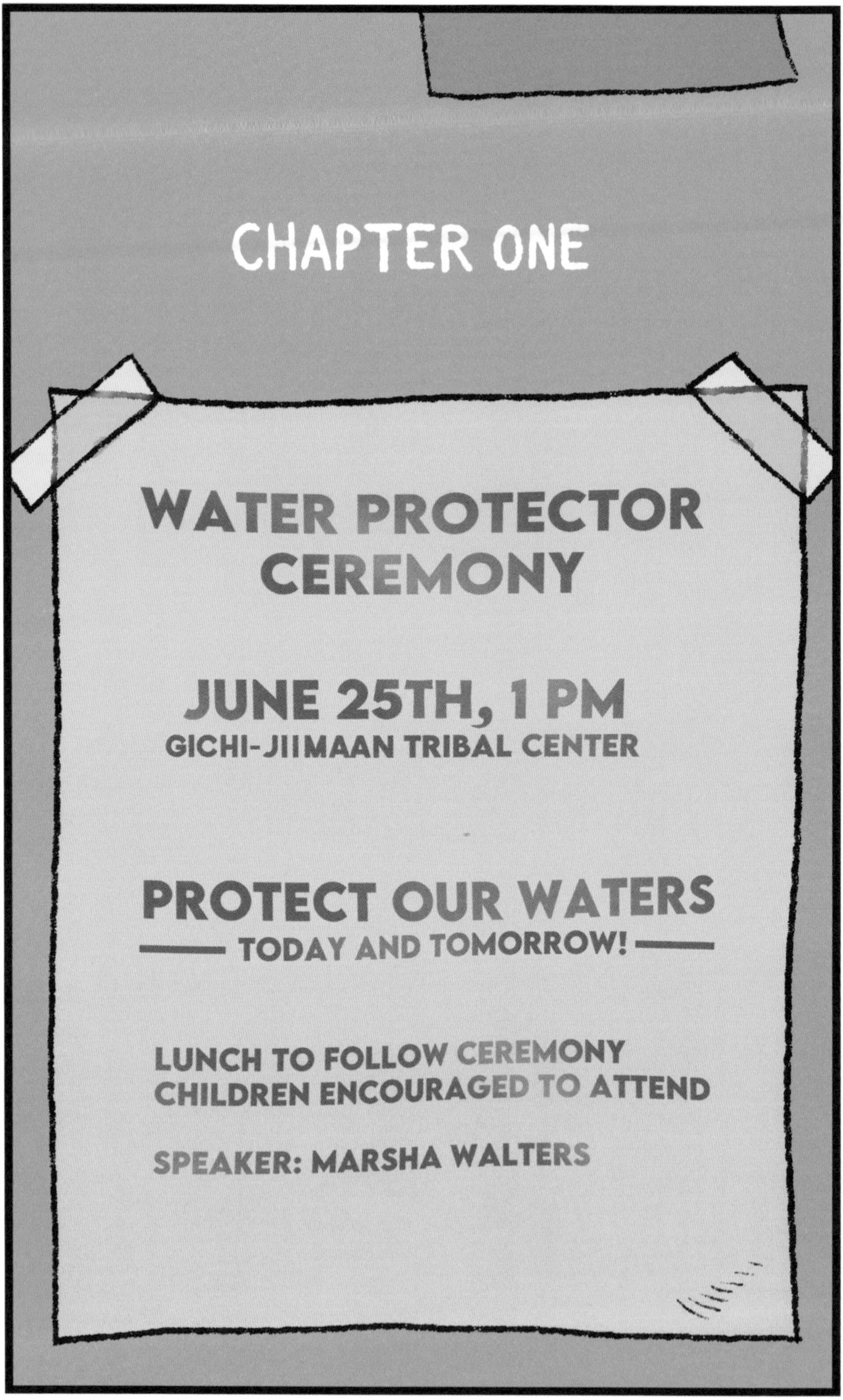
CHAPTER ONE
WATER PROTECTOR CEREMONY
JUNE 25TH, 1 PM
GICHI-JIIMAAN TRIBAL CENTER
PROTECT OUR WATERS
TODAY AND TOMORROW!
LUNCH TO FOLLOW CEREMONY
CHILDREN ENCOURAGED TO ATTEND
SPEAKER: MARSHA WALTERS

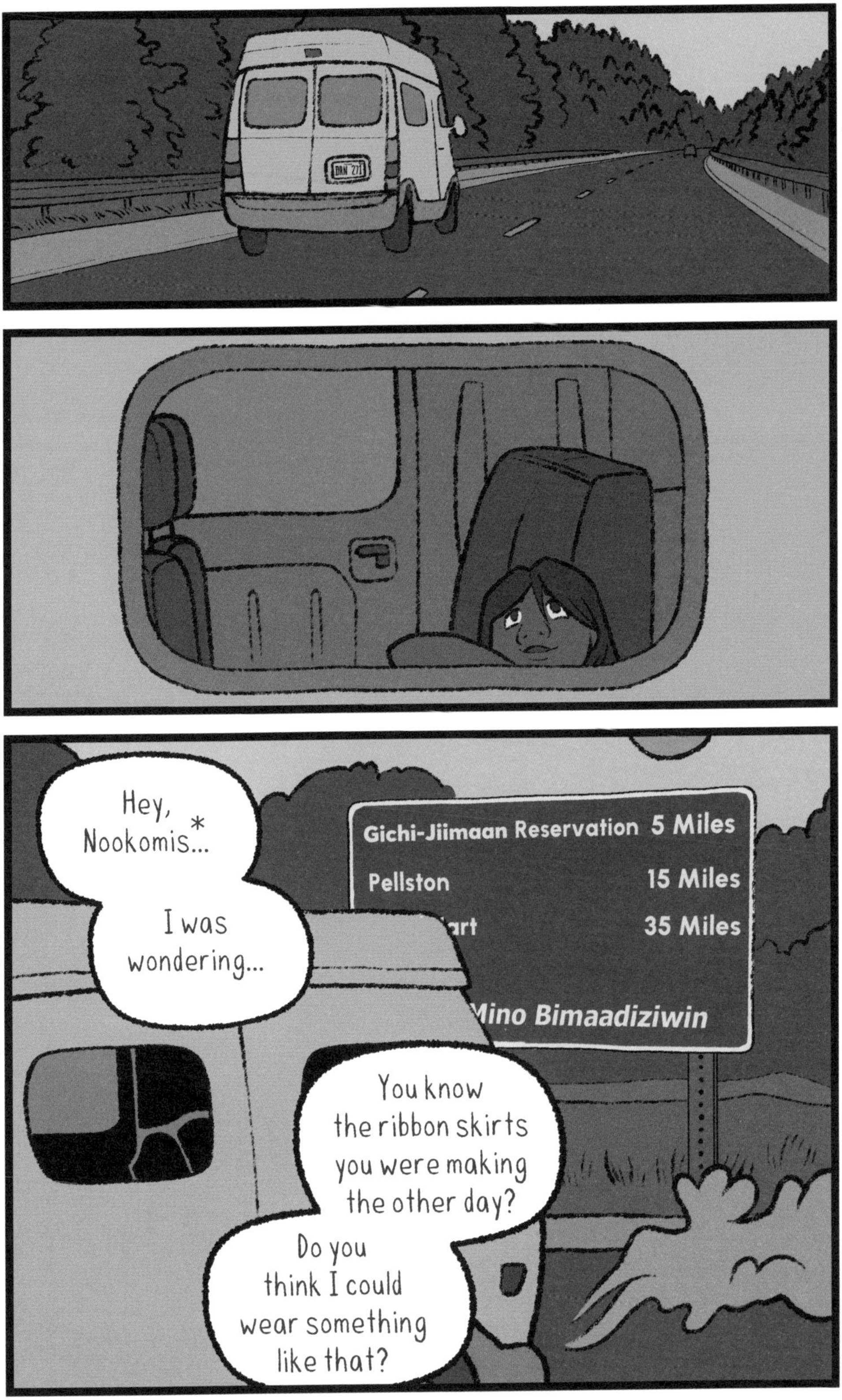
Gichi-Jiimaan Reservation 5 Miles
Pellston 15 Miles
35 Miles
Mino Bimaadiziwin
Hey, Nookomis...*
I was wondering...
You know the ribbon skirts you were making the other day?
Do you think I could wear something like that?

*Grandmother

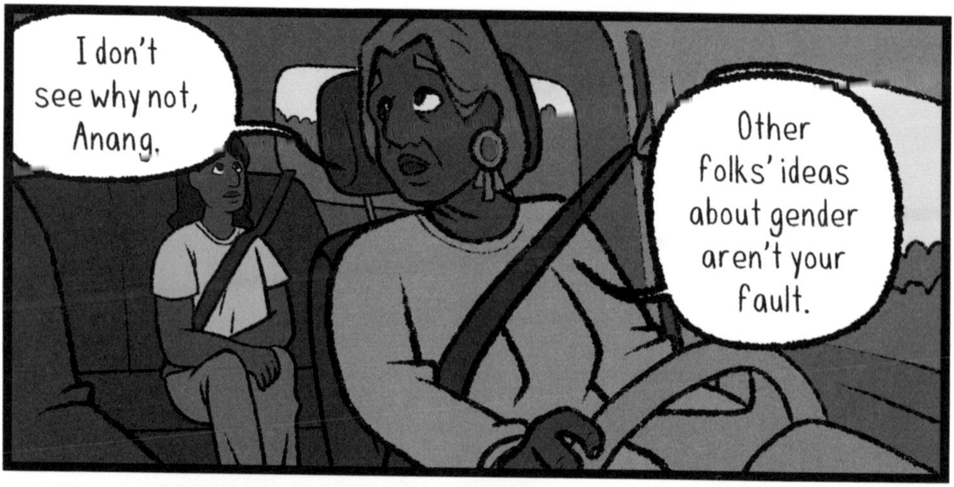
I don't see why not, Anang.
Other folks' ideas about gender aren't your fault.

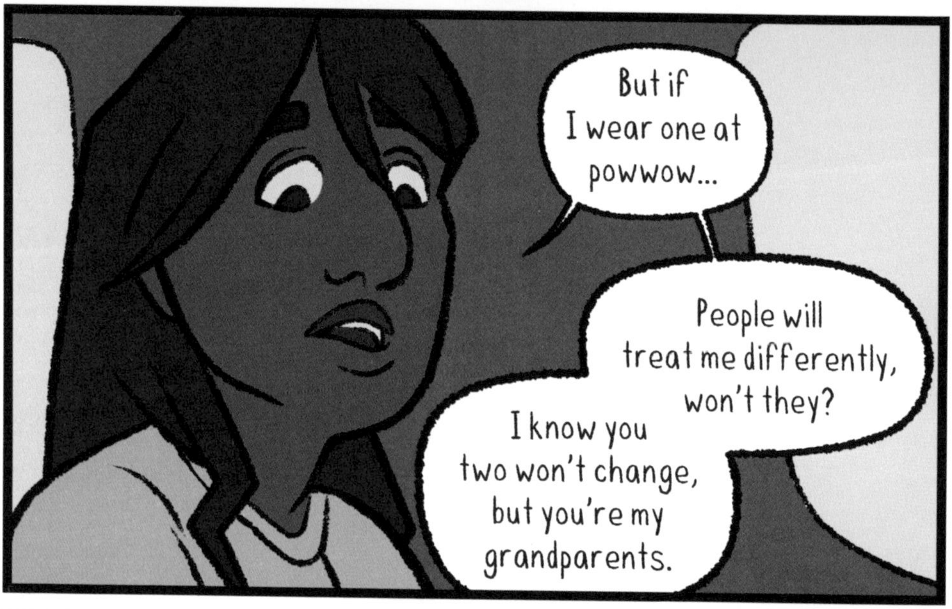
But if I wear one at powwow...
People will treat me differently, won't they?
I know you two won't change, but you're my grandparents.

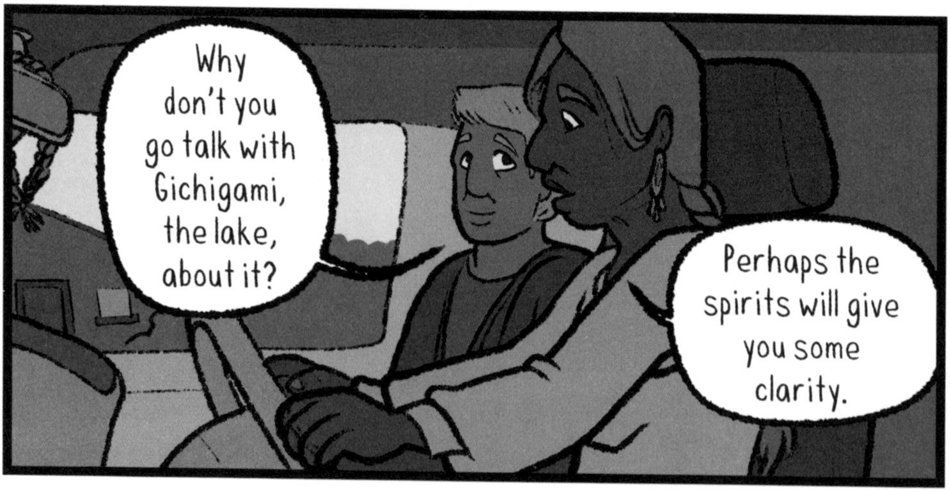
Why don't you go talk with Gichigami, the lake, about it?
Perhaps the spirits will give you some clarity.

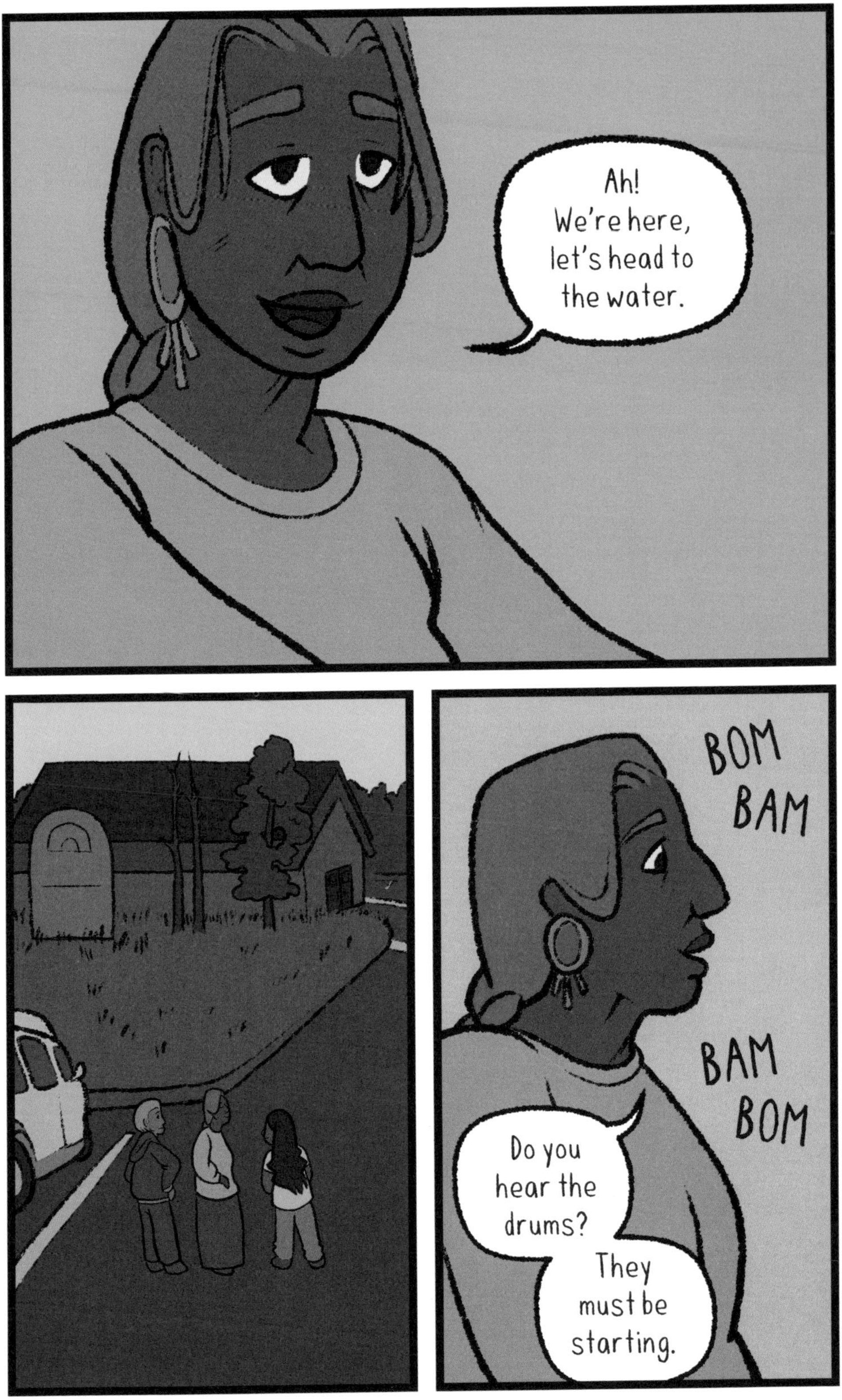
Ah! We're here, let's head to the water.
BOM BAM
BAM BOM
Do you hear the drums?
They must be starting.

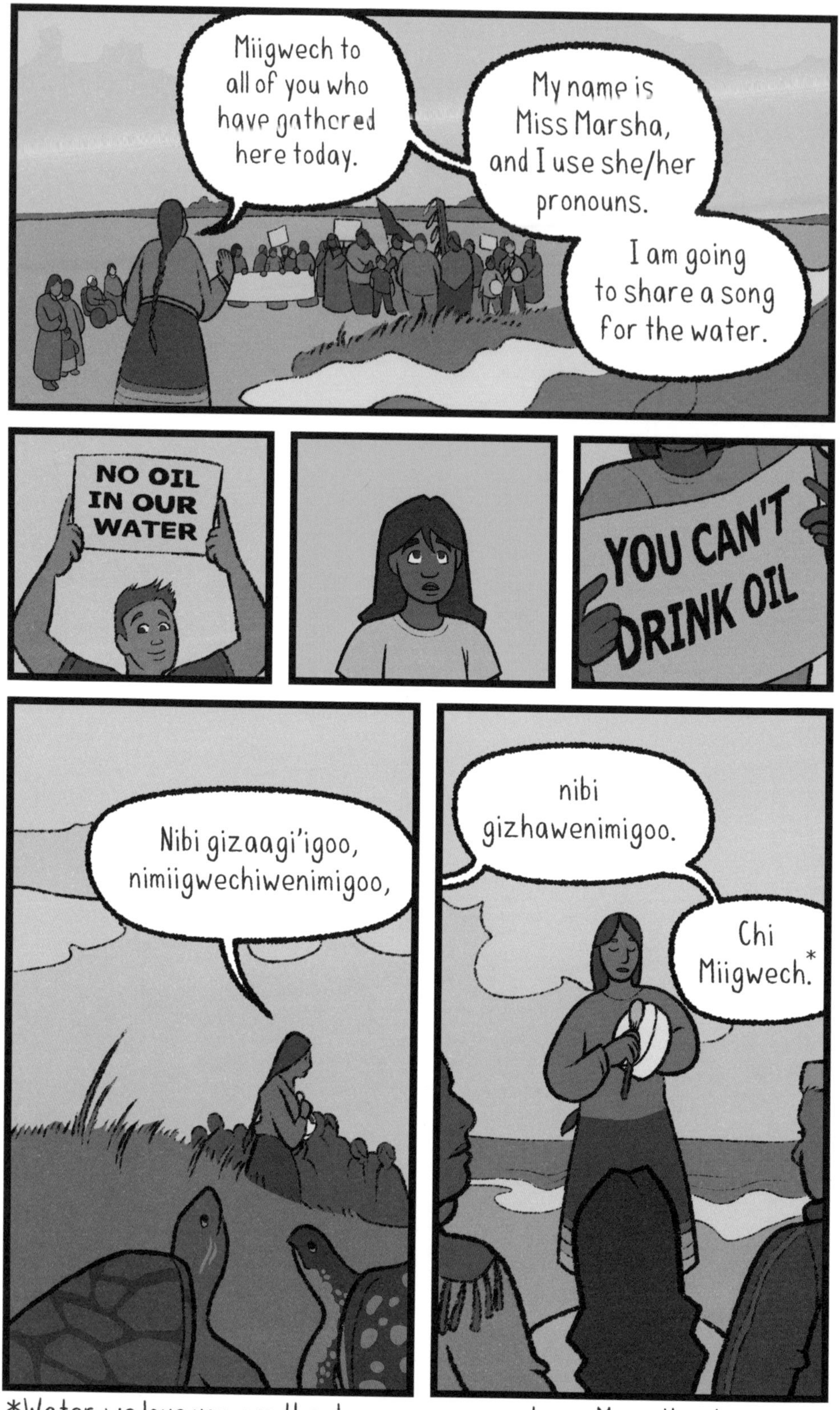
Miigwech to all of you who have gathered here today.
My name is Miss Marsha, and I use she/her pronouns.
I am going to share a song for the water.
NO OIL IN OUR WATER
YOU CAN'T DRINK OIL
Nibi gizaagi'igoo, nimiigwechiwenimigoo,
nibi gizhawenimigoo.
Chi Miigwech.*

*Water, we love you, we thank you, we respect you. Many thanks.

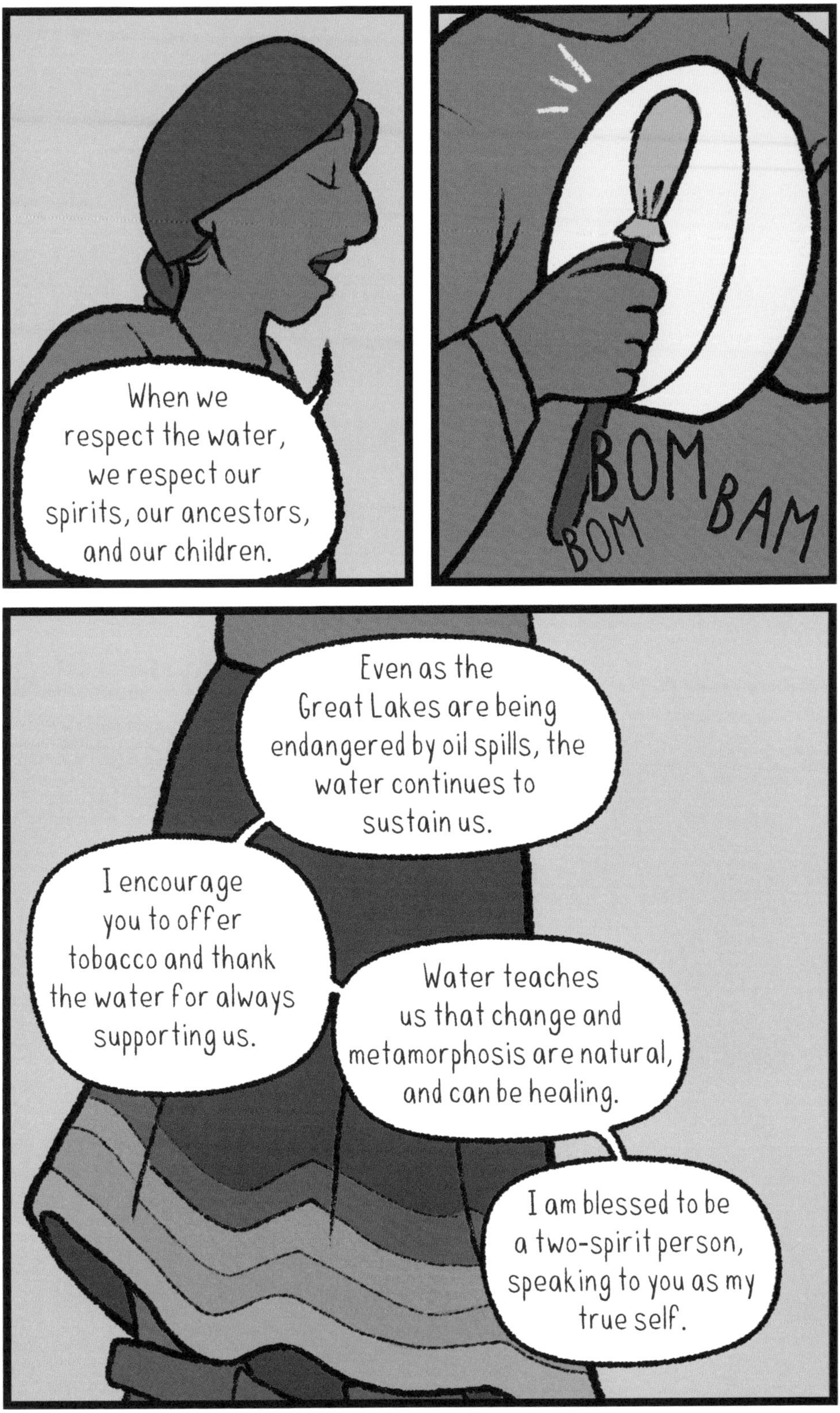
When we respect the water, we respect our spirits, our ancestors, and our children.
BOM
BOM
BAM
Even as the Great Lakes are being endangered by oil spills, the water continues to sustain us.
I encourage you to offer tobacco and thank the water for always supporting us.
Water teaches us that change and metamorphosis are natural, and can be healing.
I am blessed to be a two-spirit person, speaking to you as my true self.

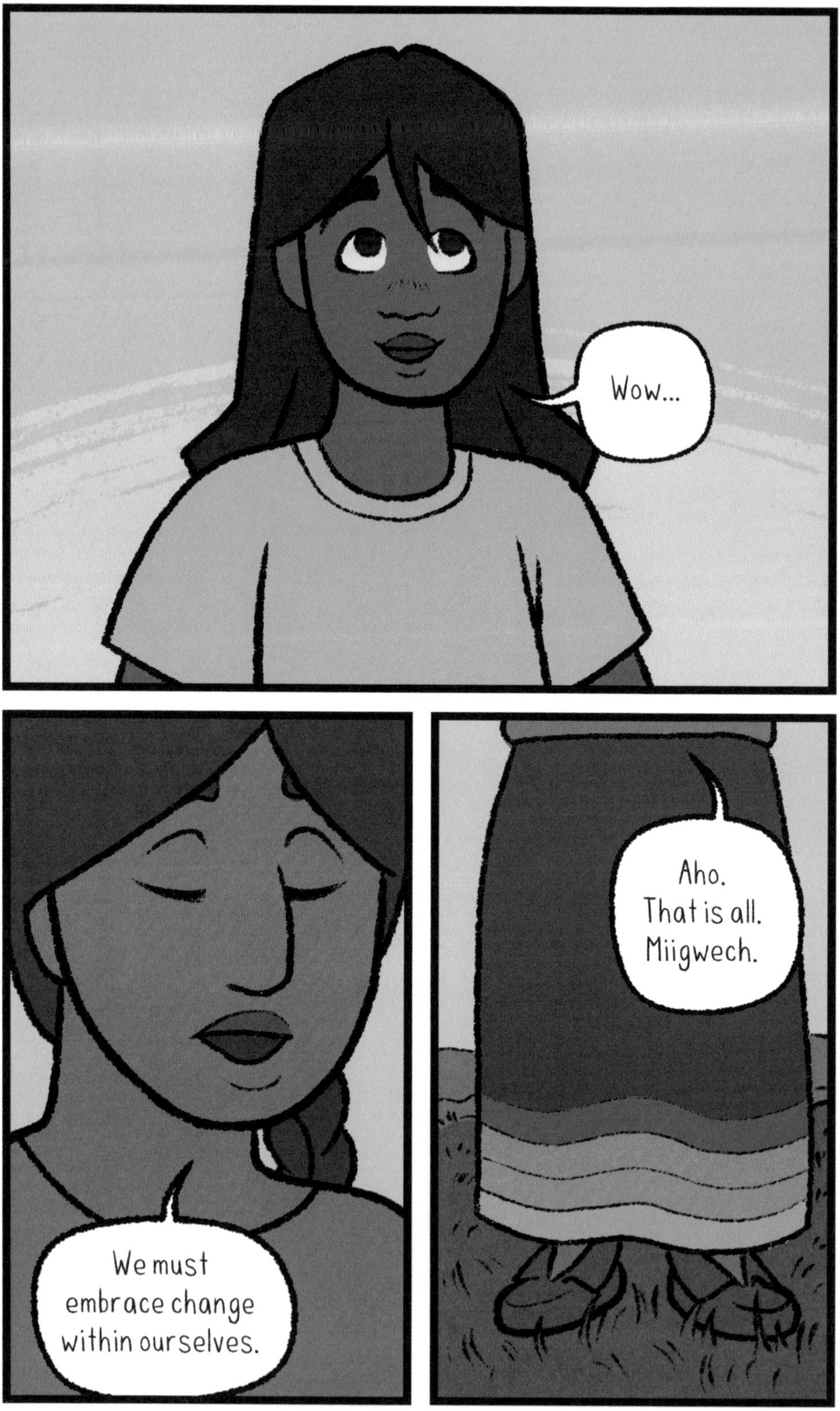
Wow...
We must embrace change within ourselves.
Aho. That is all. Miigwech.

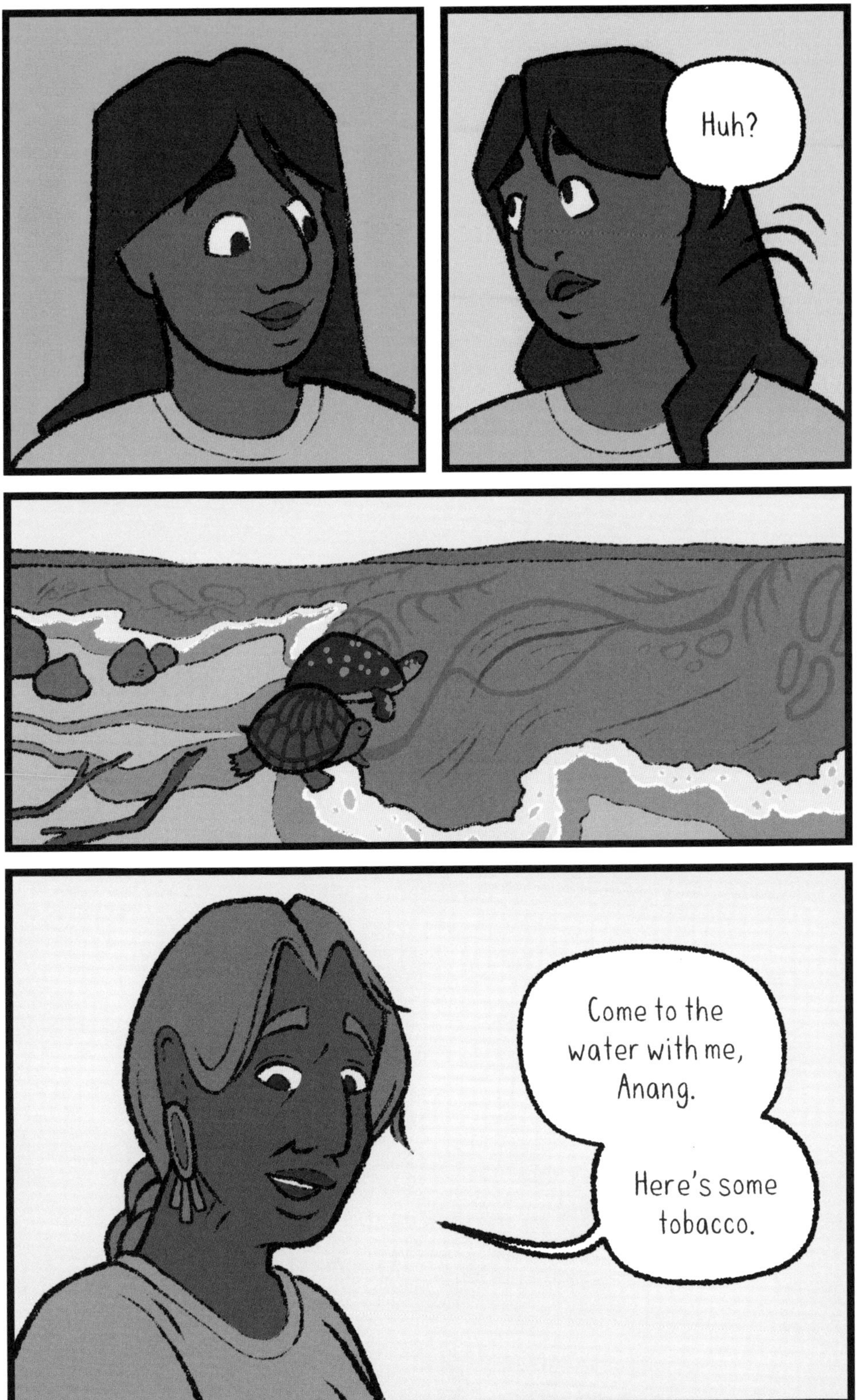
Huh?
Come to the water with me, Anang.
Here's some tobacco.

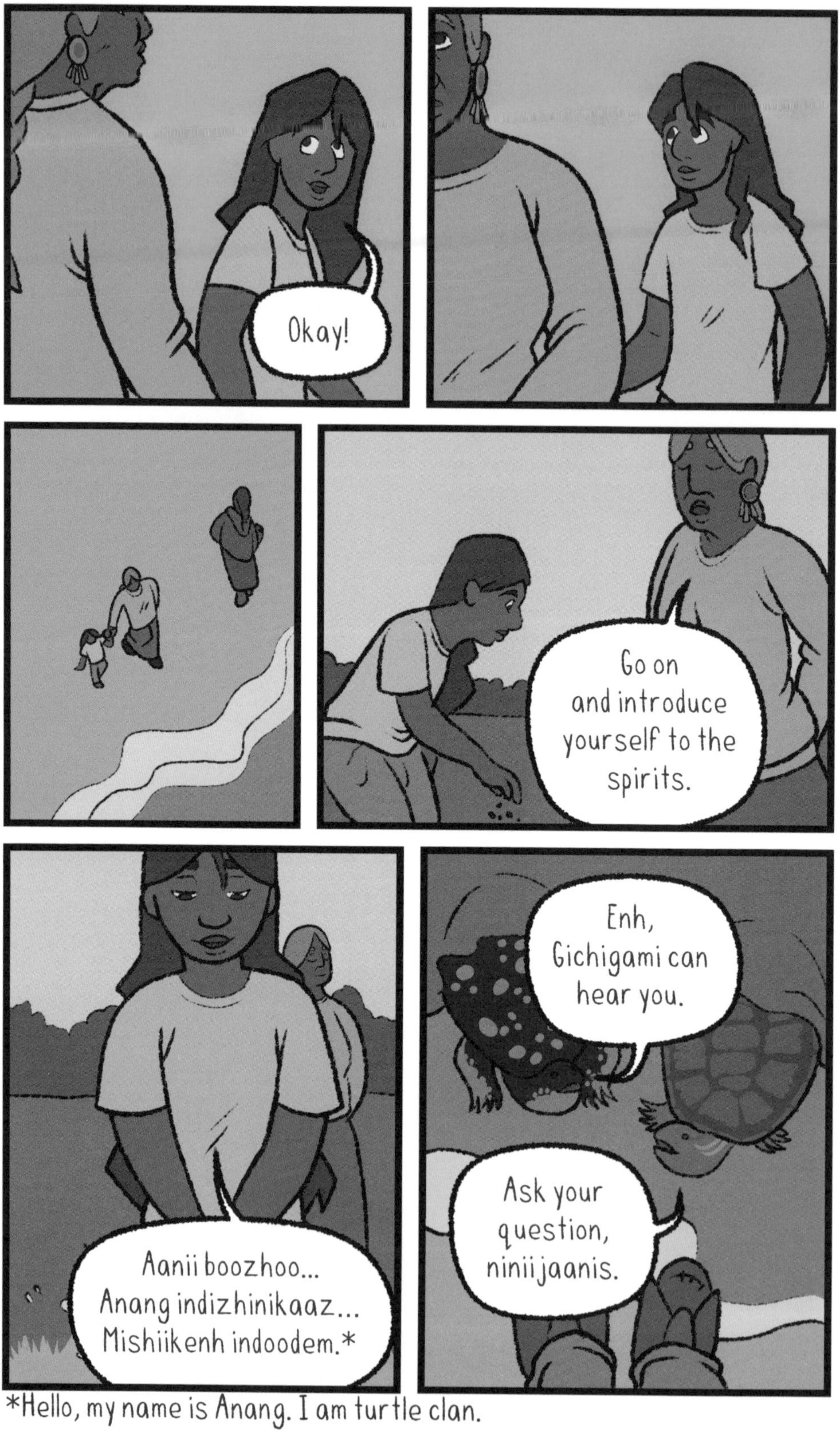
Okay!
Go on and introduce yourself to the spirits.
Aanii boozhoo... Anang indizhinikaaz... Mishiikenh indoodem.*
Enh, Gichigami can hear you.
Ask your question, niniijaanis.

*Hello, my name is Anang. I am turtle clan.

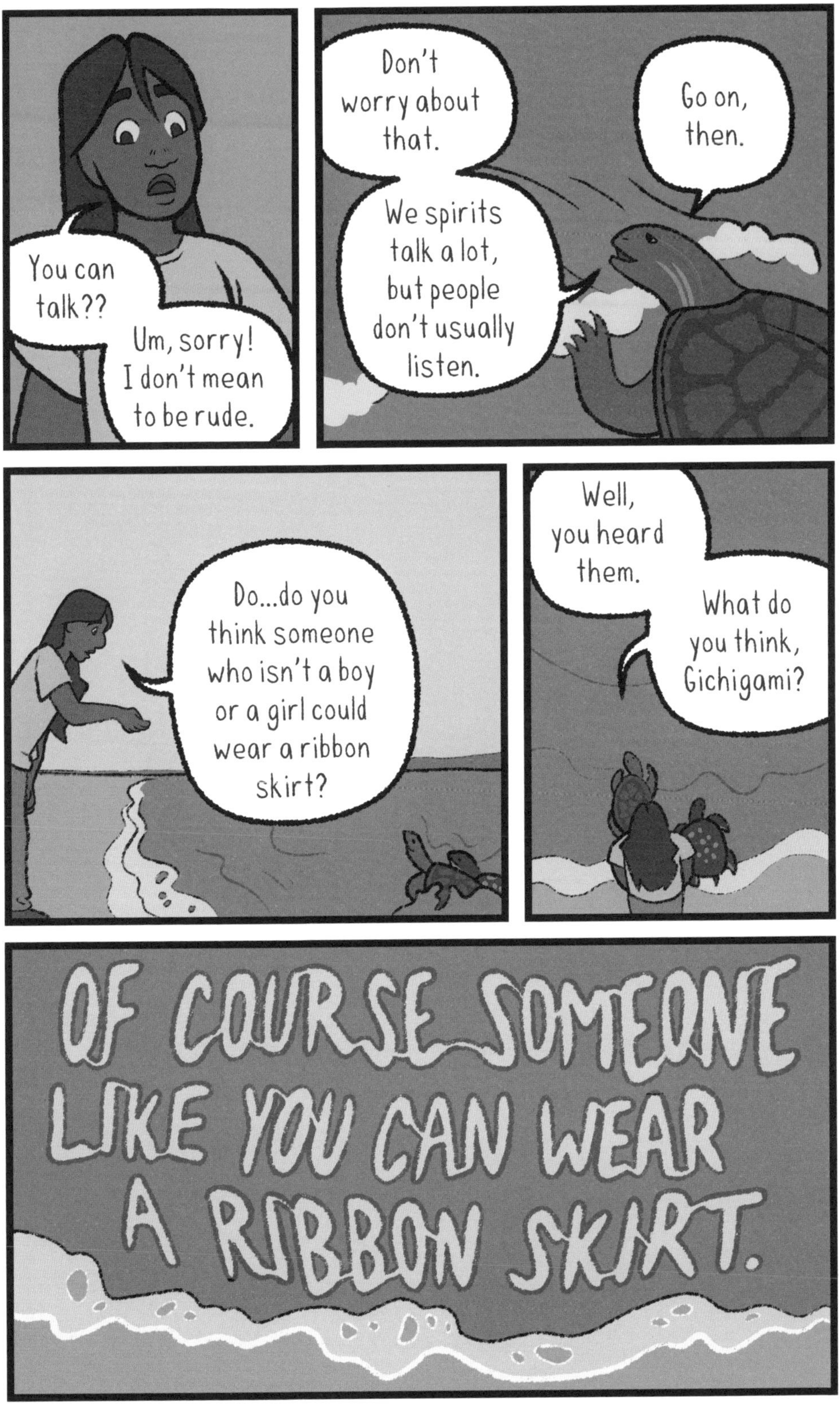
You can talk??
Um, sorry! I don't mean to be rude.
Don't worry about that.
We spirits talk a lot, but people don't usually listen.
Go on, then.
Do...do you think someone who isn't a boy or a girl could wear a ribbon skirt?
Well, you heard them.
What do you think, Gichigami?
OF COURSE SOMEONE LIKE YOU CAN WEAR A RIBBON SKIRT.

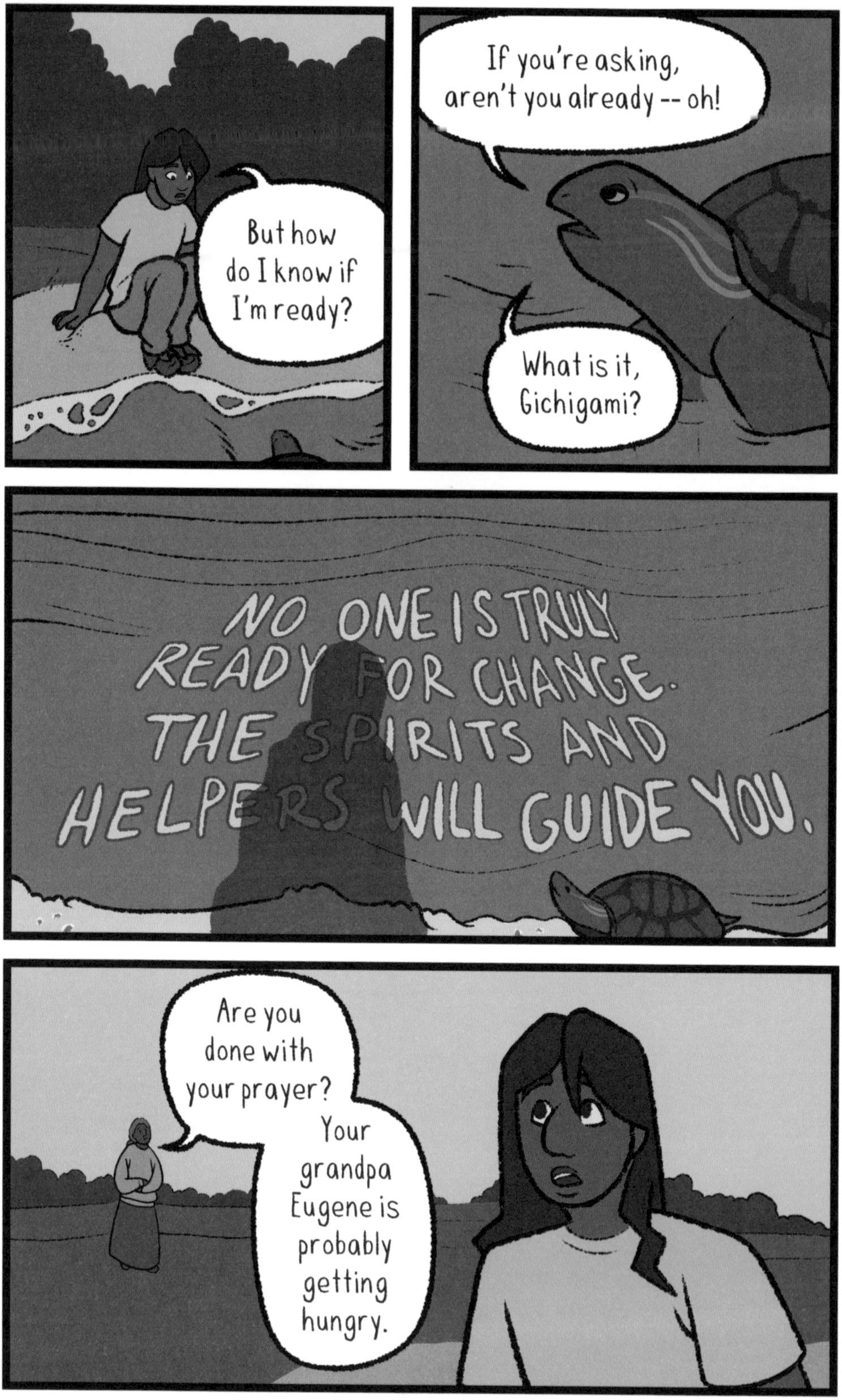
But how do I know if I'm ready?
If you're asking, aren't you already -- oh!
What is it, Gichigami?
NO ONE IS TRULY READY FOR CHANGE. THE SPIRITS AND HELPERS WILL GUIDE YOU.
Are you done with your prayer?
Your grandpa Eugene is probably getting hungry.

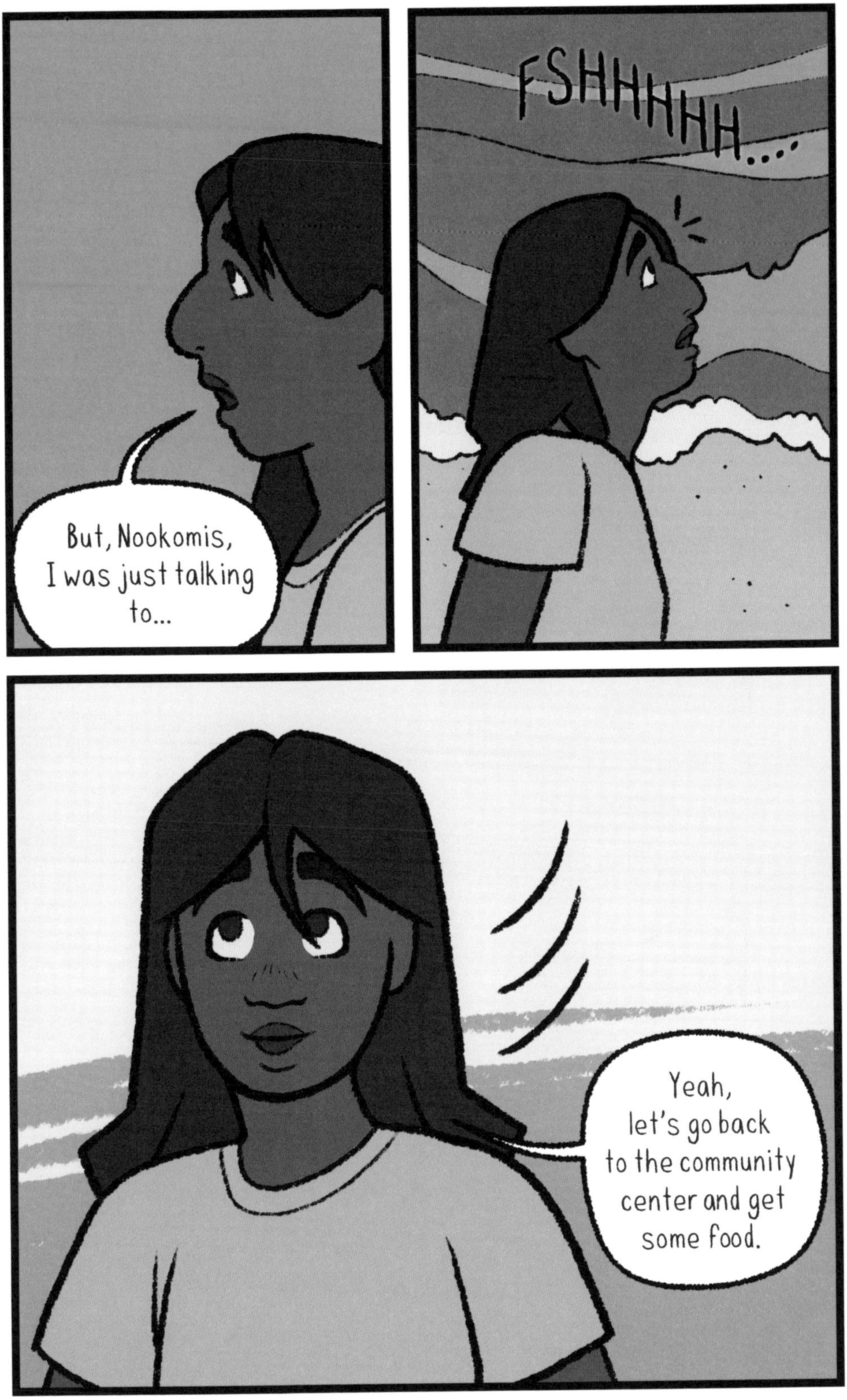
But, Nookomis, I was just talking to...
FSHHHHH....
Yeah, let's go back to the community center and get some food.

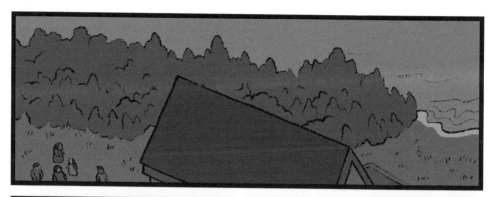

Sherry!

Look who's trying to talk to you!

Oh my gosh, is that Anang? You know, the boy-girl.

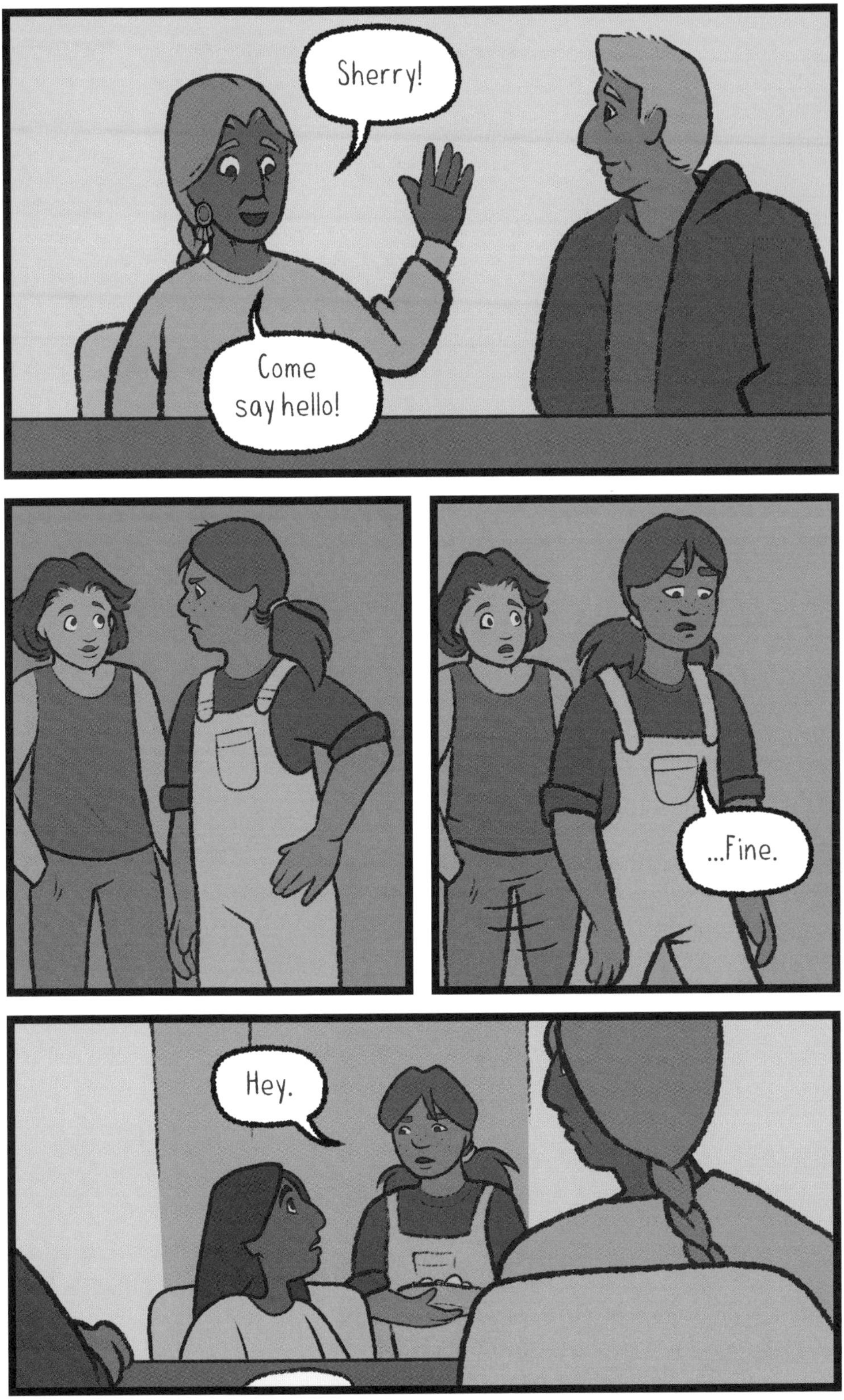
Sherry!
Come say hello!
...Fine.
Hey.

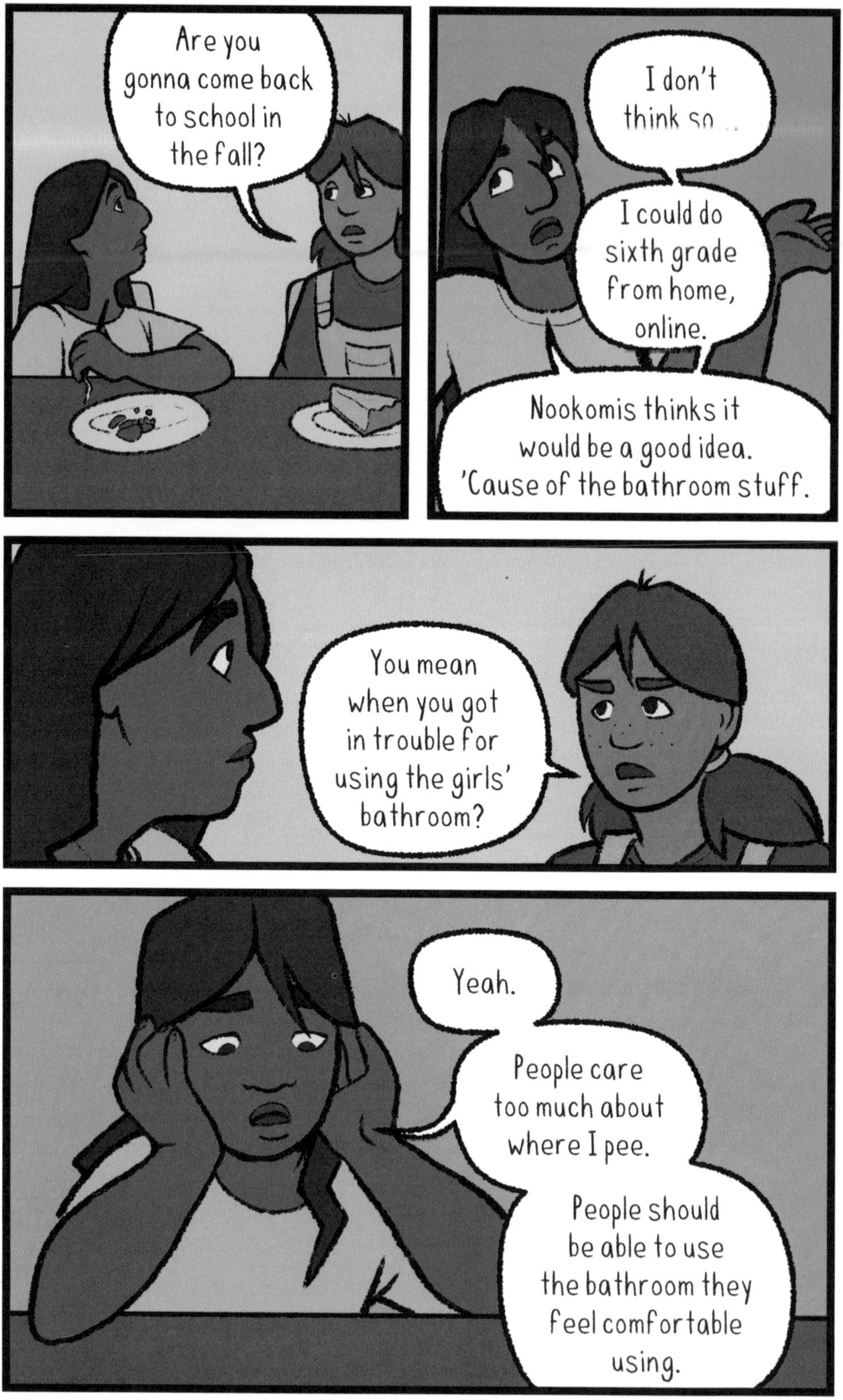

Are you gonna come back to school in the fall?
I don't think so . . .
I could do sixth grade from home, online.
Nookomis thinks it would be a good idea. 'Cause of the bathroom stuff.
You mean when you got in trouble for using the girls' bathroom?
Yeah.
People care too much about where I pee.
People should be able to use the bathroom they feel comfortable using.

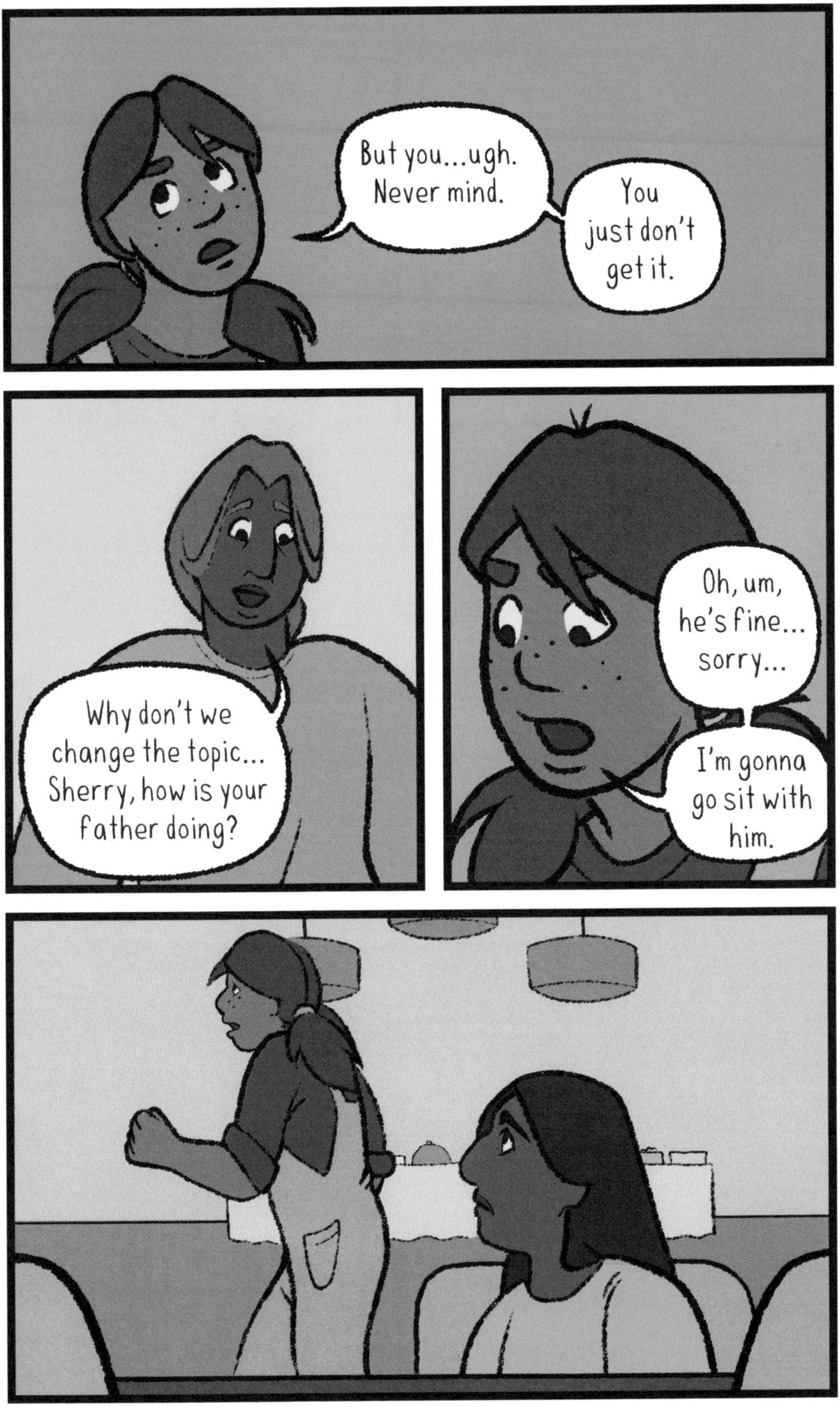
But you...ugh. Never mind.
You just don't get it.
Why don't we change the topic... Sherry, how is your father doing?
Oh, um, he's fine... sorry...
I'm gonna go sit with him.

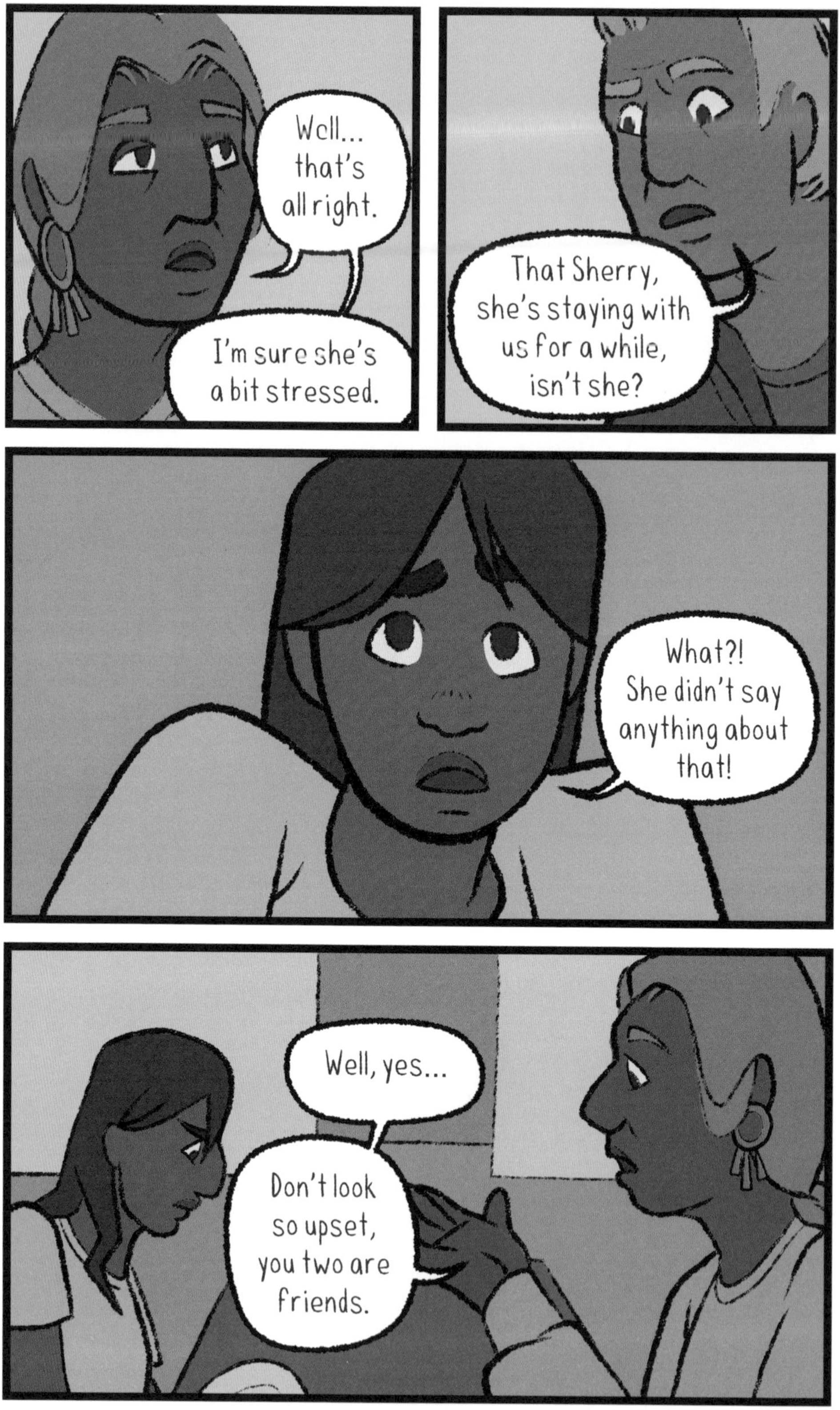
Well... that's all right.
I'm sure she's a bit stressed.
That Sherry, she's staying with us for a while, isn't she?
What?! She didn't say anything about that!
Well, yes...
Don't look so upset, you two are friends.

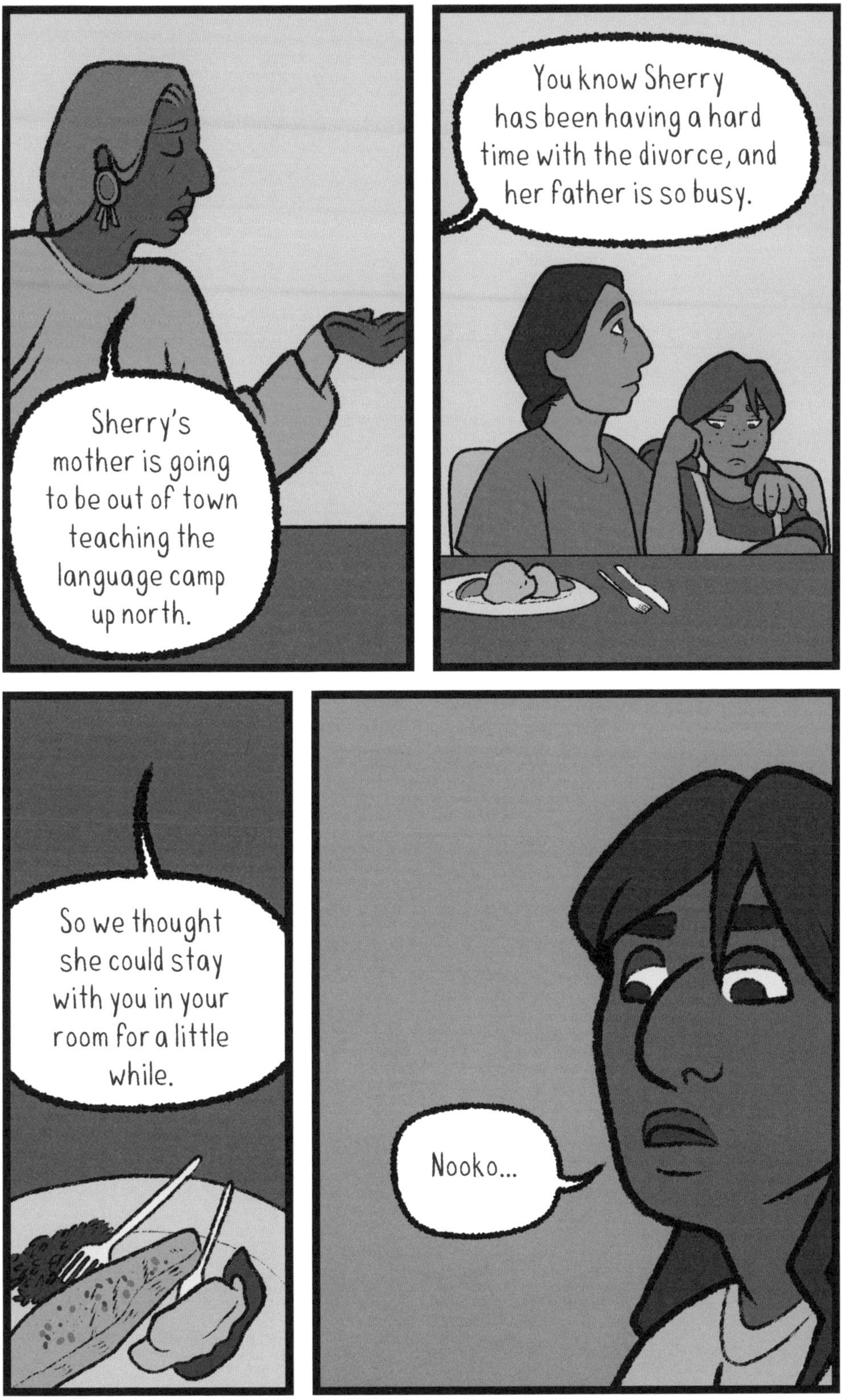
Sherry's mother is going to be out of town teaching the language camp up north.
You know Sherry has been having a hard time with the divorce, and her father is so busy.
So we thought she could stay with you in your room for a little while.
Nooko...

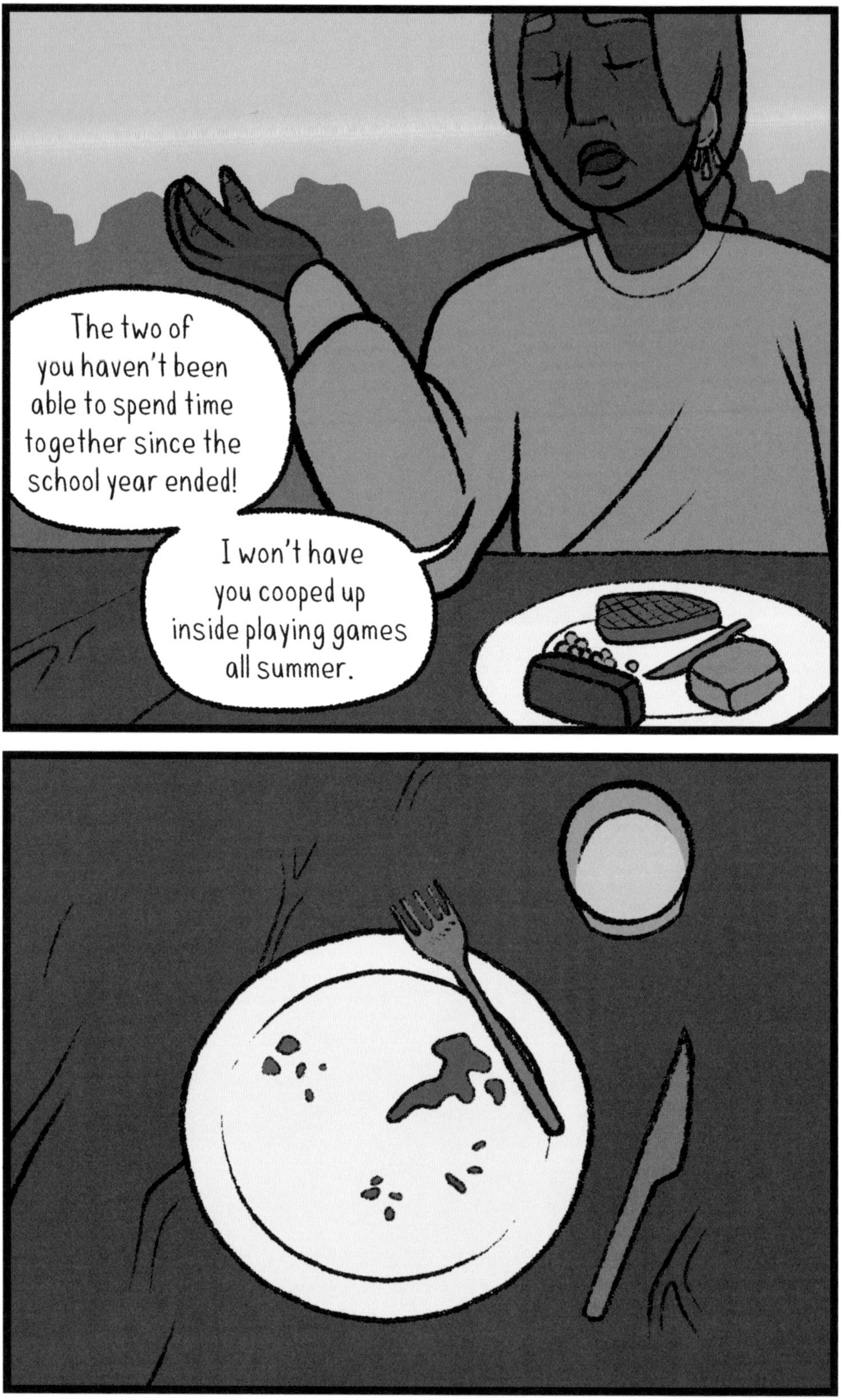
The two of you haven't been able to spend time together since the school year ended!
I won't have you cooped up inside playing games all summer.

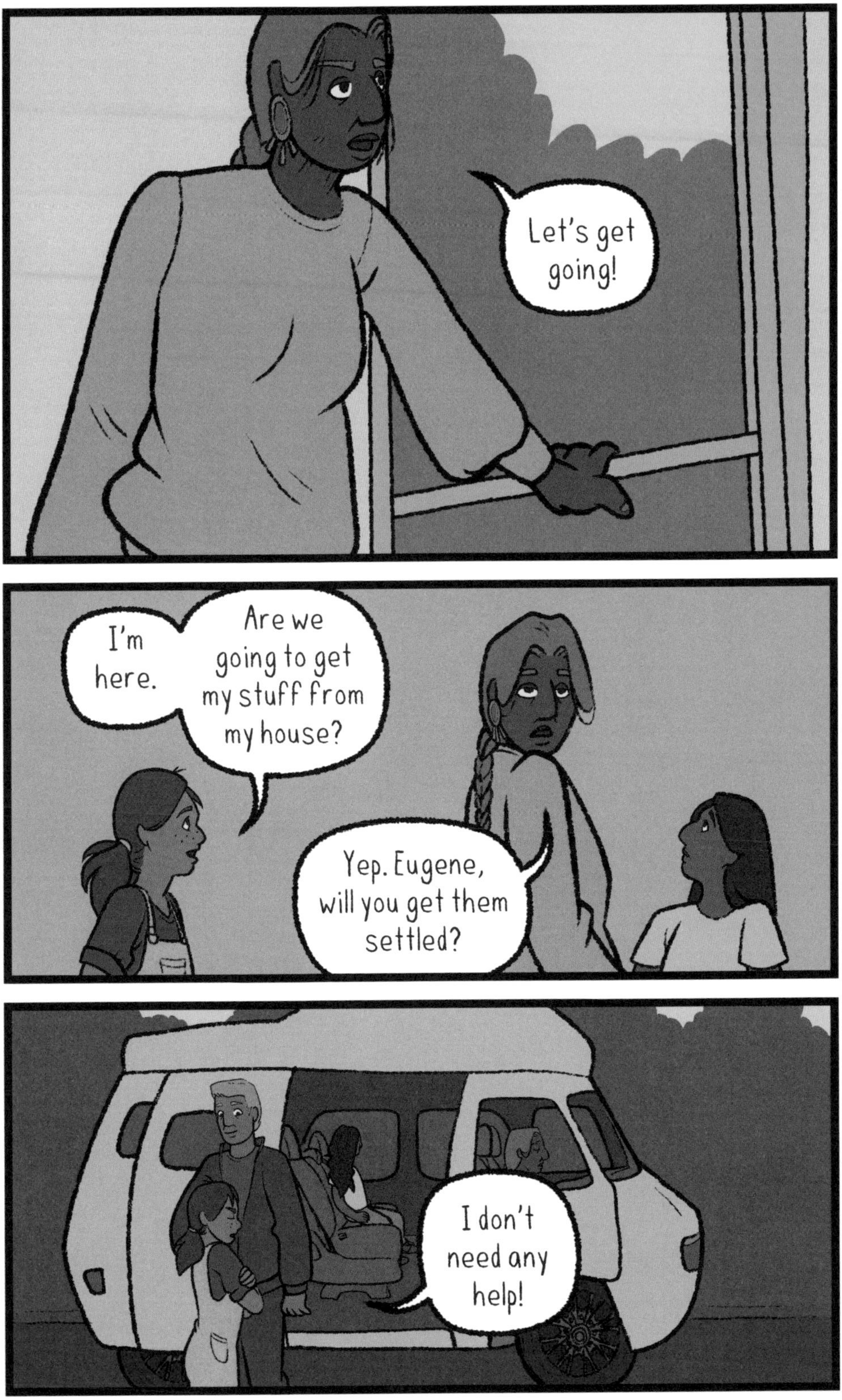
Let's get going!
I'm here.
Are we going to get my stuff from my house?
Yep. Eugene, will you get them settled?
I don't need any help!

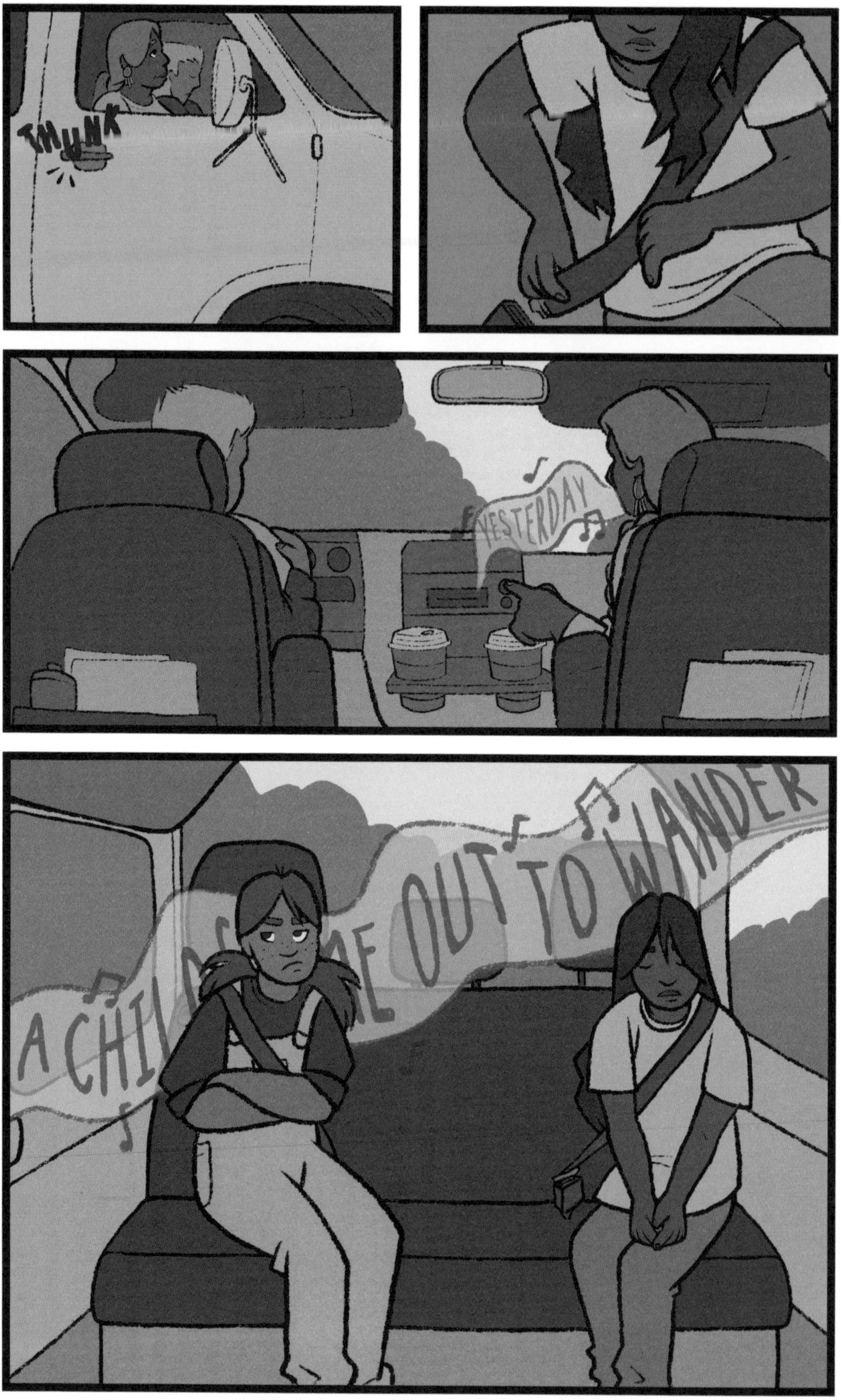
THUNK
YESTERDAY
A CHI ME OUT TO WANDER

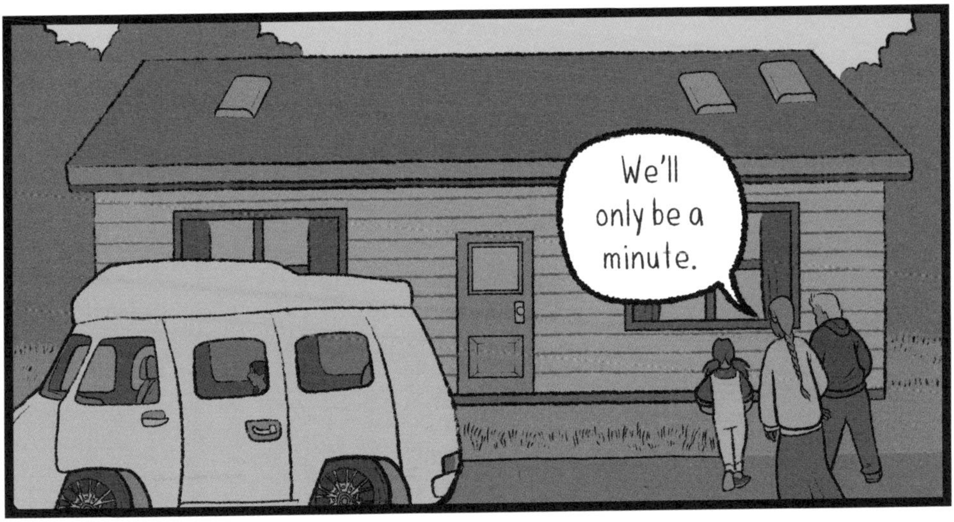
We'll only be a minute.

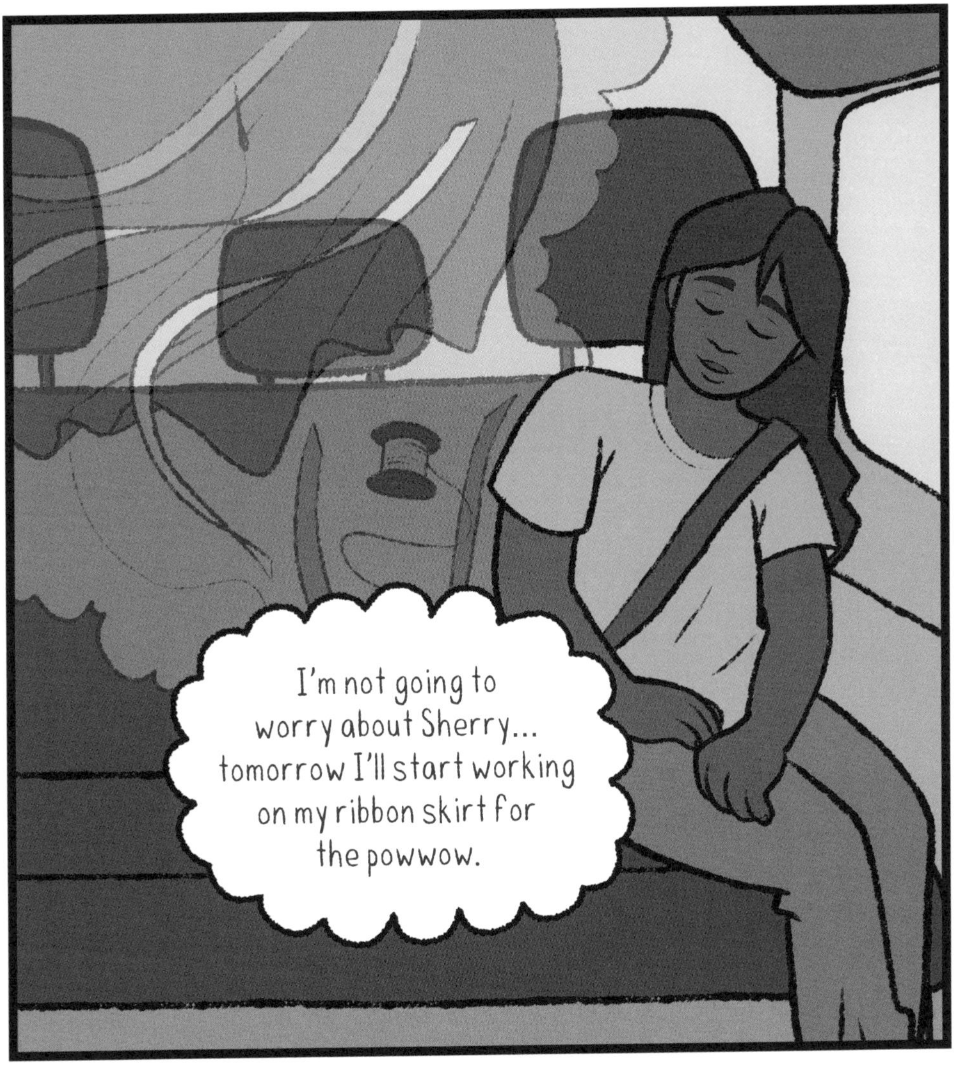
I'm not going to worry about Sherry... tomorrow I'll start working on my ribbon skirt for the powwow.

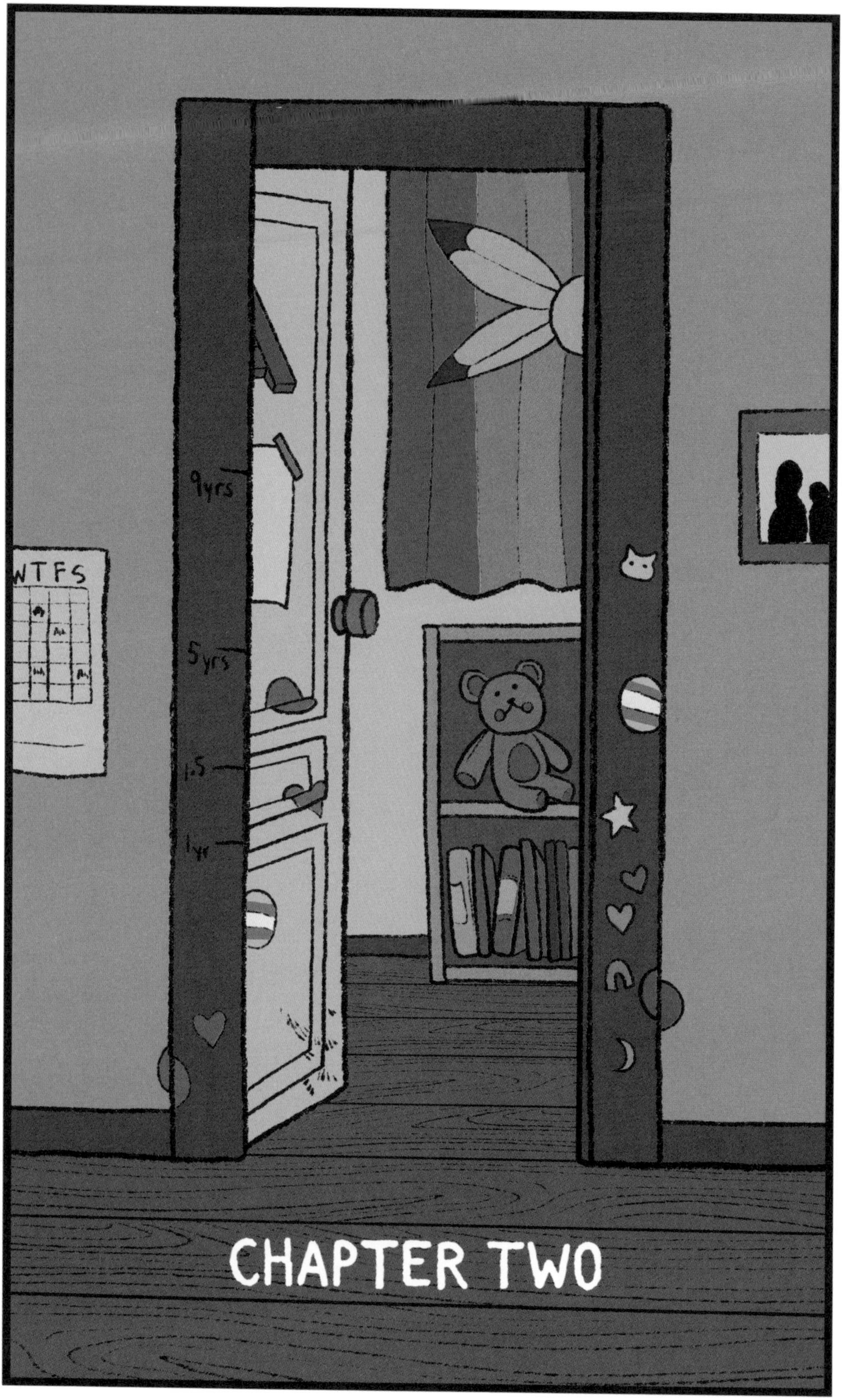
9yrs
5yrs
1.5
1yr
WTFS
CHAPTER TWO

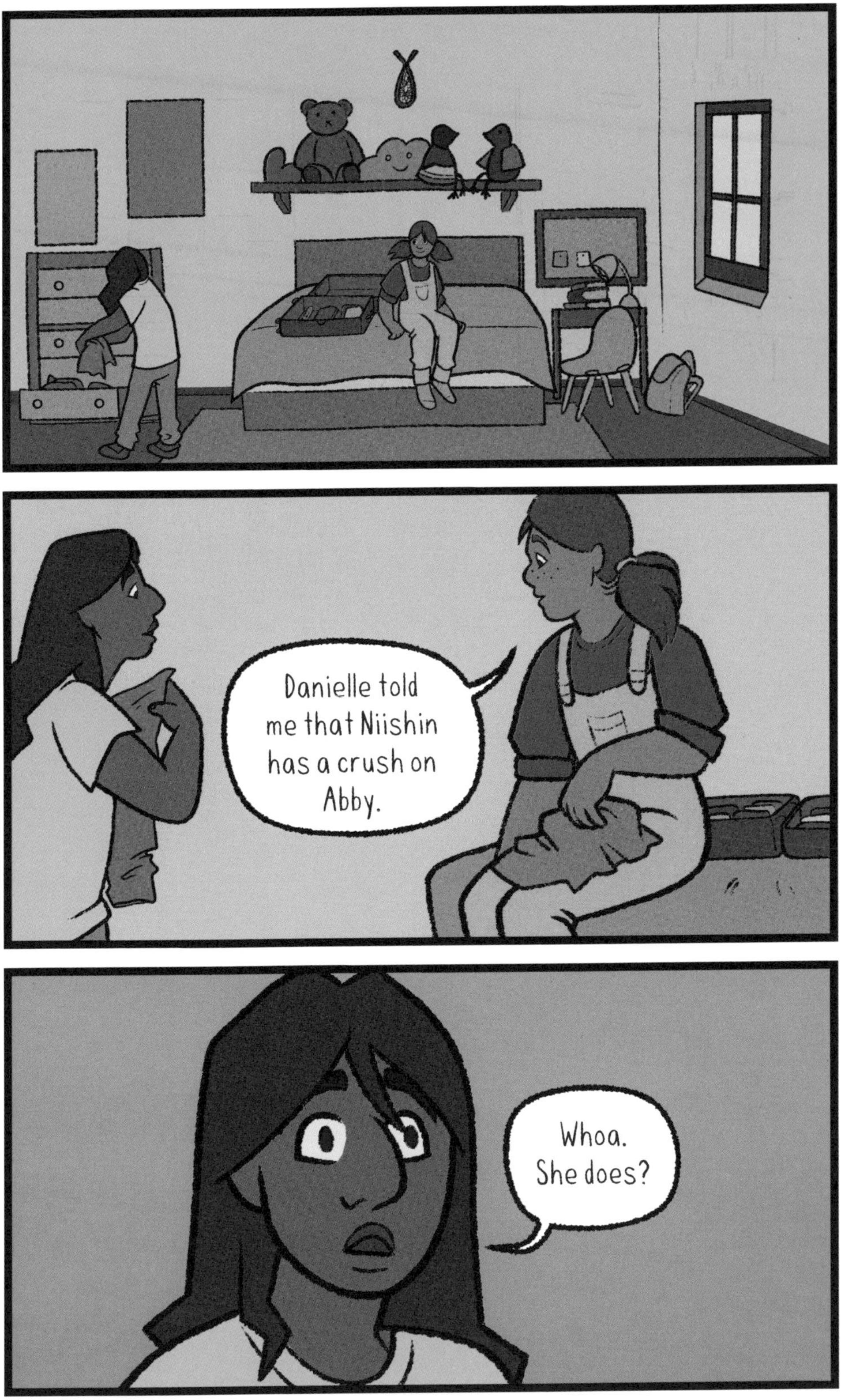
Danielle told me that Niishin has a crush on Abby.
Whoa. She does?

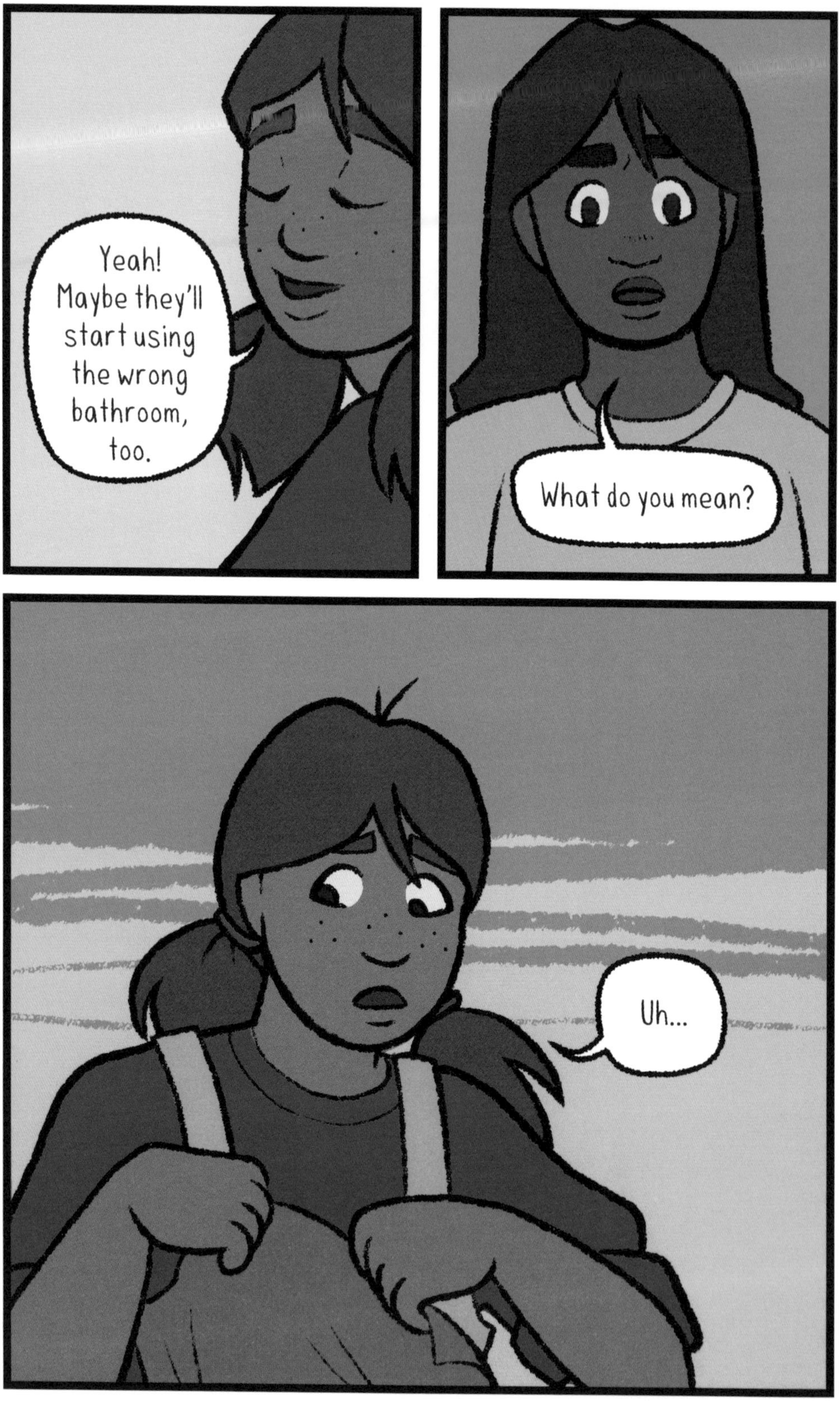
Yeah! Maybe they'll start using the wrong bathroom, too.
What do you mean?
Uh...

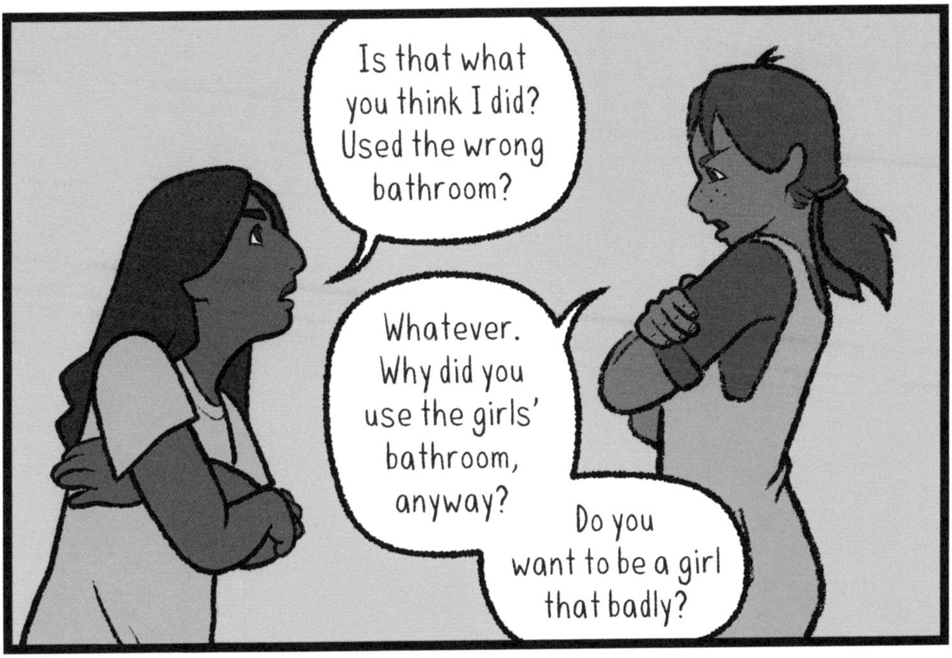
Is that what you think I did? Used the wrong bathroom?
Whatever. Why did you use the girls' bathroom, anyway?
Do you want to be a girl that badly?

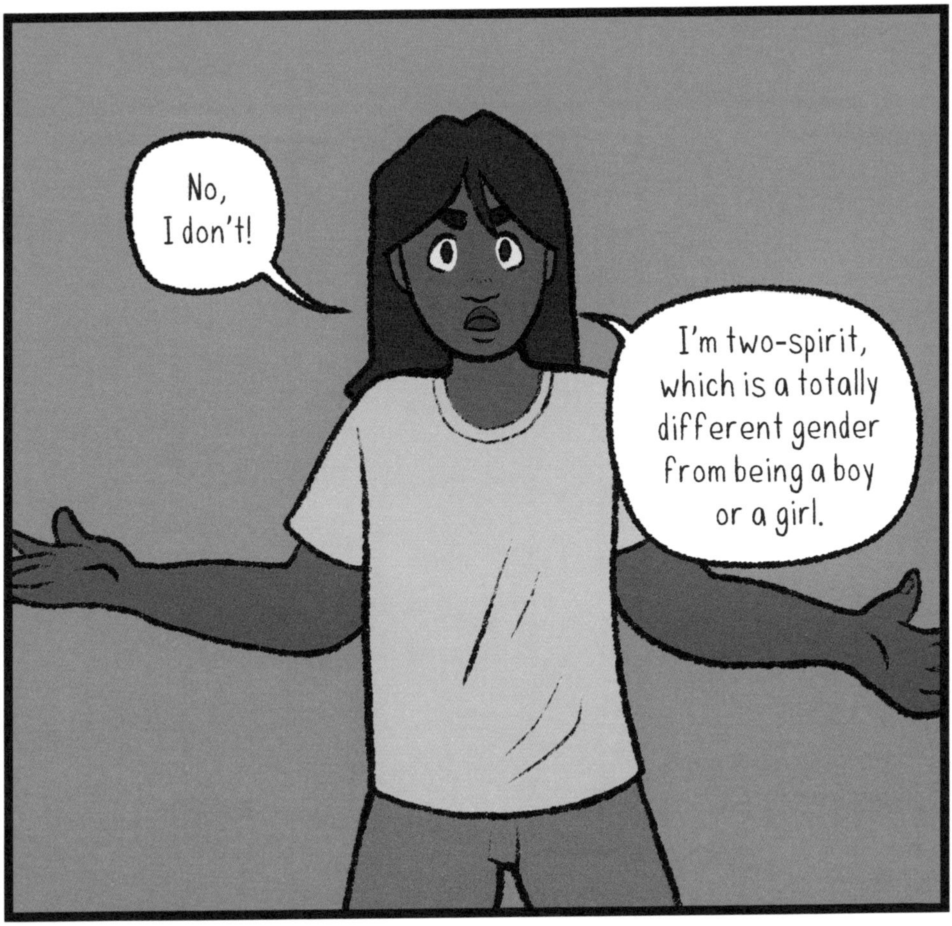
No, I don't!
I'm two-spirit, which is a totally different gender from being a boy or a girl.

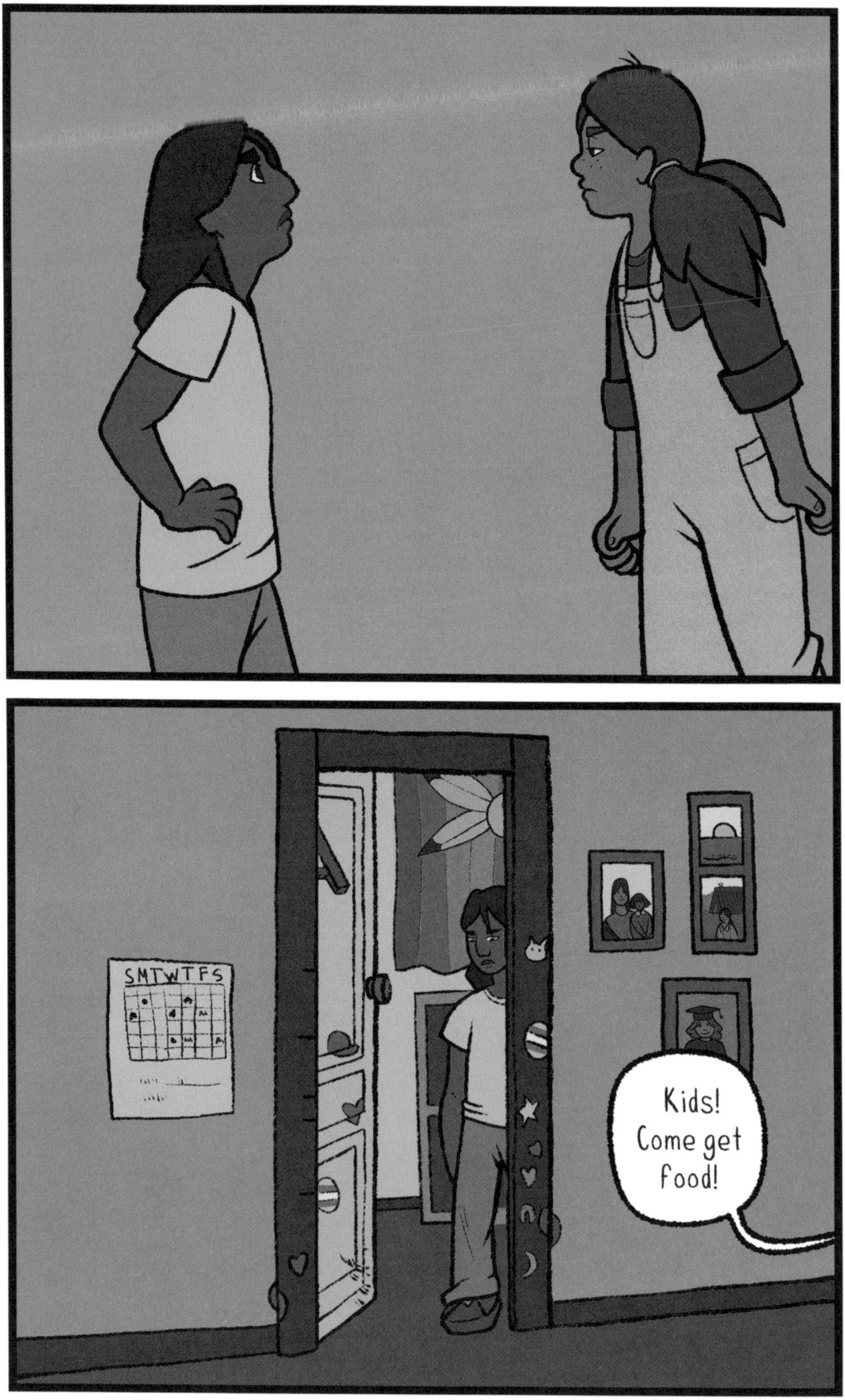
SMTWTFS
Kids! Come get food!

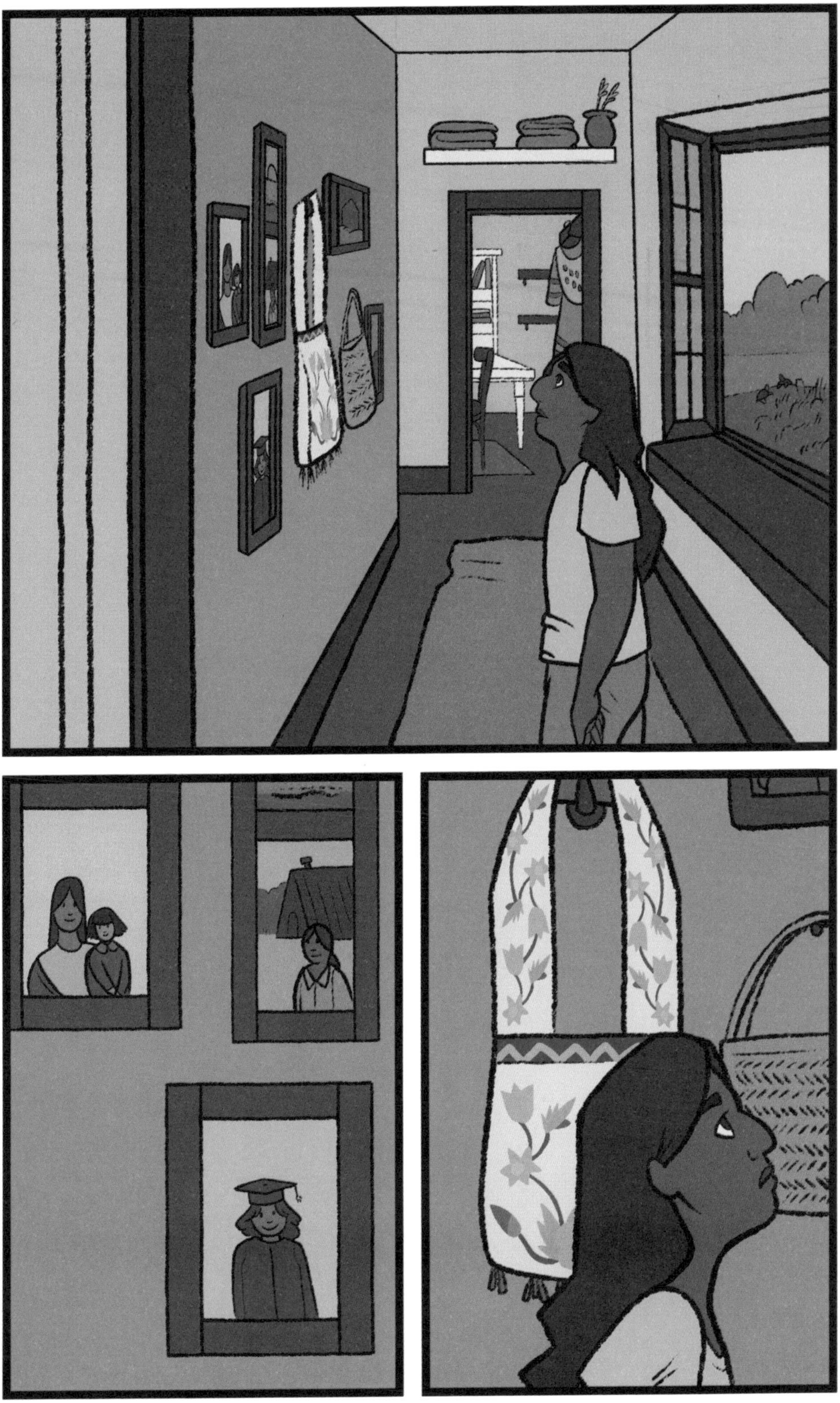

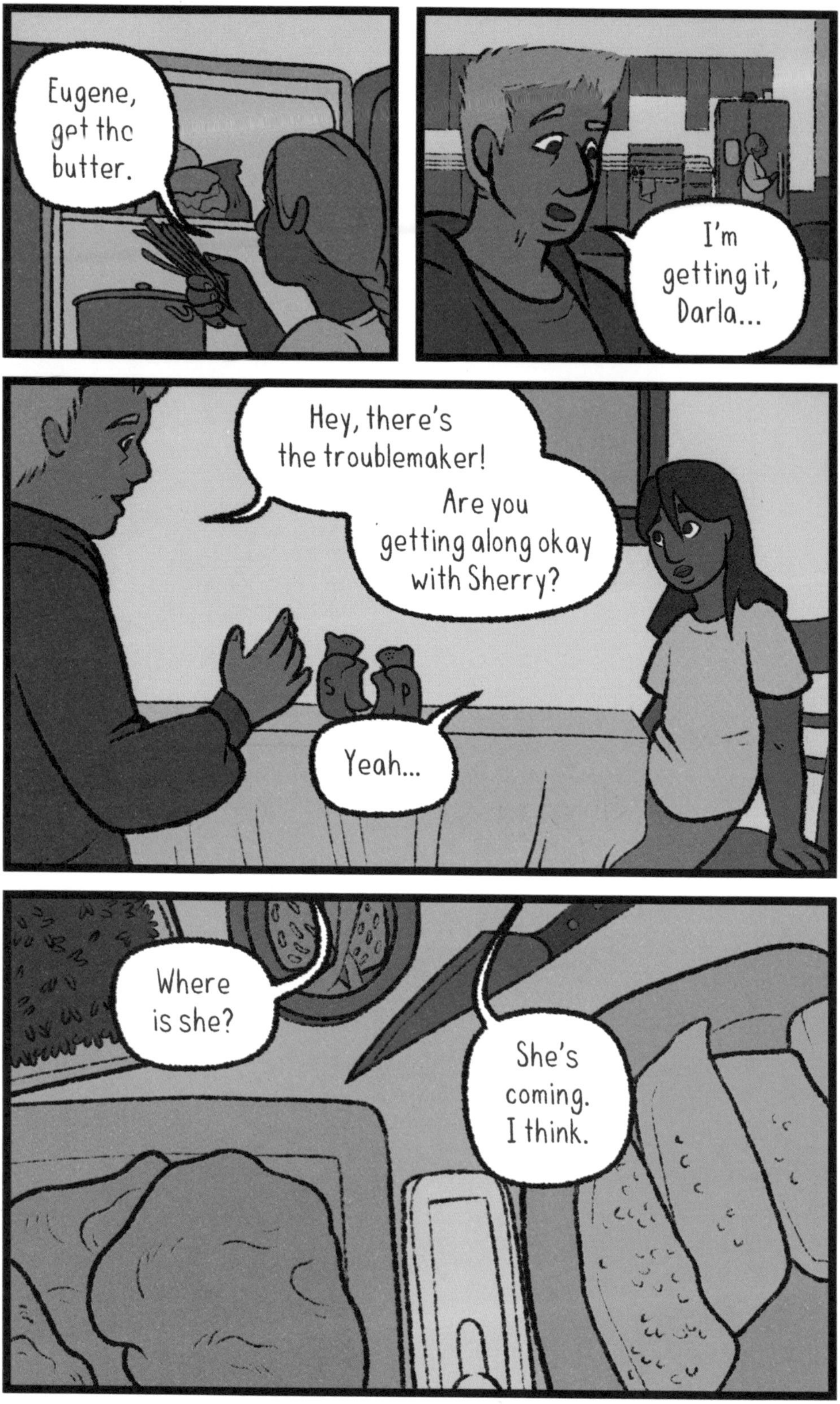
Eugene, get the butter.
I'm getting it, Darla...
Hey, there's the troublemaker!
Are you getting along okay with Sherry?
Yeah...
Where is she?
She's coming. I think.

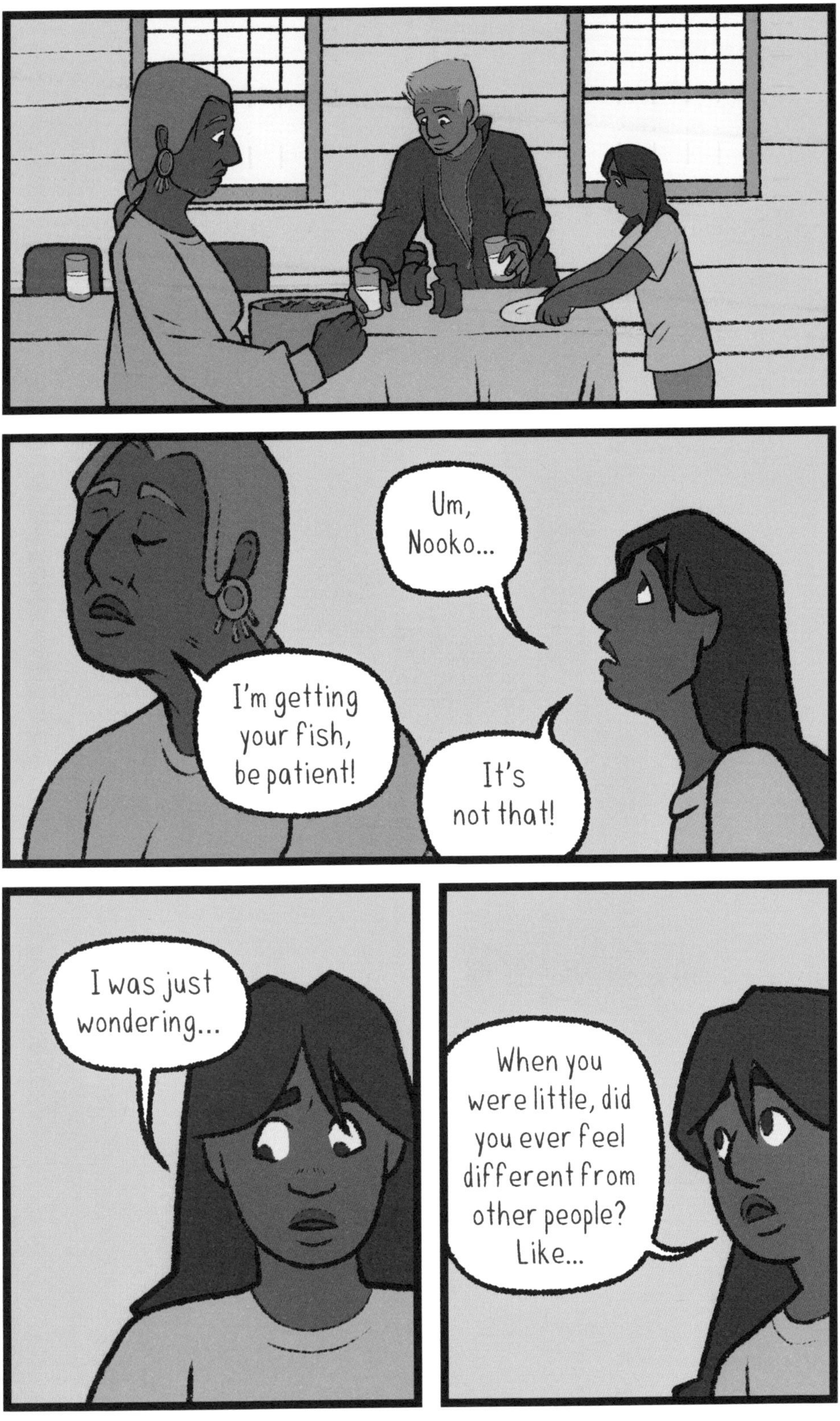
Um, Nooko...
I'm getting your fish, be patient!
It's not that!
I was just wondering...
When you were little, did you ever feel different from other people? Like...

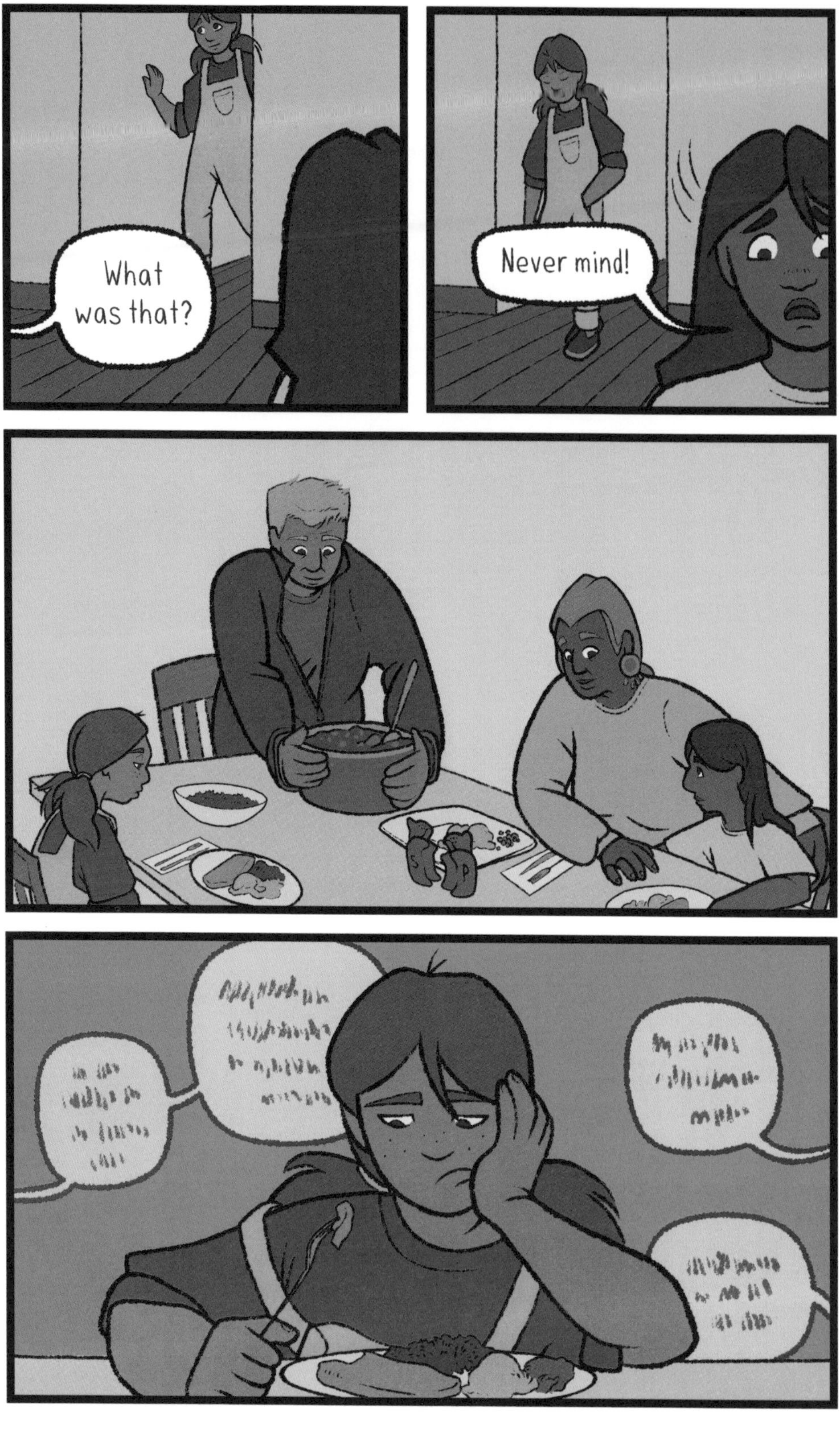
What was that?
Never mind!

All right.
I've got regalia orders to finish putting together, so you two have to go play outside.
What? But I want to stay and watch cartoons.
Plus we're too old to play outside!
Too old...
You're never too old to play, Anang.
And put your shoes on.
Aw...

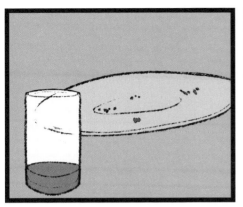

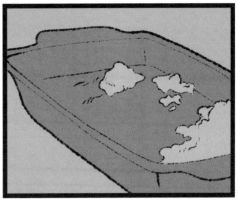

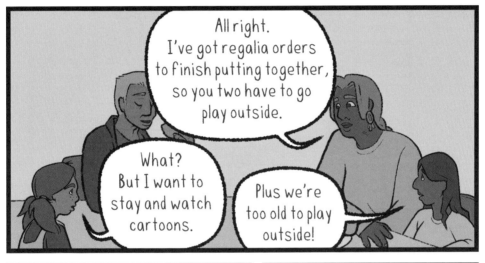

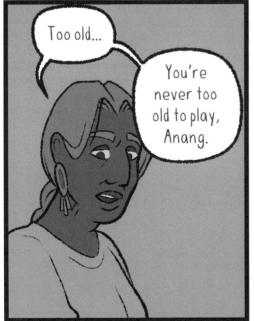

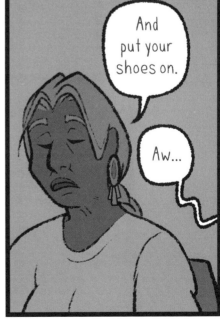

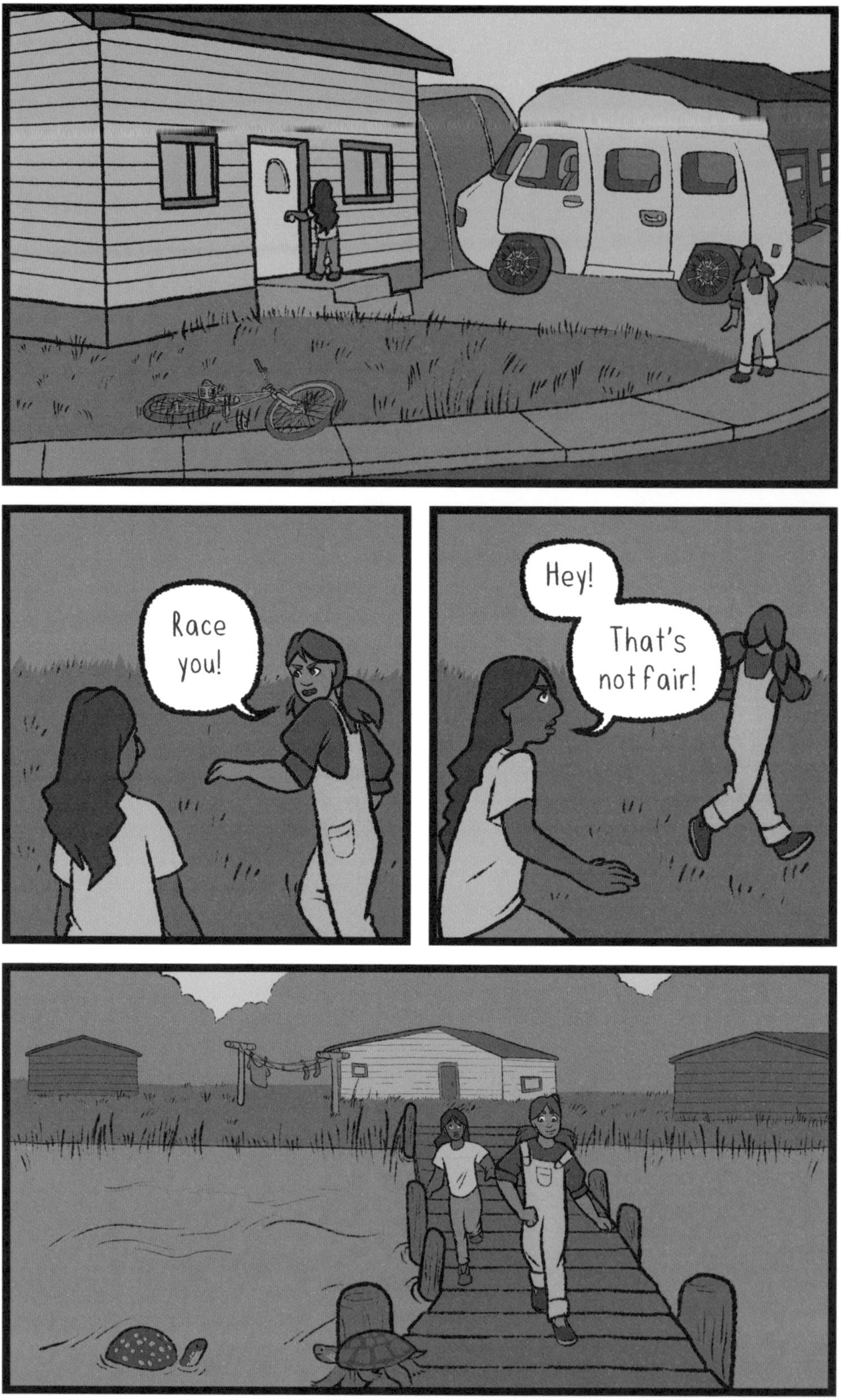
Race you!
Hey!
That's not fair!

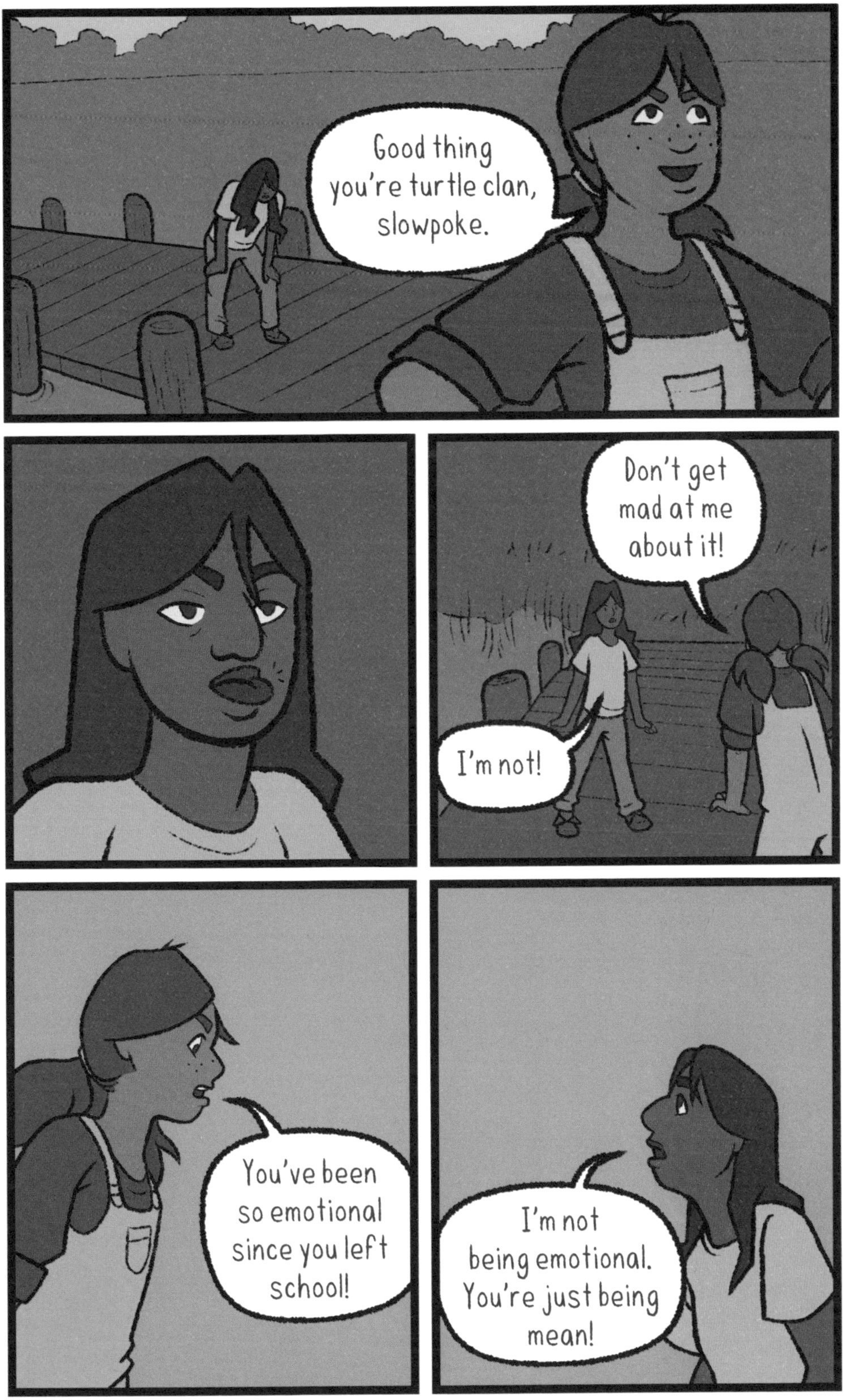
Good thing you're turtle clan, slowpoke.
Don't get mad at me about it!
I'm not!
You've been so emotional since you left school!
I'm not being emotional. You're just being mean!

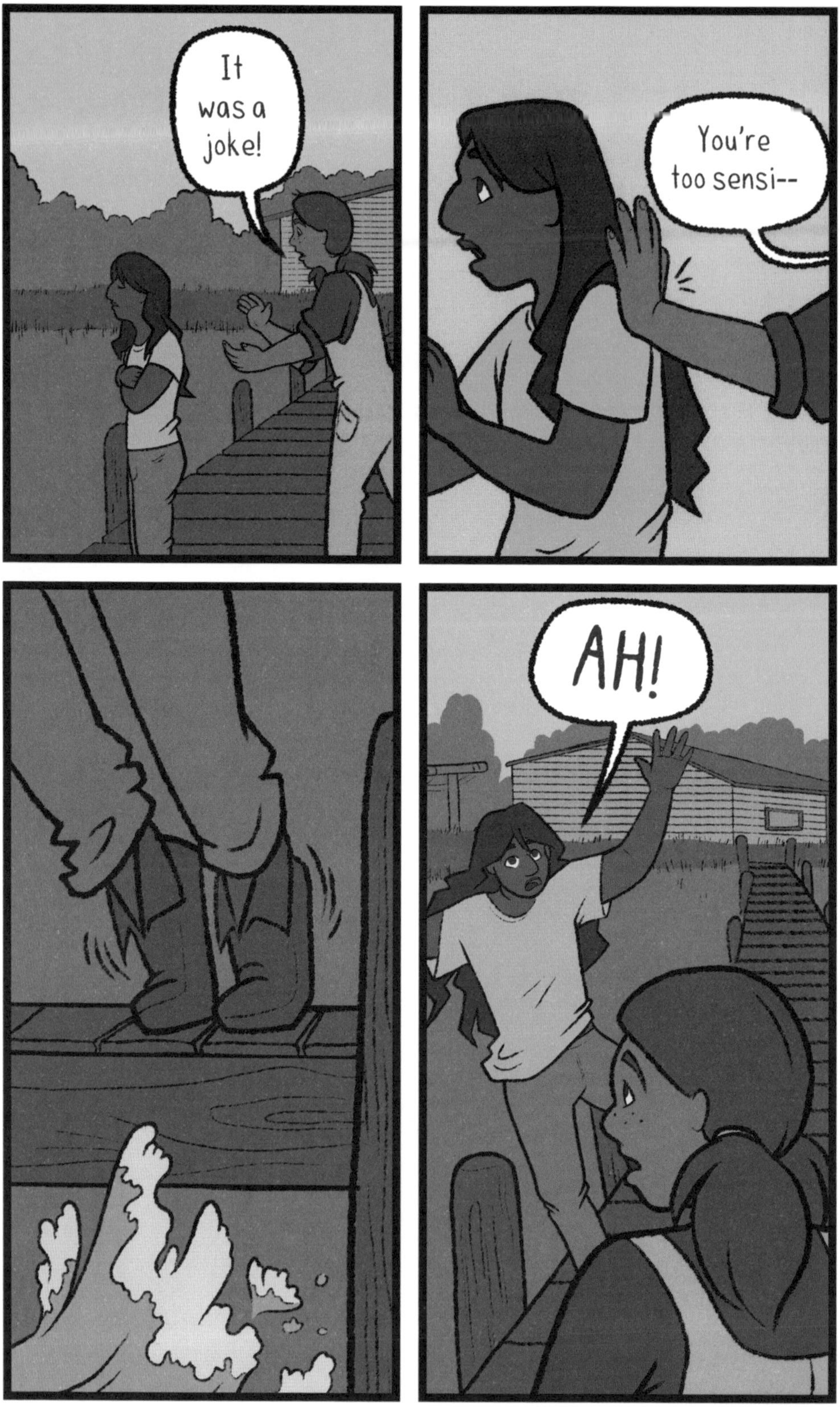
It was a joke!
You're too sensi--
AH!

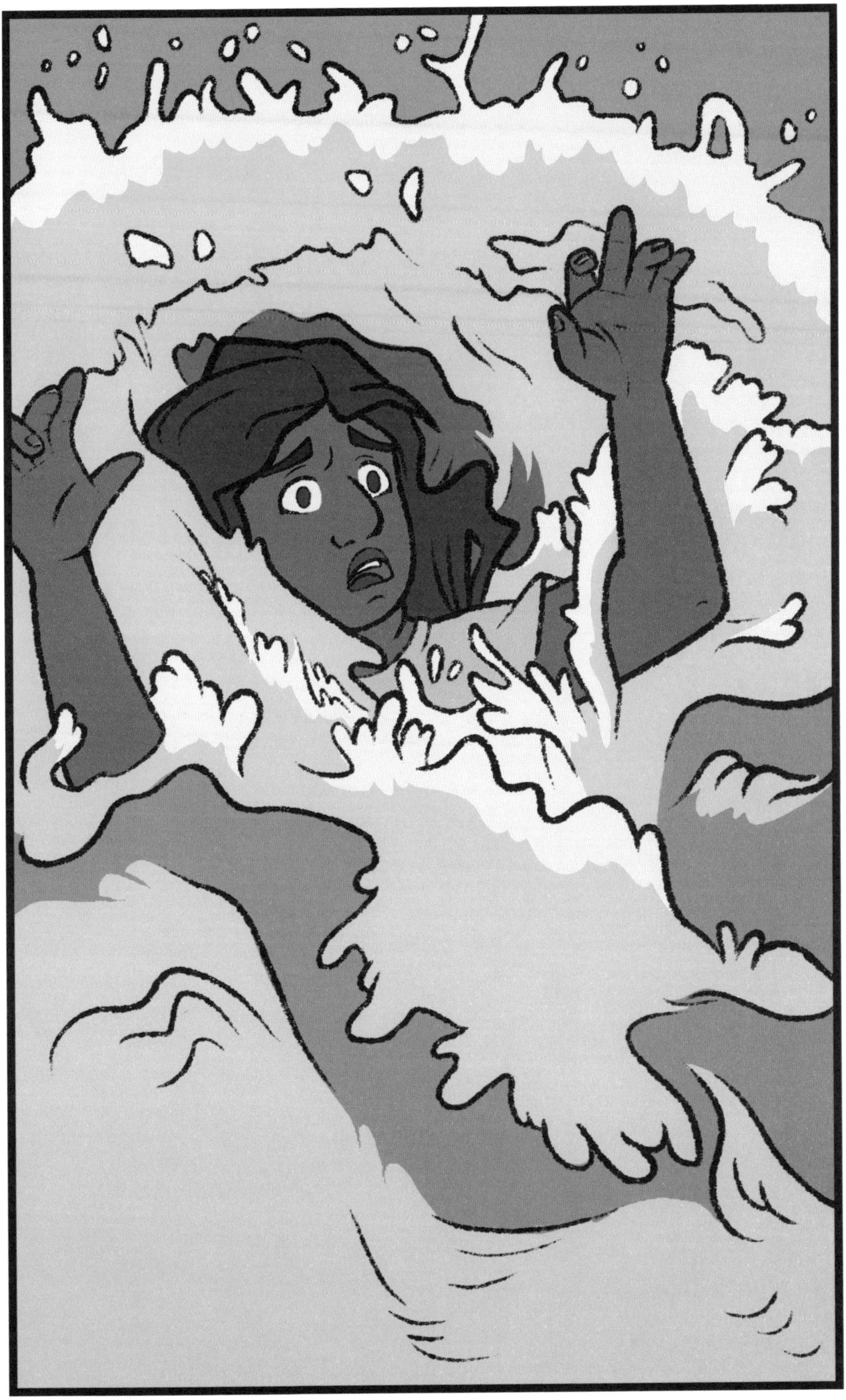

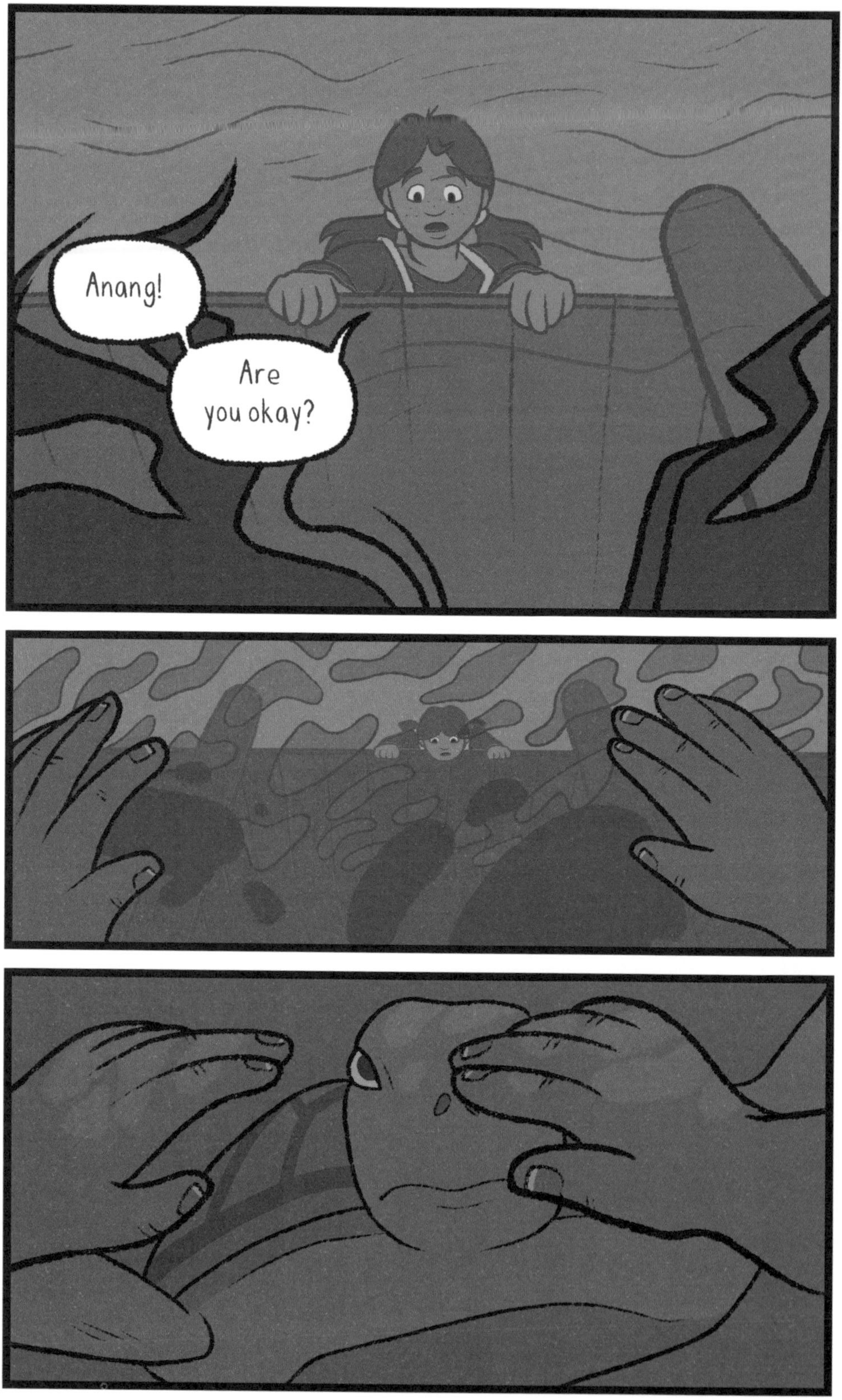
Anang!
Are you okay?

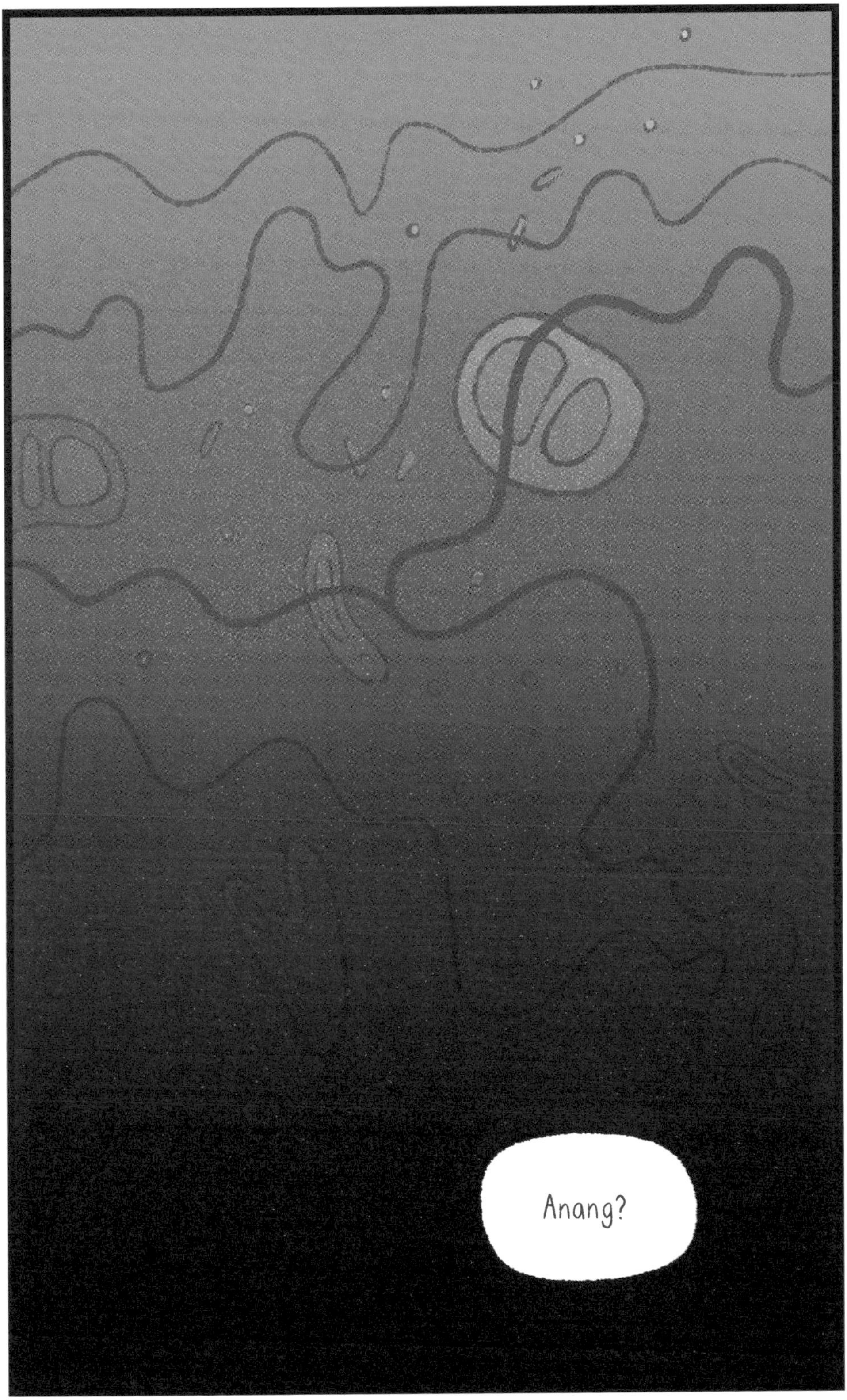
Anang?

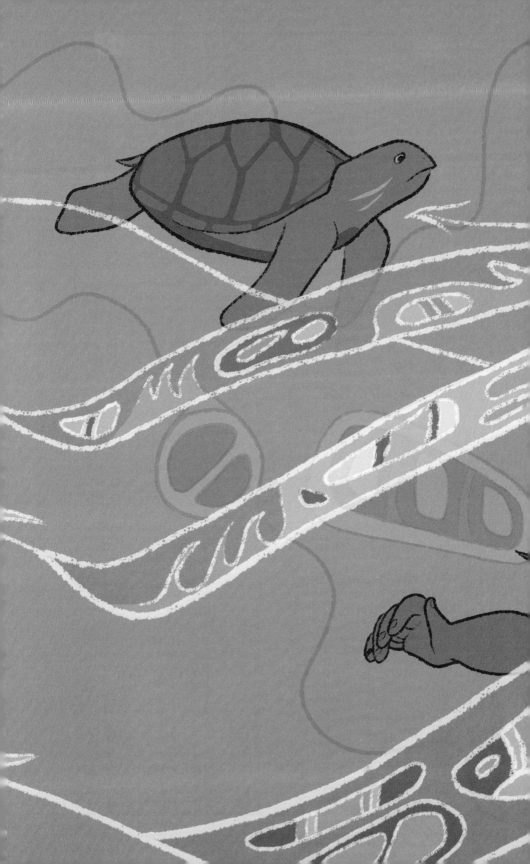

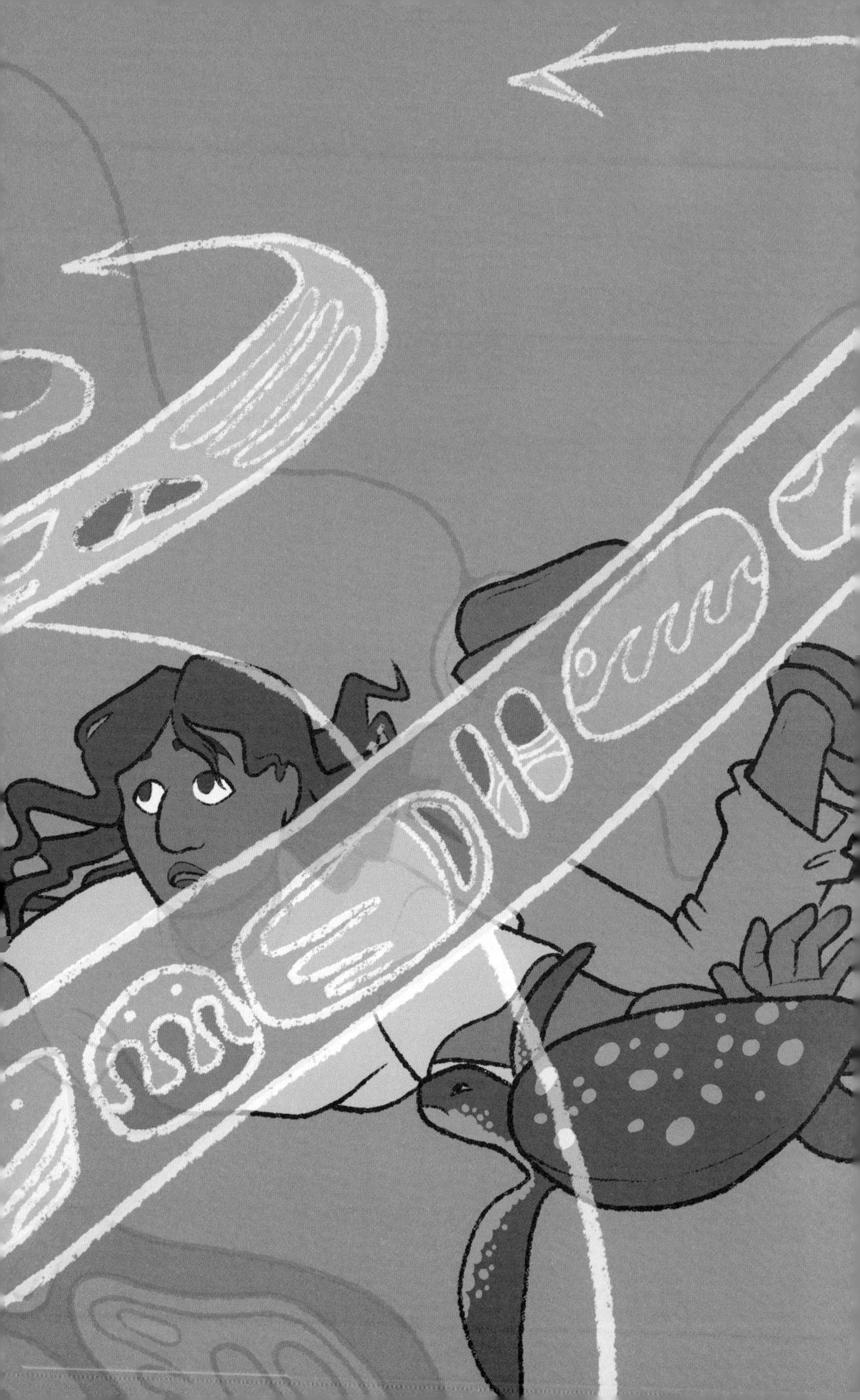

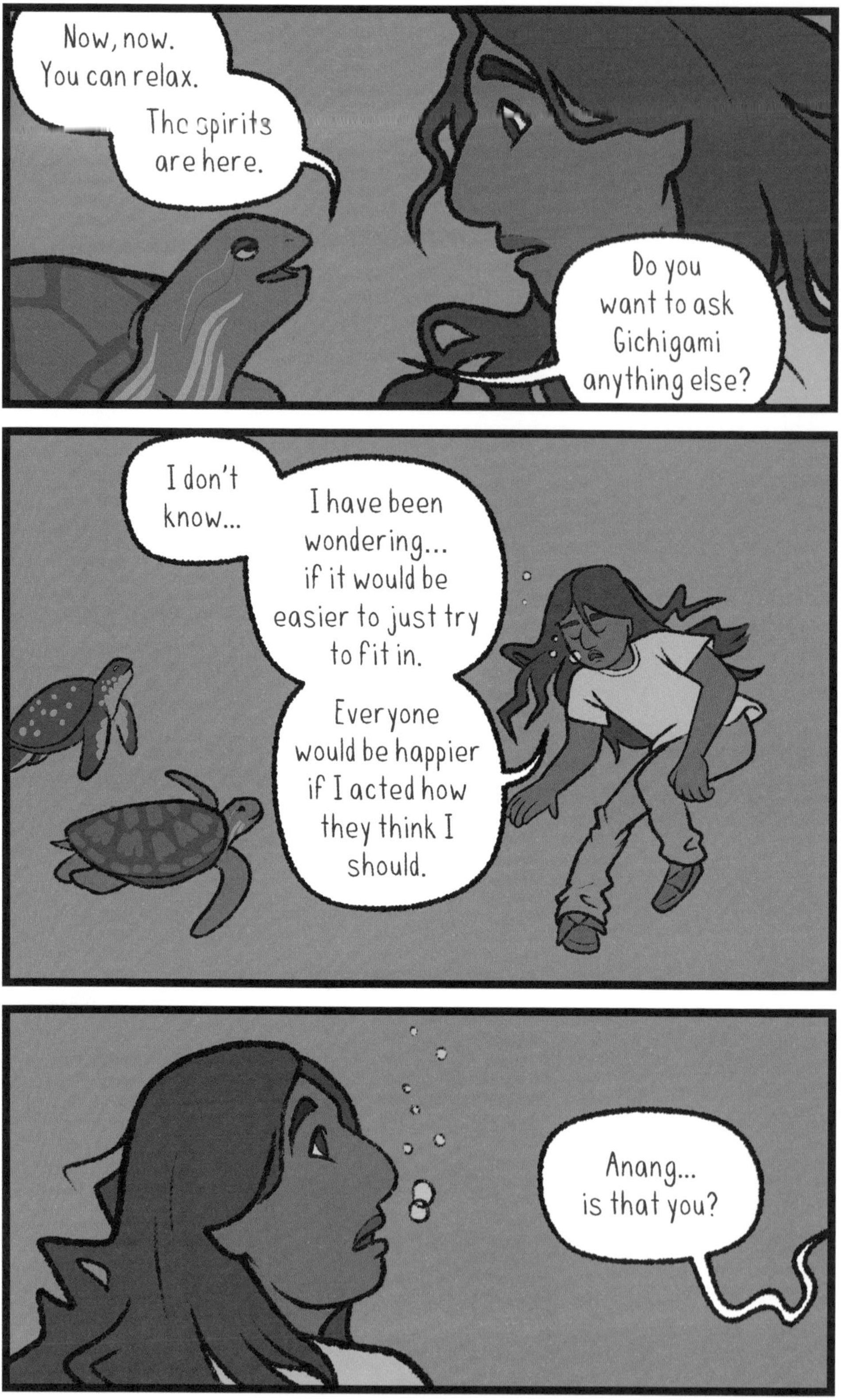
Now, now. You can relax.
The spirits are here.
Do you want to ask Gichigami anything else?
I don't know...
I have been wondering... if it would be easier to just try to fit in.
Everyone would be happier if I acted how they think I should.
Anang... is that you?

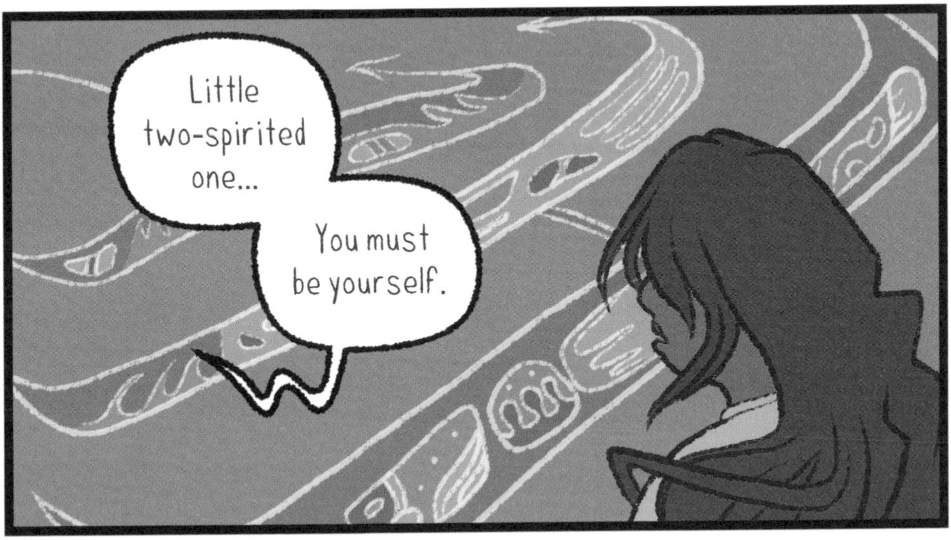
Little two-spirited one...
You must be yourself.

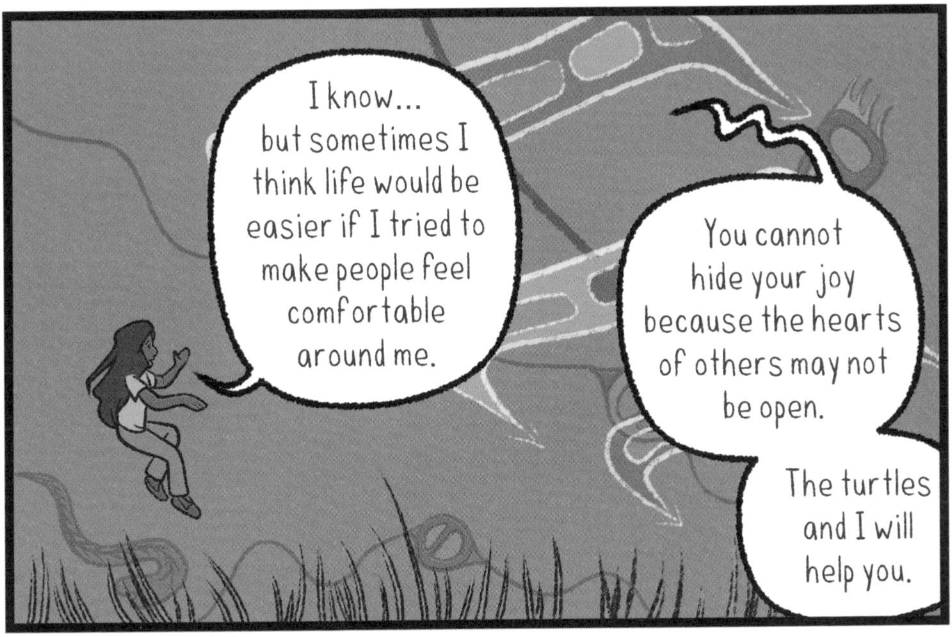
I know... but sometimes I think life would be easier if I tried to make people feel comfortable around me.
You cannot hide your joy because the hearts of others may not be open.
The turtles and I will help you.

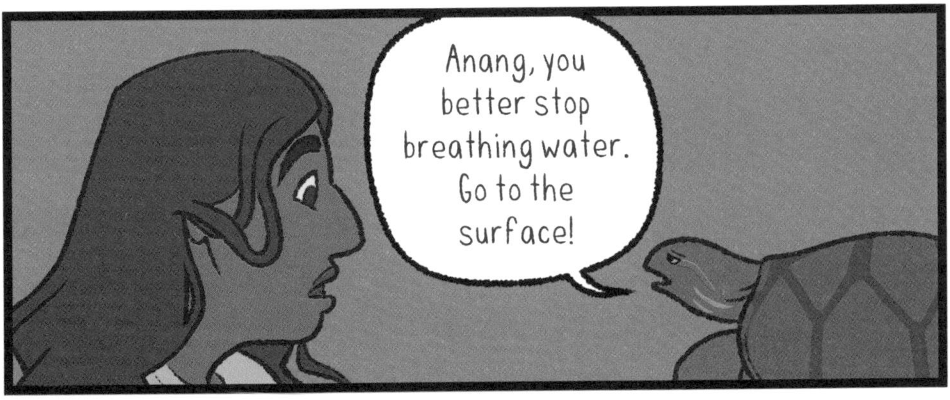
Anang, you better stop breathing water. Go to the surface!

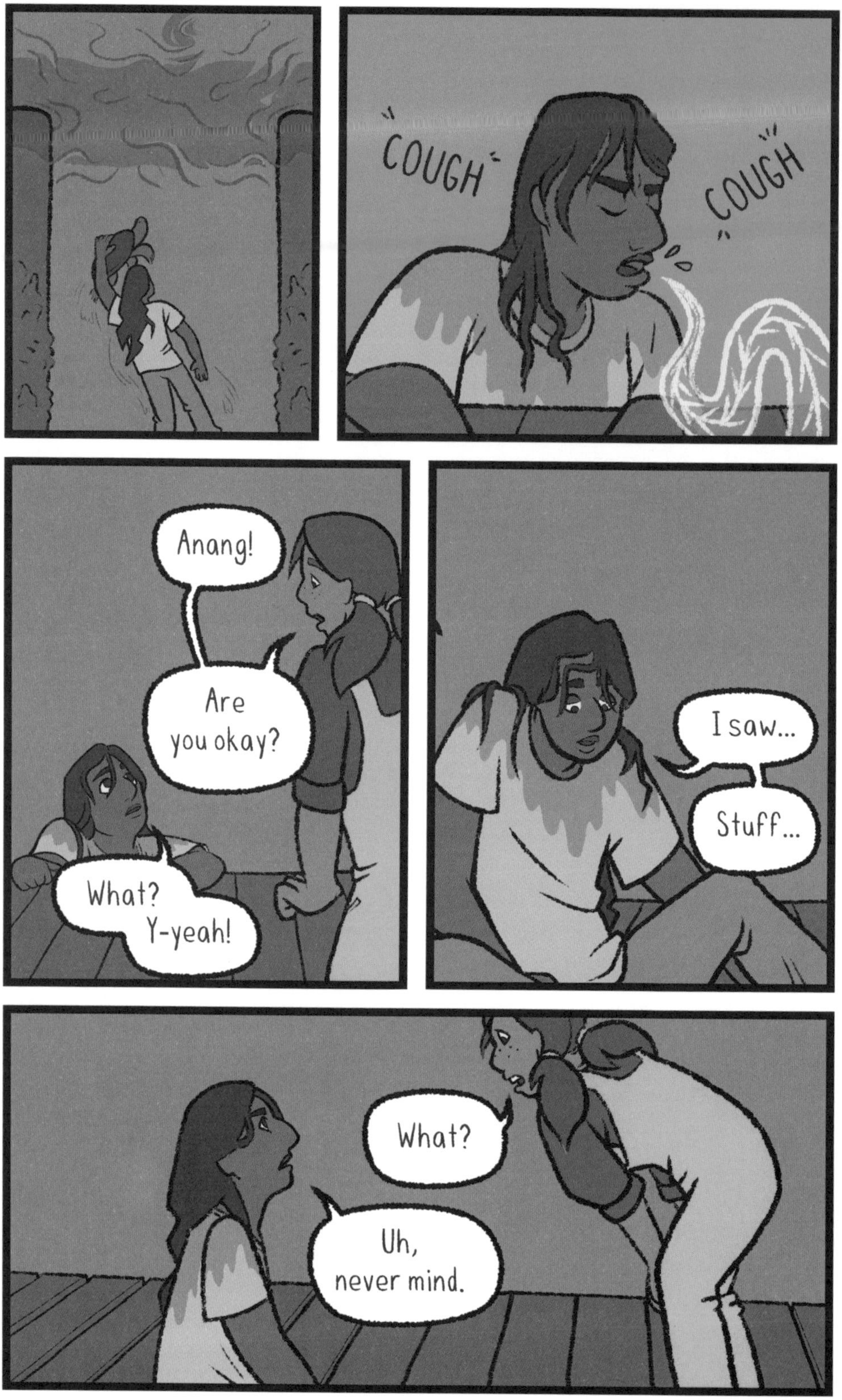
COUGH
COUGH
Anang!
Are you okay?
What? Y-yeah!
I saw...
Stuff...
What?
Uh, never mind.

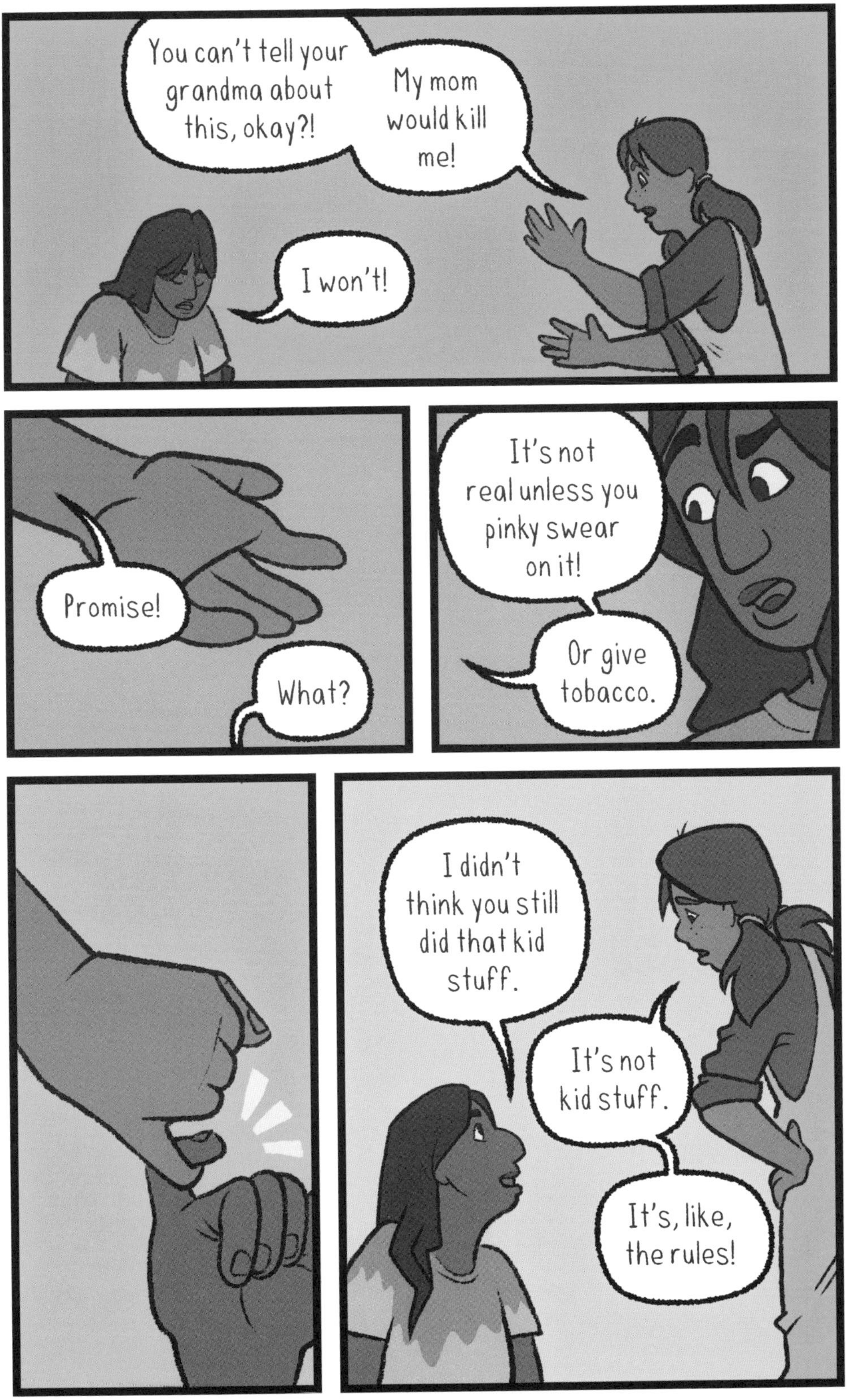
You can't tell your grandma about this, okay?!
My mom would kill me!
I won't!
Promise!
What?
It's not real unless you pinky swear on it!
Or give tobacco.
I didn't think you still did that kid stuff.
It's not kid stuff.
It's, like, the rules!

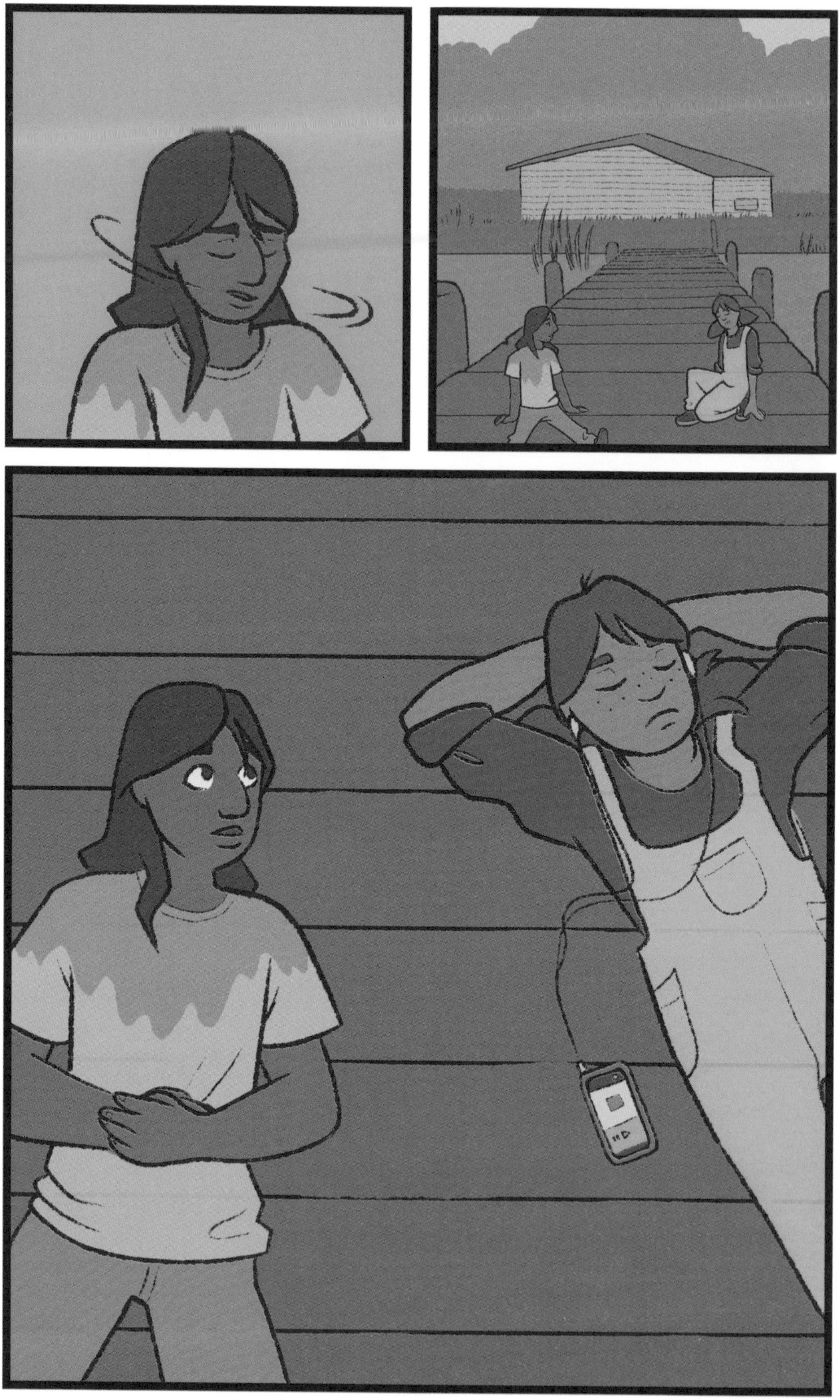

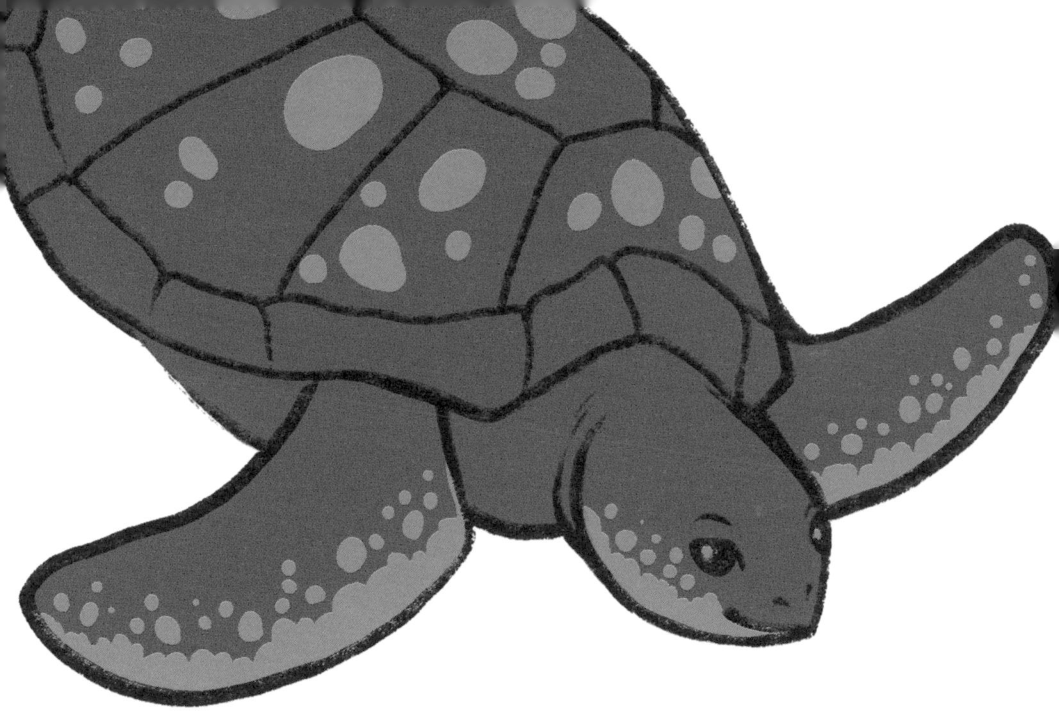

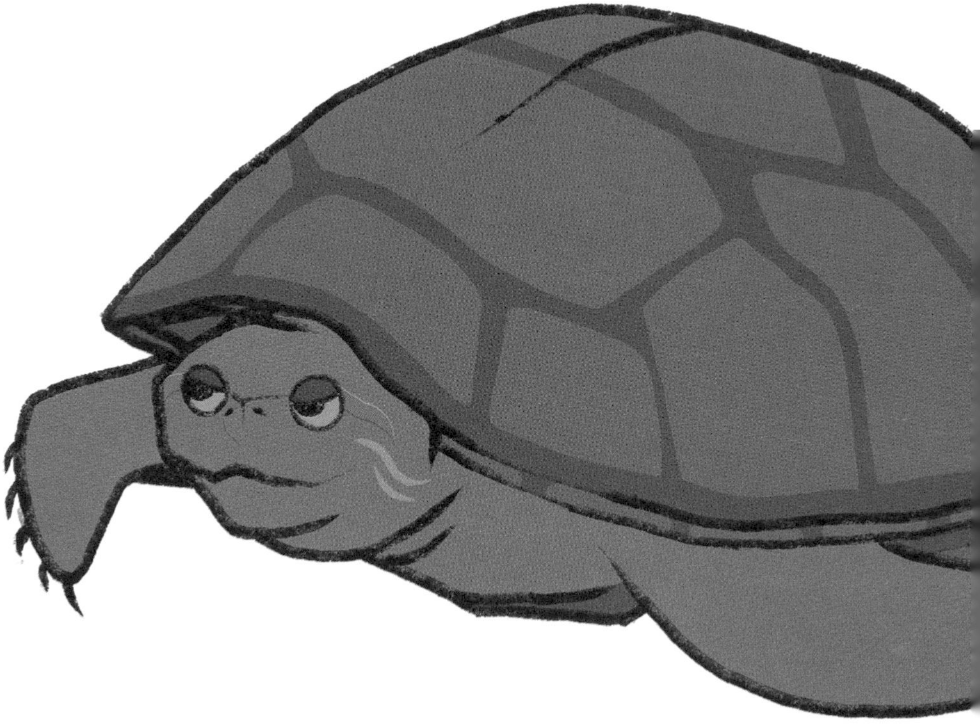

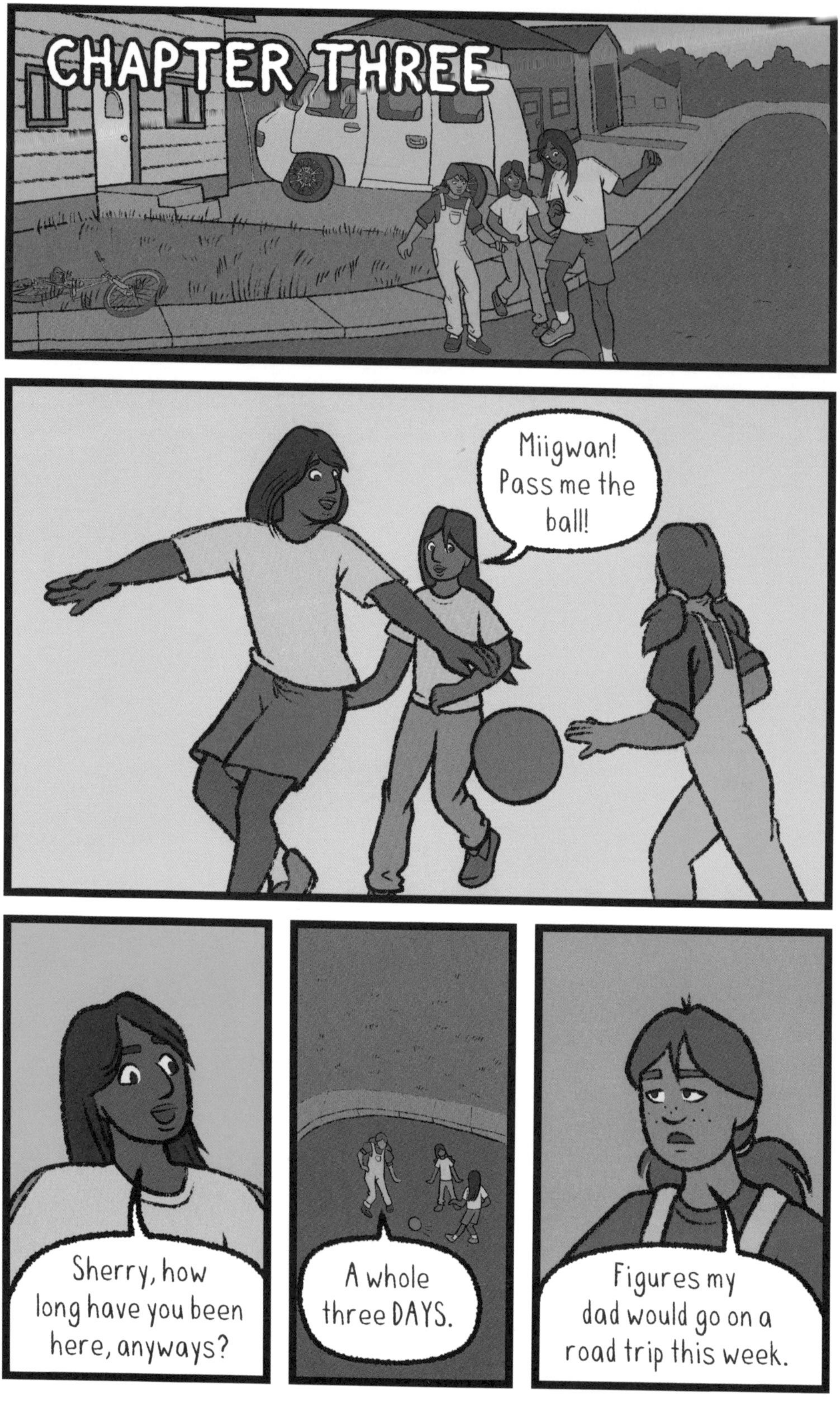
CHAPTER THREE
Miigwan! Pass me the ball!
Sherry, how long have you been here, anyways?
A whole three DAYS.
Figures my dad would go on a road trip this week.

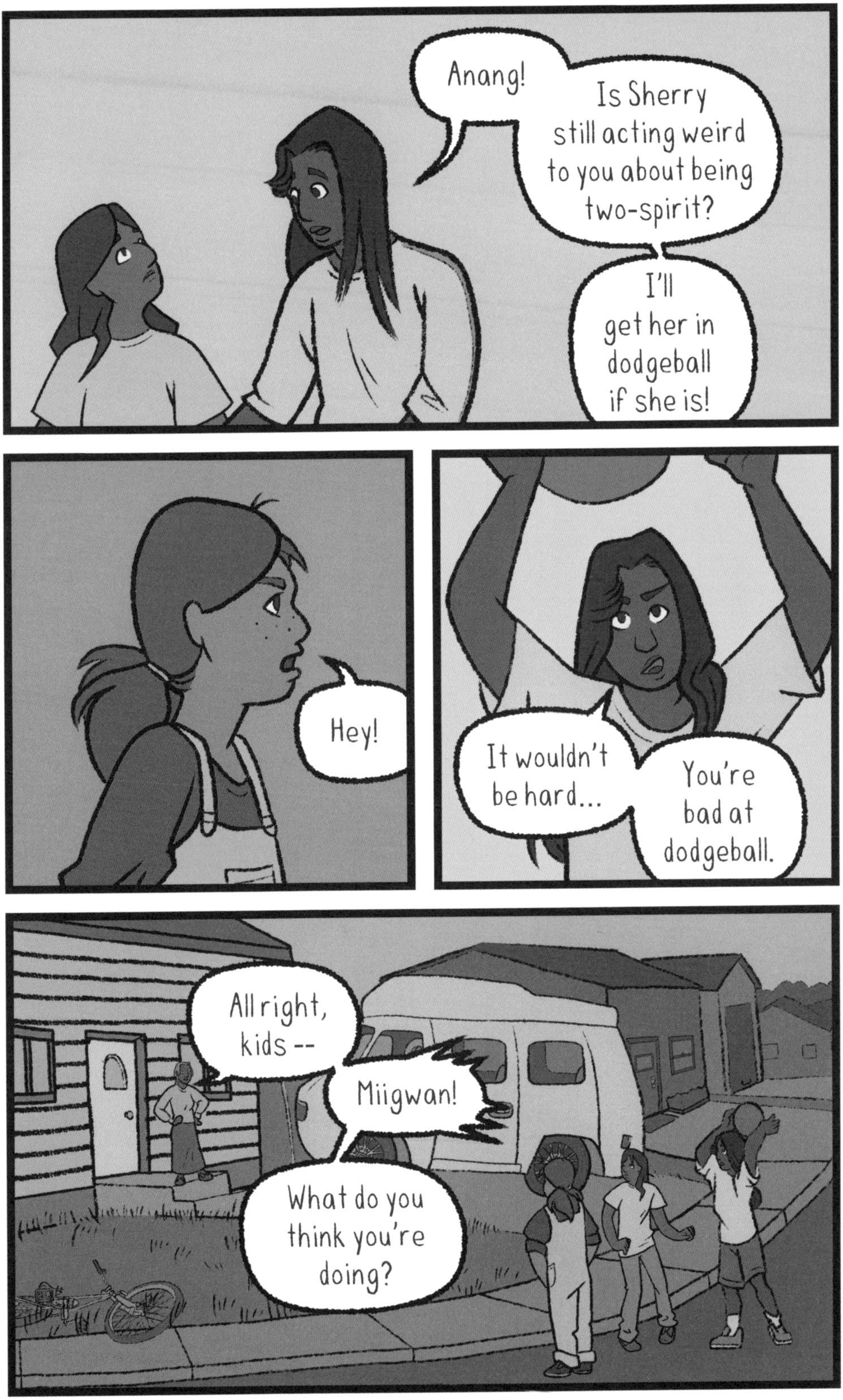
Anang!
Is Sherry still acting weird to you about being two-spirit?
I'll get her in dodgeball if she is!
Hey!
It wouldn't be hard...
You're bad at dodgeball.
All right, kids --
Miigwan!
What do you think you're doing?

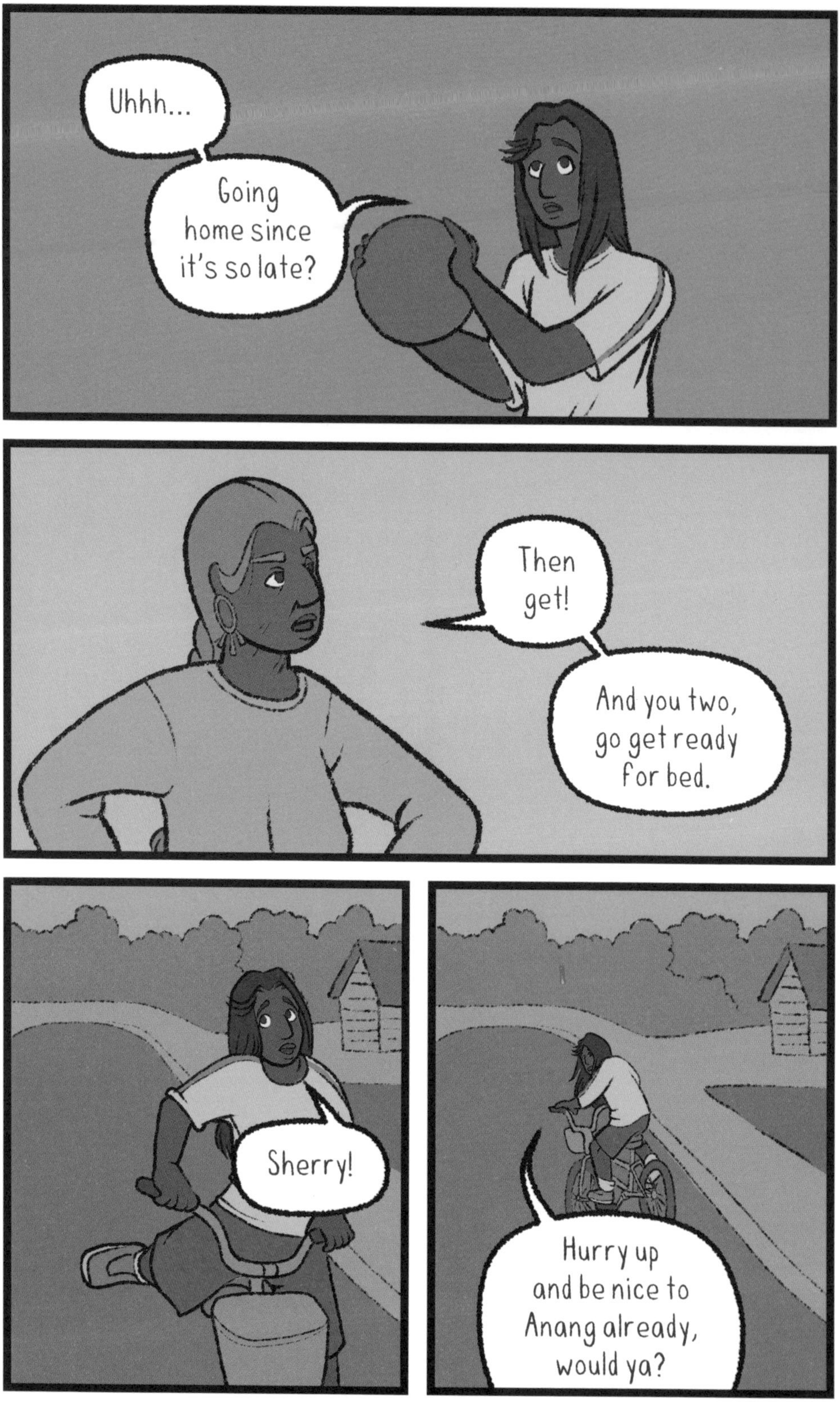
Uhhh...
Going home since it's so late?
Then get!
And you two, go get ready for bed.
Sherry!
Hurry up and be nice to Anang already, would ya?

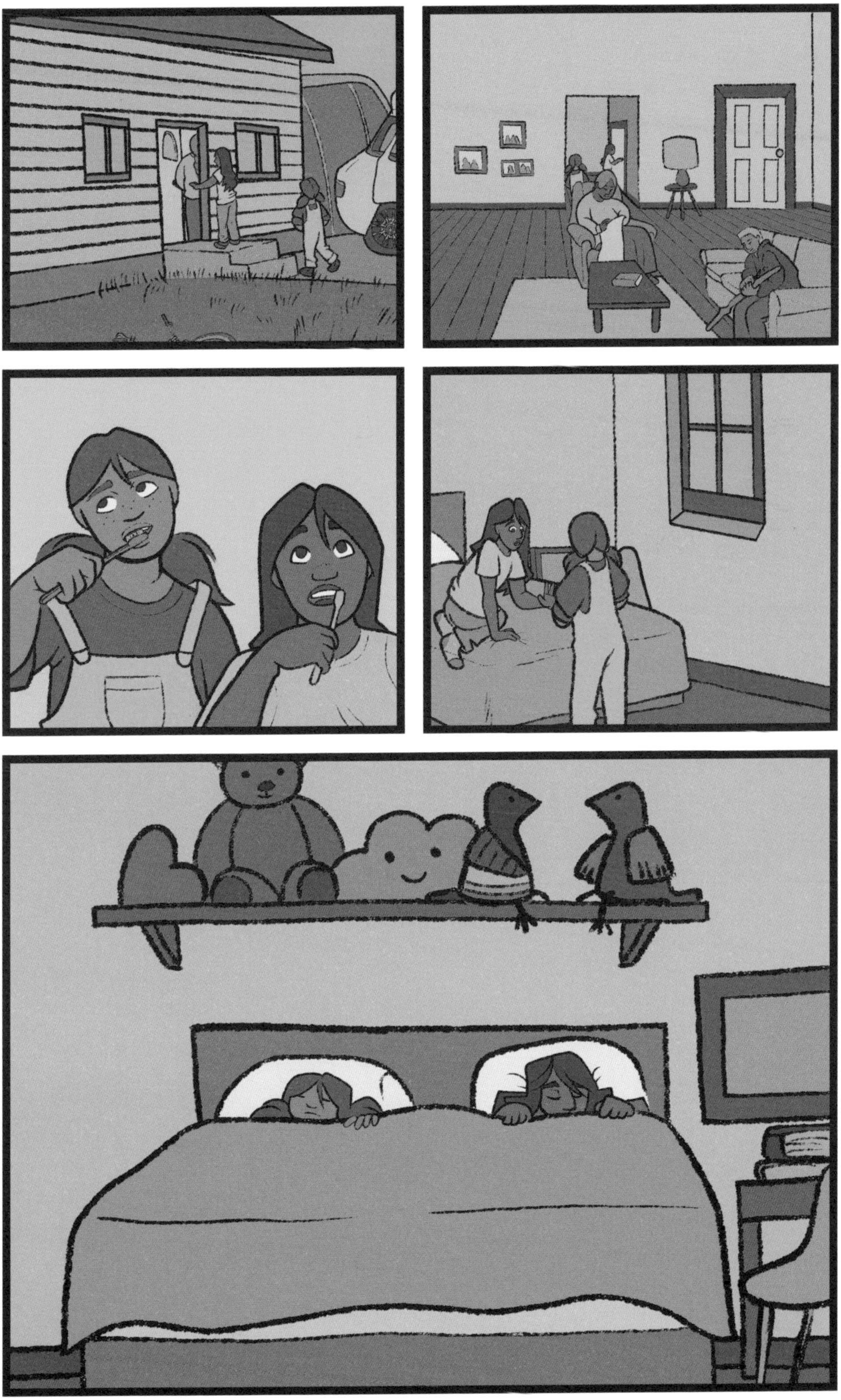

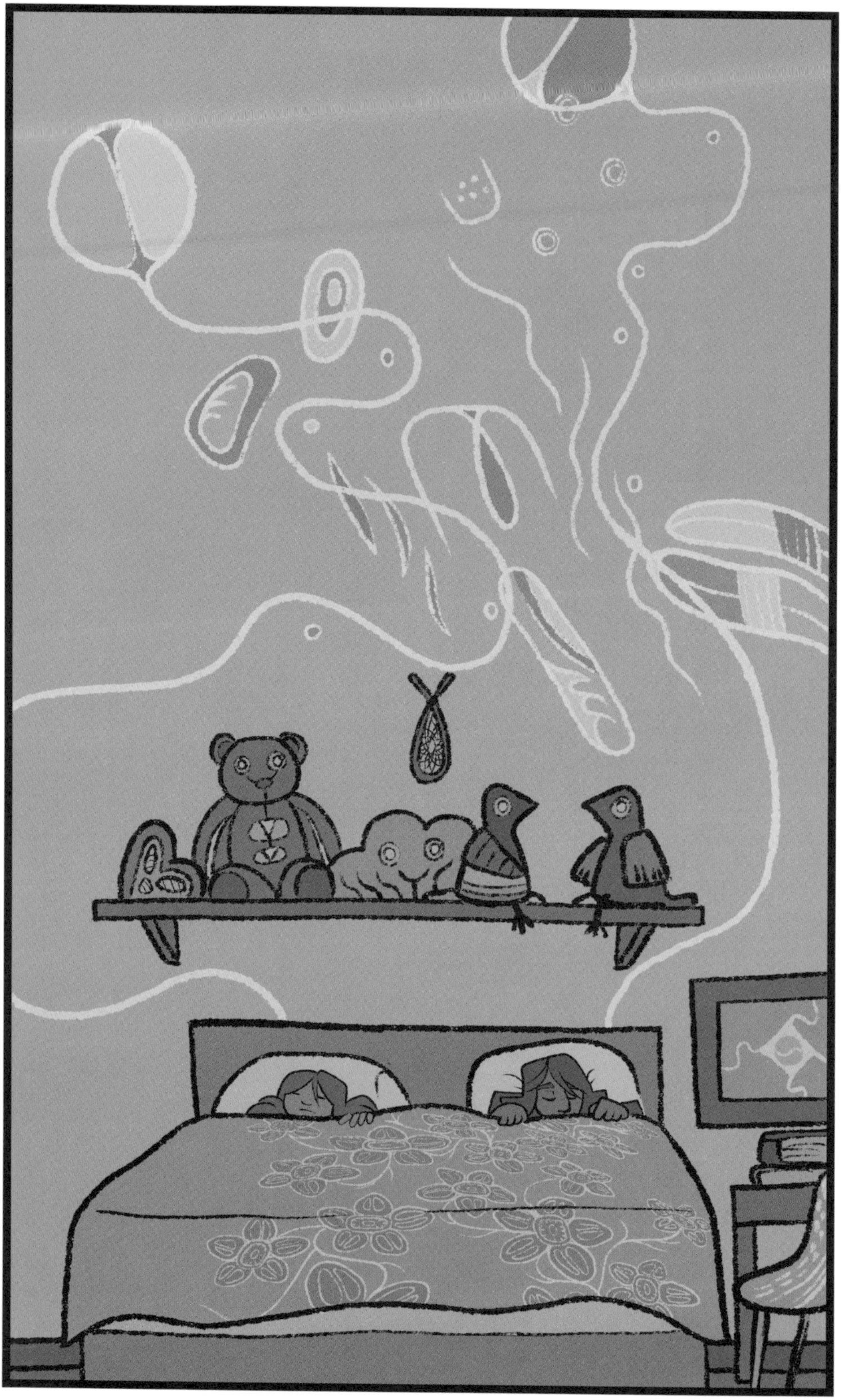

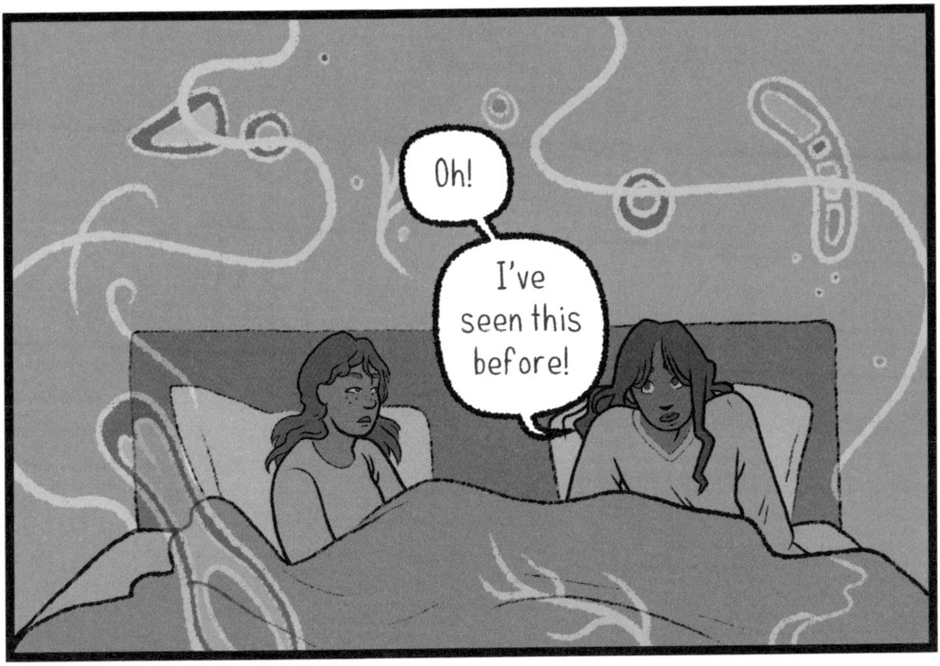
Oh!
I've seen this before!

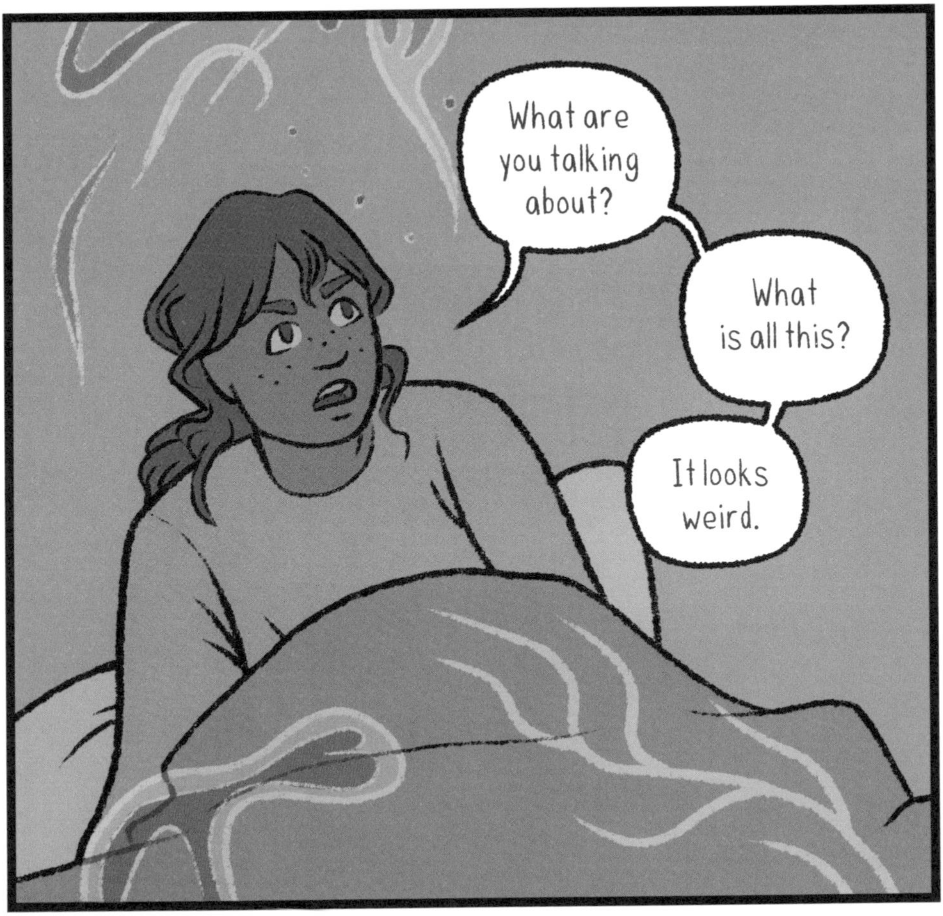
What are you talking about?
What is all this?
It looks weird.

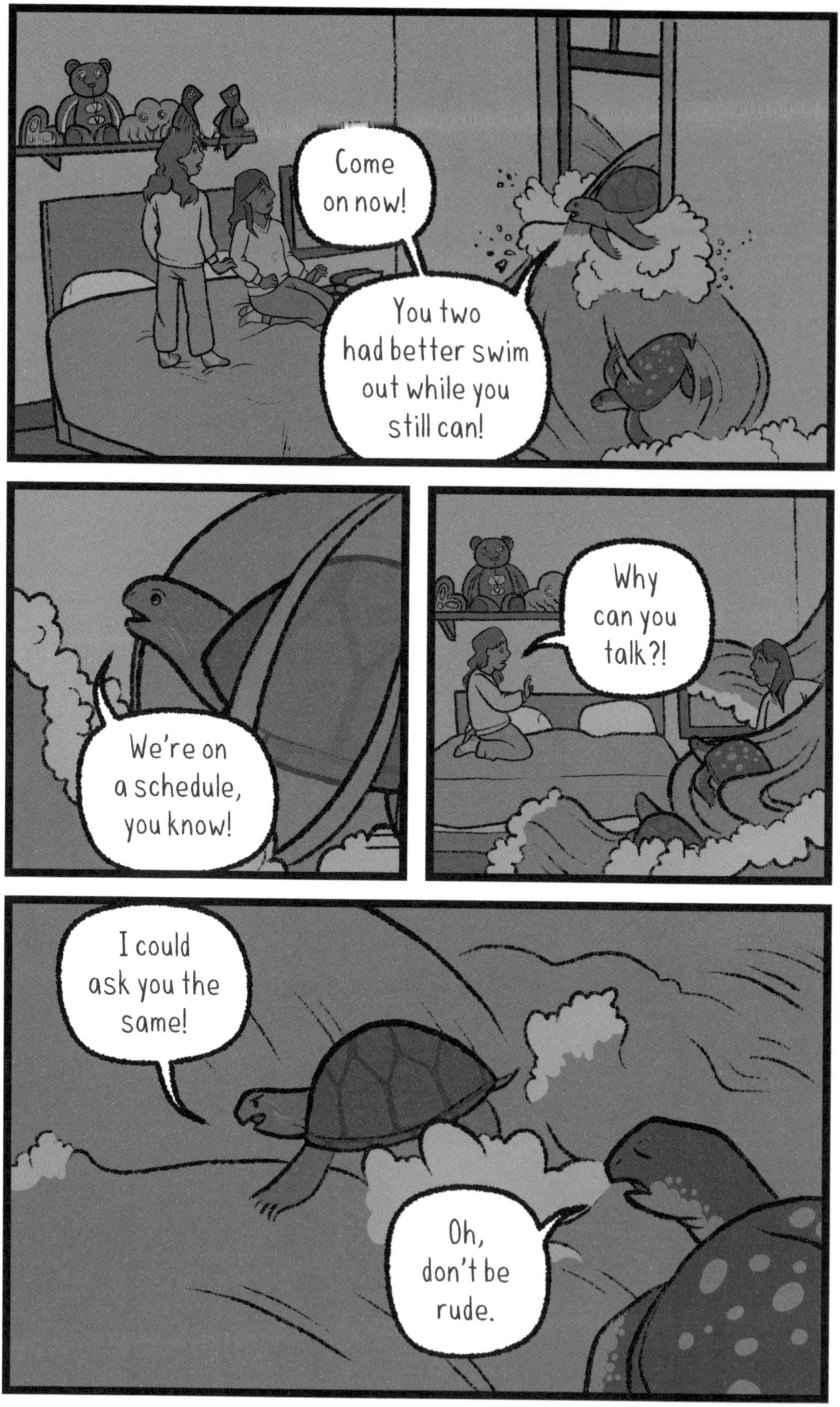
Come on now!
You two had better swim out while you still can!
We're on a schedule, you know!
Why can you talk?!
I could ask you the same!
Oh, don't be rude.

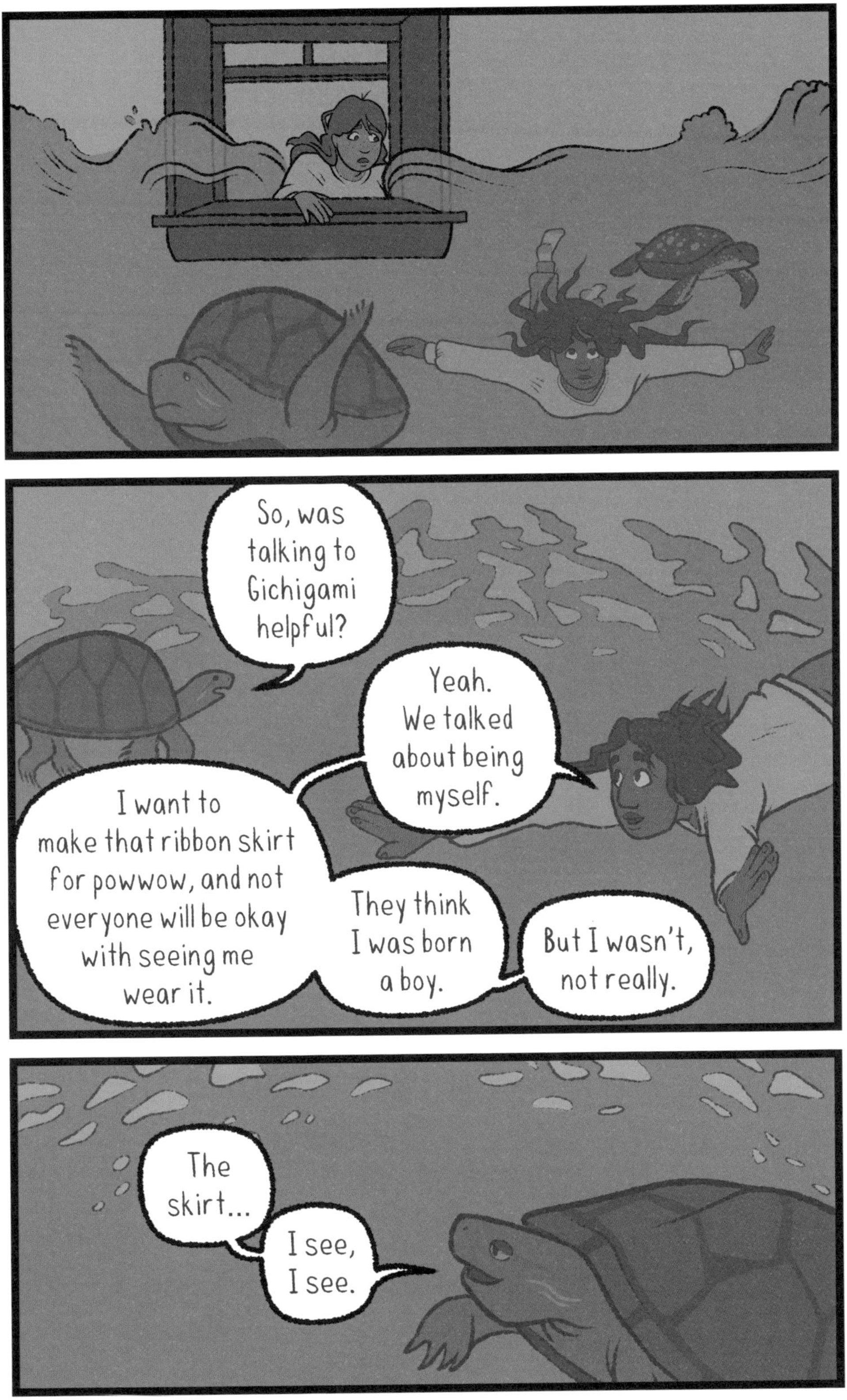
So, was talking to Gichigami helpful?
Yeah. We talked about being myself.
I want to make that ribbon skirt for powwow, and not everyone will be okay with seeing me wear it.
They think I was born a boy.
But I wasn't, not really.
The skirt...
I see, I see.

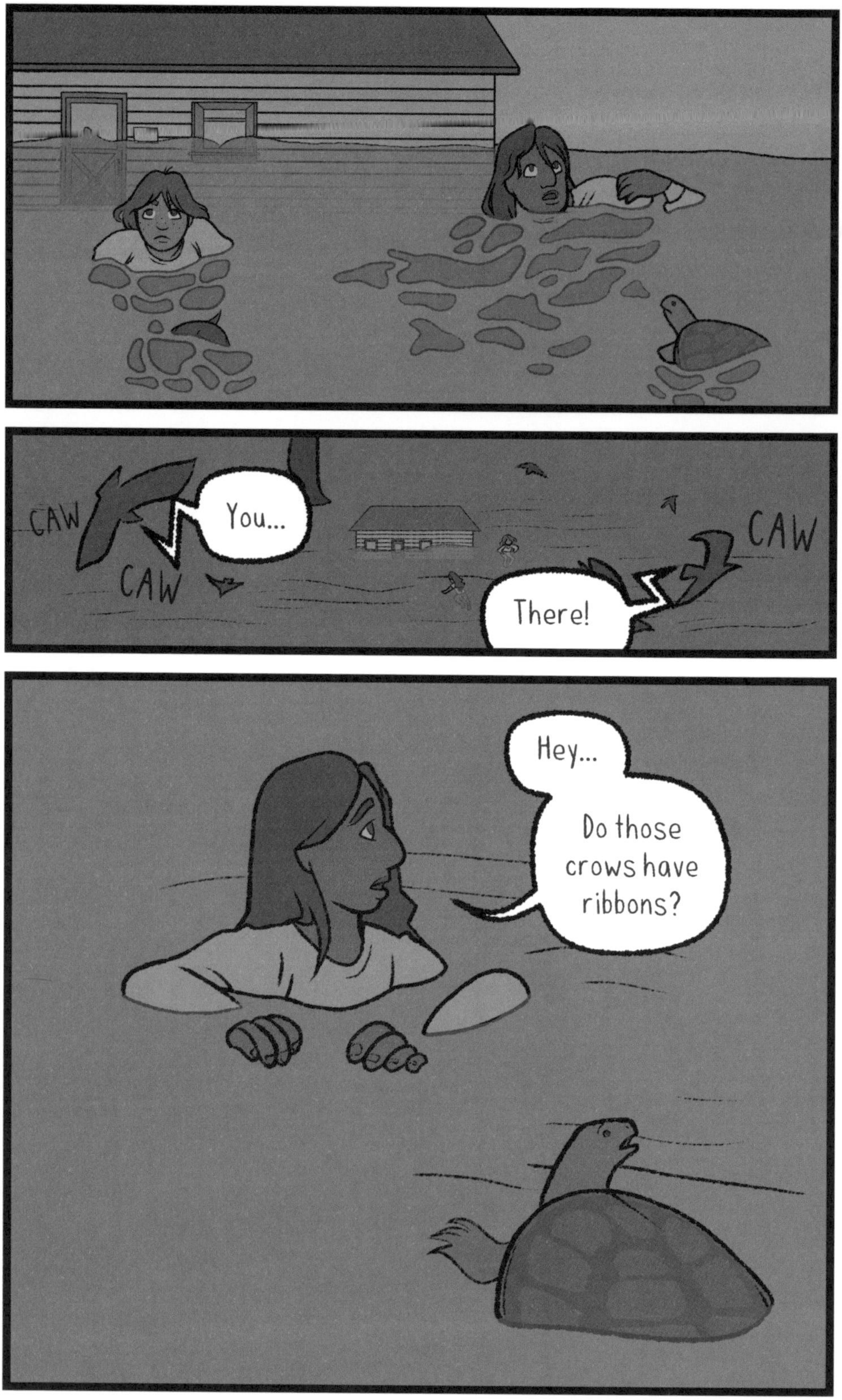
CAW
You...
CAW
CAW
There!
Hey...
Do those crows have ribbons?

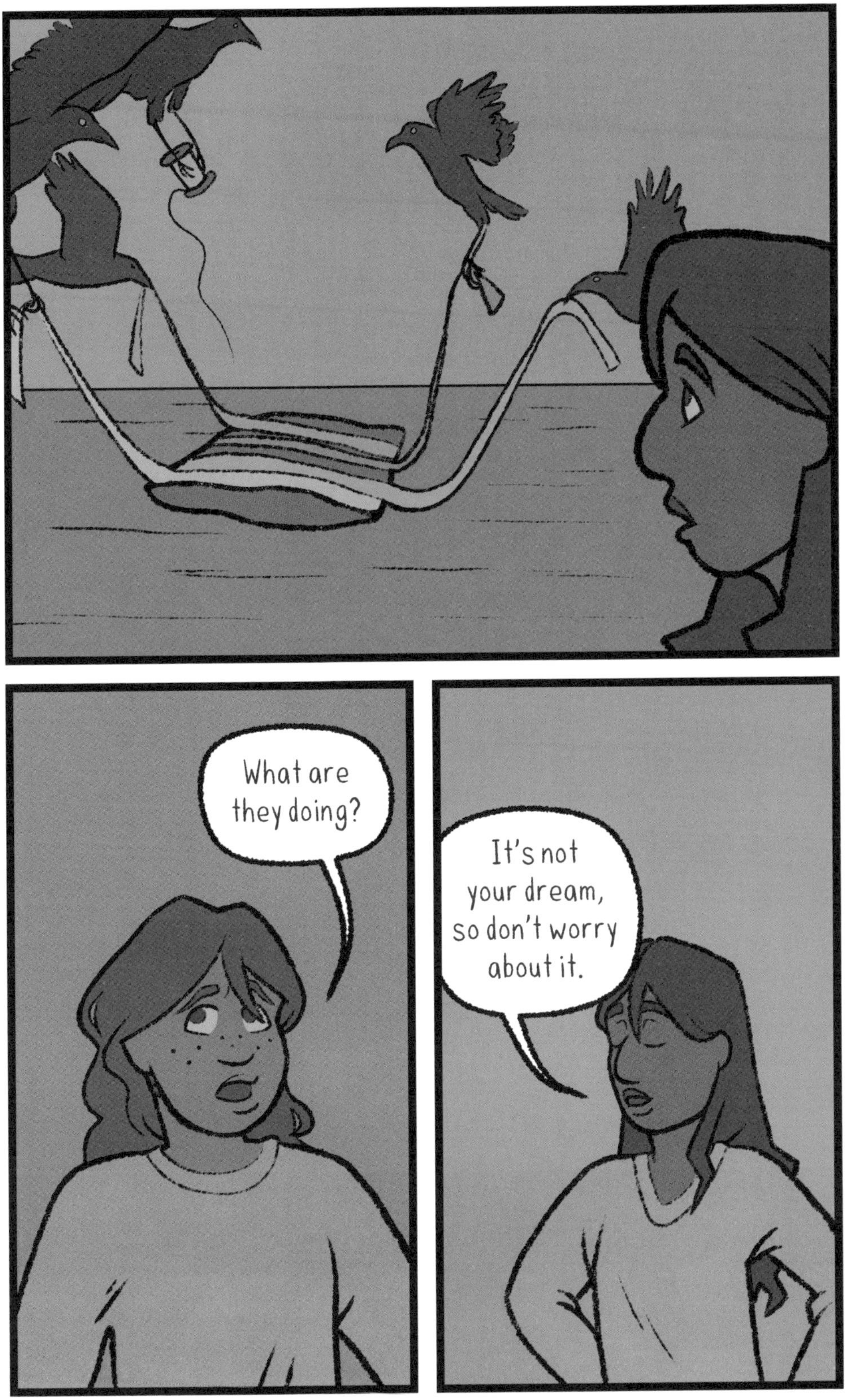
What are they doing?
It's not your dream, so don't worry about it.

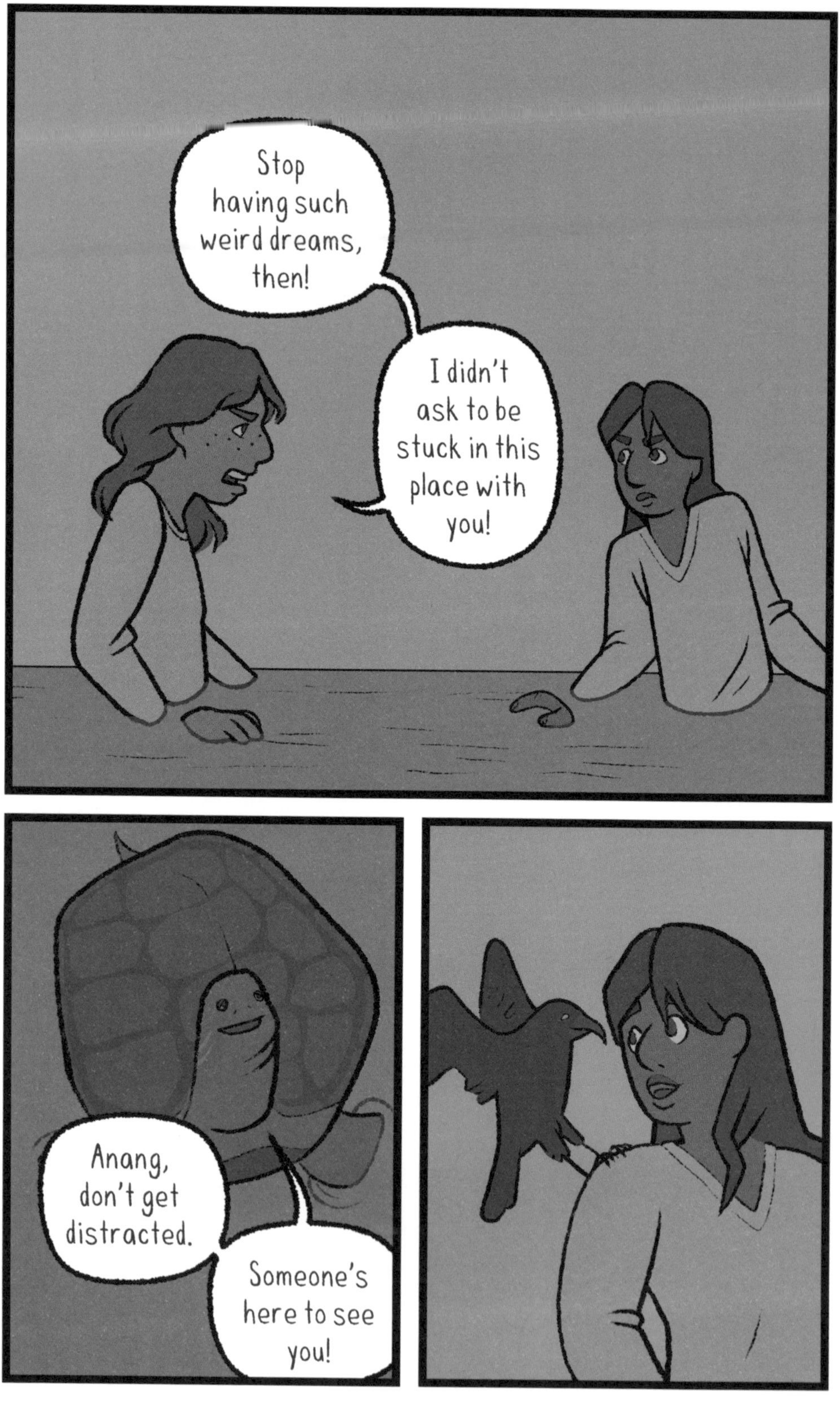
Stop having such weird dreams, then!
I didn't ask to be stuck in this place with you!
Anang, don't get distracted.
Someone's here to see you!

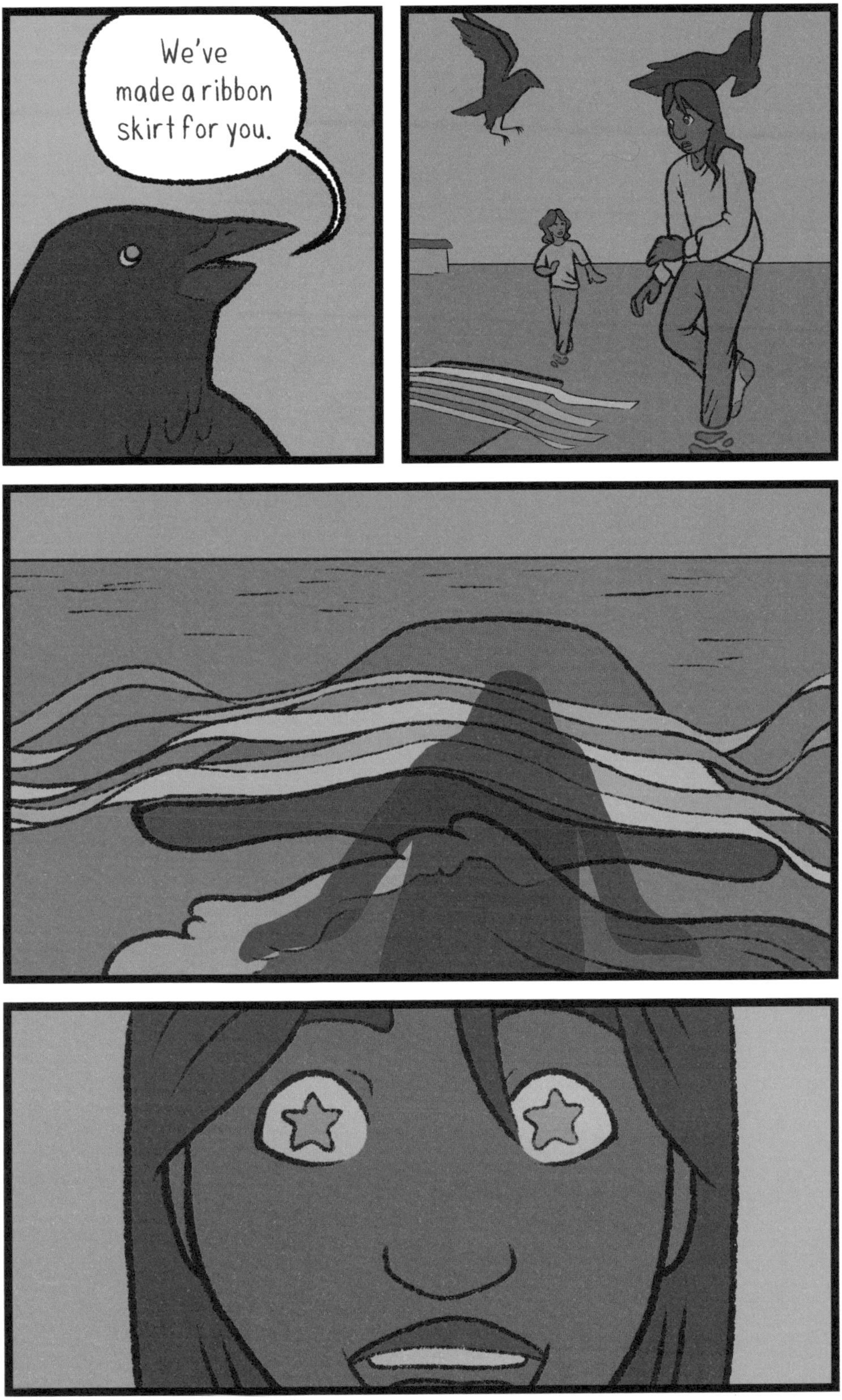
We've made a ribbon skirt for you.

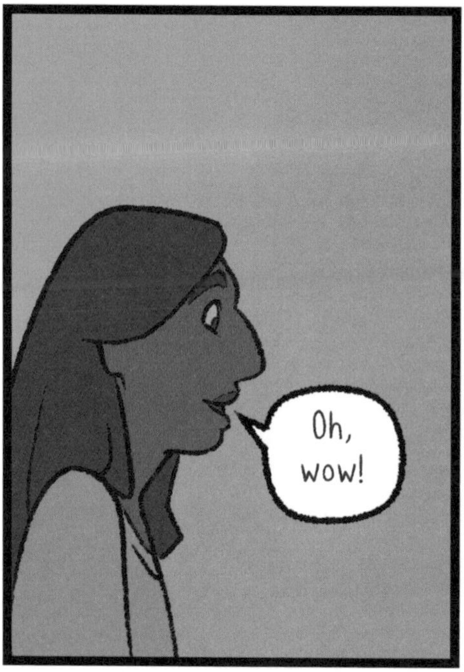
Oh,
wow!

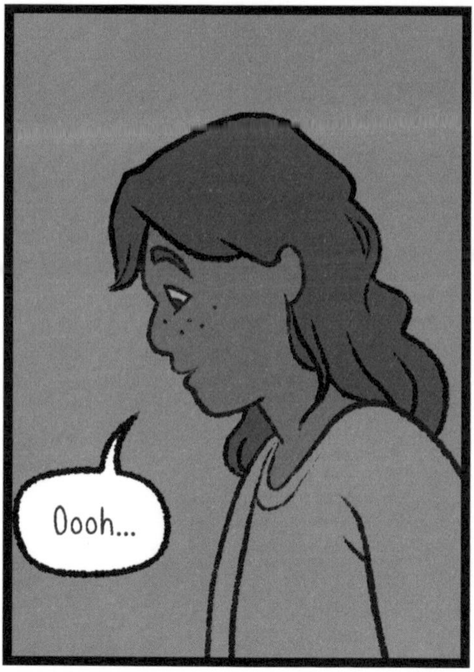
Oooh...

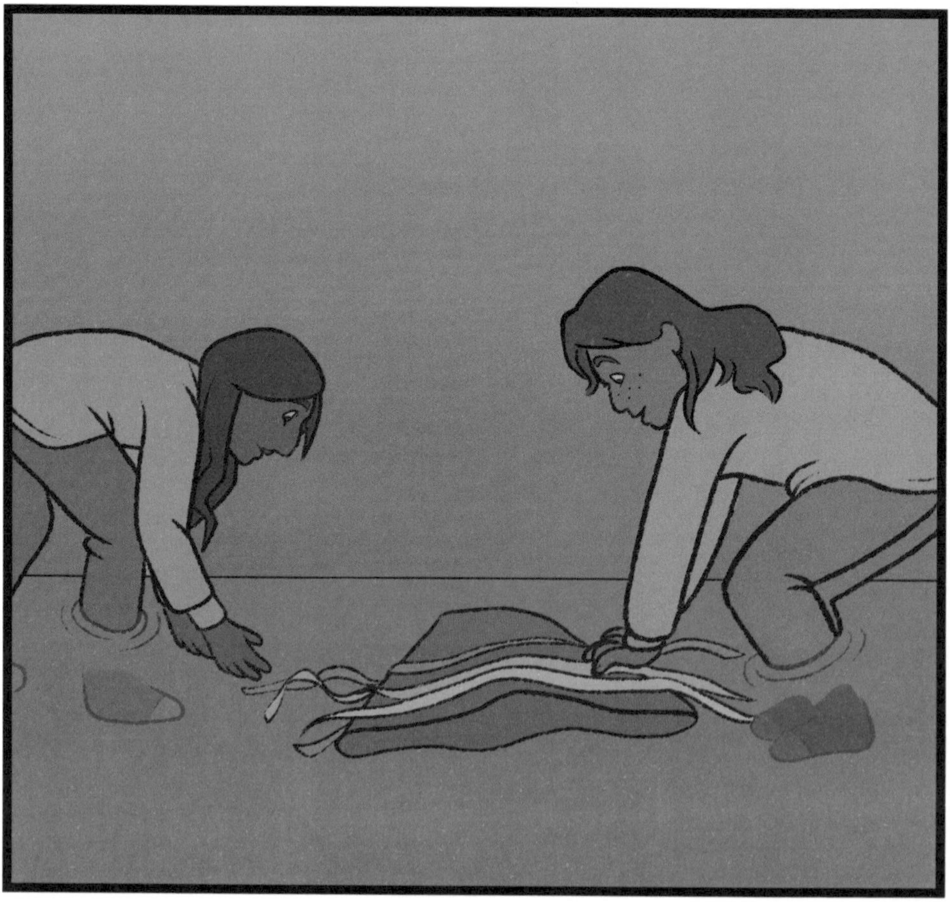

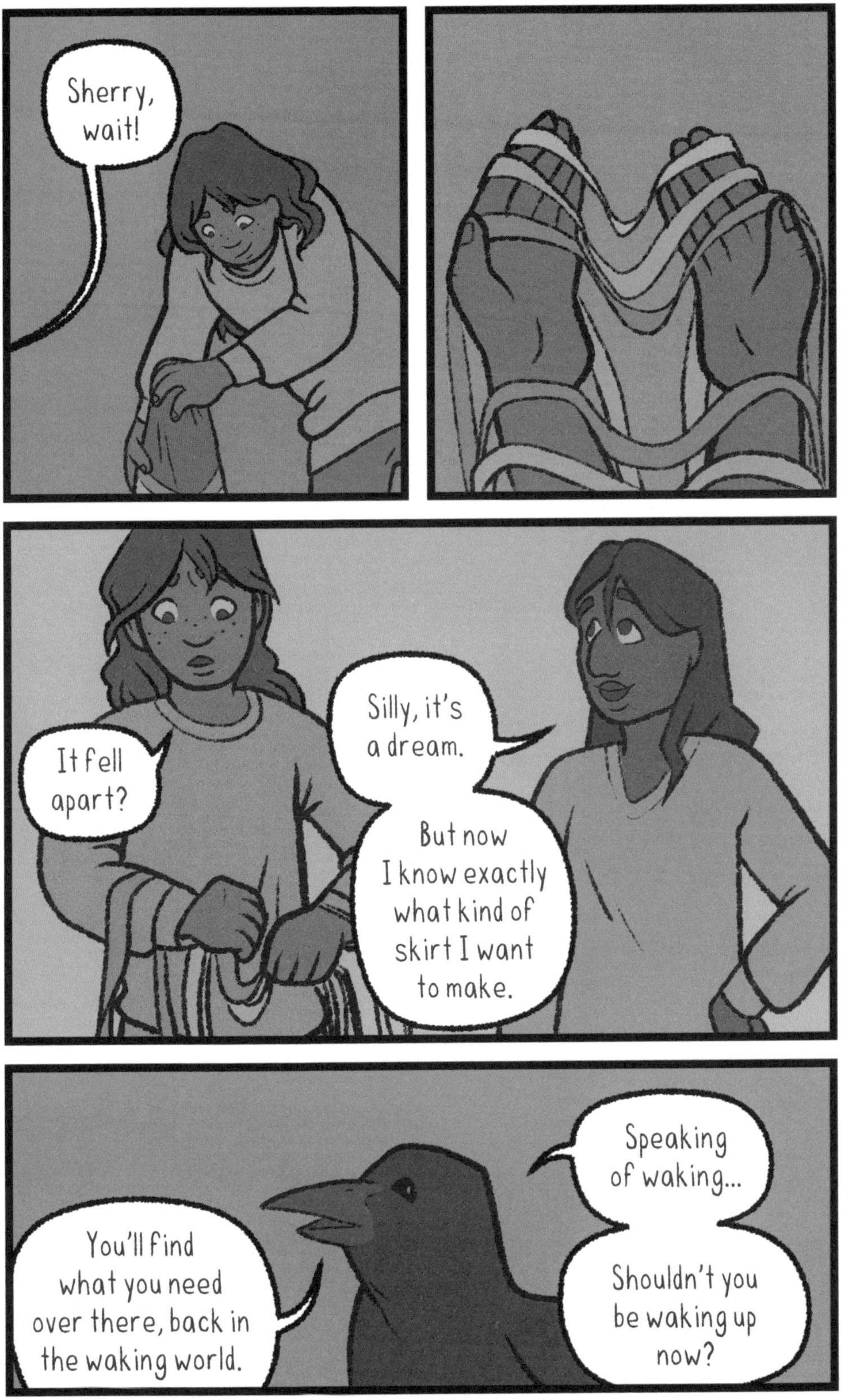
Sherry, wait!
It fell apart?
Silly, it's a dream.
But now I know exactly what kind of skirt I want to make.
Speaking of waking...
Shouldn't you be waking up now?
You'll find what you need over there, back in the waking world.

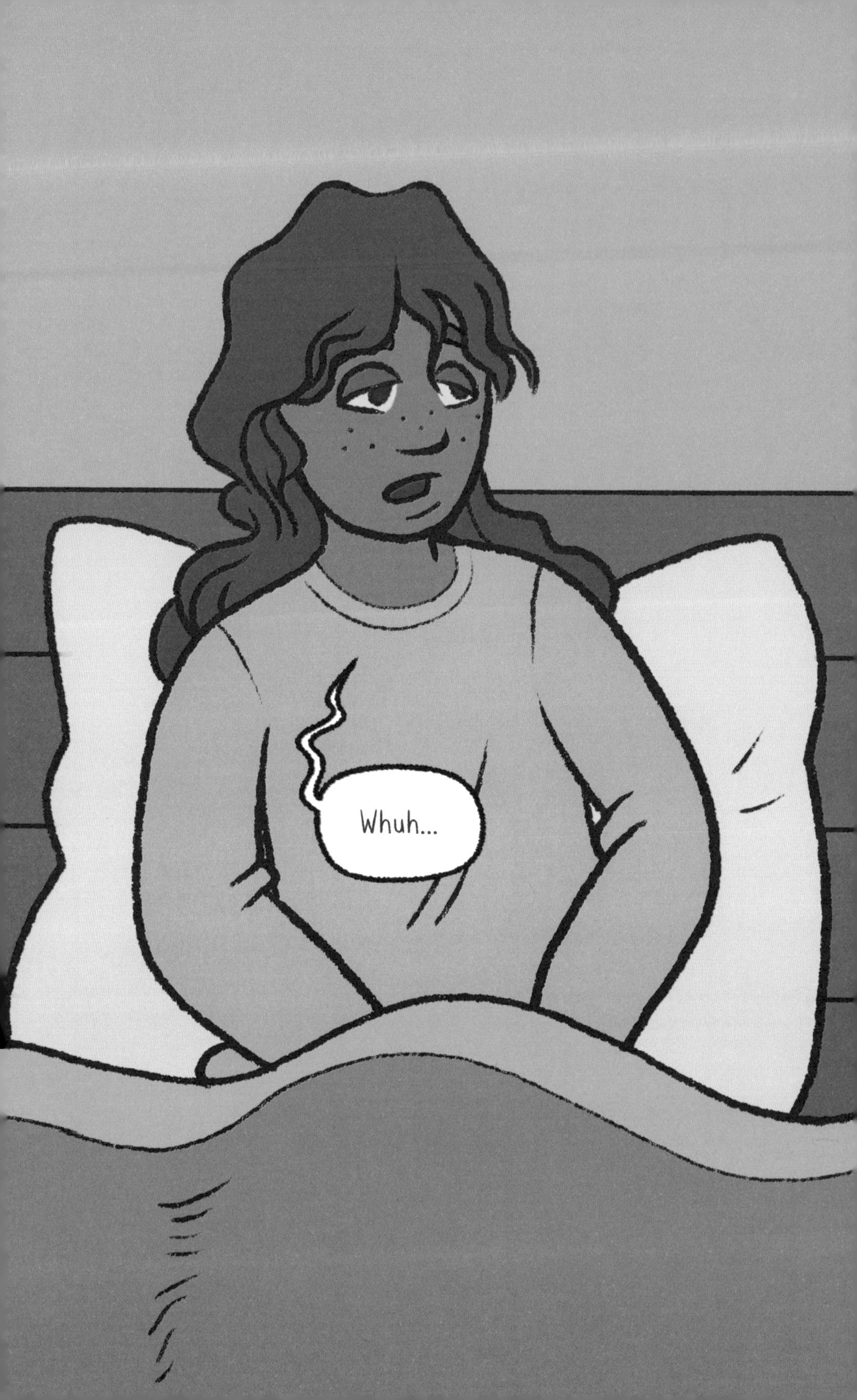
Whuh...

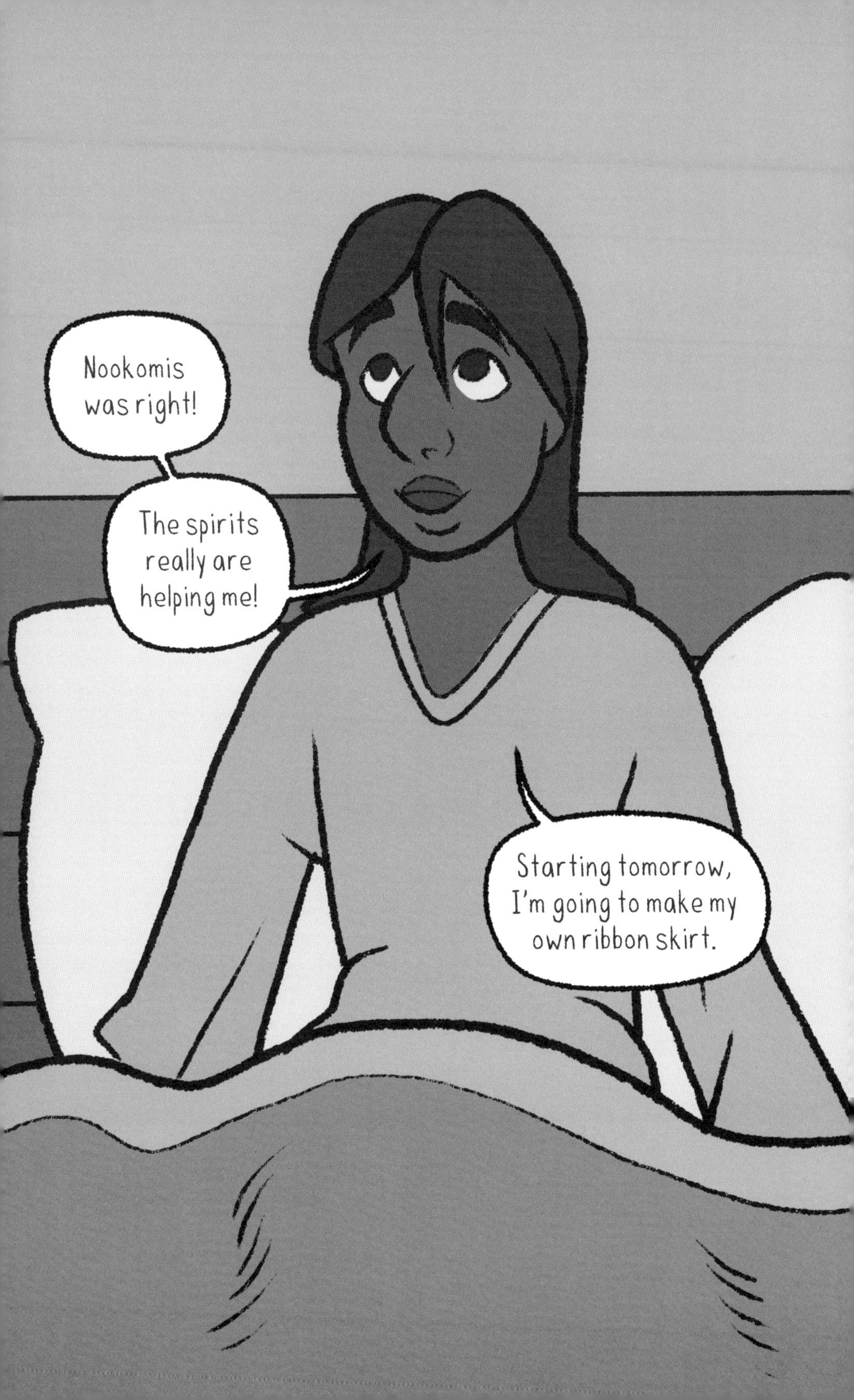
Nookomis was right!
The spirits really are helping me!
Starting tomorrow, I'm going to make my own ribbon skirt.

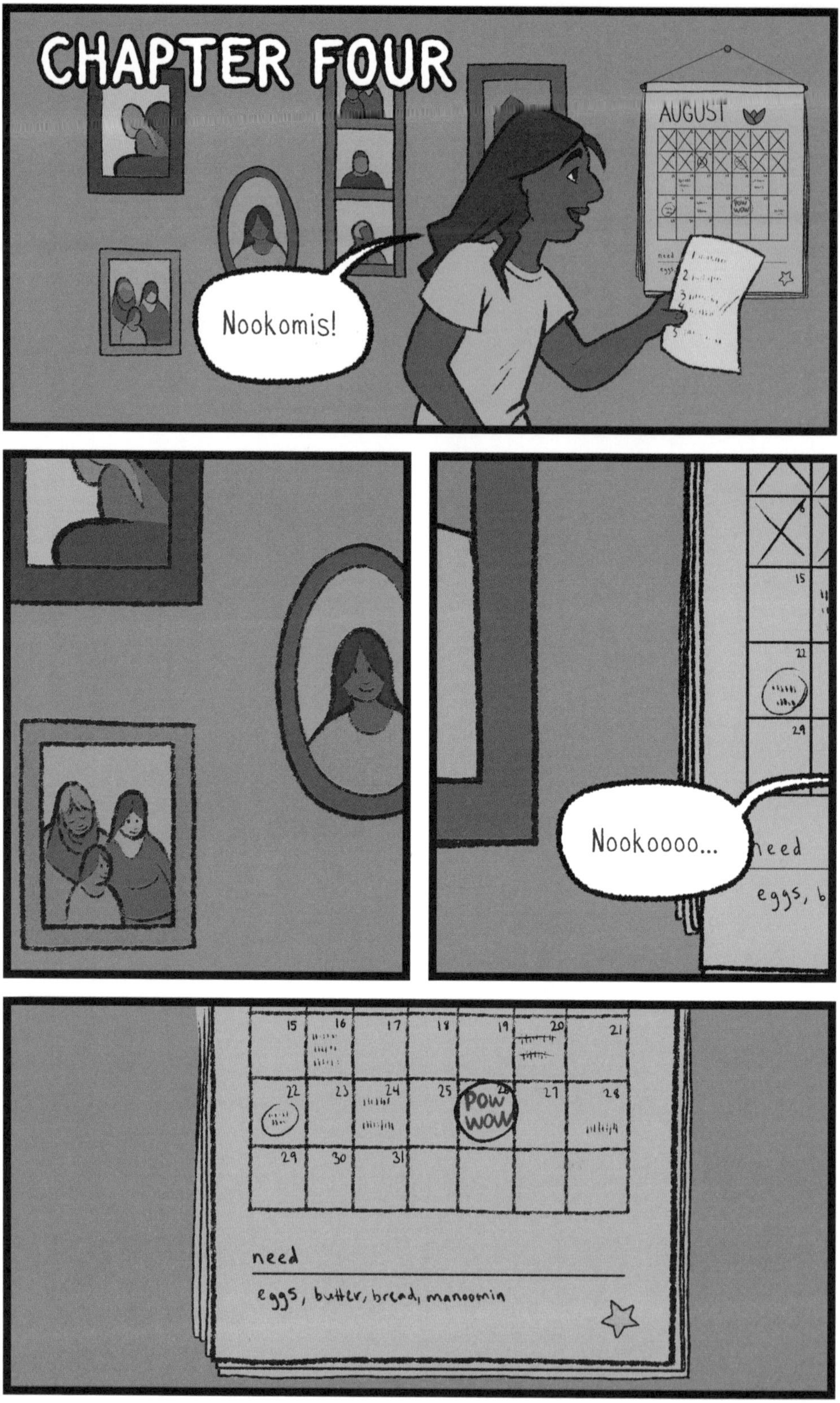

CHAPTER FOUR
AUGUST
Nookomis!
Nookoooo...
POW WOW
need
eggs, butter, bread, manoomin

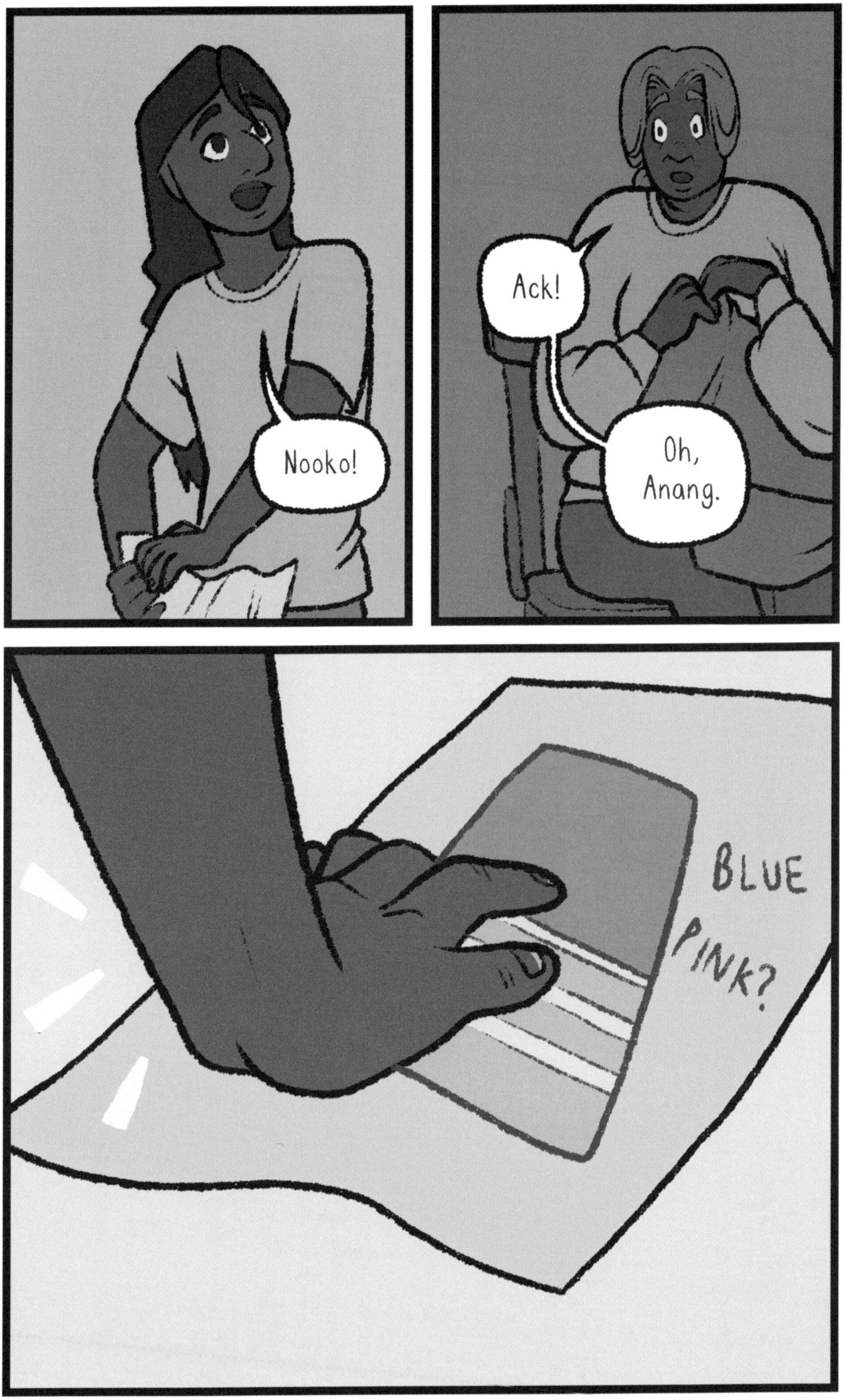
Nooko!
Ack!
Oh, Anang.
BLUE
PINK?

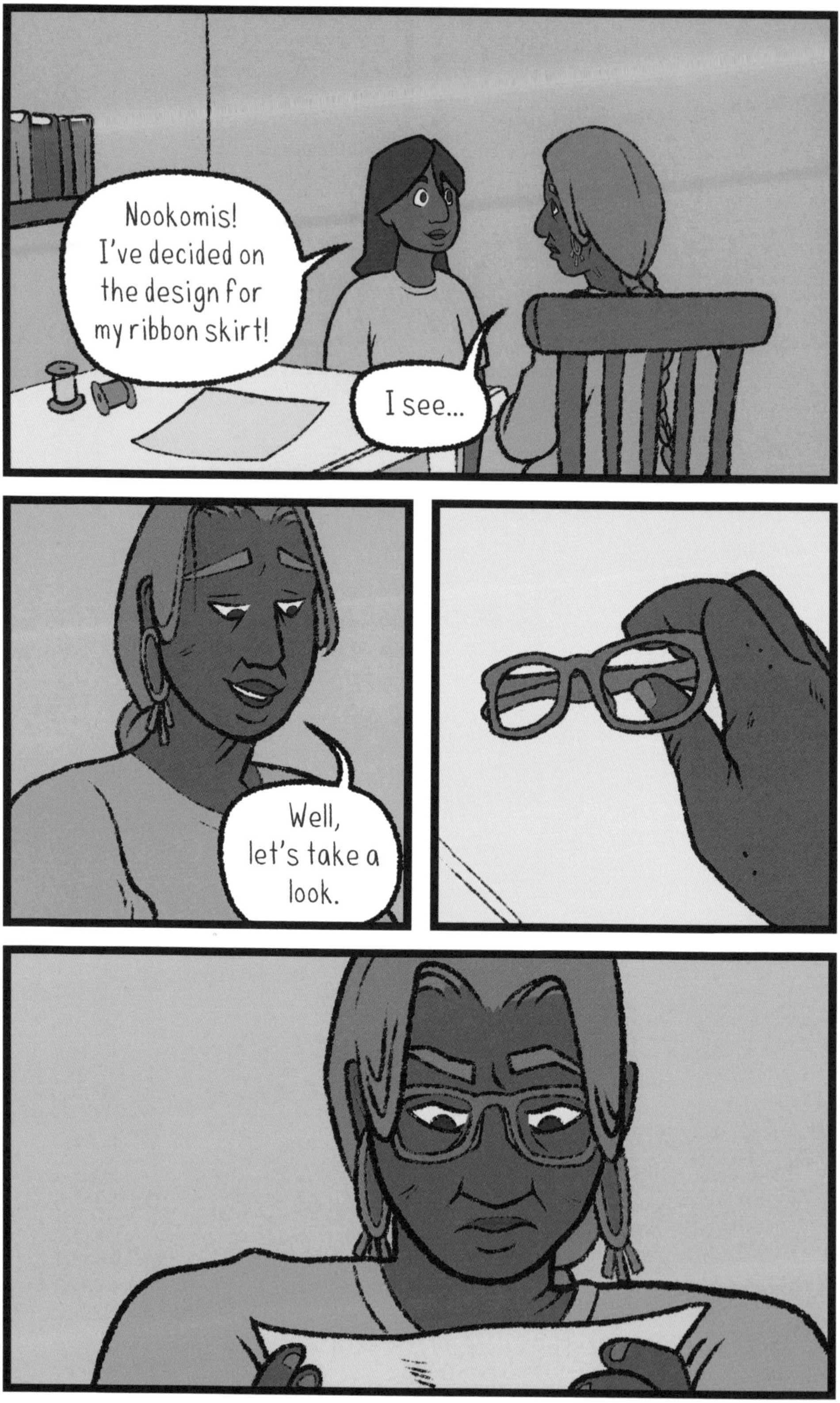
Nookomis! I've decided on the design for my ribbon skirt!
I see...
Well, let's take a look.

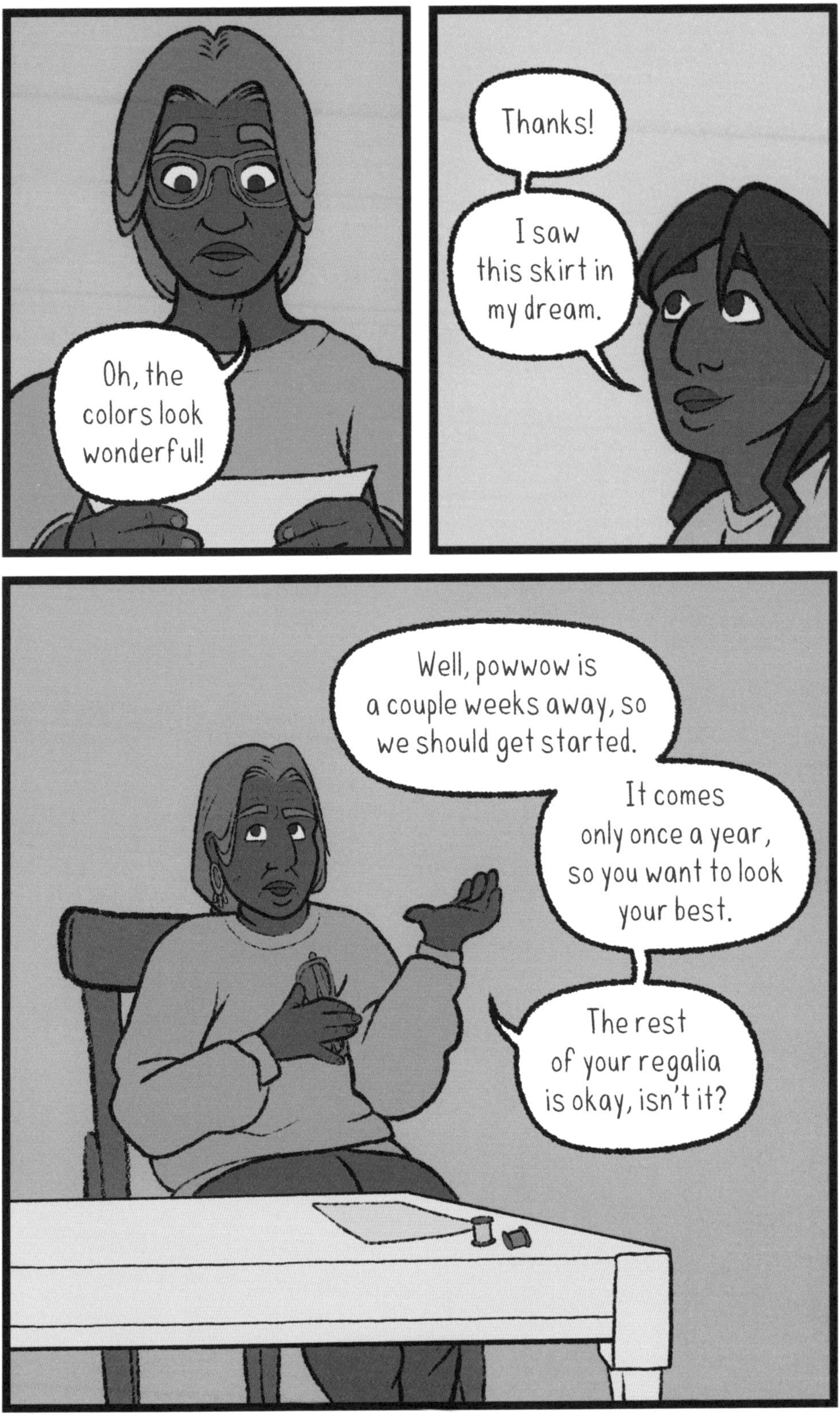
Oh, the colors look wonderful!
Thanks!
I saw this skirt in my dream.
Well, powwow is a couple weeks away, so we should get started.
It comes only once a year, so you want to look your best.
The rest of your regalia is okay, isn't it?

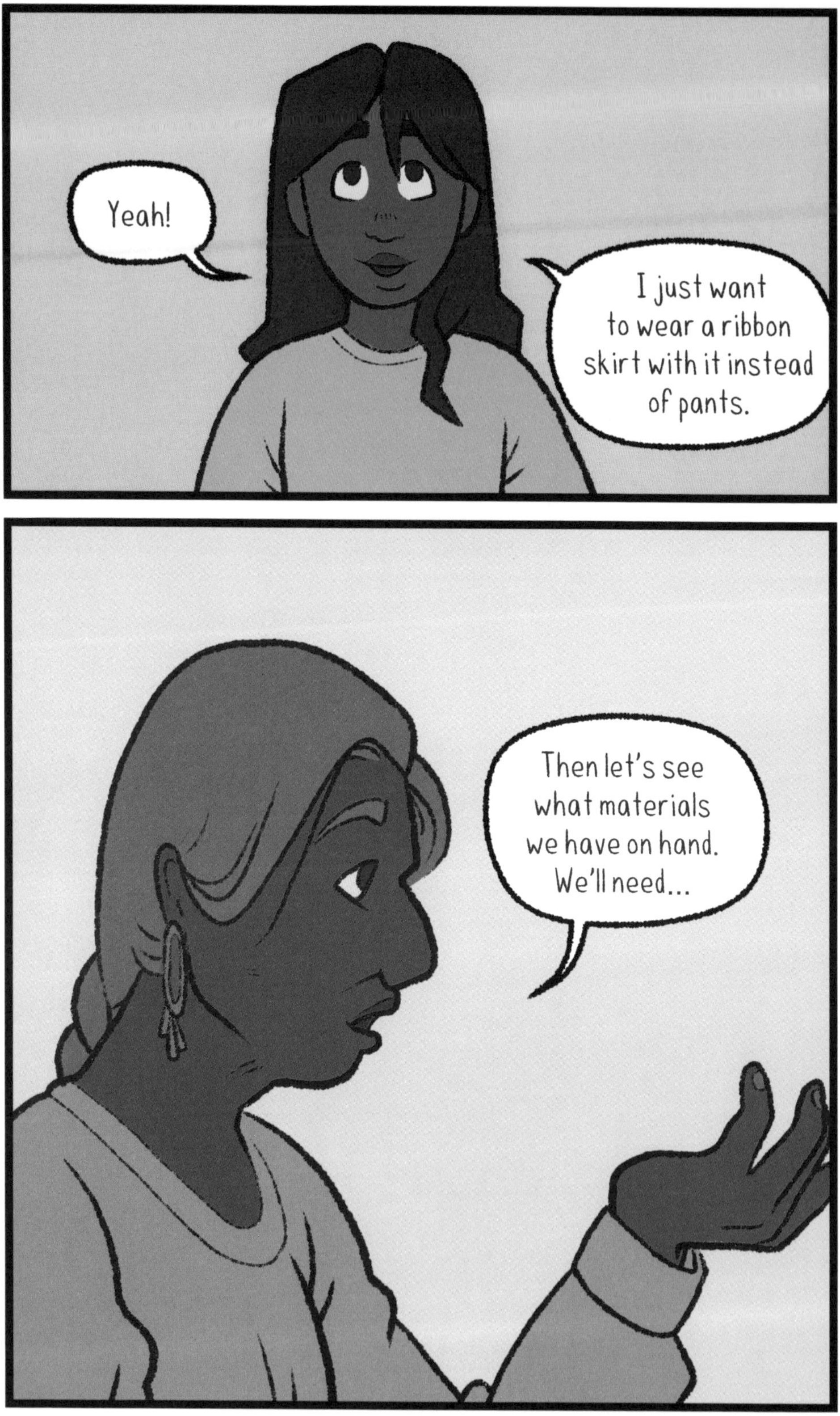
Yeah!
I just want to wear a ribbon skirt with it instead of pants.
Then let's see what materials we have on hand. We'll need...

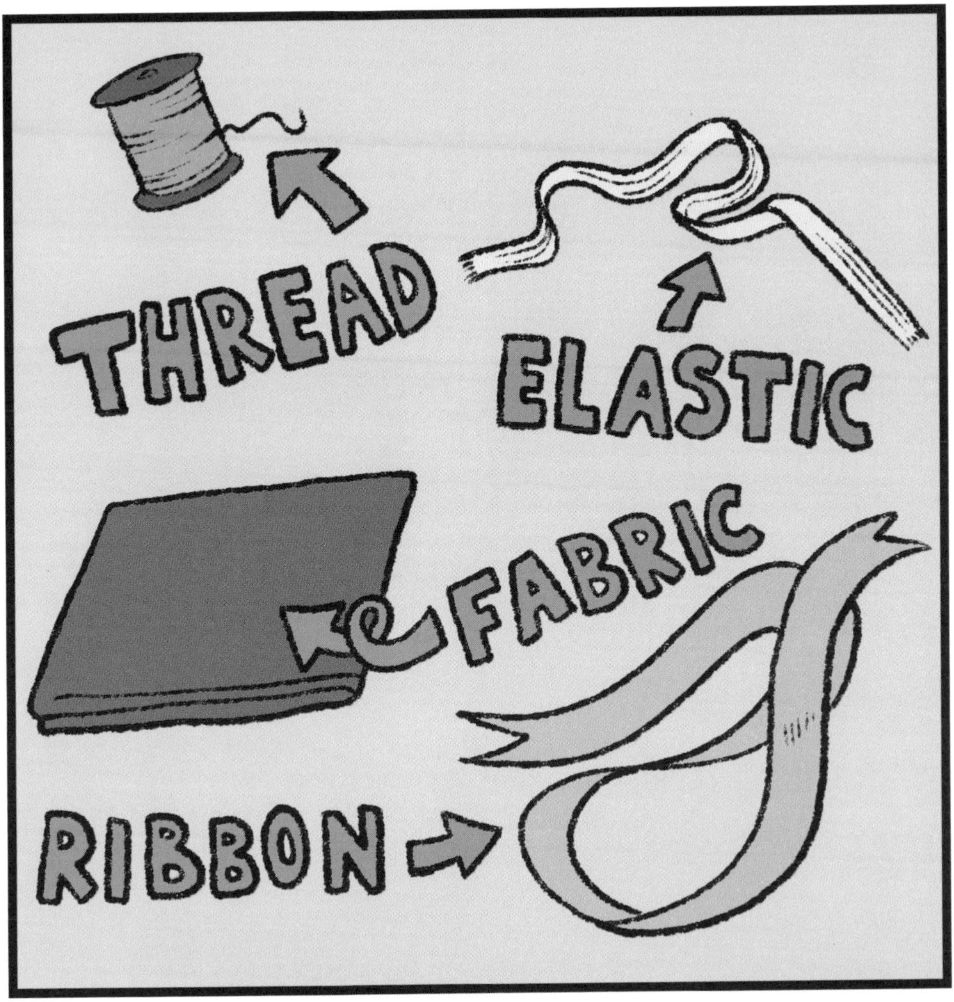
THREAD
ELASTIC
FABRIC
RIBBON

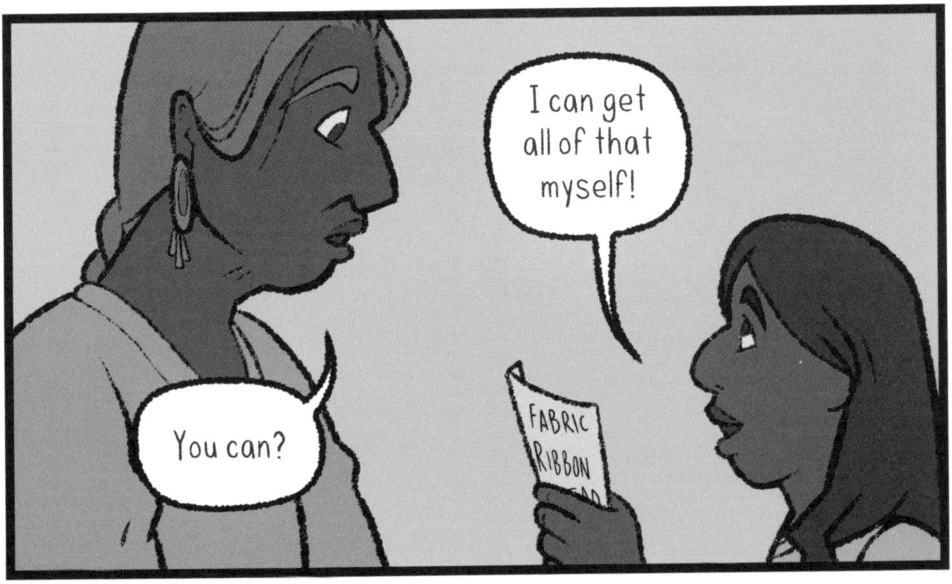
I can get all of that myself!
You can?
FABRIC
RIBBON

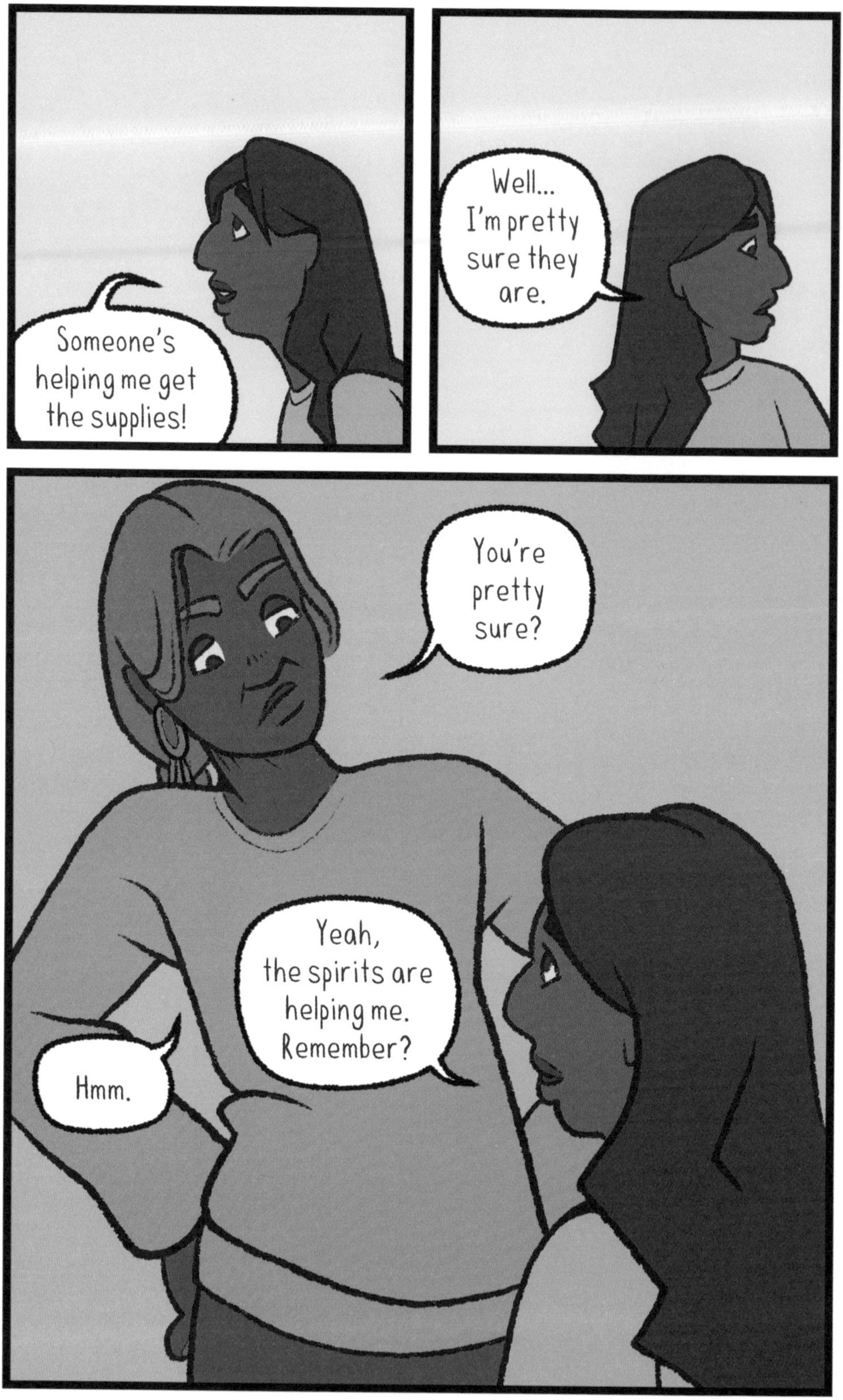
Someone's helping me get the supplies!
Well... I'm pretty sure they are.
You're pretty sure?
Yeah, the spirits are helping me. Remember?
Hmm.

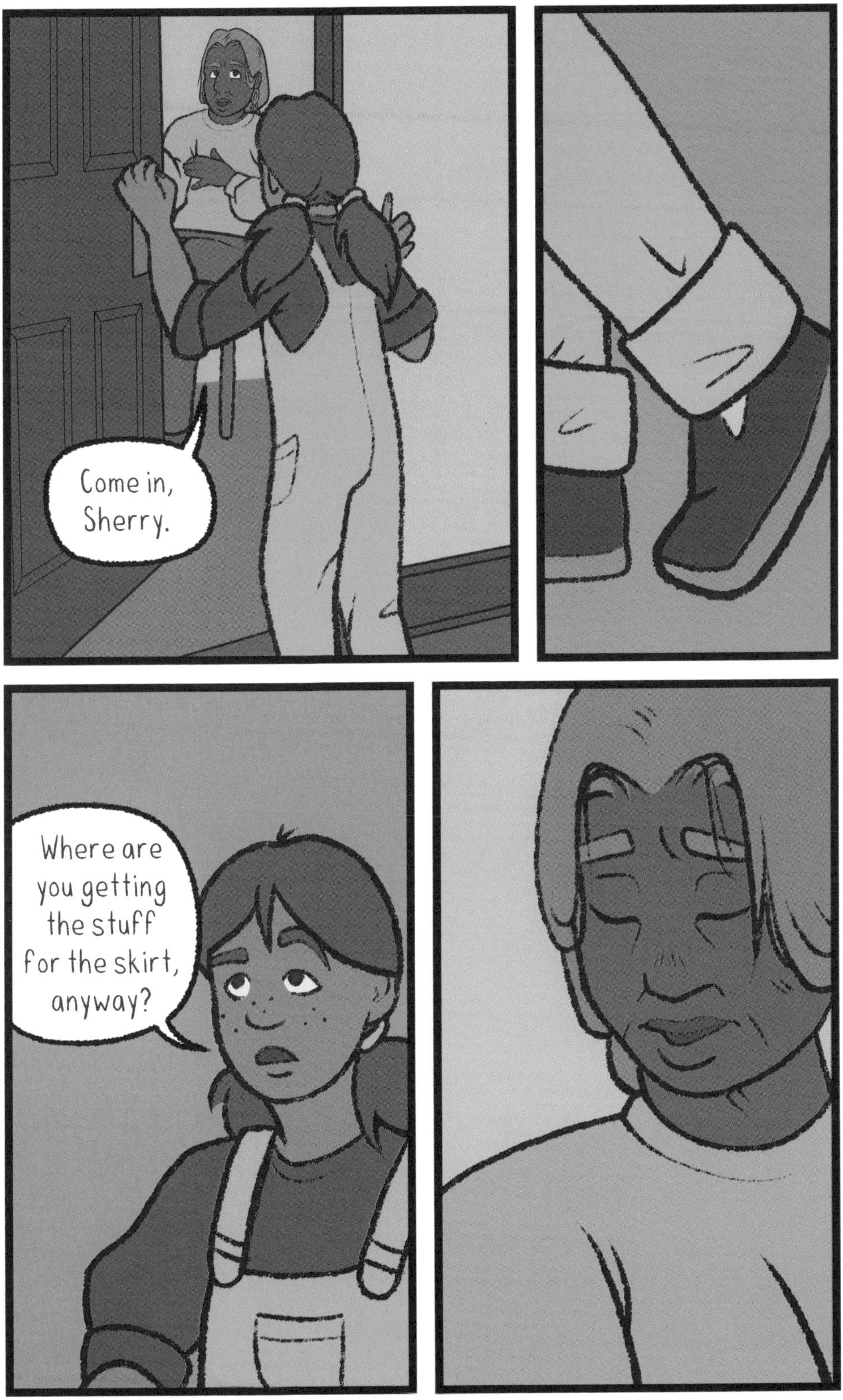
Come in, Sherry.
Where are you getting the stuff for the skirt, anyway?

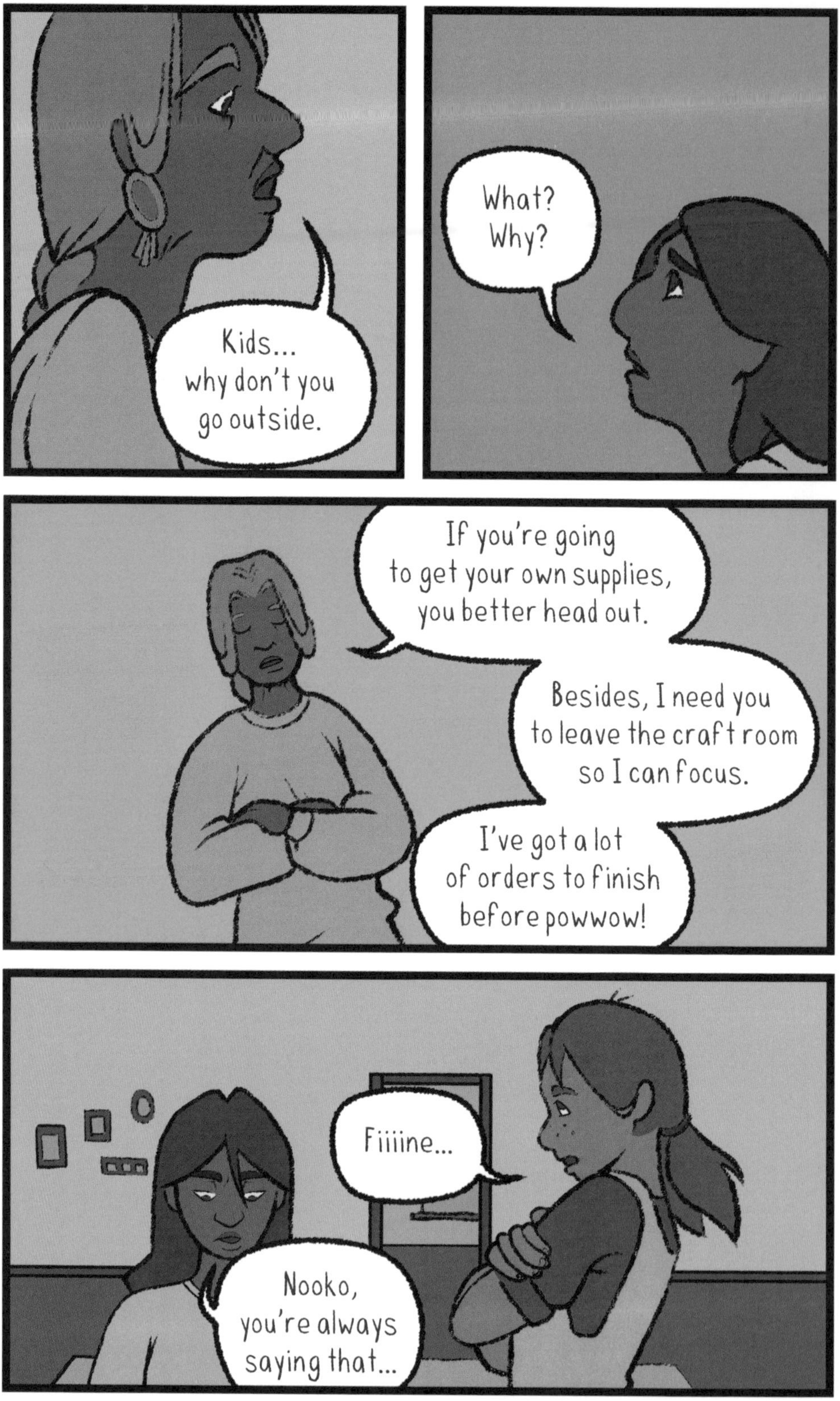
Kids...
why don't you
go outside.
What?
Why?
If you're going
to get your own supplies,
you better head out.
Besides, I need you
to leave the craft room
so I can focus.
I've got a lot
of orders to finish
before powwow!
Fiiiine...
Nooko,
you're always
saying that...

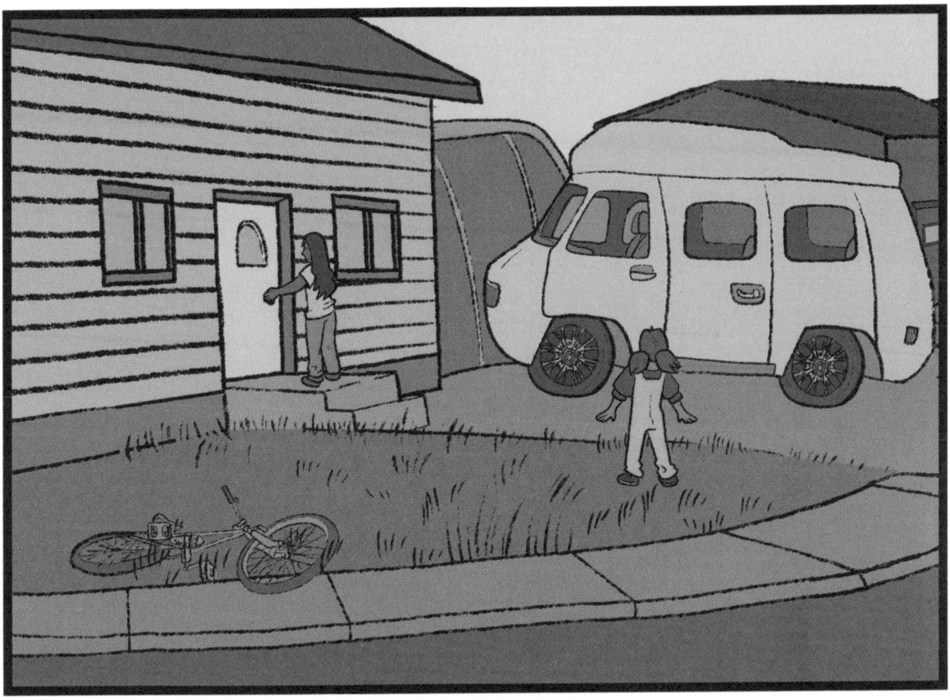

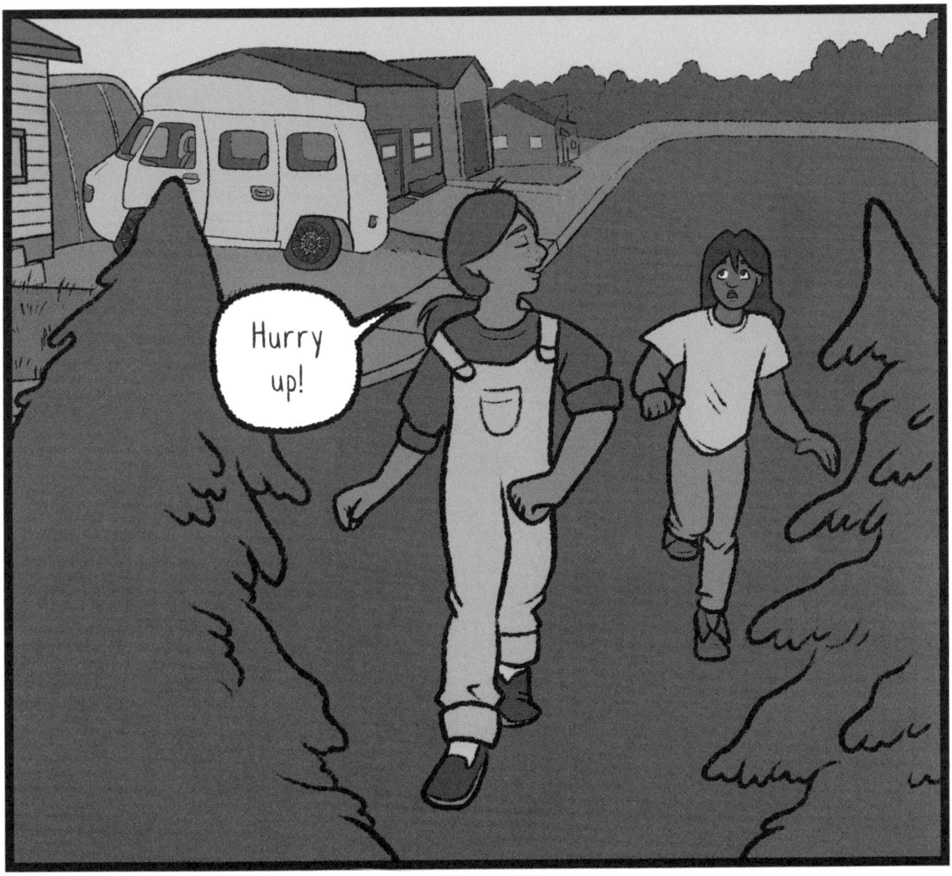
Hurry up!

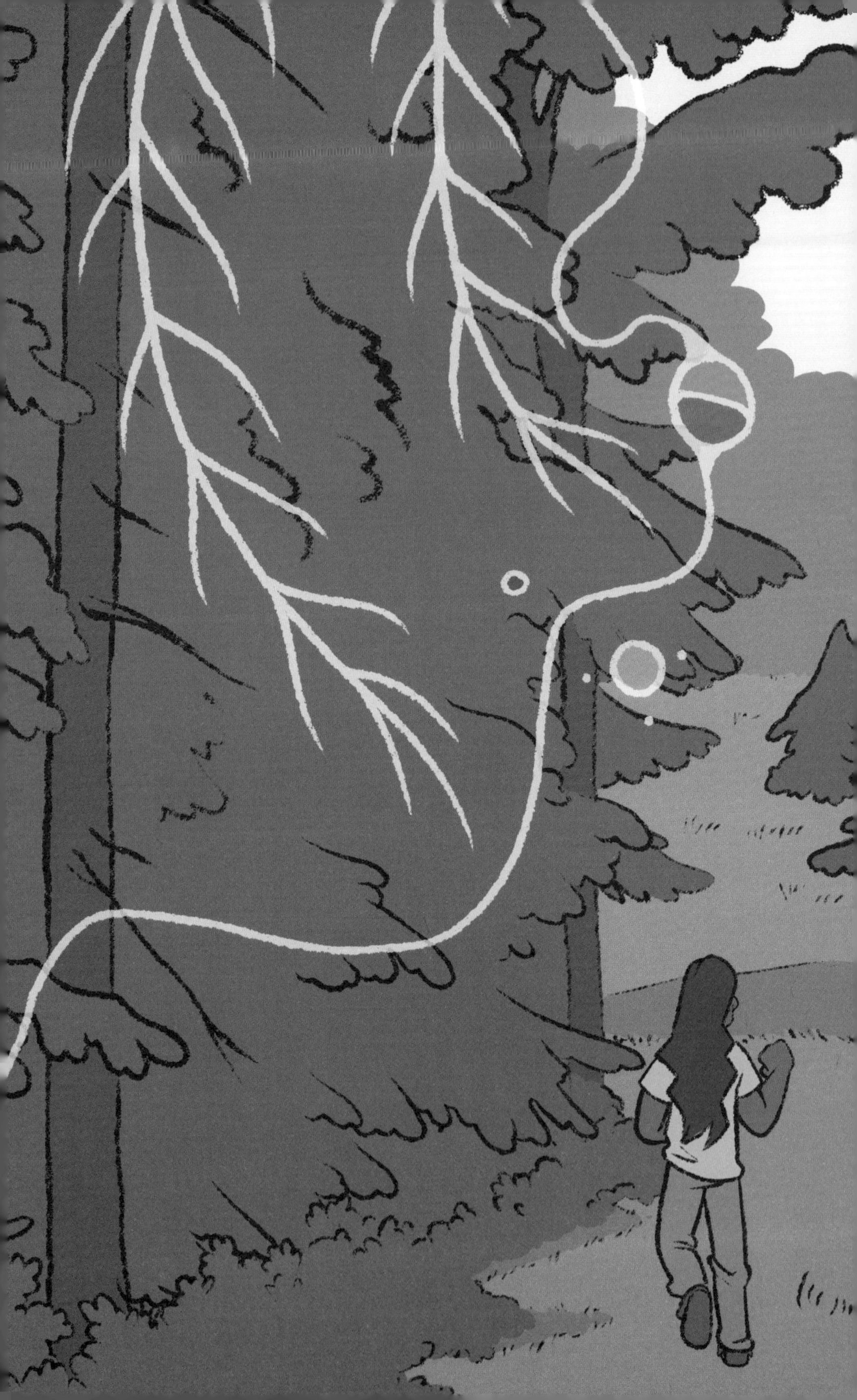

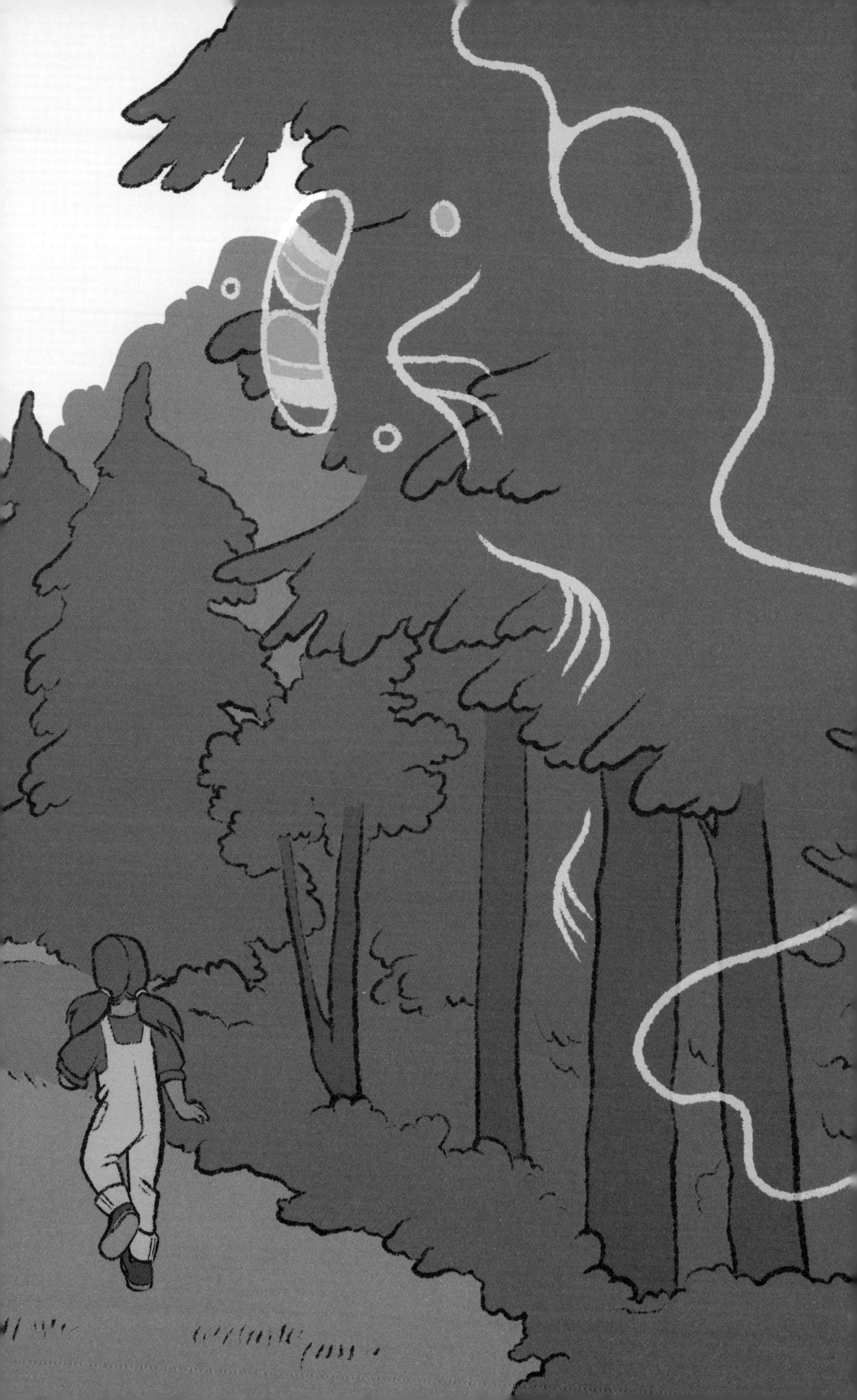

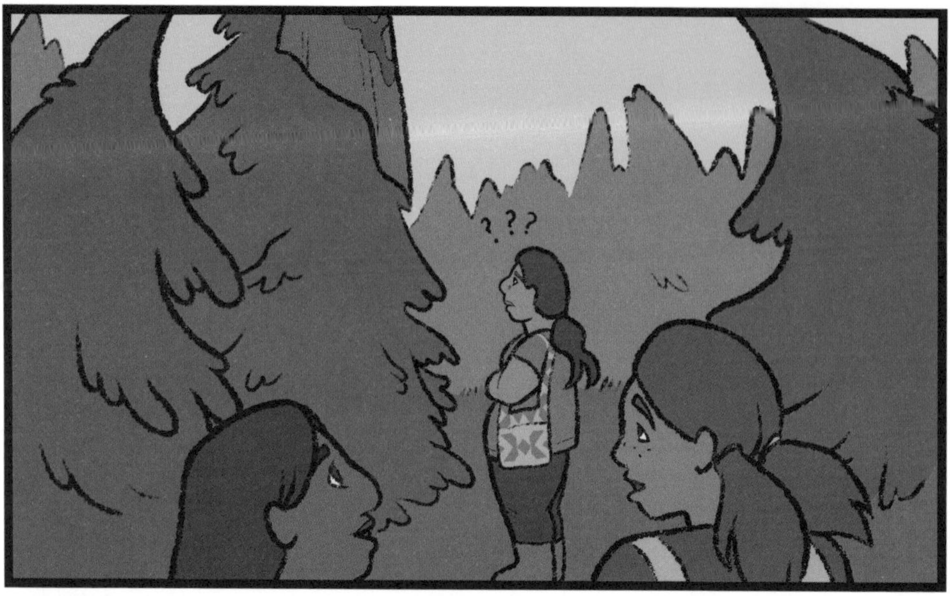
???

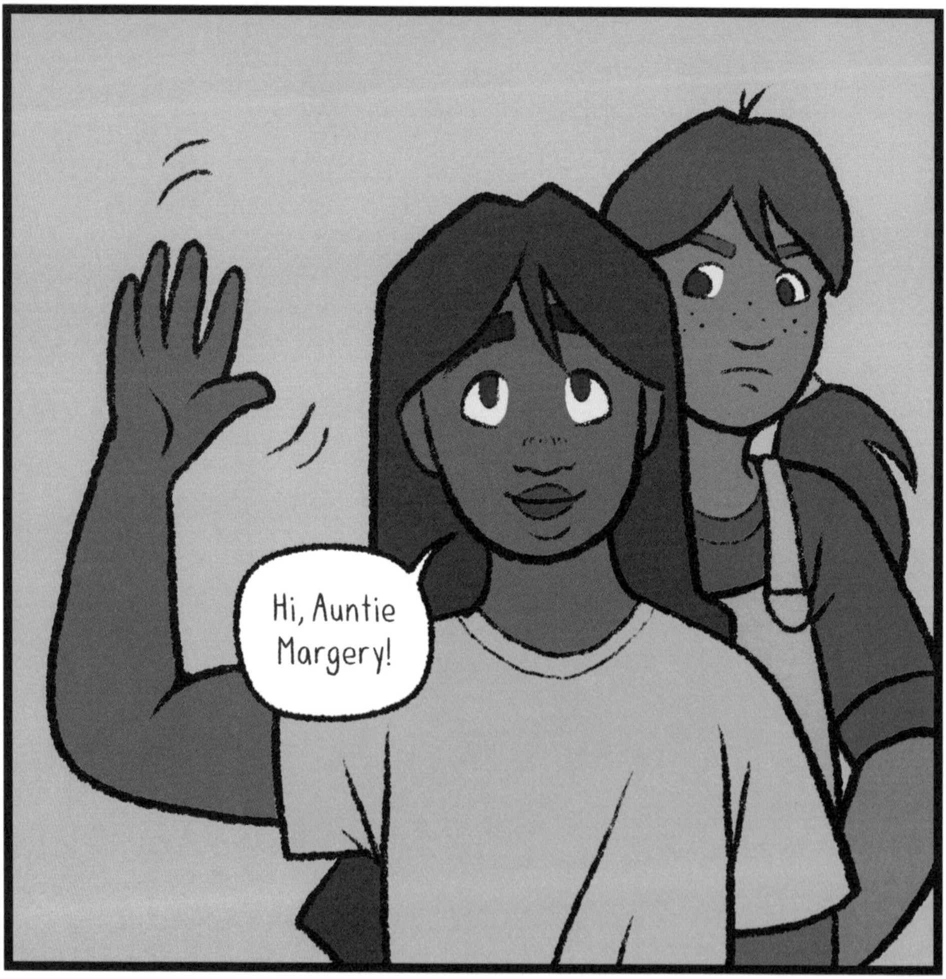
Hi, Auntie Margery!

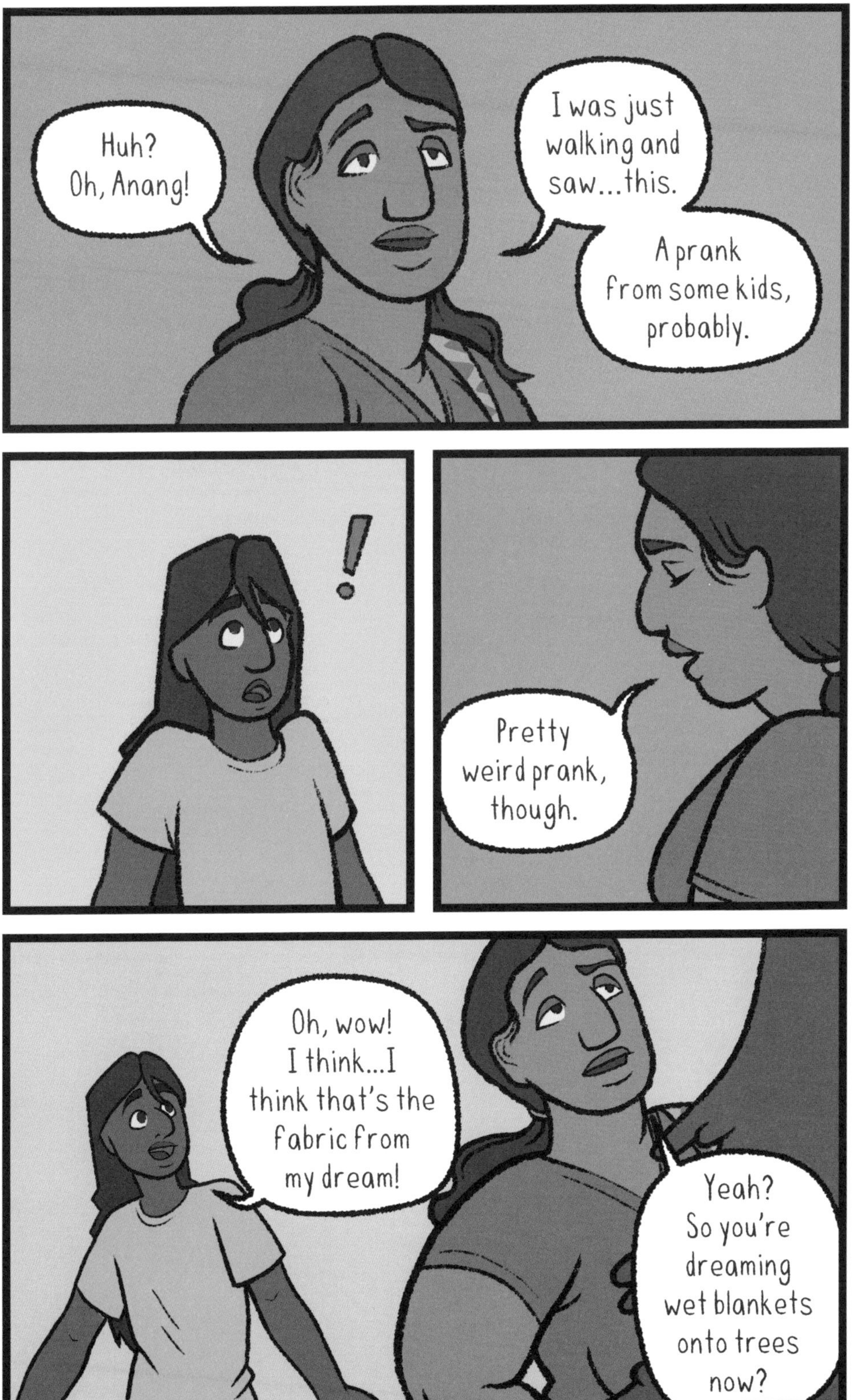
Huh? Oh, Anang!
I was just walking and saw...this.
A prank from some kids, probably.
!
Pretty weird prank, though.
Oh, wow! I think...I think that's the fabric from my dream!
Yeah? So you're dreaming wet blankets onto trees now?

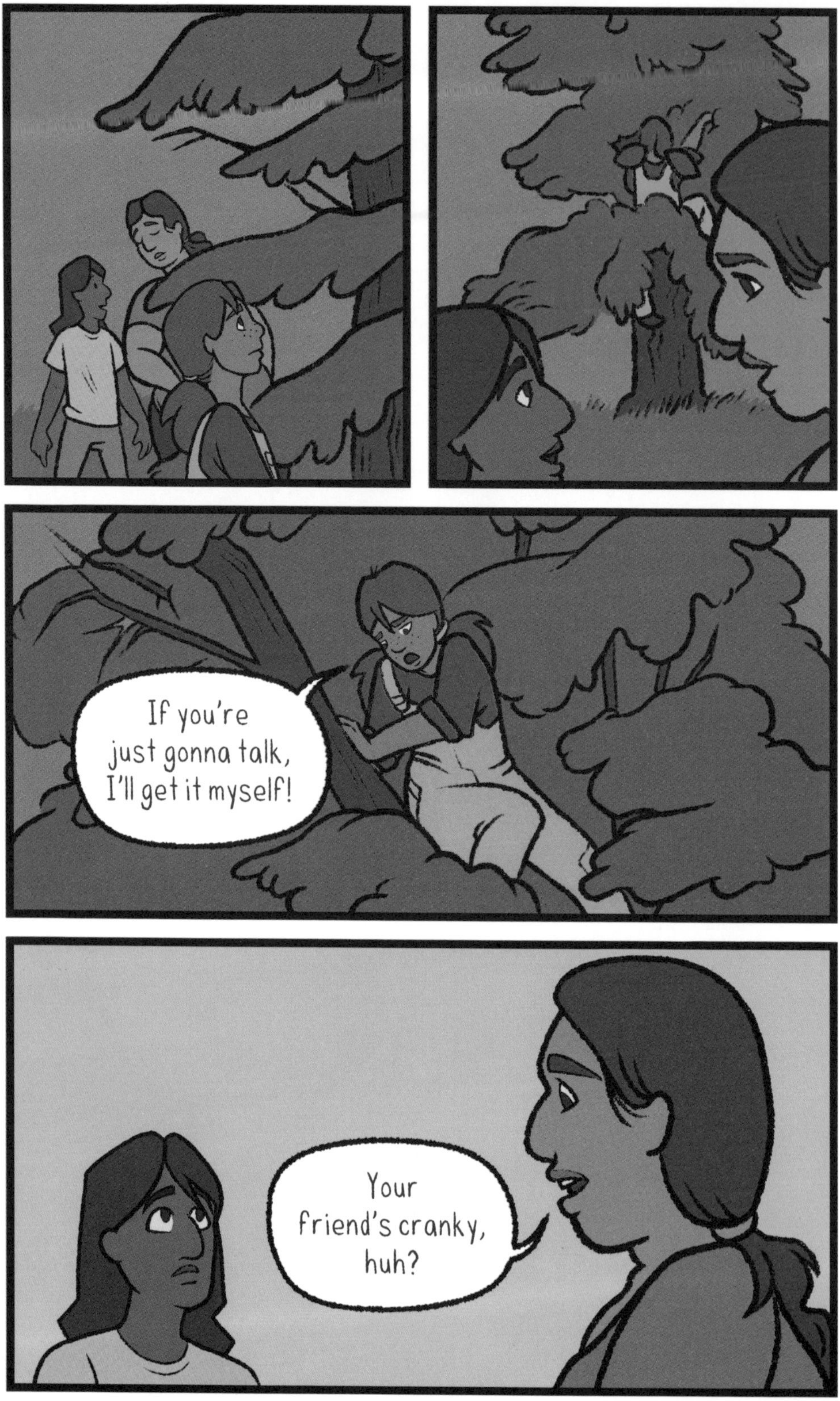
If you're just gonna talk, I'll get it myself!
Your friend's cranky, huh?

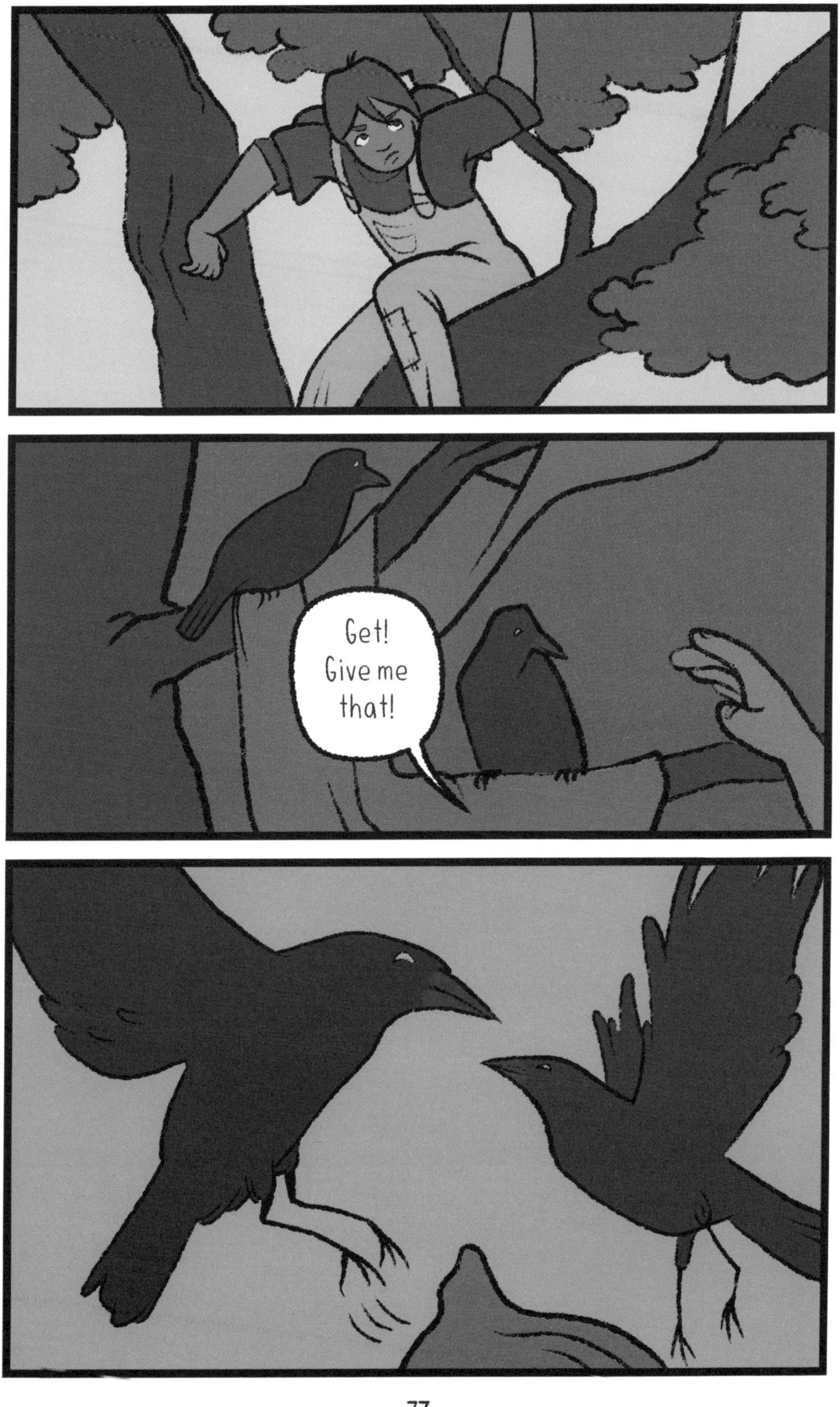
Get! Give me that!

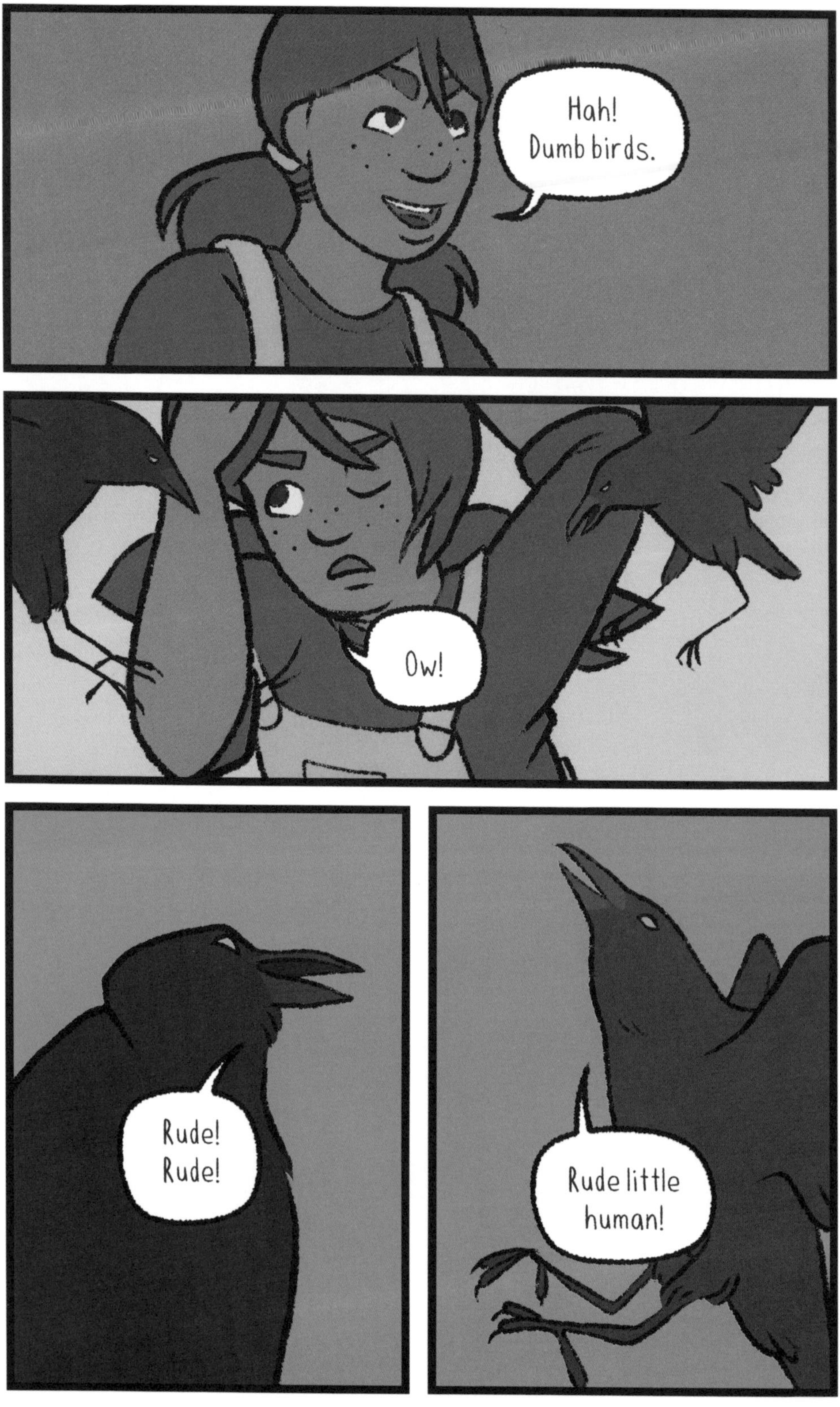
Hah!
Dumb birds.
Ow!
Rude!
Rude!
Rude little
human!

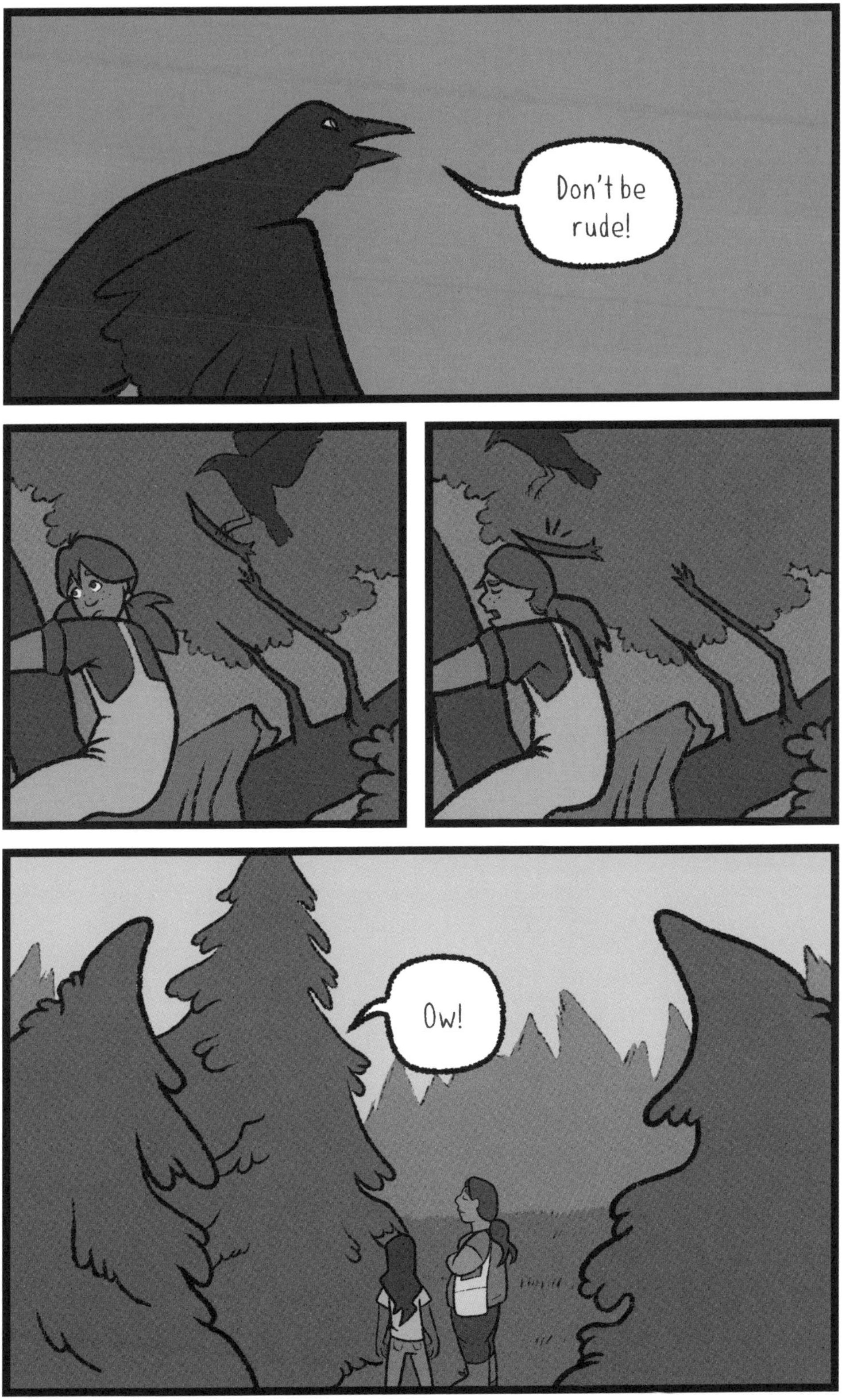
Don't be rude!
Ow!

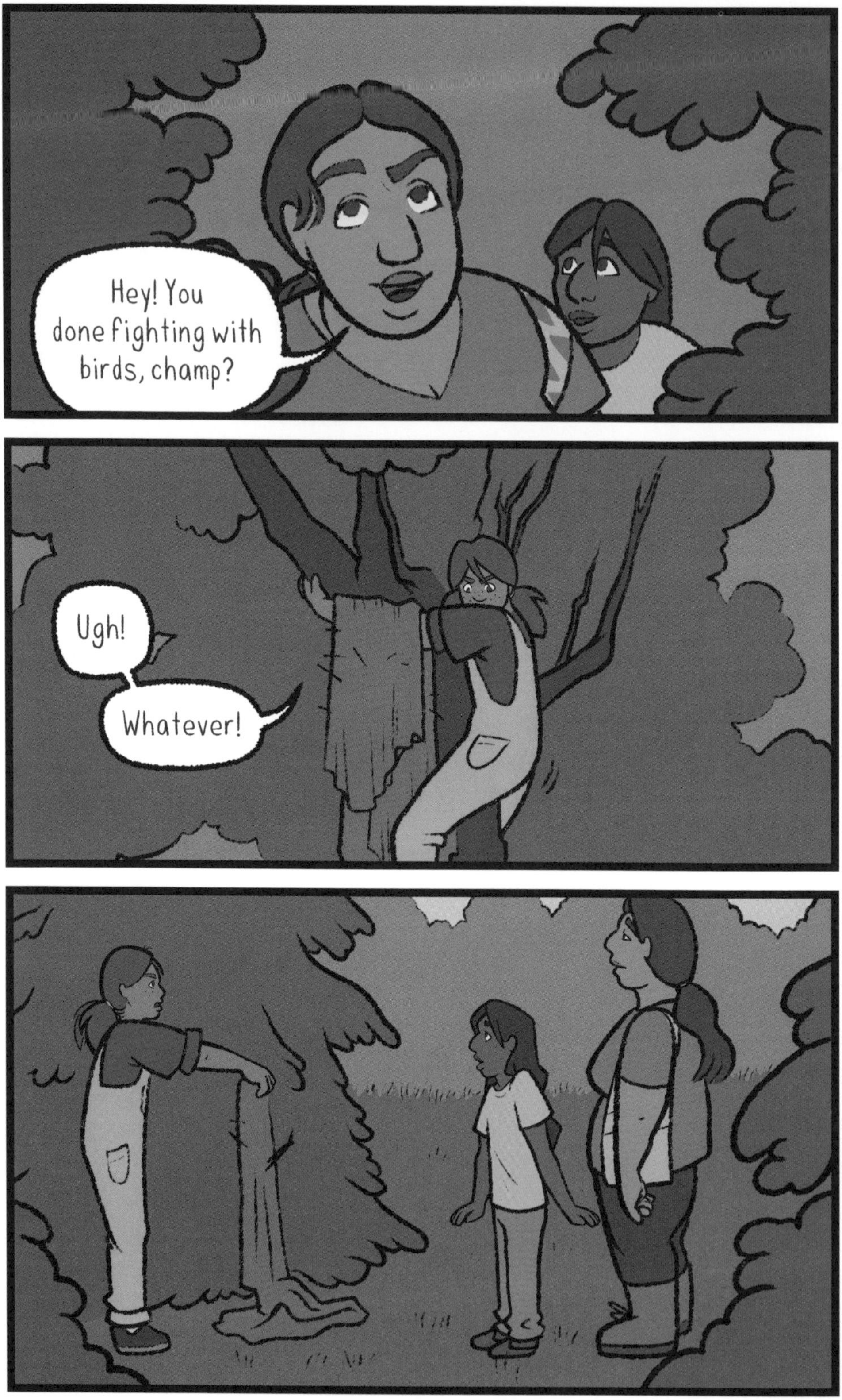
Hey! You done fighting with birds, champ?
Ugh!
Whatever!

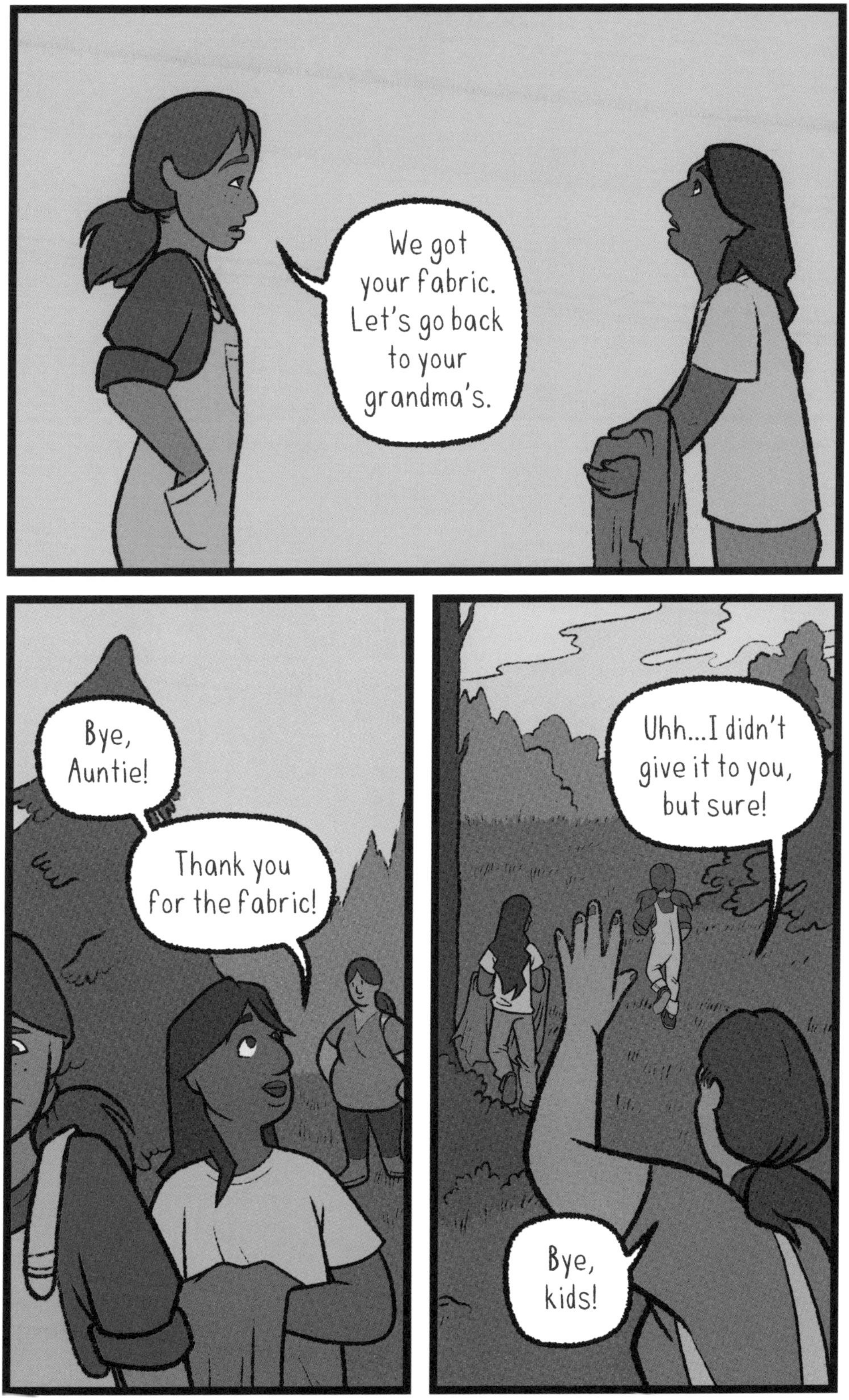
We got your fabric. Let's go back to your grandma's.
Bye, Auntie!
Thank you for the fabric!
Uhh...I didn't give it to you, but sure!
Bye, kids!

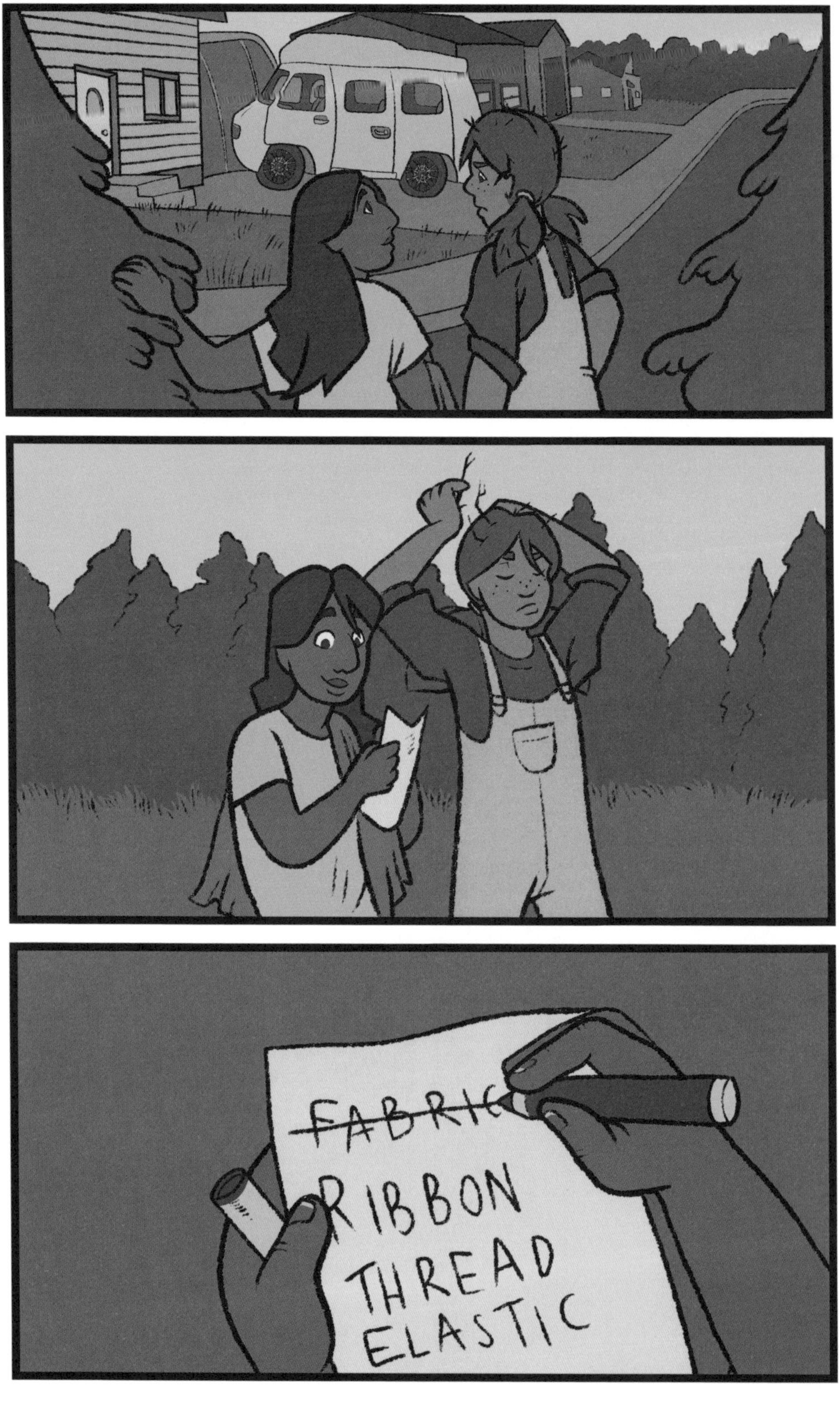
FABRIC
RIBBON
THREAD
ELASTIC

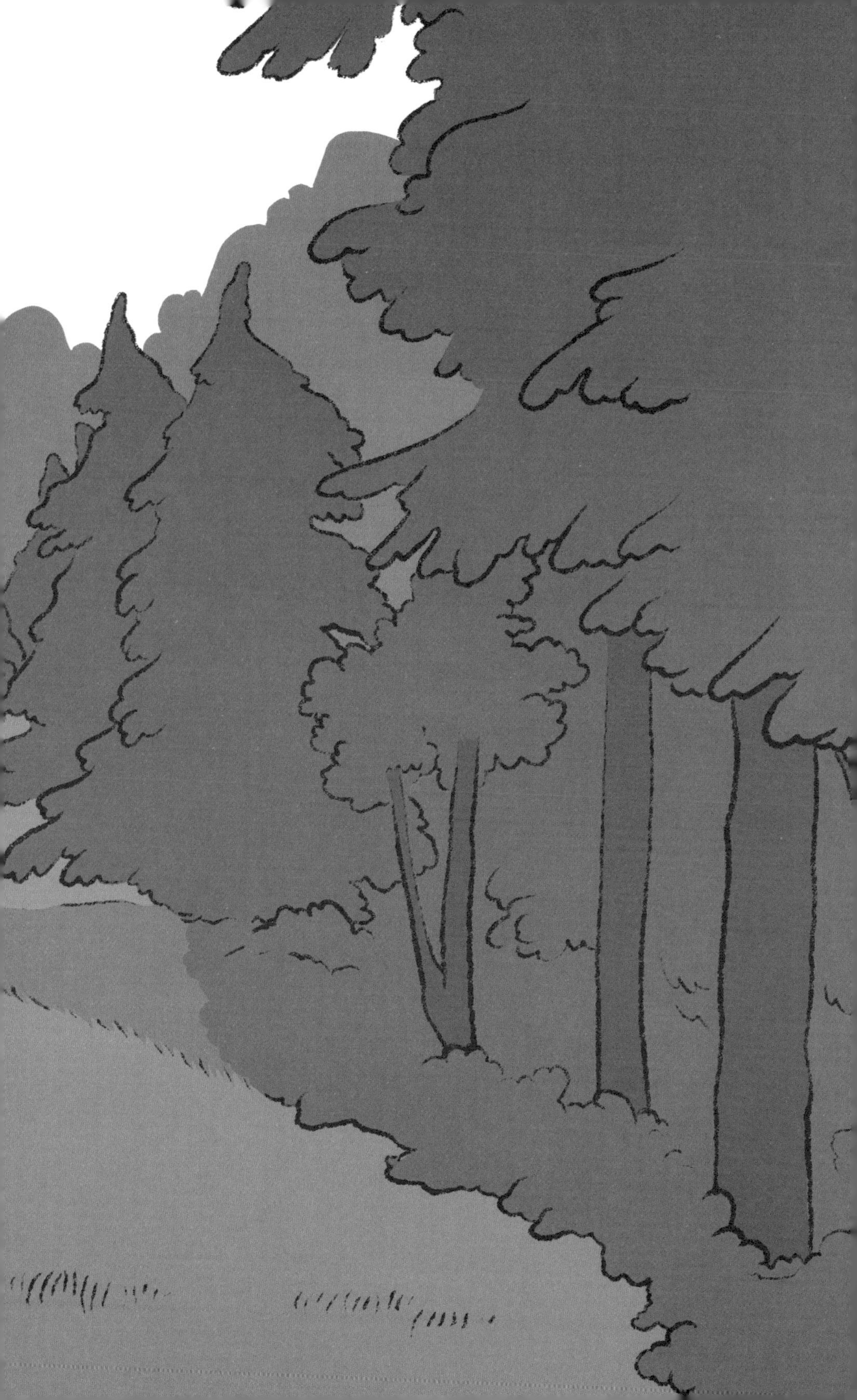

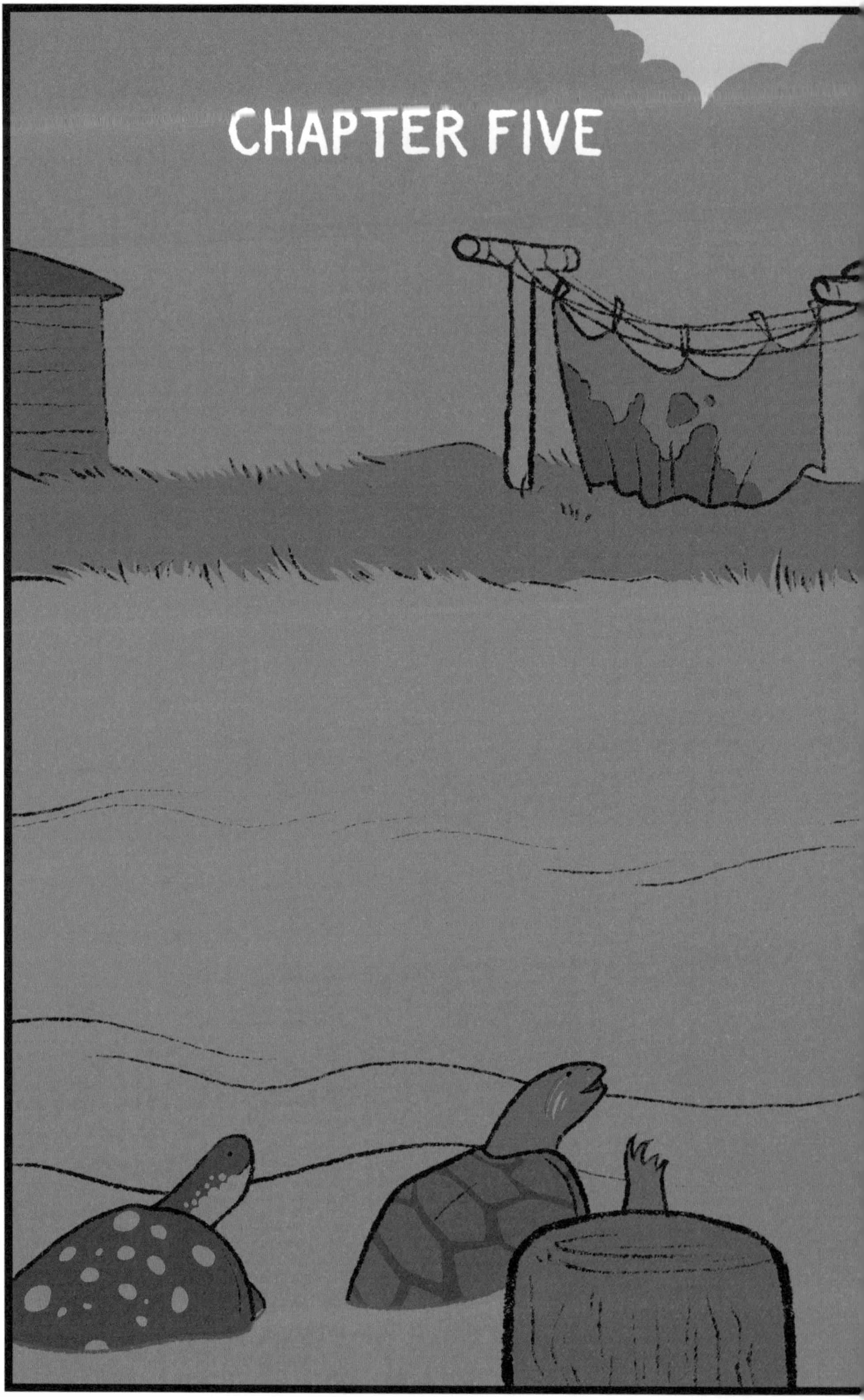
CHAPTER FIVE

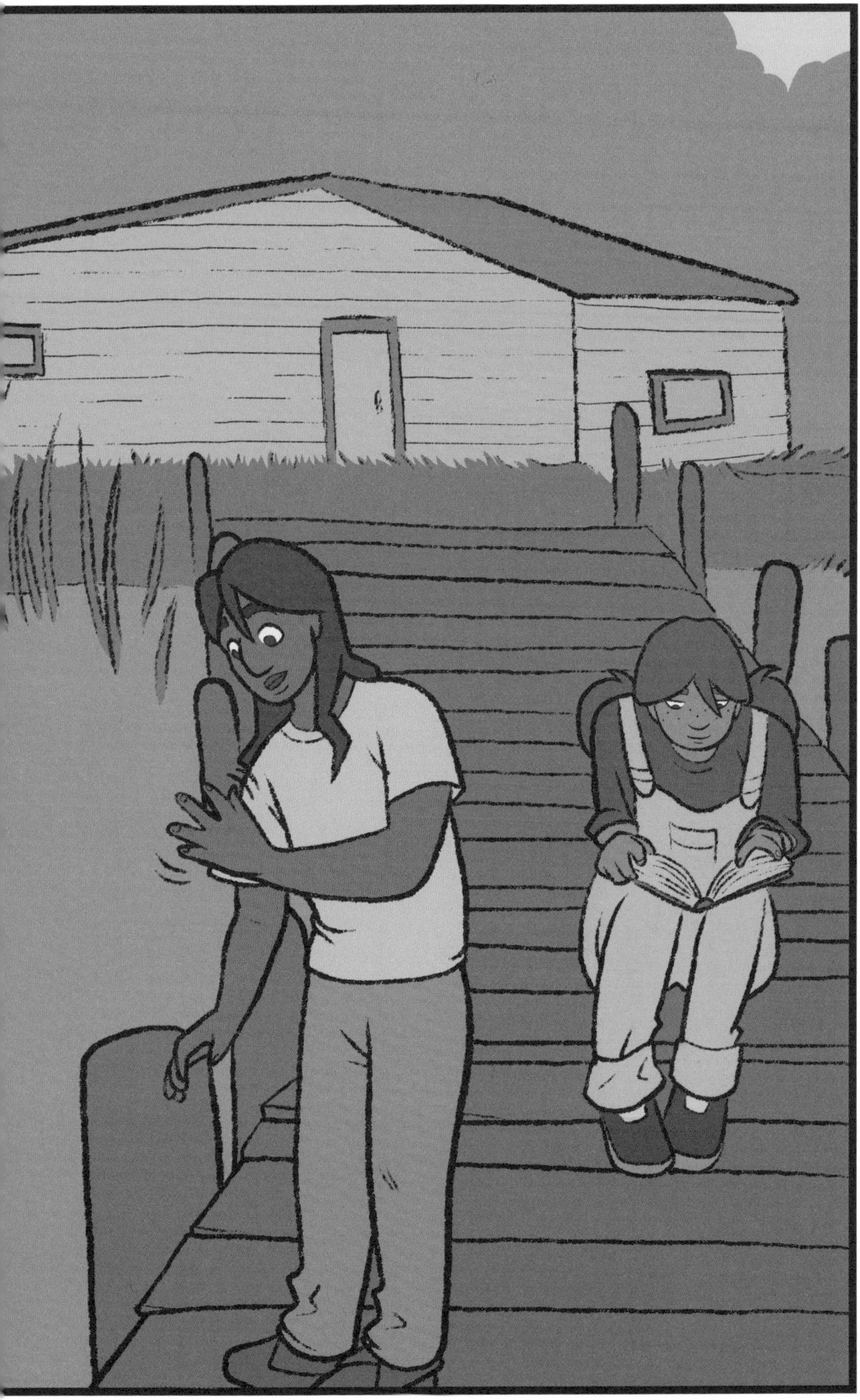

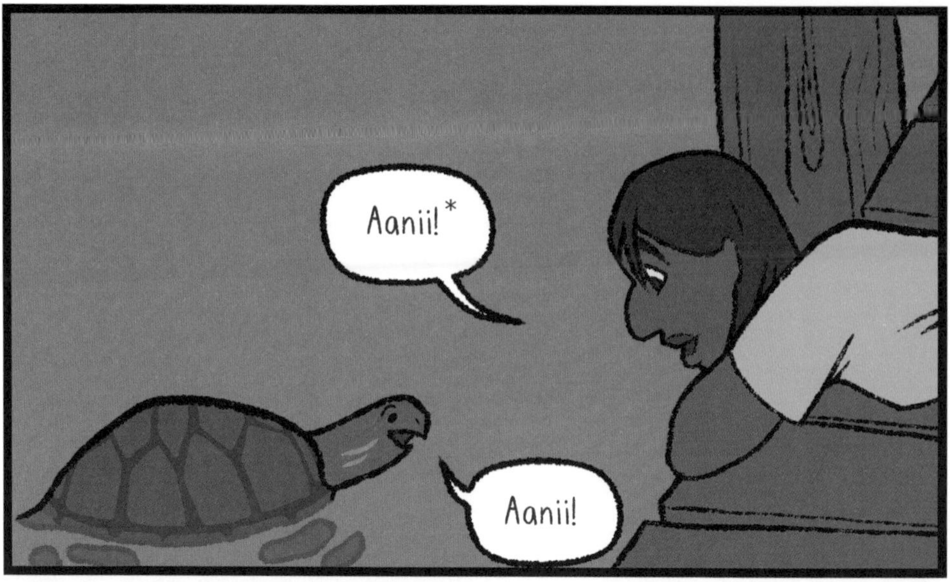
Aanii!*
Aanii!

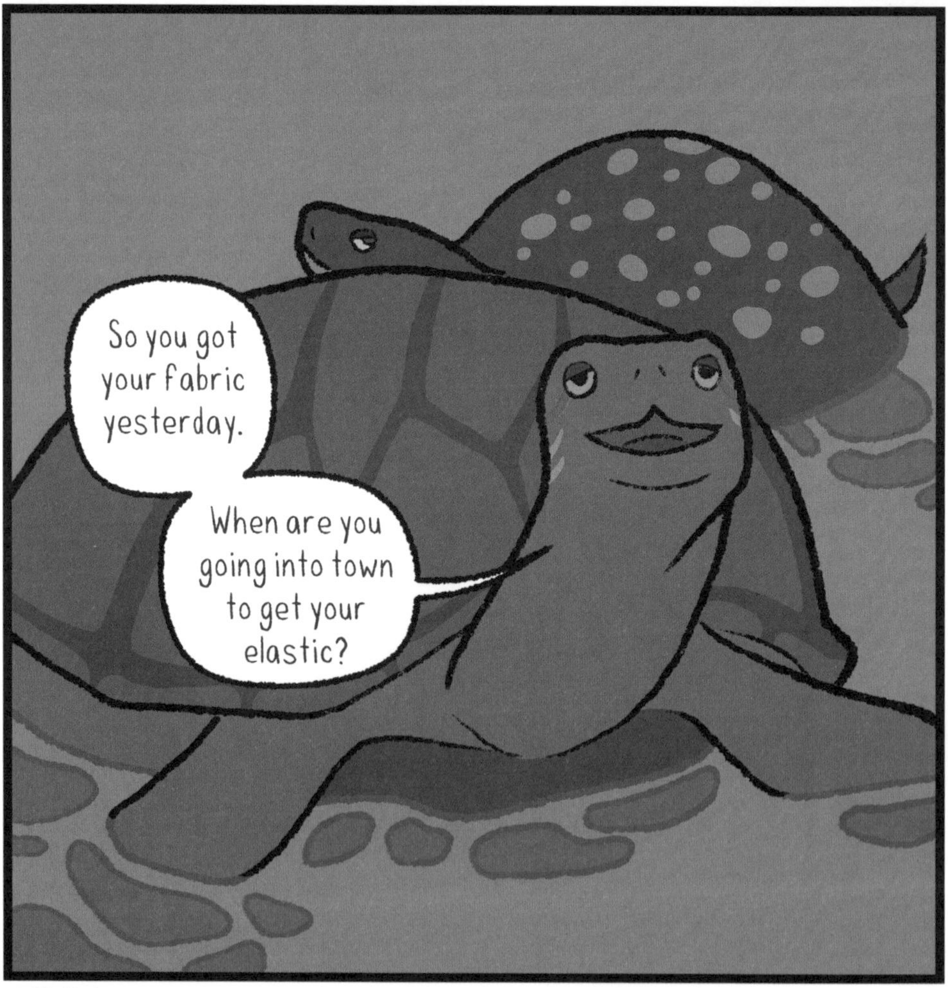
So you got your fabric yesterday.
When are you going into town to get your elastic?

* Hello!

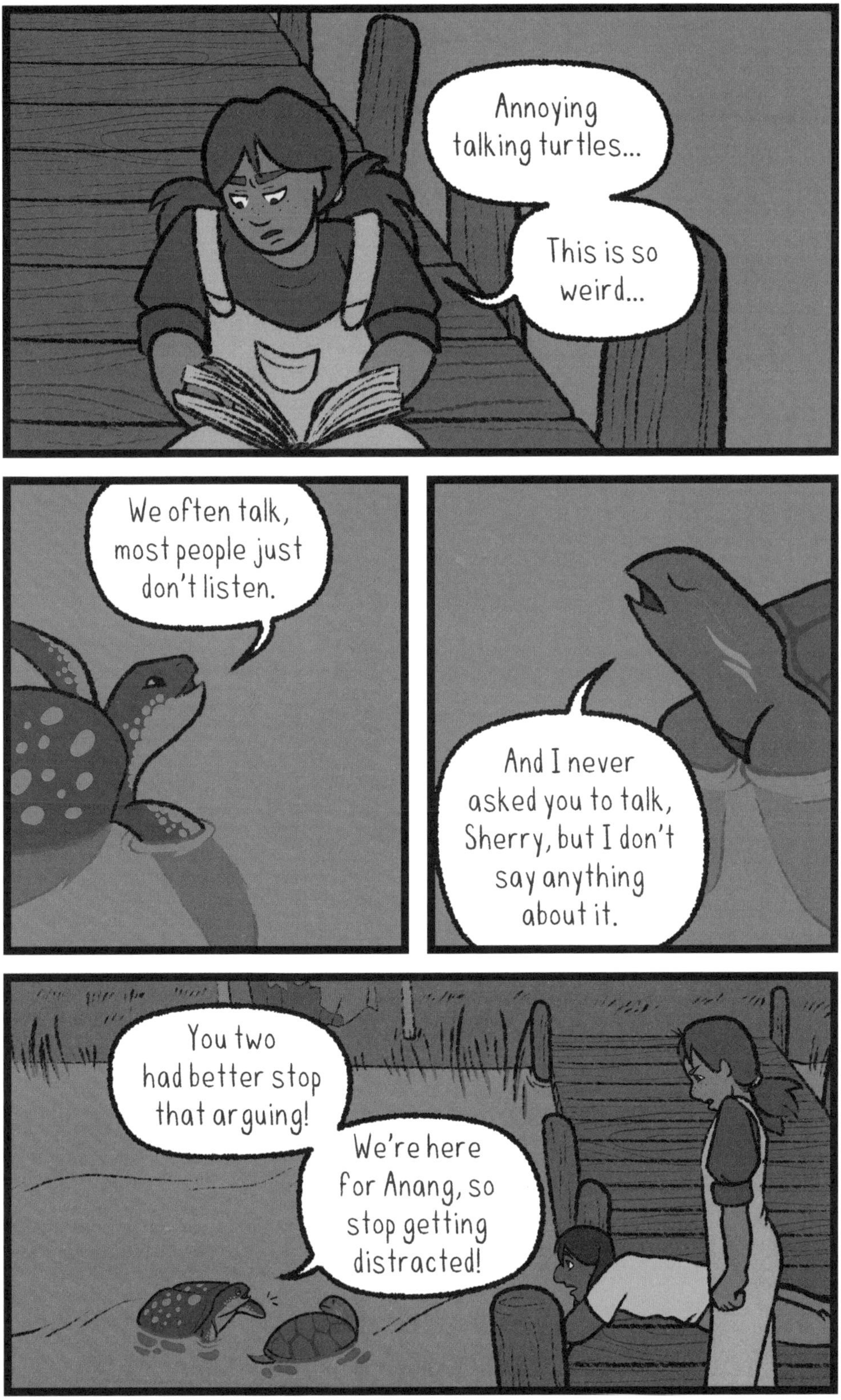
Annoying talking turtles...
This is so weird...
We often talk, most people just don't listen.
And I never asked you to talk, Sherry, but I don't say anything about it.
You two had better stop that arguing!
We're here for Anang, so stop getting distracted!

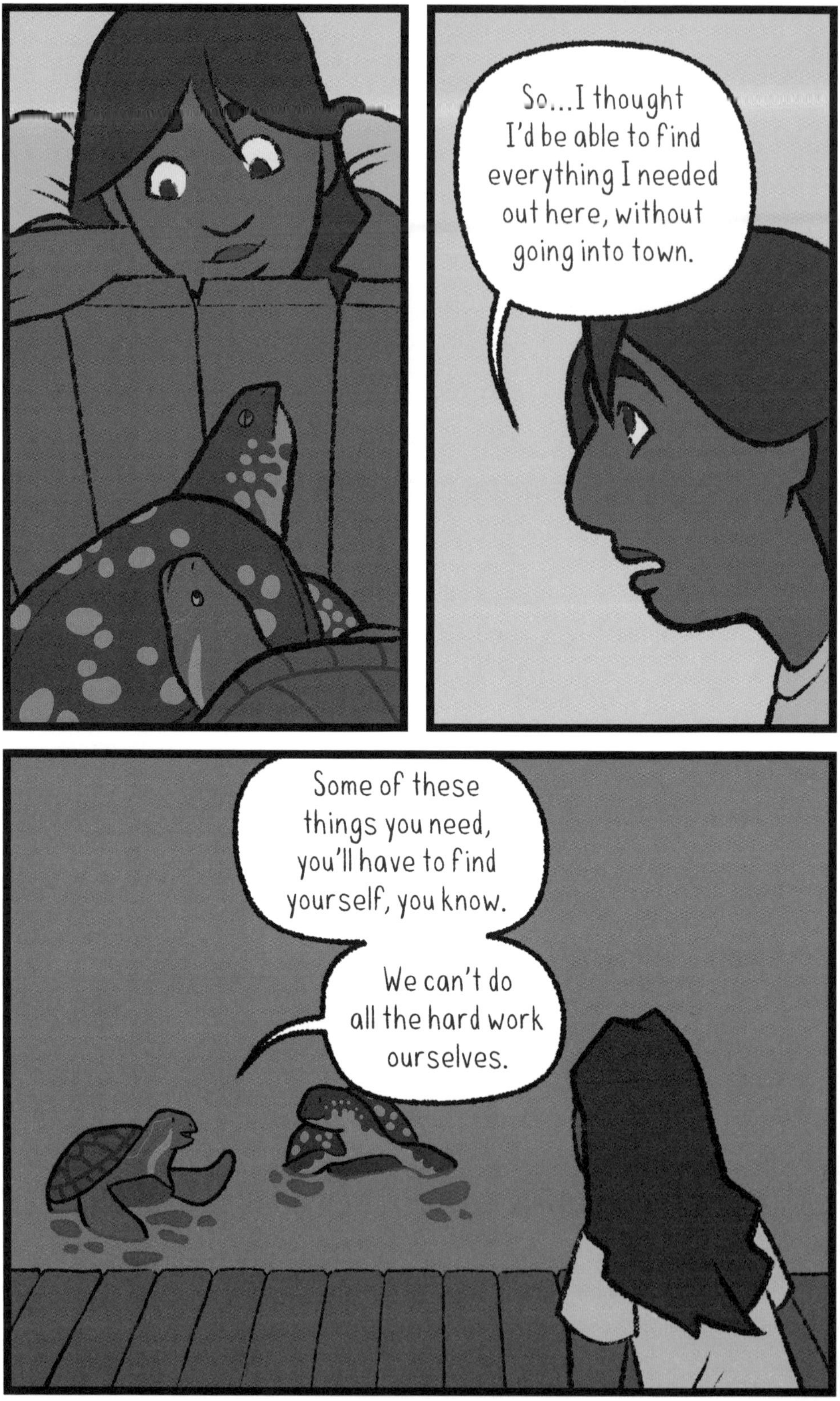
So...I thought I'd be able to find everything I needed out here, without going into town.
Some of these things you need, you'll have to find yourself, you know.
We can't do all the hard work ourselves.

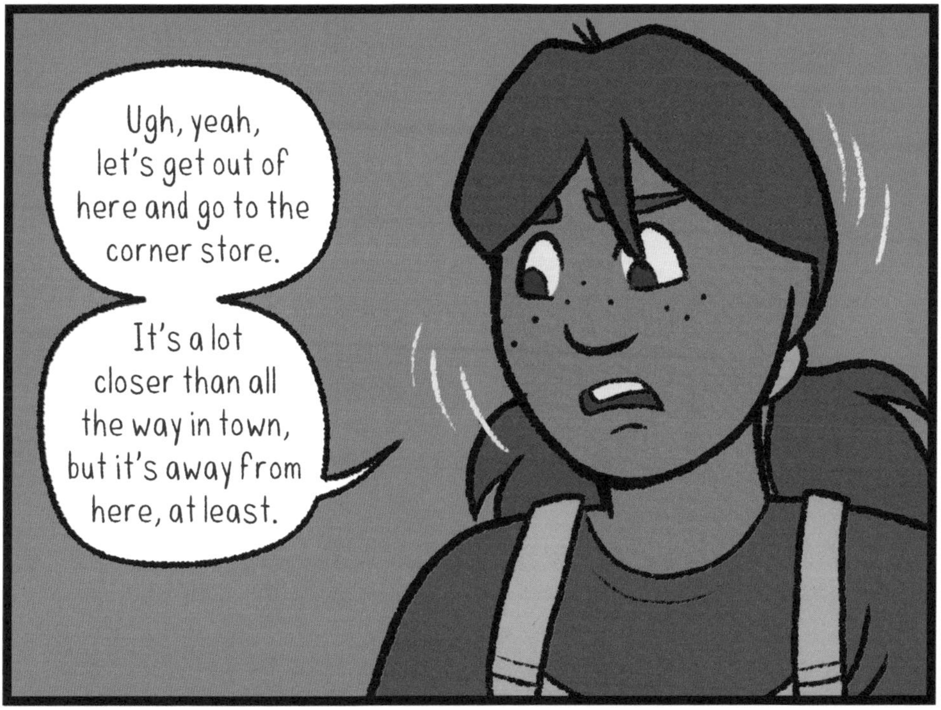
Ugh, yeah, let's get out of here and go to the corner store.
It's a lot closer than all the way in town, but it's away from here, at least.

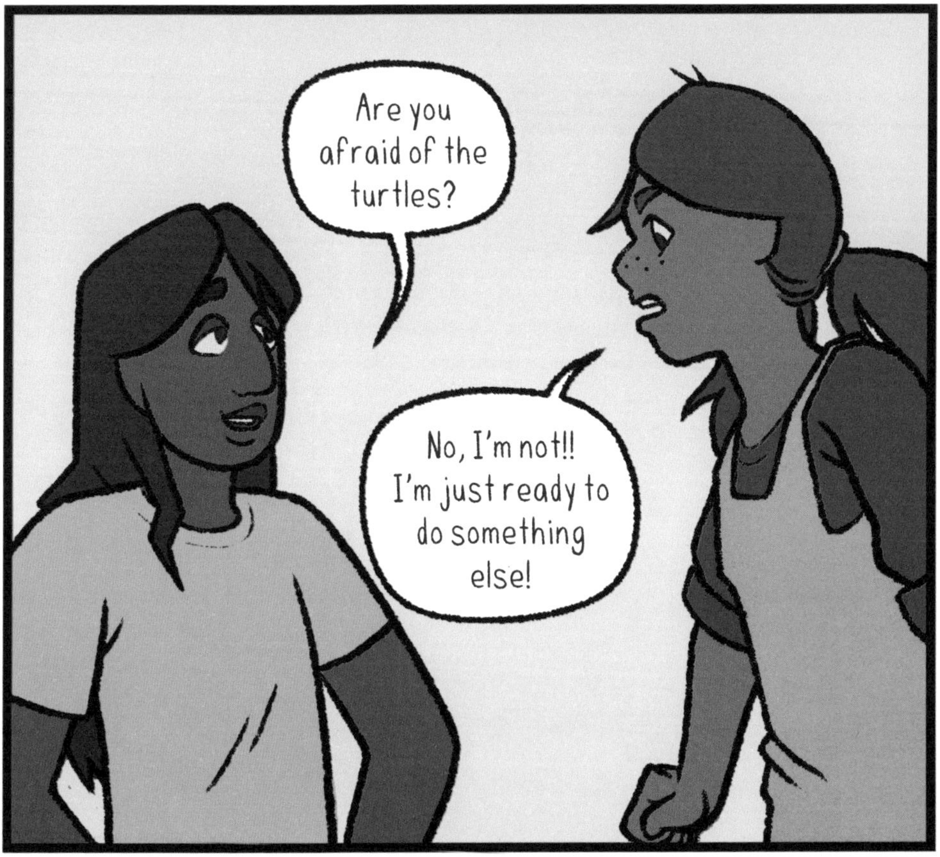
Are you afraid of the turtles?
No, I'm not!! I'm just ready to do something else!

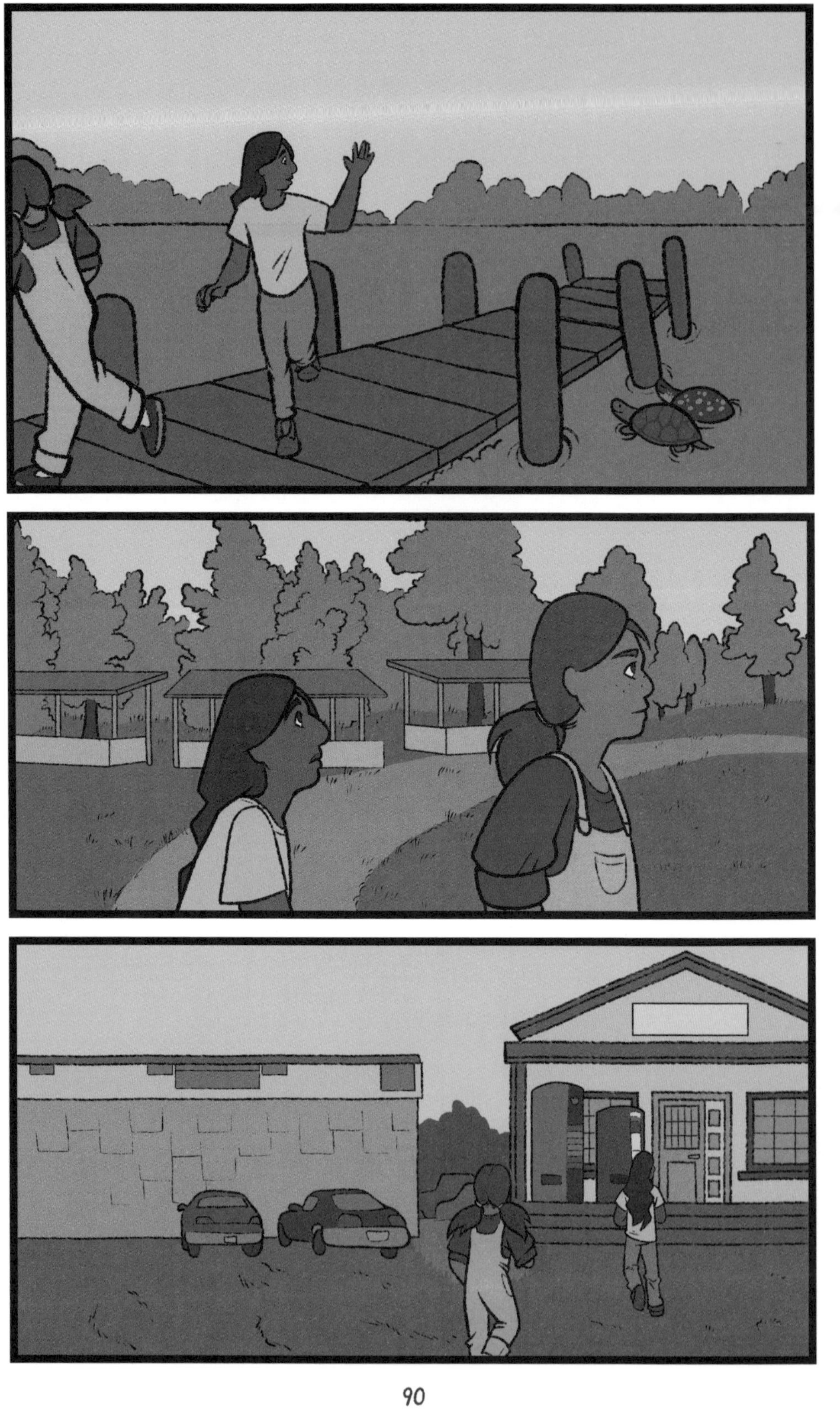

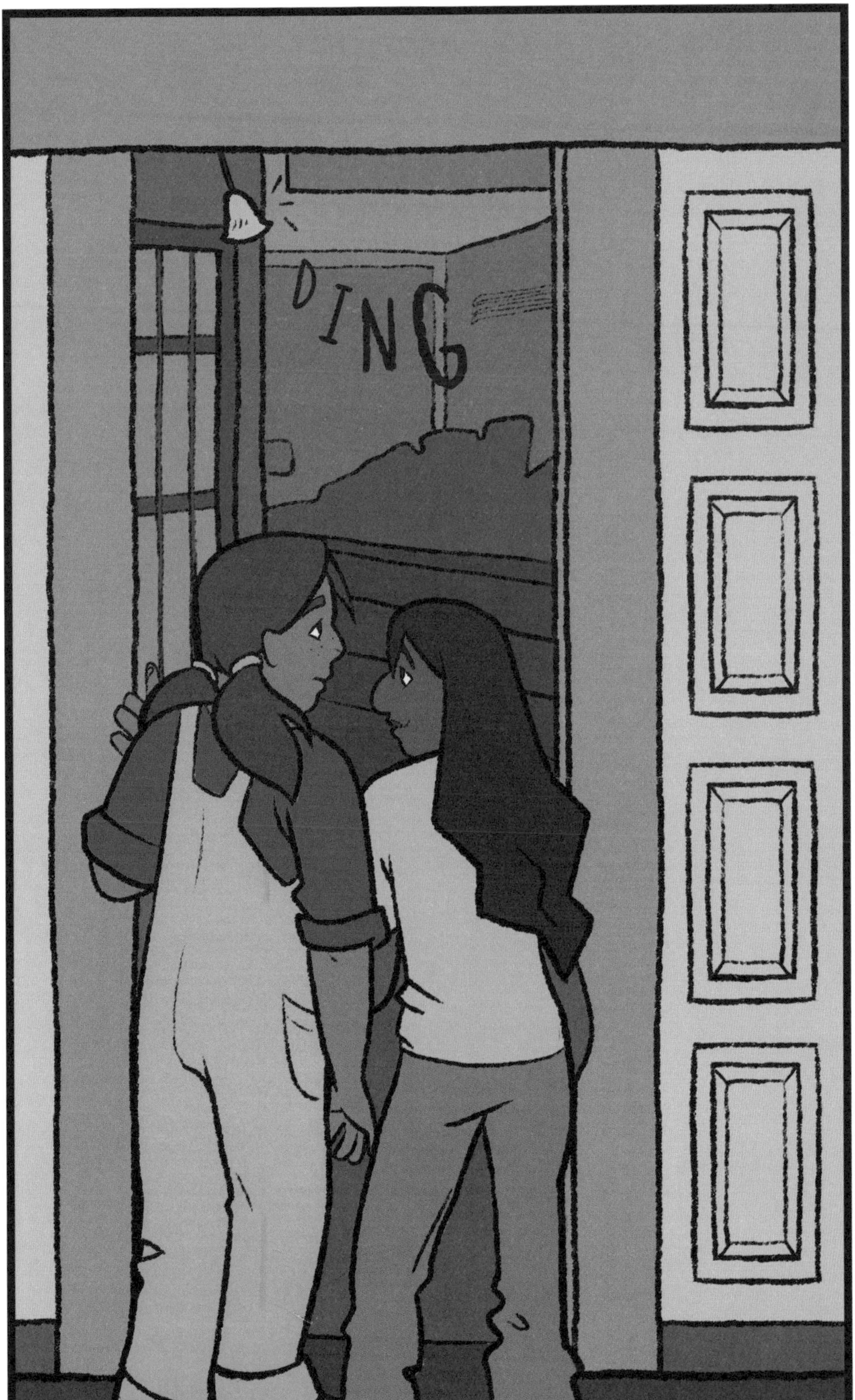
DING

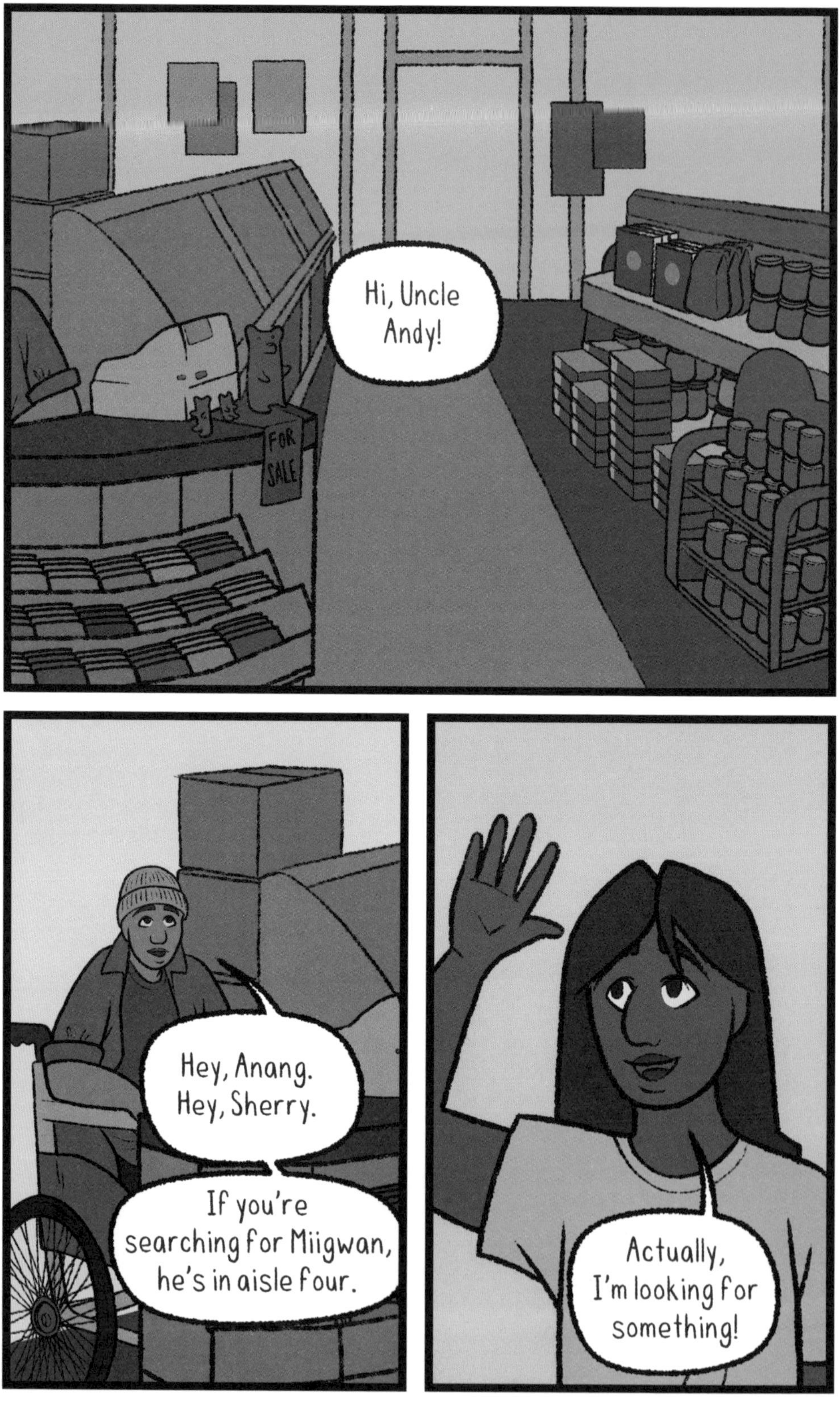
FOR SALE
Hi, Uncle Andy!
Hey, Anang. Hey, Sherry.
If you're searching for Miigwan, he's in aisle four.
Actually, I'm looking for something!

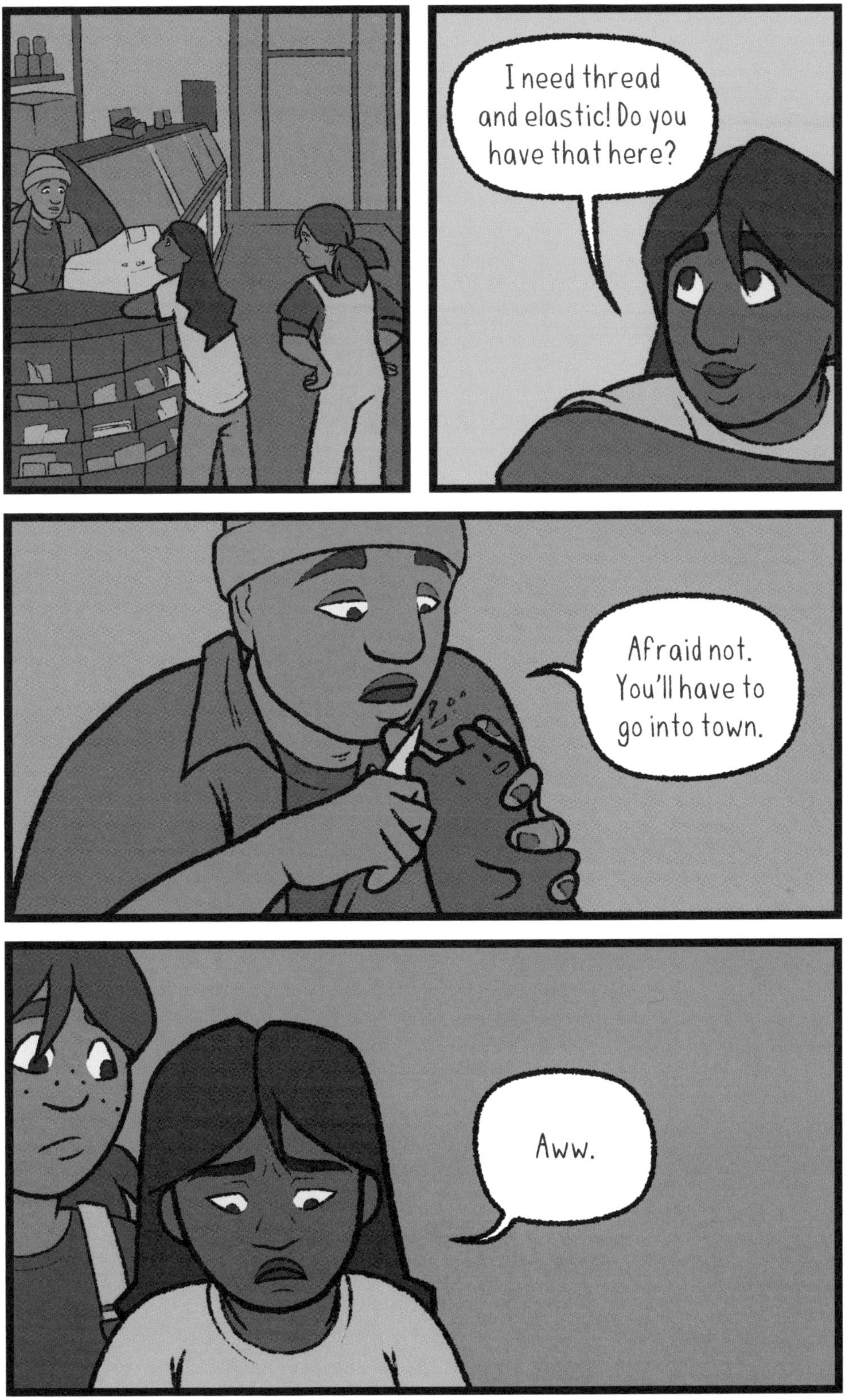
I need thread and elastic! Do you have that here?
Afraid not. You'll have to go into town.
Aww.

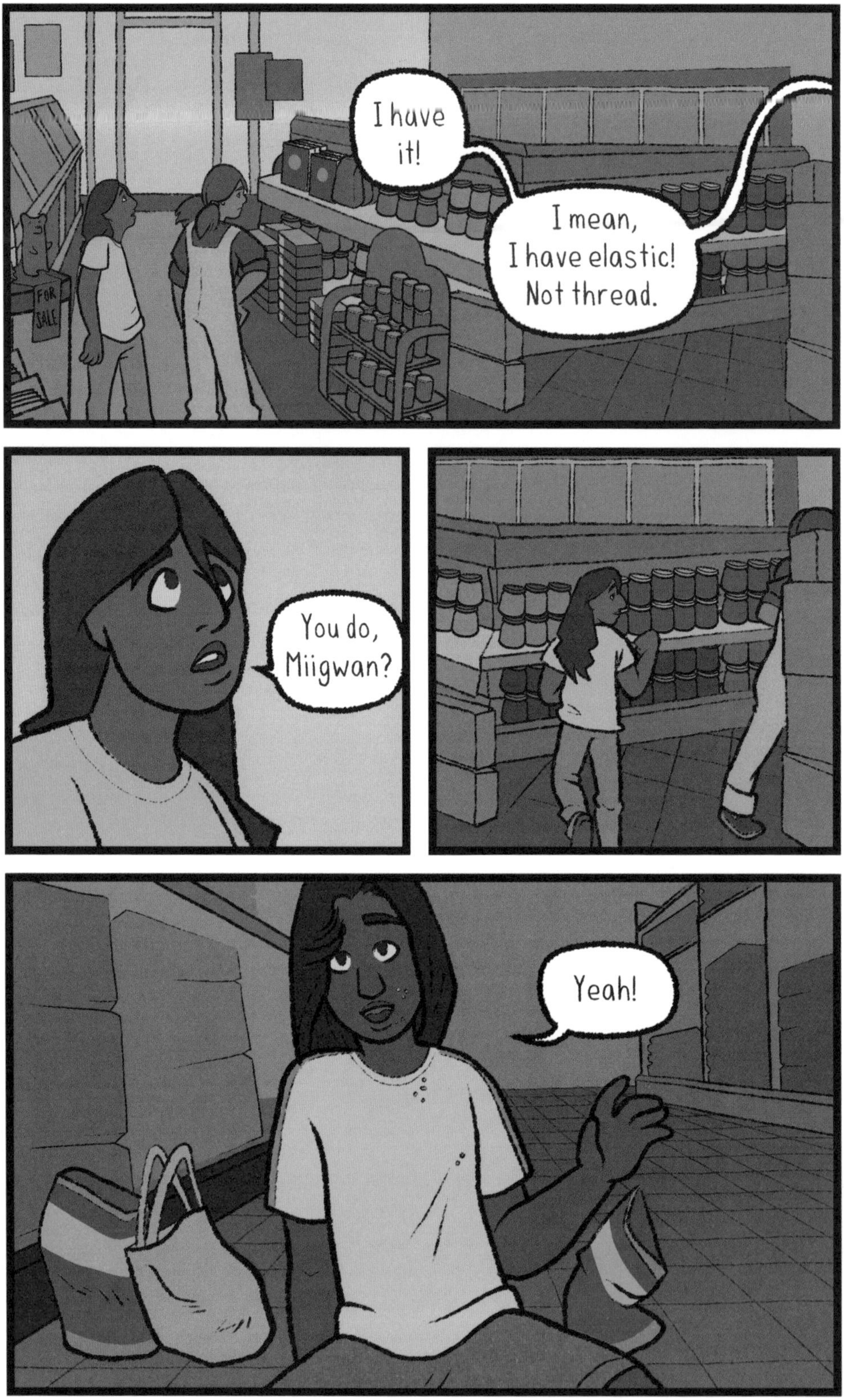
FOR SALE
I have it!
I mean, I have elastic! Not thread.
You do, Miigwan?
Yeah!

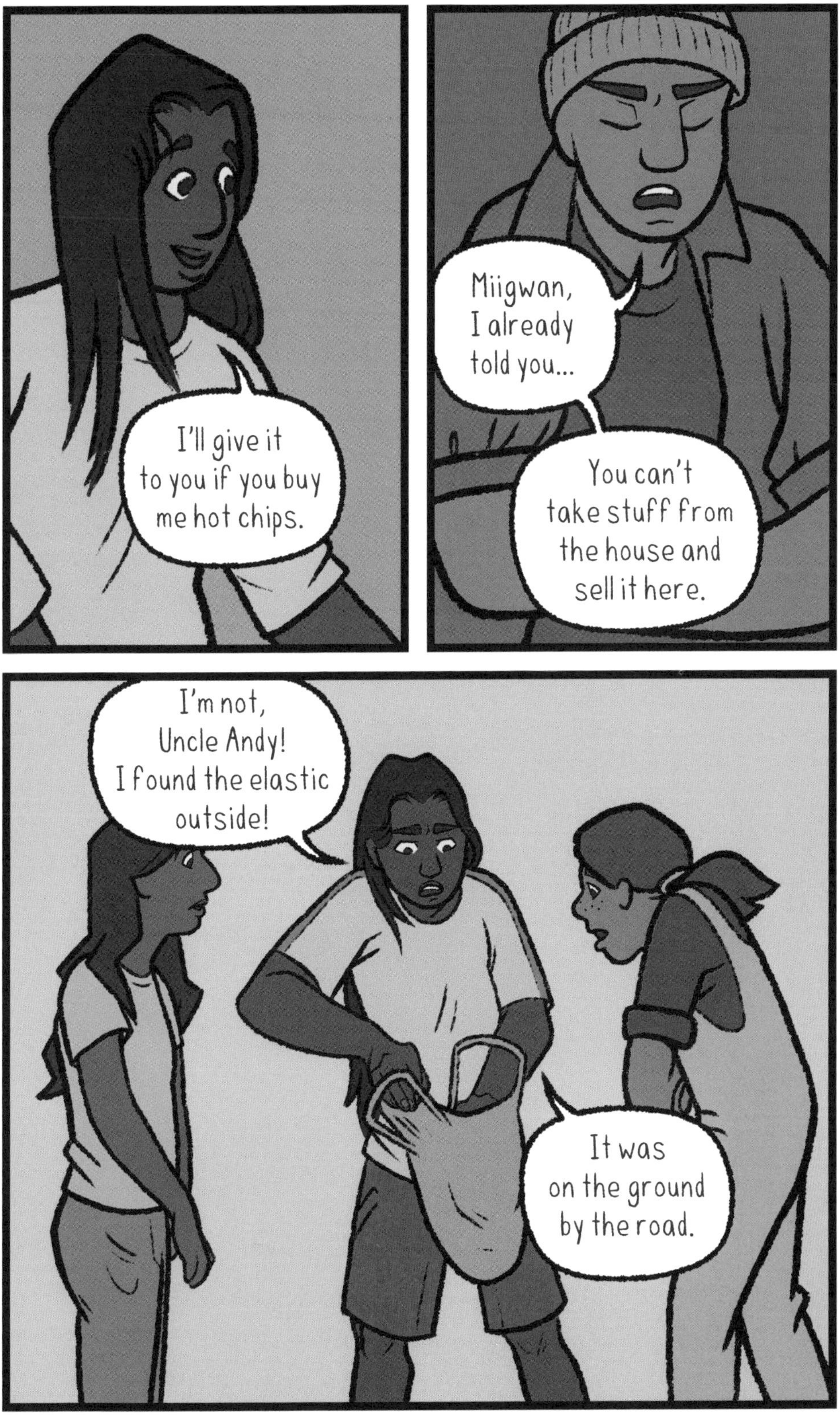
I'll give it to you if you buy me hot chips.
Miigwan, I already told you...
You can't take stuff from the house and sell it here.
I'm not, Uncle Andy! I found the elastic outside!
It was on the ground by the road.

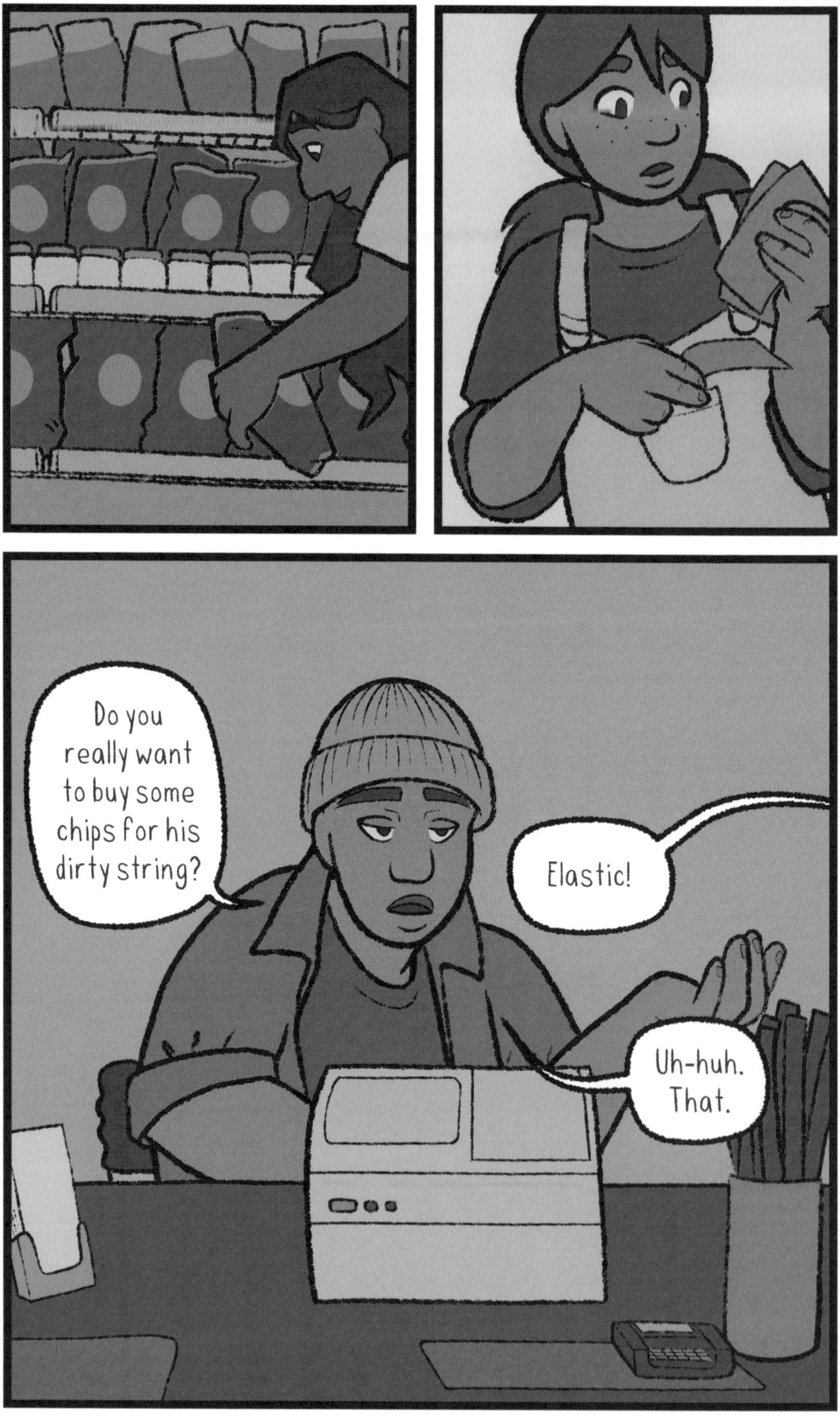
Do you really want to buy some chips for his dirty string?
Elastic!
Uh-huh. That.

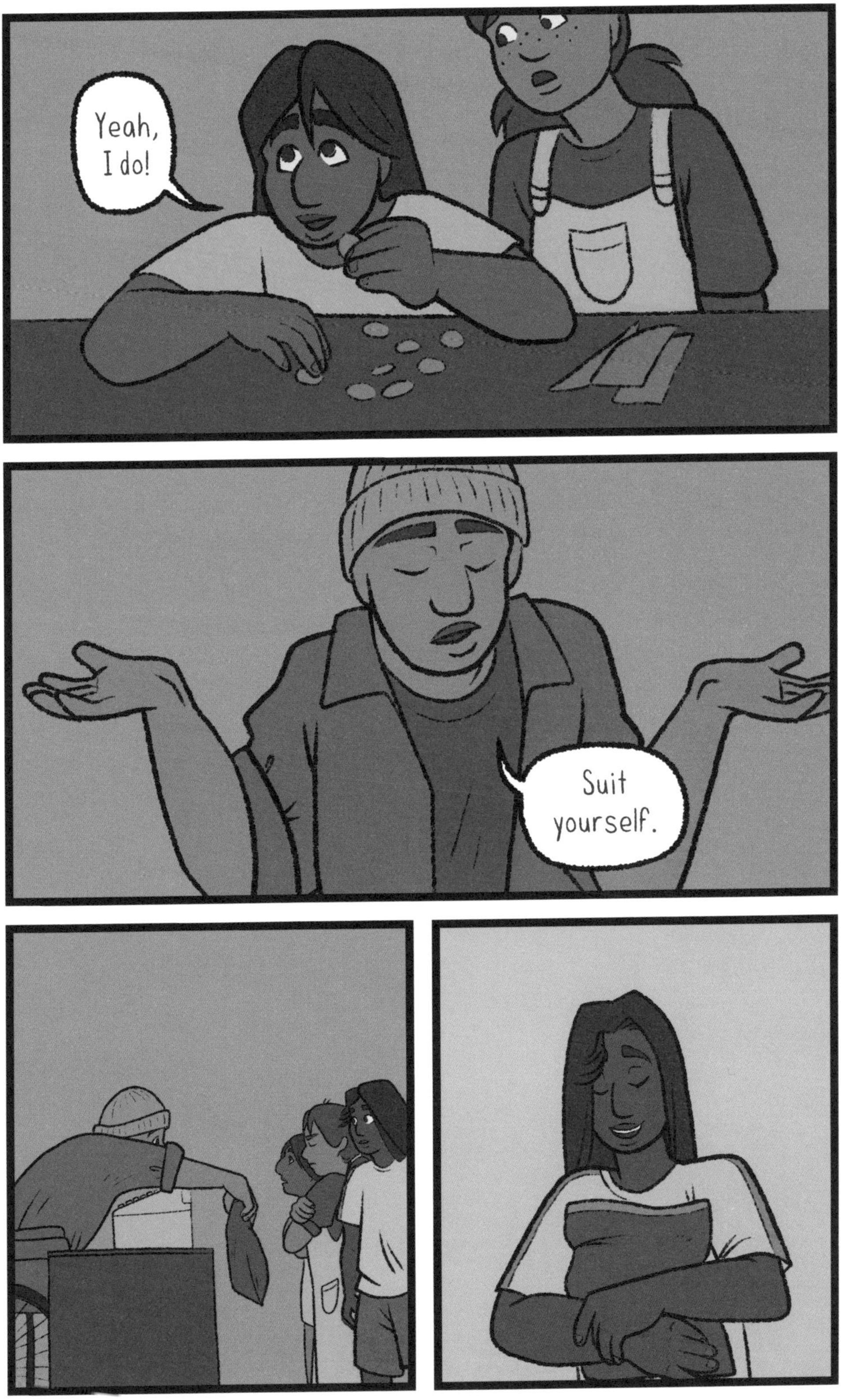
Yeah, I do!
Suit yourself.

Now will you please go outside and stop bothering customers?

Okaaaay!

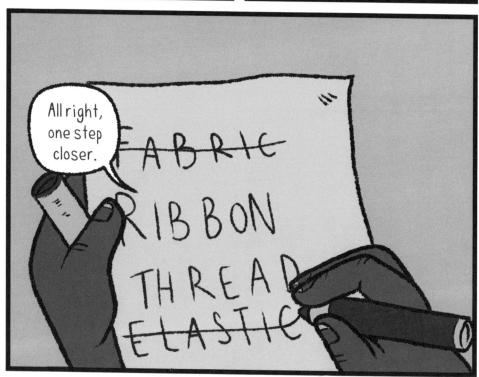

All right, one step closer.

FABRIC

RIBBON

THREAD

ELASTIC

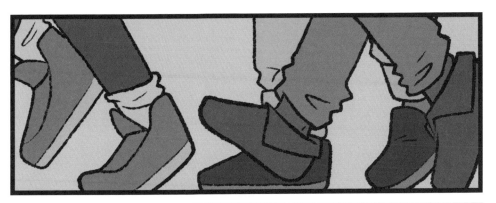

Let's go to the dunes!

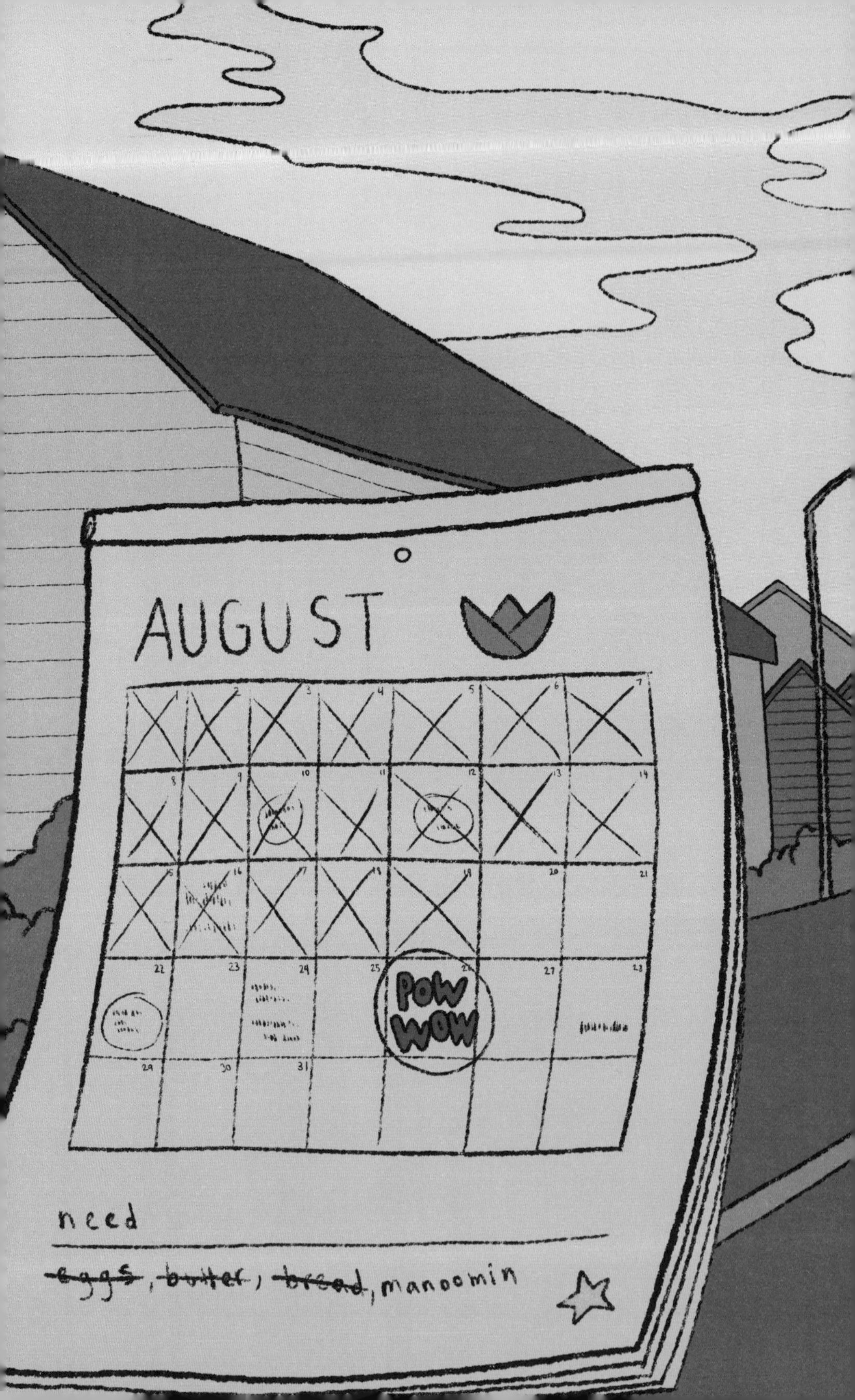
AUGUST
POW WOW
need
eggs, butter, bread, manoomin

CHAPTER SIX

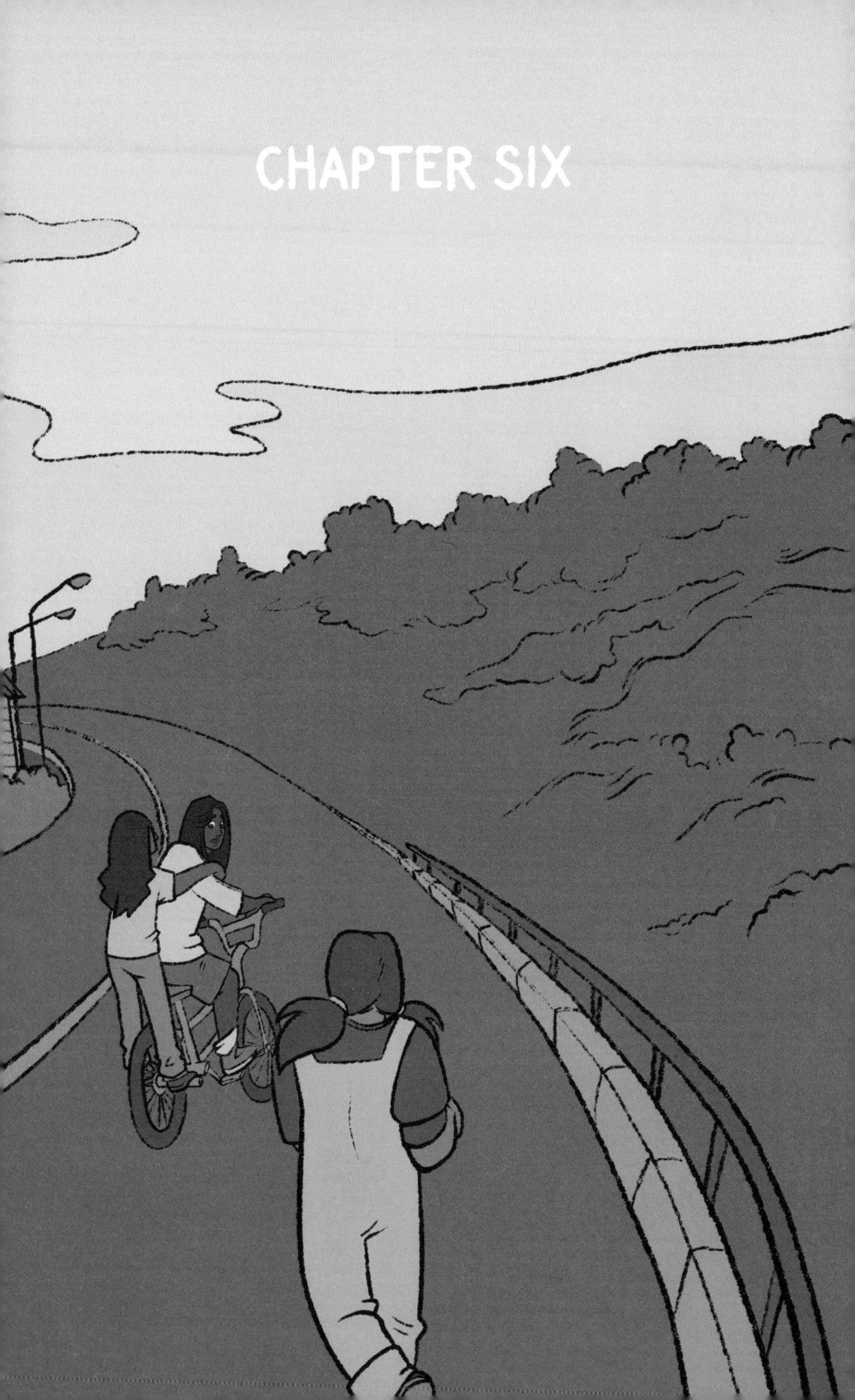

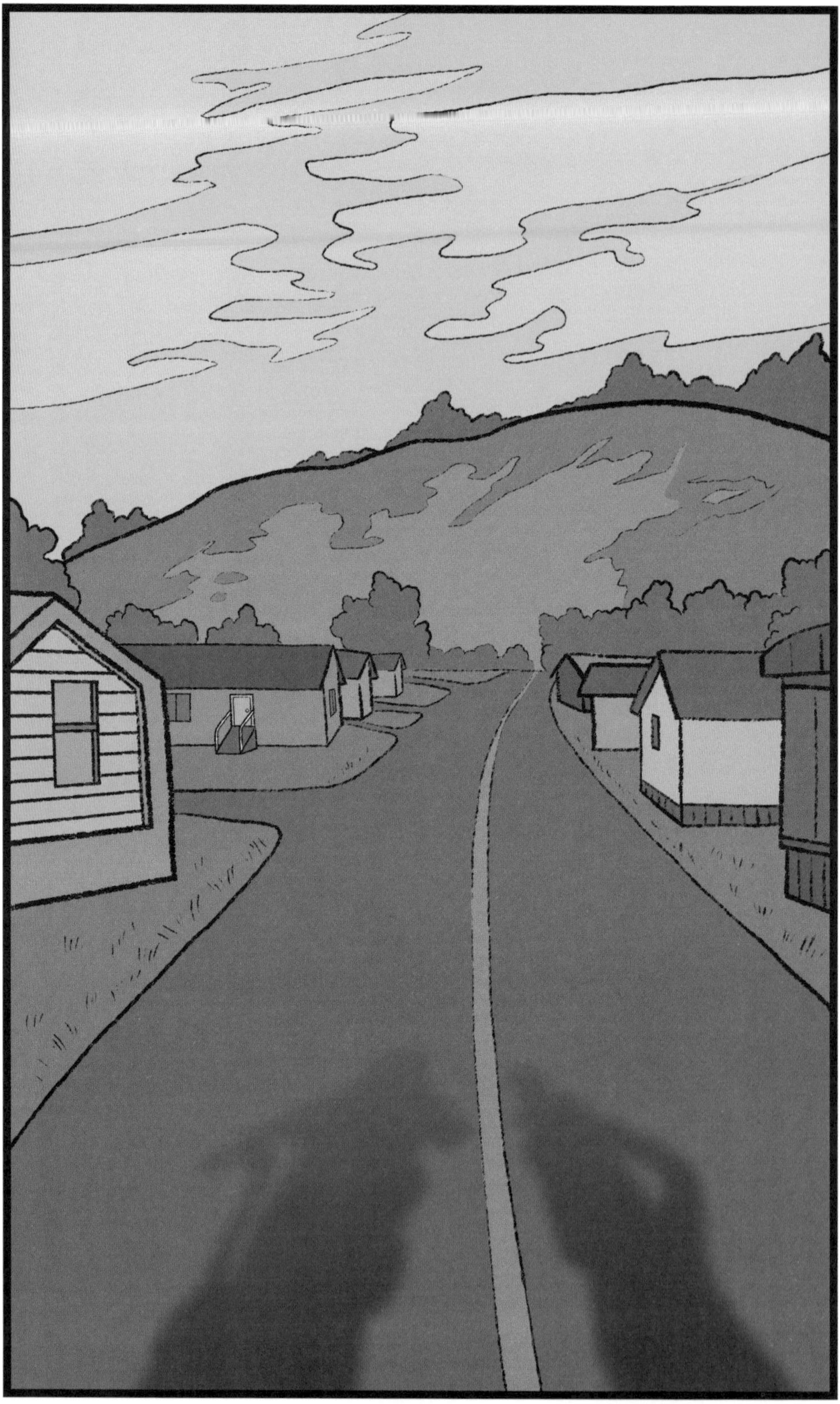

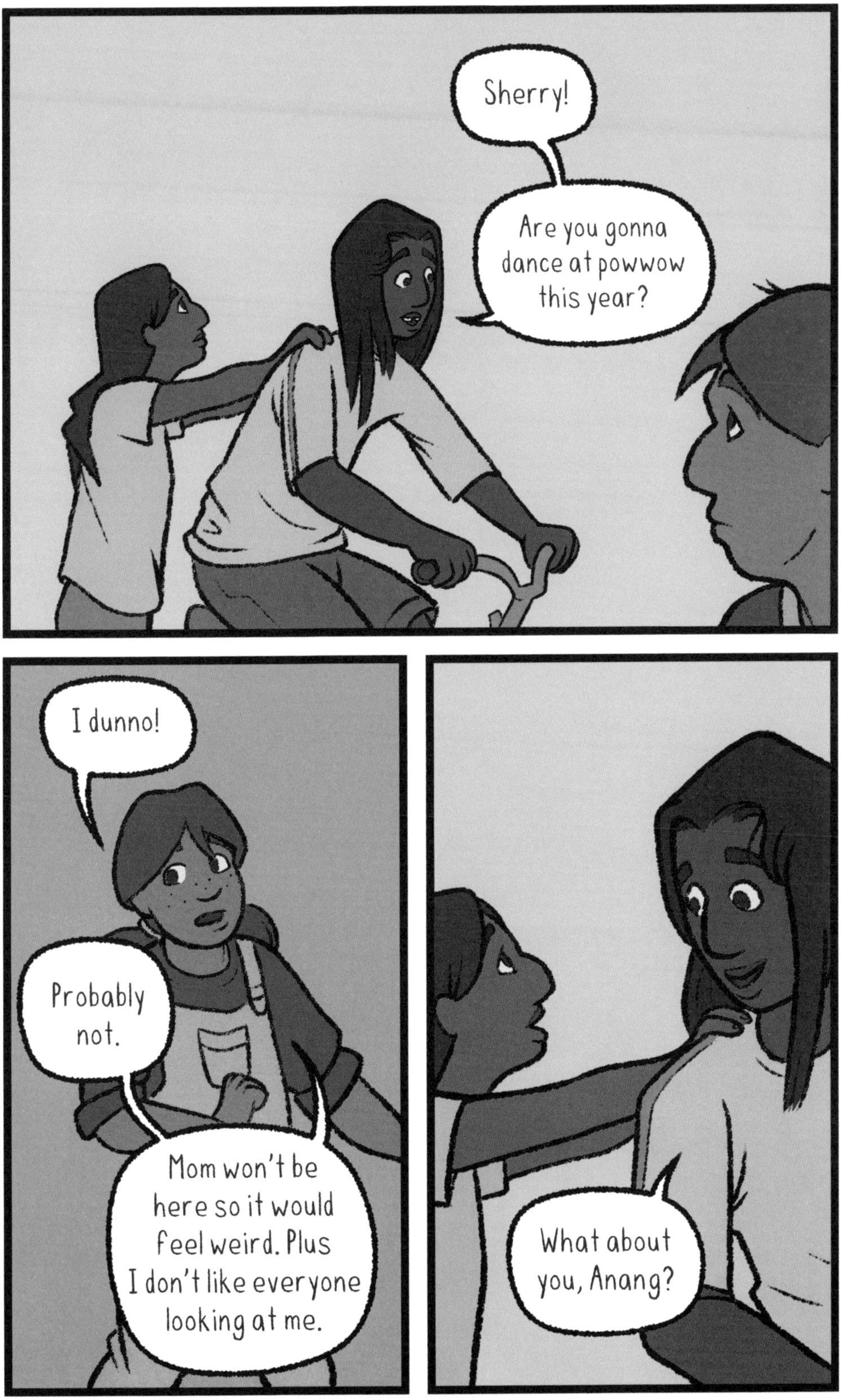
Sherry!
Are you gonna dance at powwow this year?
I dunno!
Probably not.
Mom won't be here so it would feel weird. Plus I don't like everyone looking at me.
What about you, Anang?

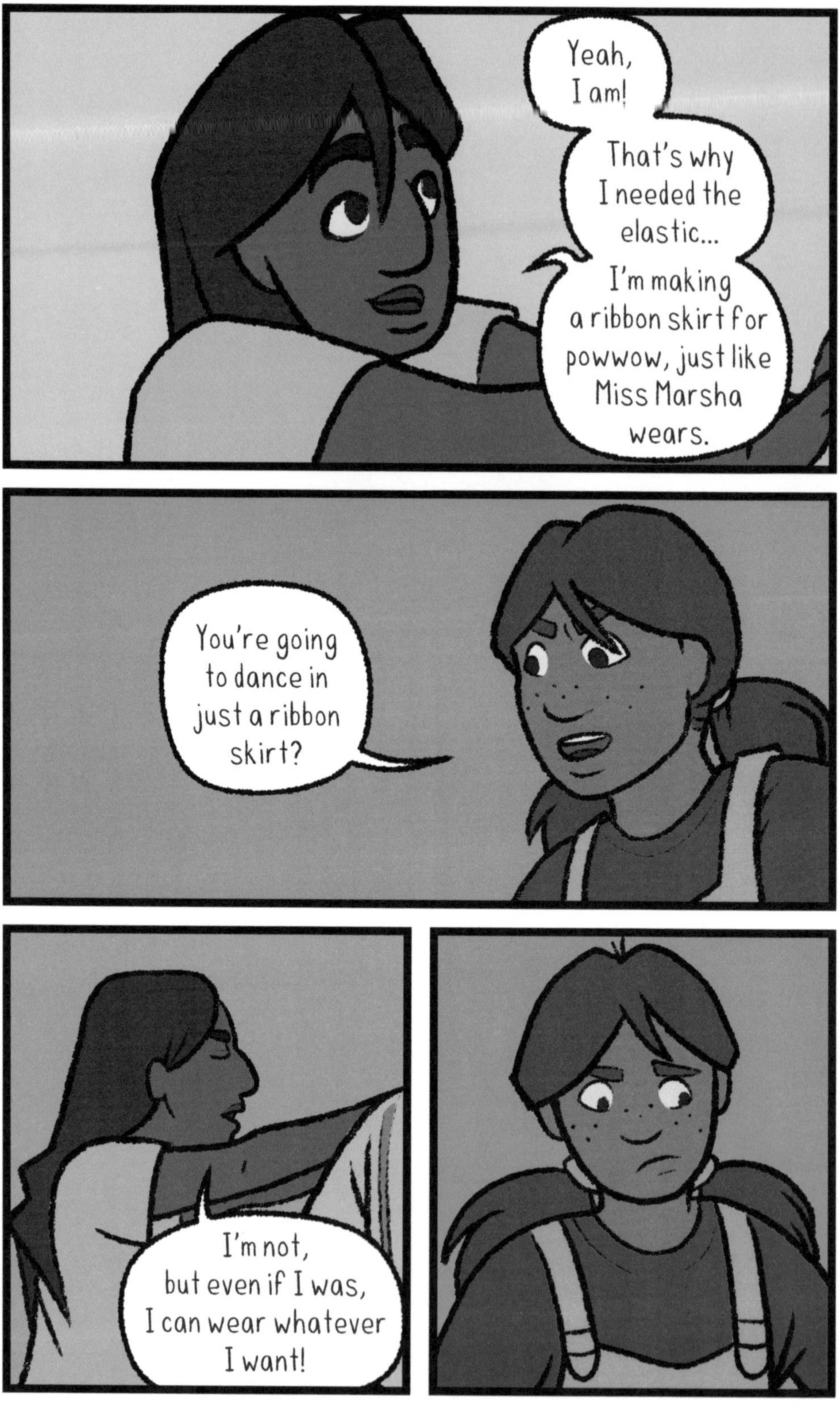
Yeah, I am!
That's why I needed the elastic...
I'm making a ribbon skirt for powwow, just like Miss Marsha wears.
You're going to dance in just a ribbon skirt?
I'm not, but even if I was, I can wear whatever I want!

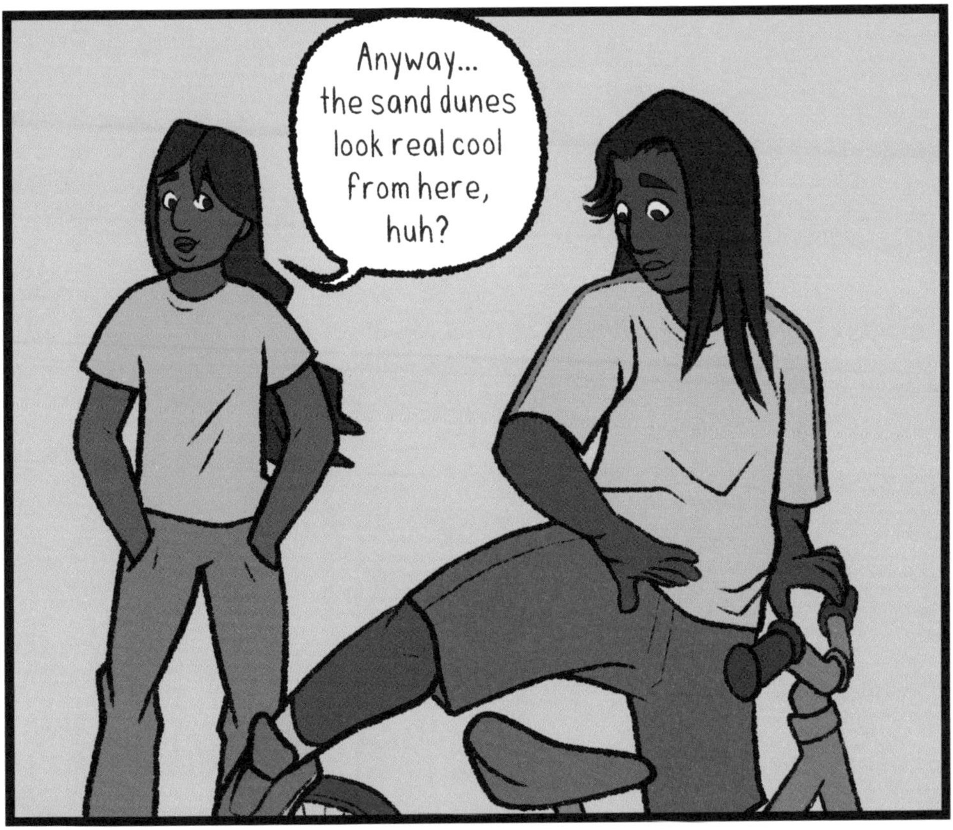
Anyway... the sand dunes look real cool from here, huh?

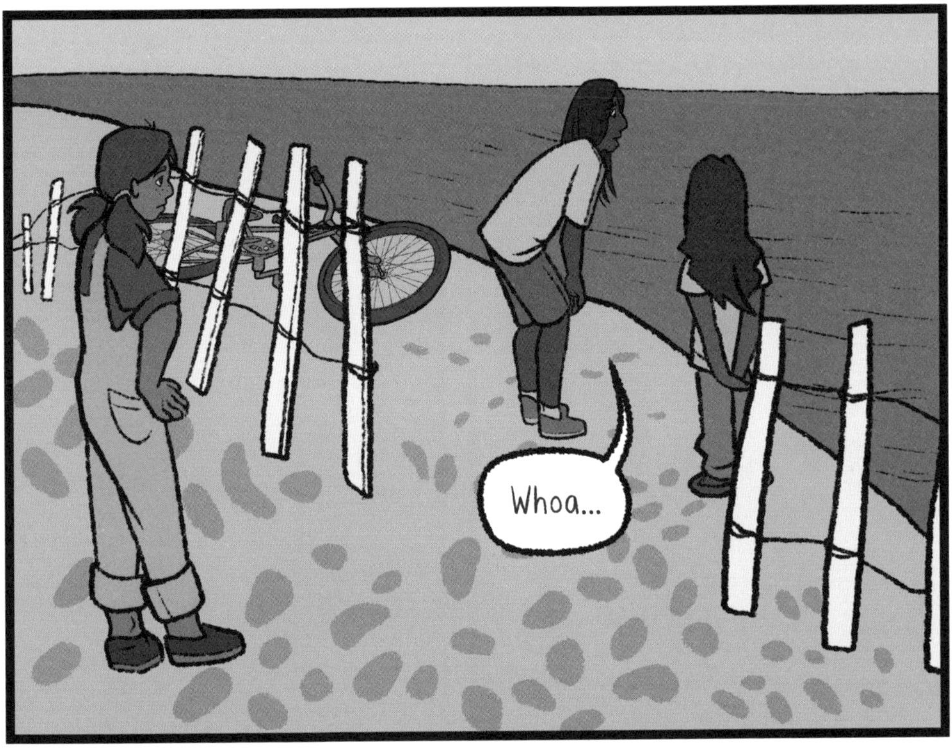
Whoa...

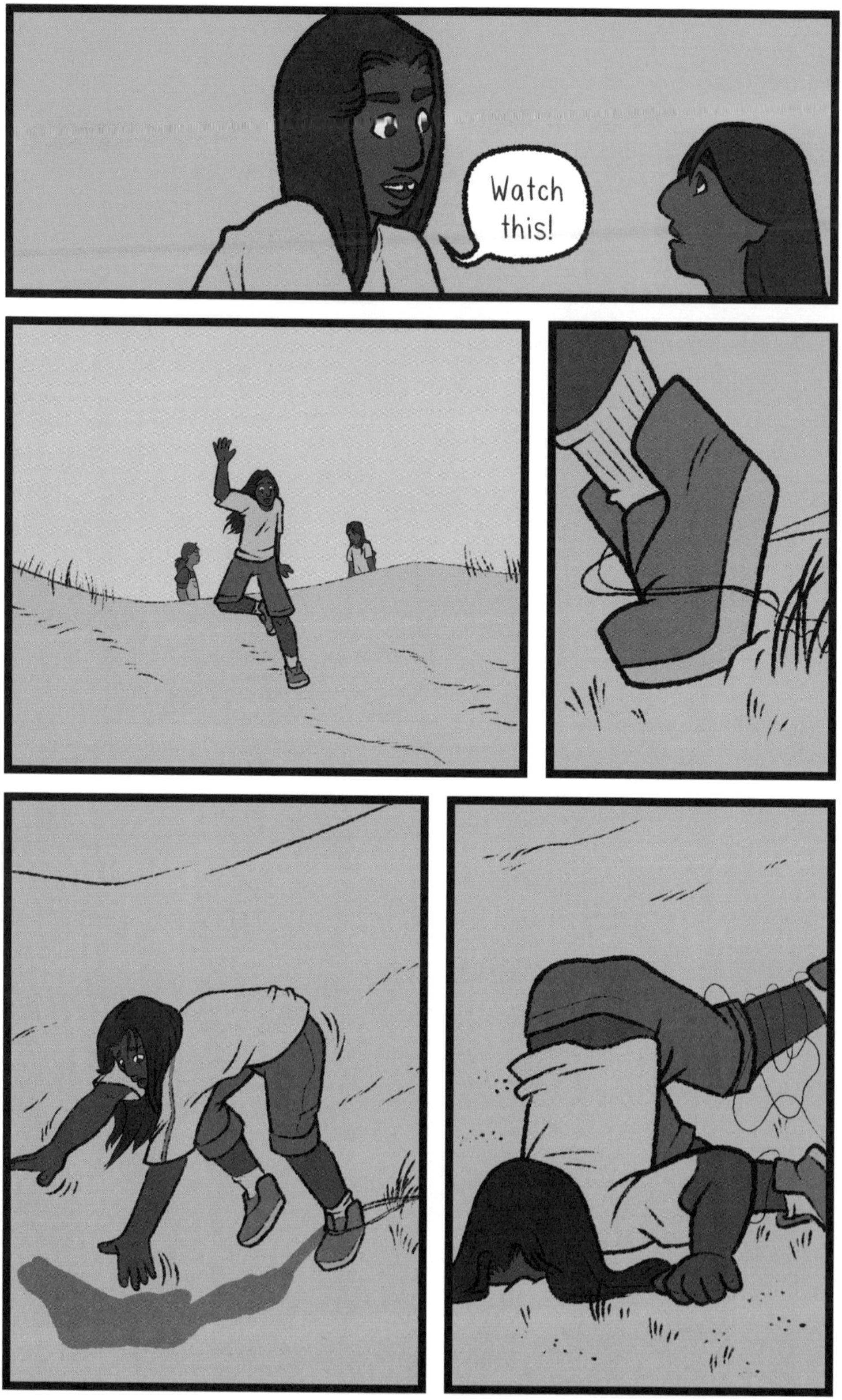
Watch this!

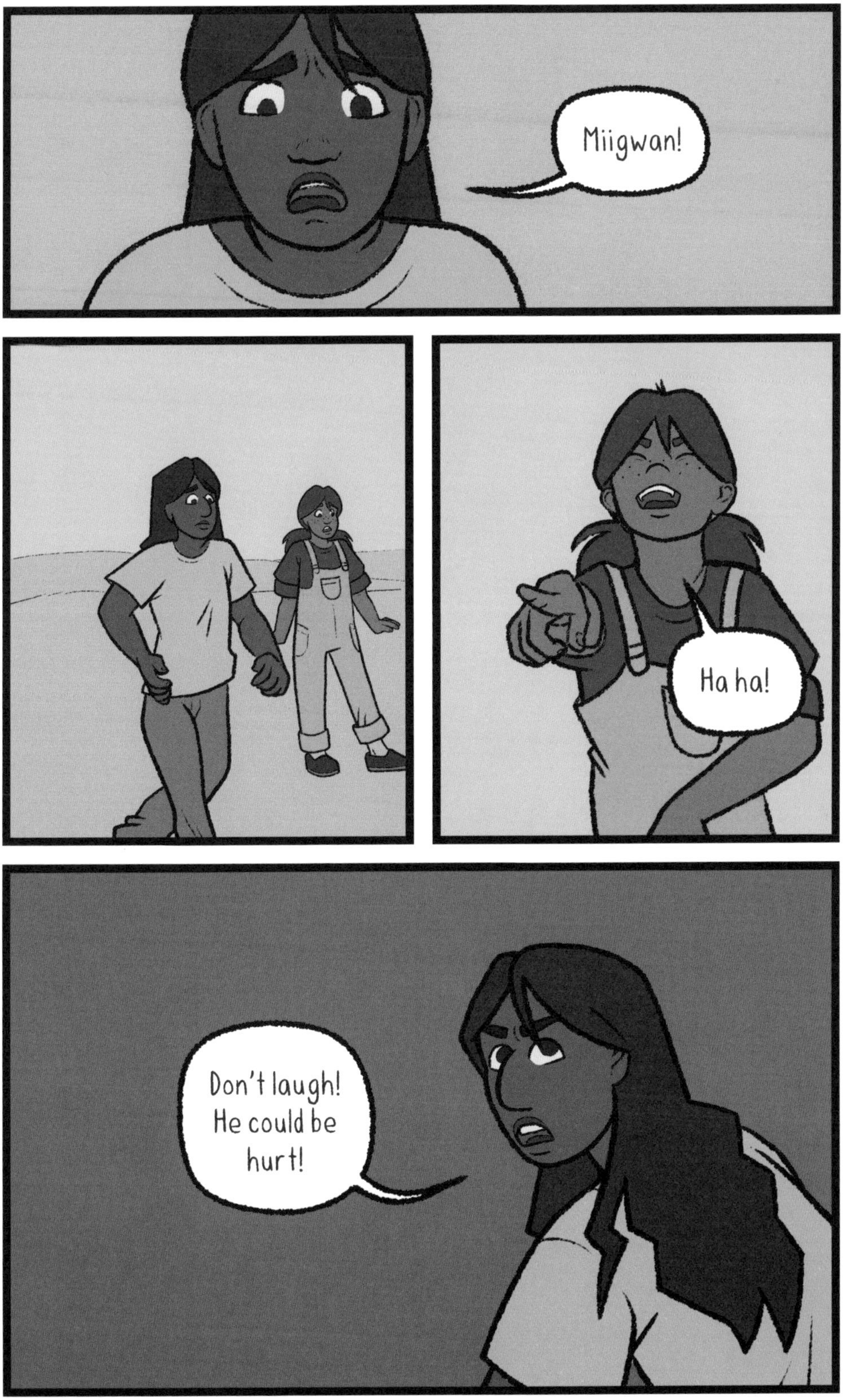
Miigwan!
Ha ha!
Don't laugh! He could be hurt!

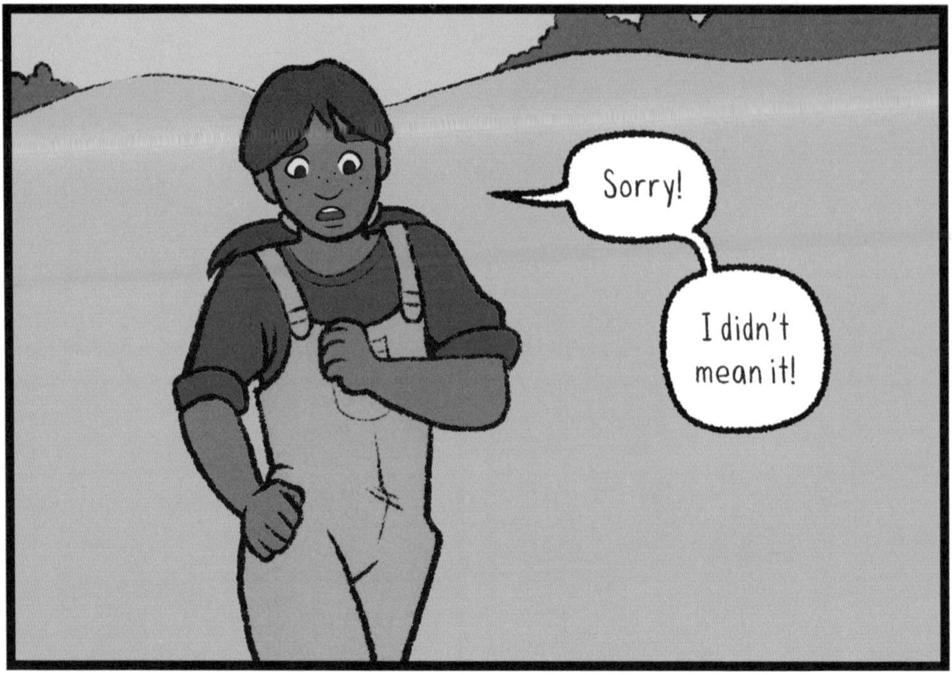
Sorry!
I didn't mean it!

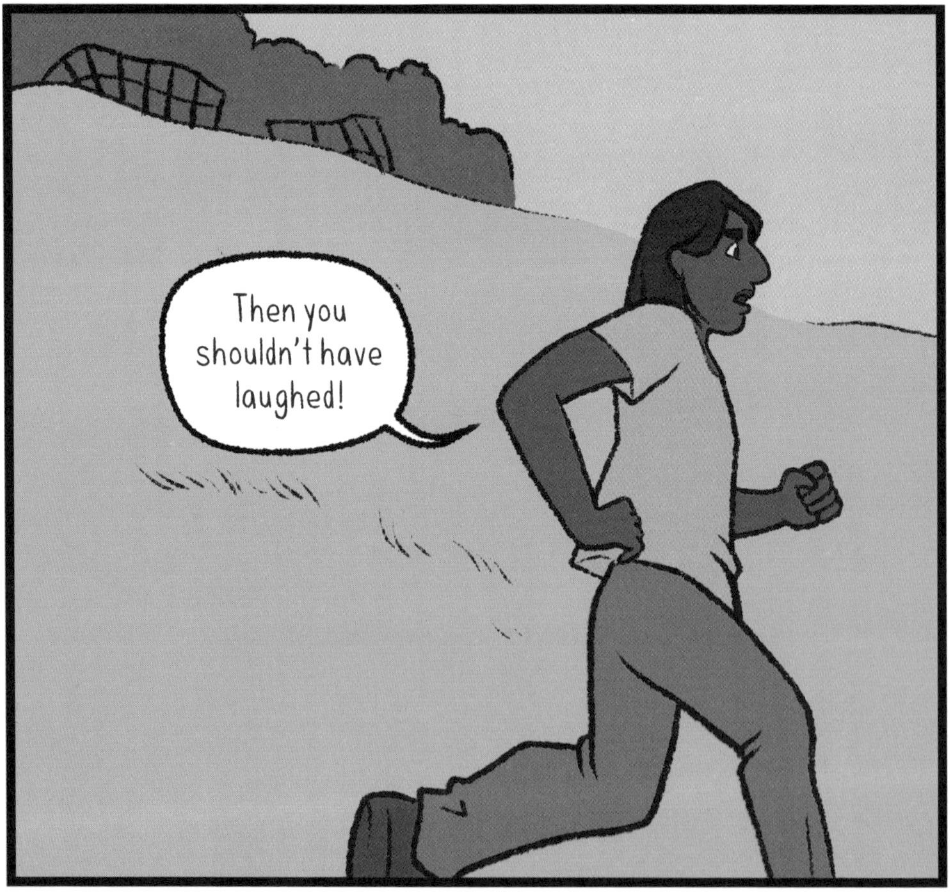
Then you shouldn't have laughed!

Anang...

Let's just help Miigwan, okay?

Is this... thread?

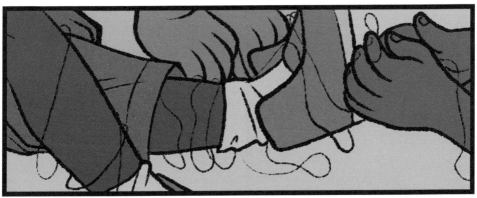

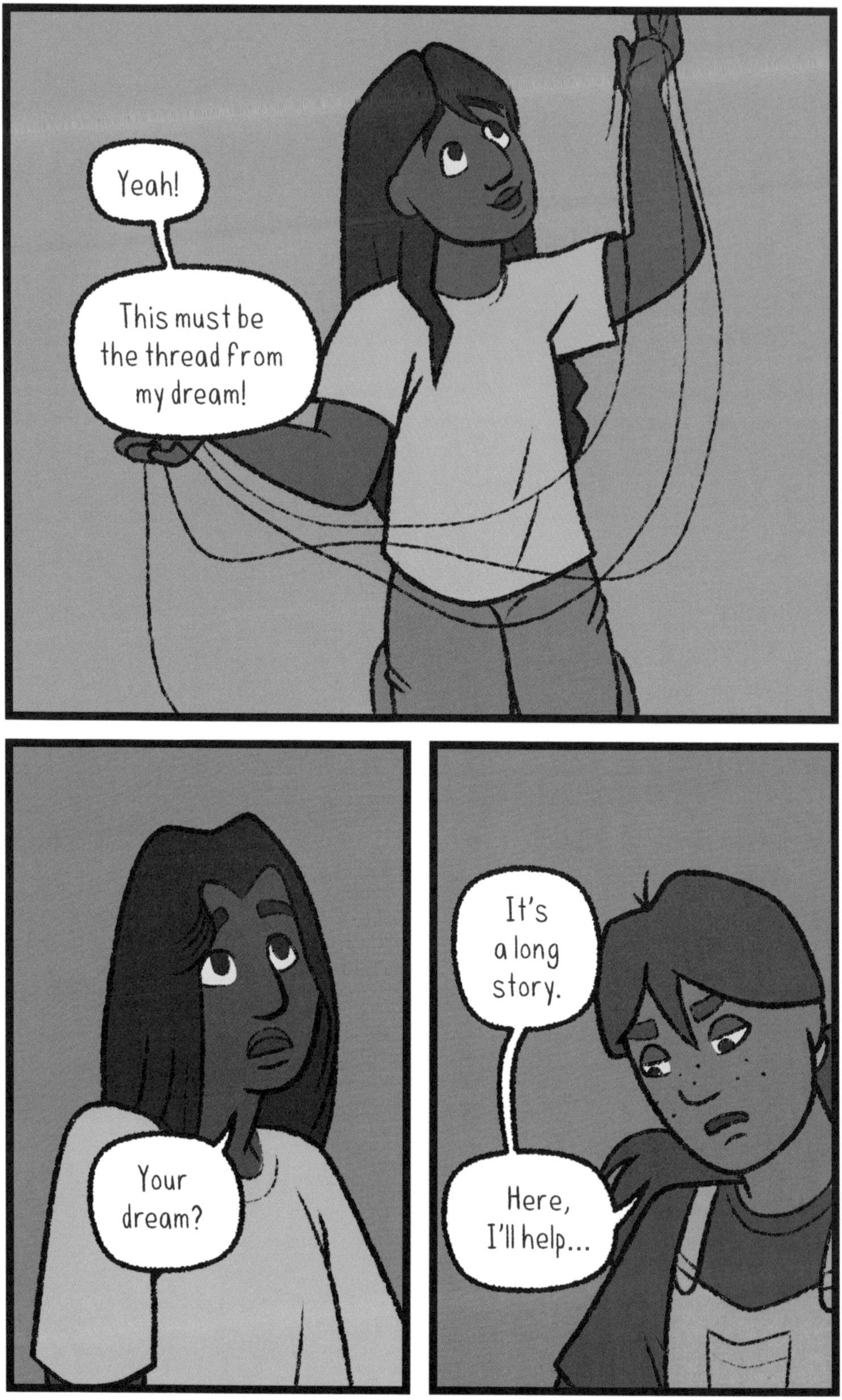
Yeah!
This must be the thread from my dream!
Your dream?
It's a long story.
Here, I'll help...

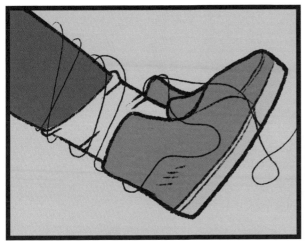

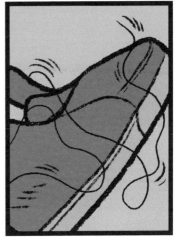

What's happening?

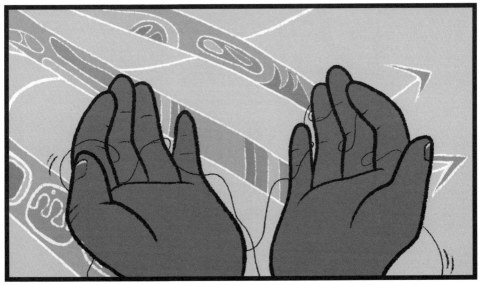

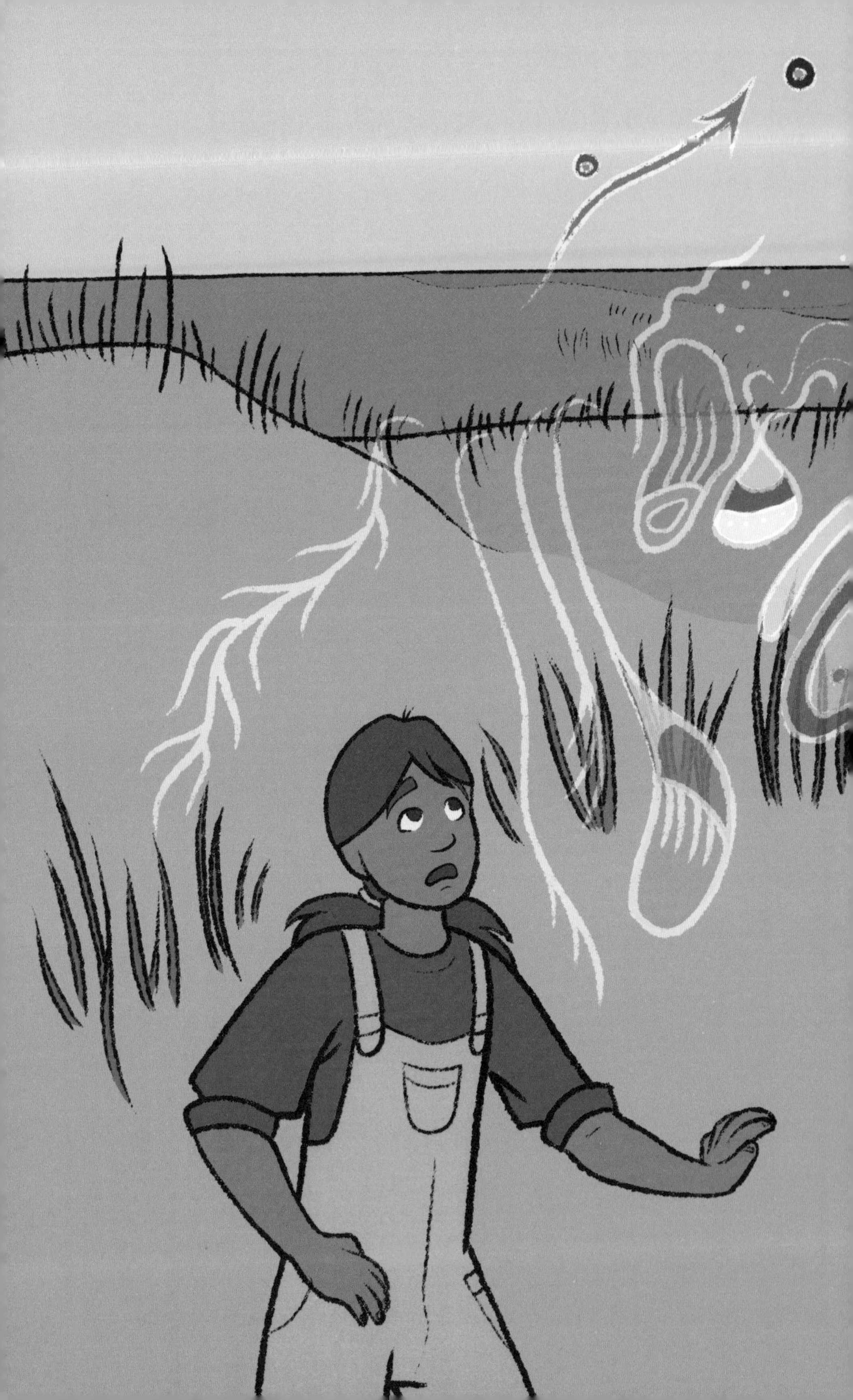

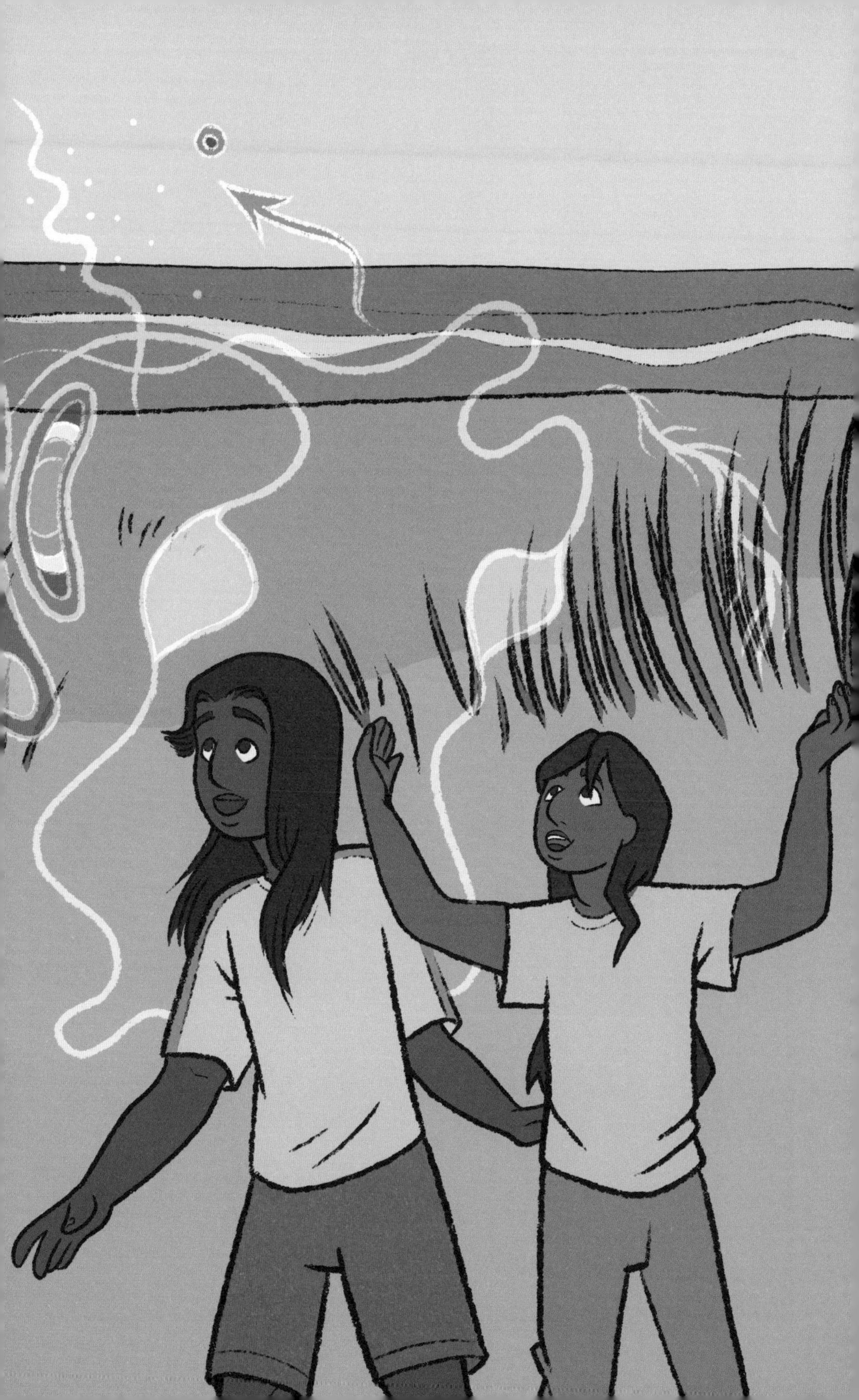

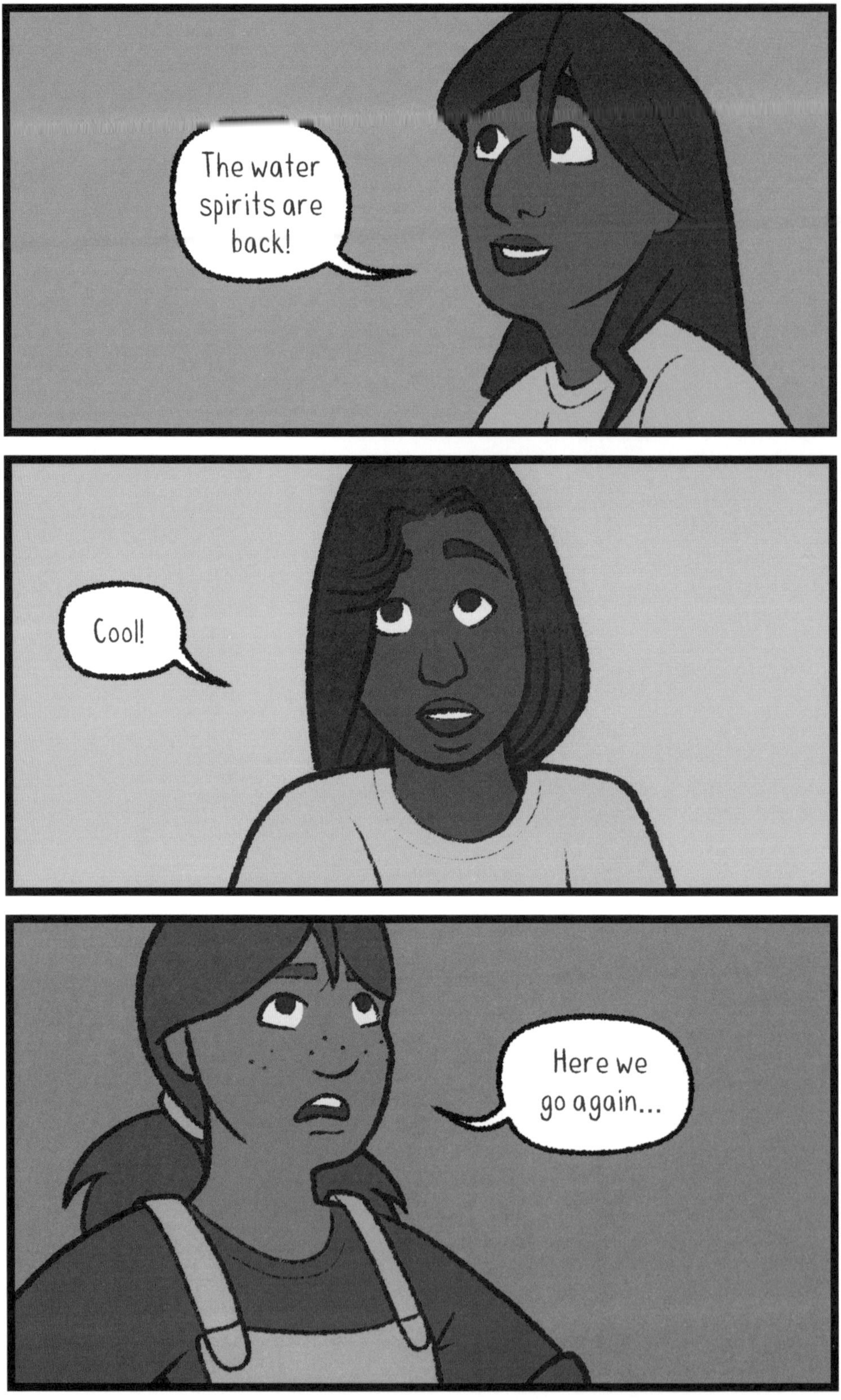
The water spirits are back!
Cool!
Here we go again...

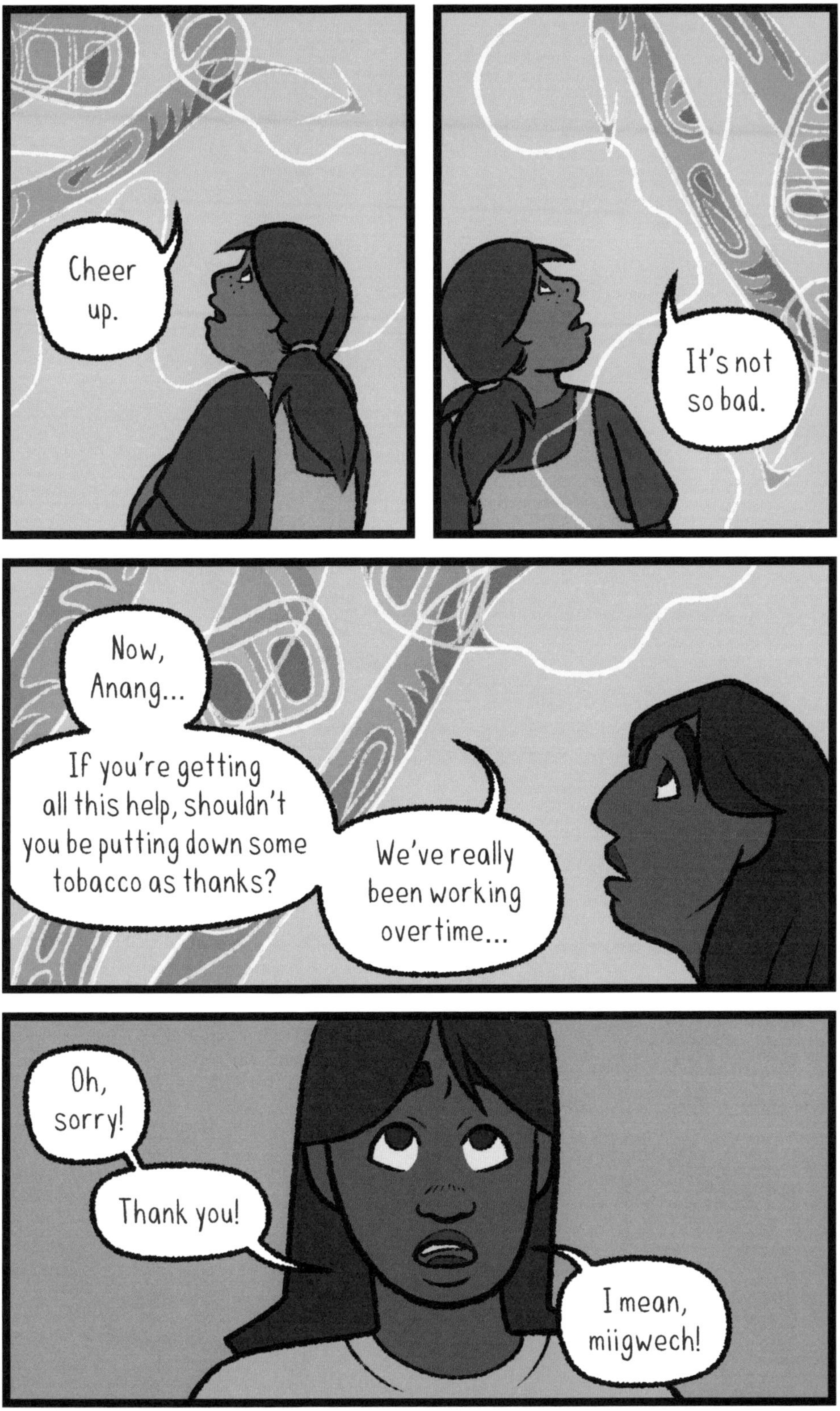
Cheer up.
It's not so bad.
Now, Anang...
If you're getting all this help, shouldn't you be putting down some tobacco as thanks?
We've really been working overtime...
Oh, sorry!
Thank you!
I mean, miigwech!

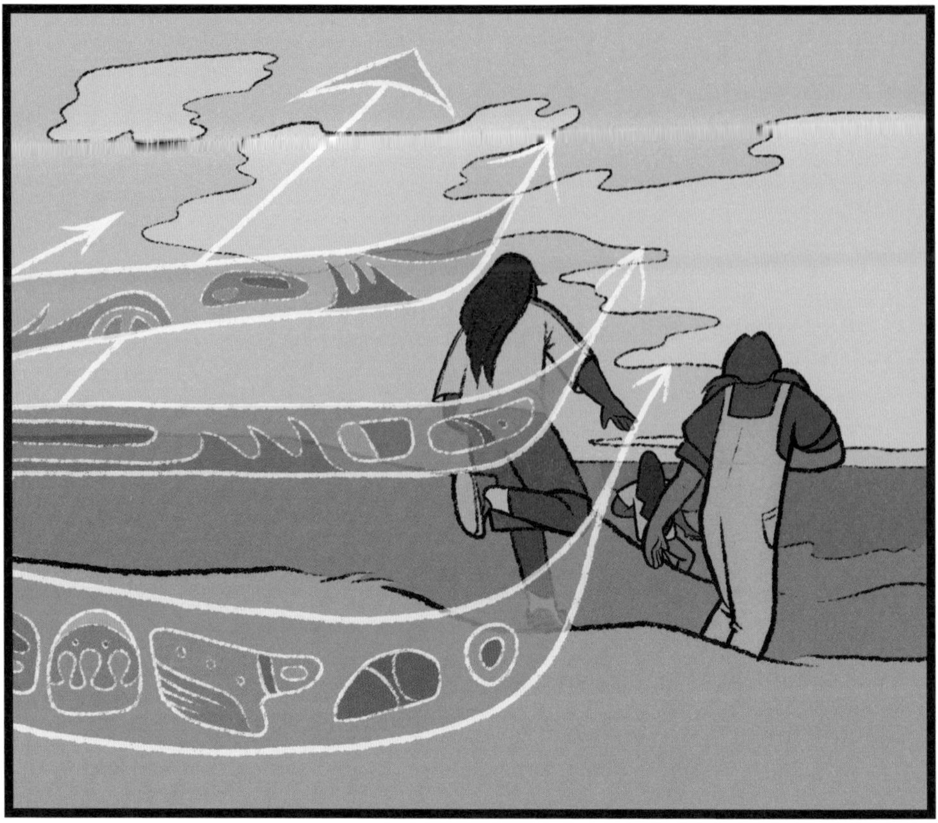

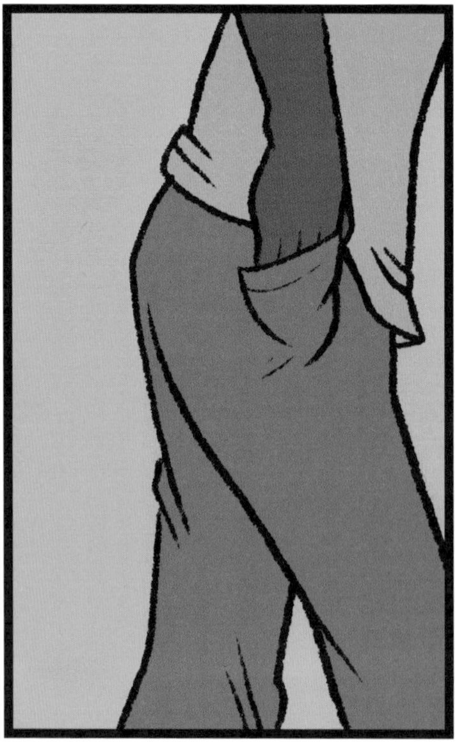

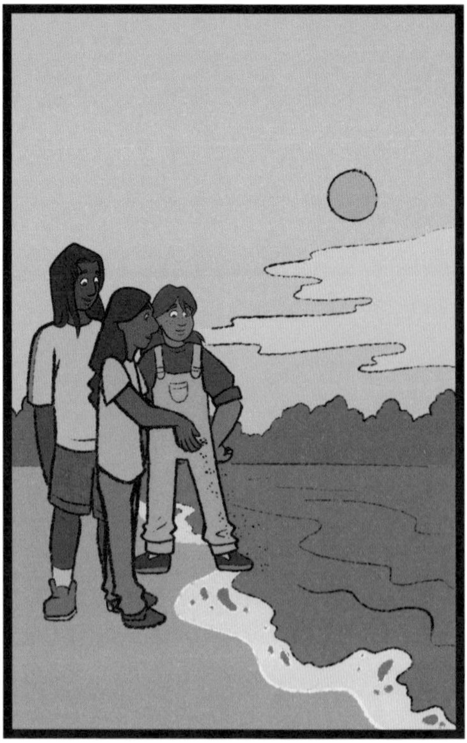

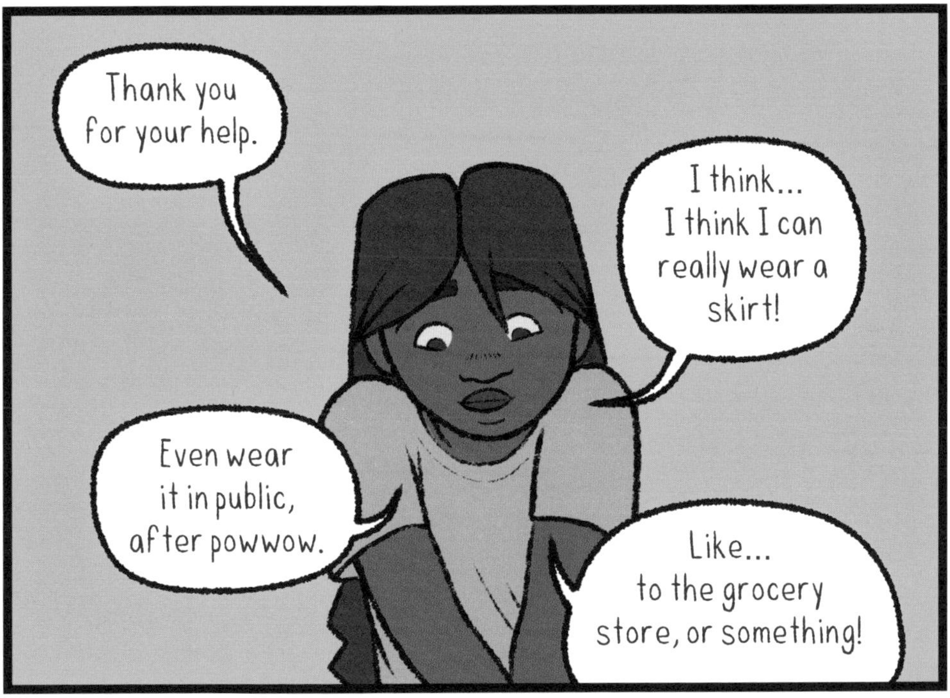
Thank you for your help.
I think... I think I can really wear a skirt!
Even wear it in public, after powwow.
Like... to the grocery store, or something!

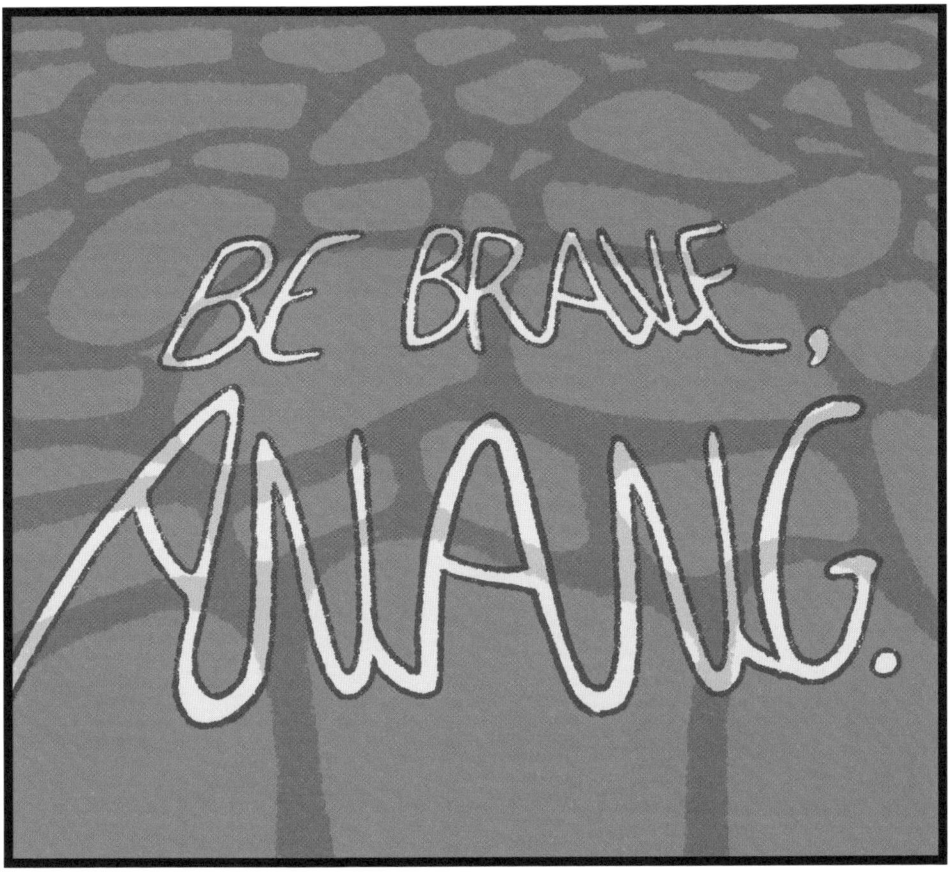
BE BRAVE, ANANG.

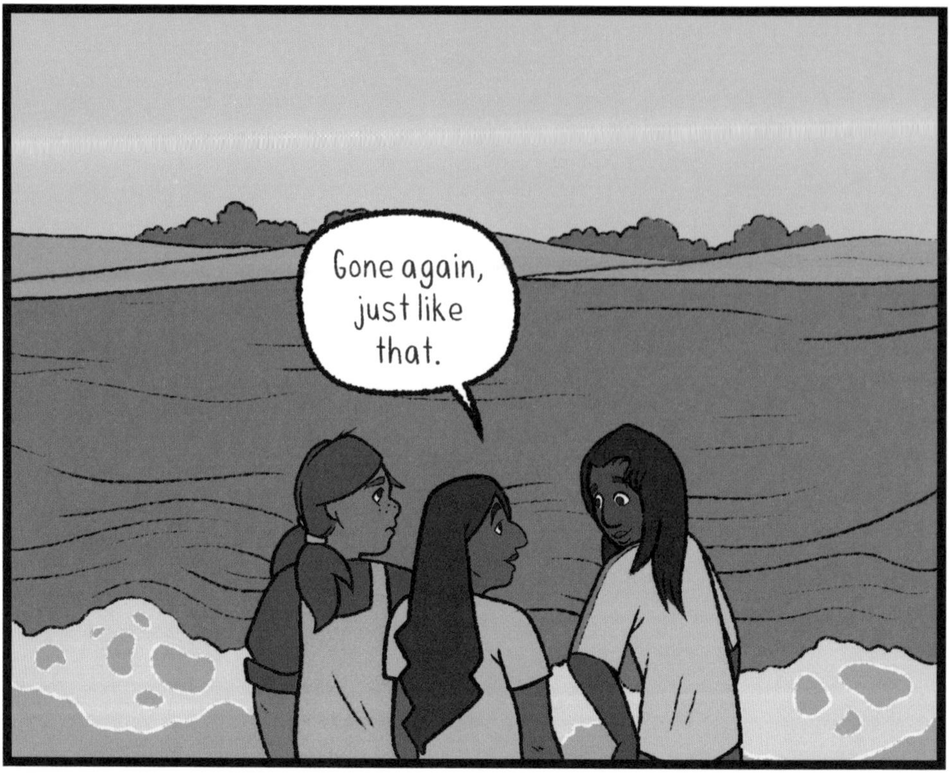
Gone again, just like that.

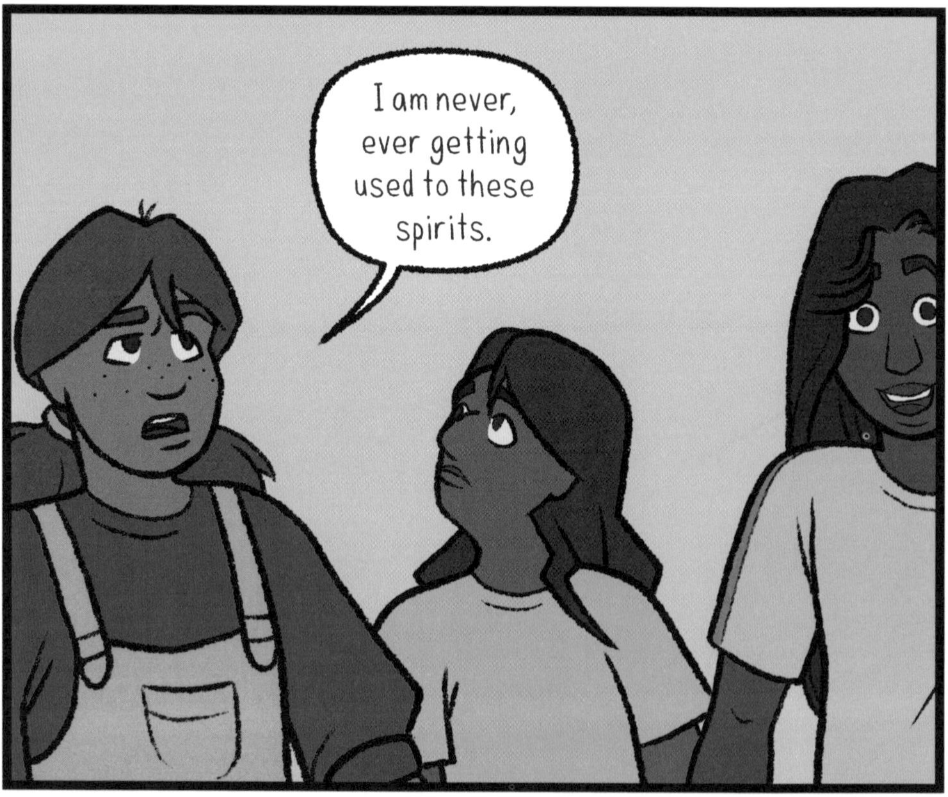
I am never, ever getting used to these spirits.

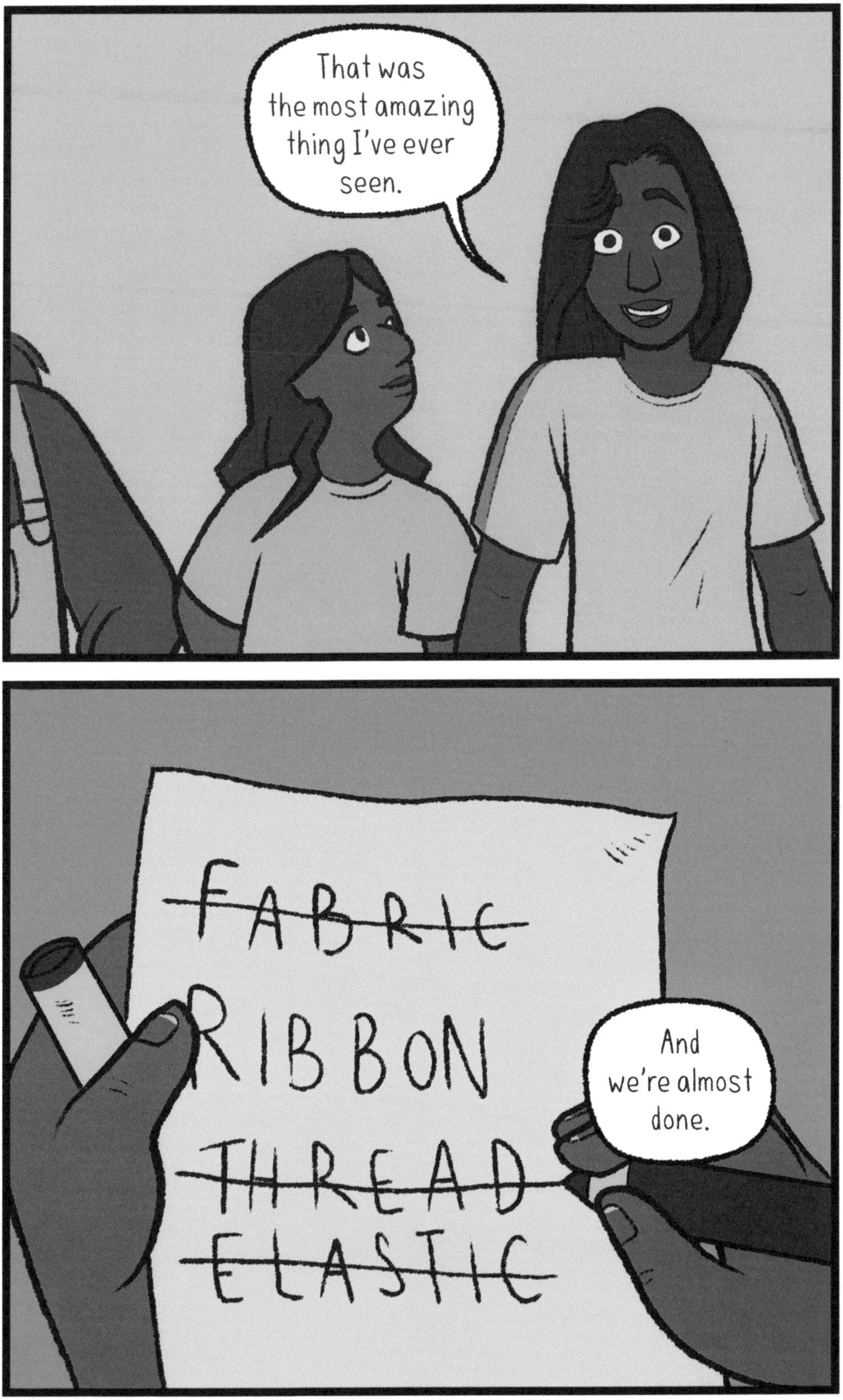
That was the most amazing thing I've ever seen.
FABRIC
RIBBON
THREAD
ELASTIC
And we're almost done.

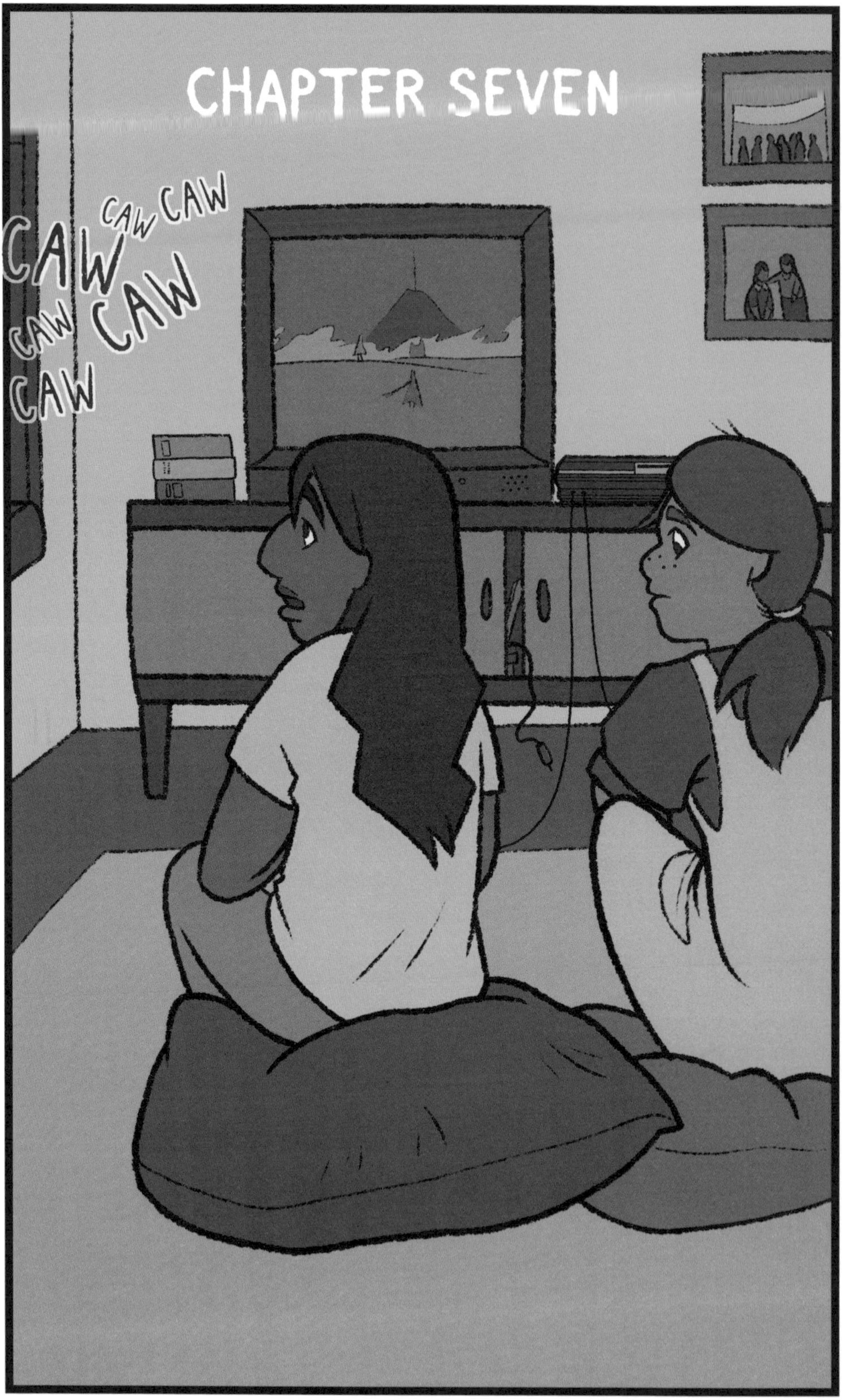
CHAPTER SEVEN
CAW CAW CAW
CAW CAW
CAW

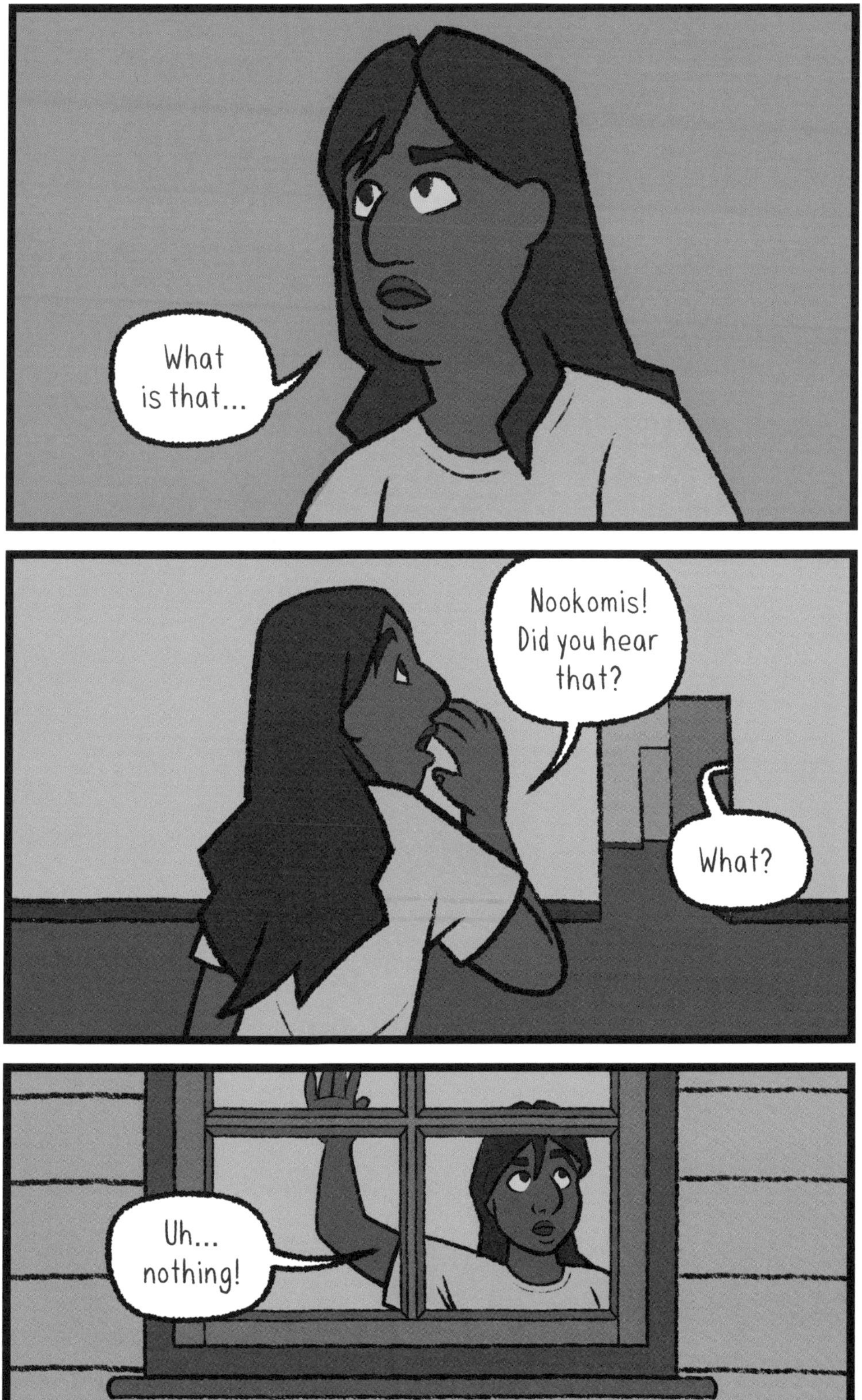
What is that...
Nookomis! Did you hear that?
What?
Uh... nothing!

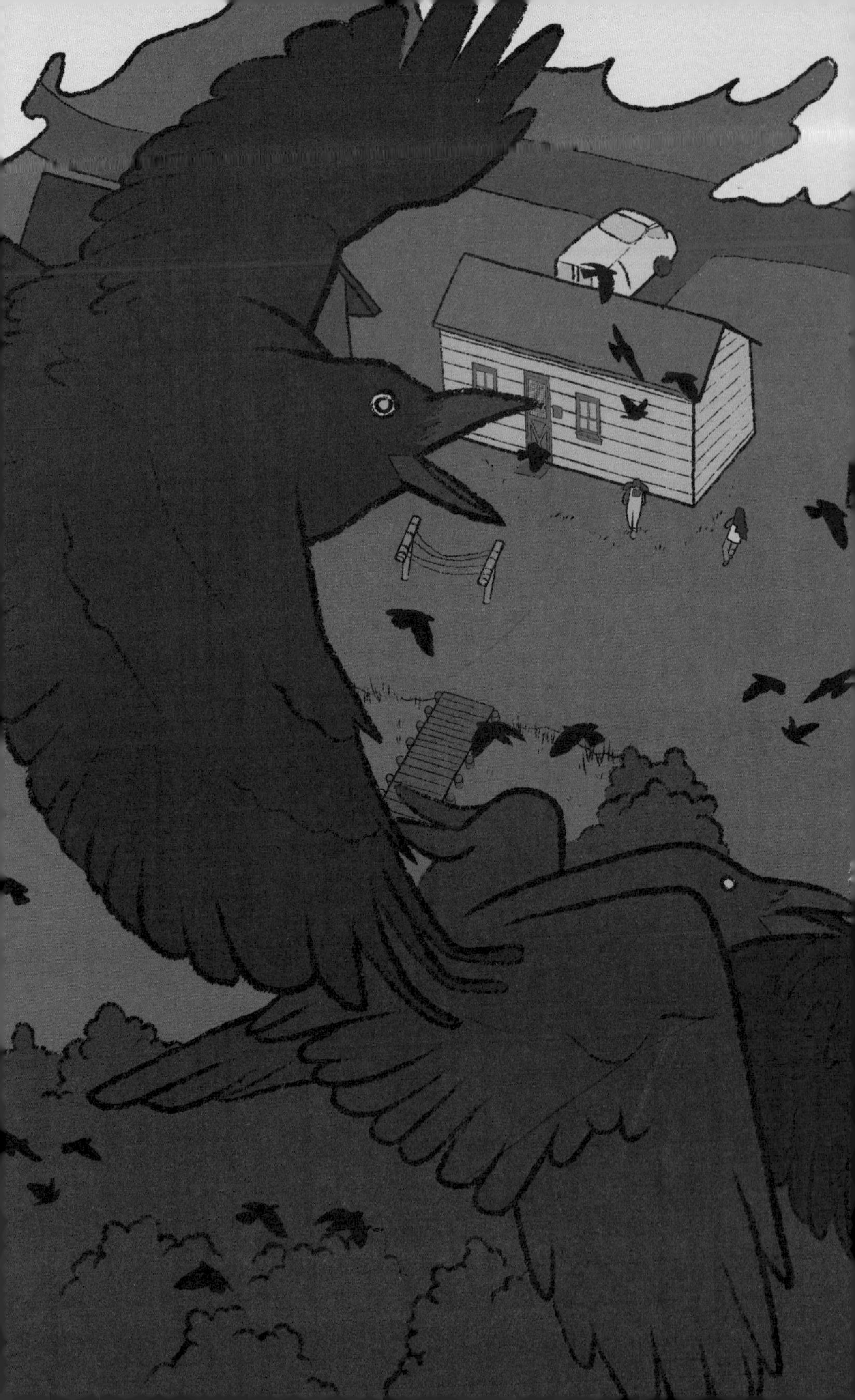

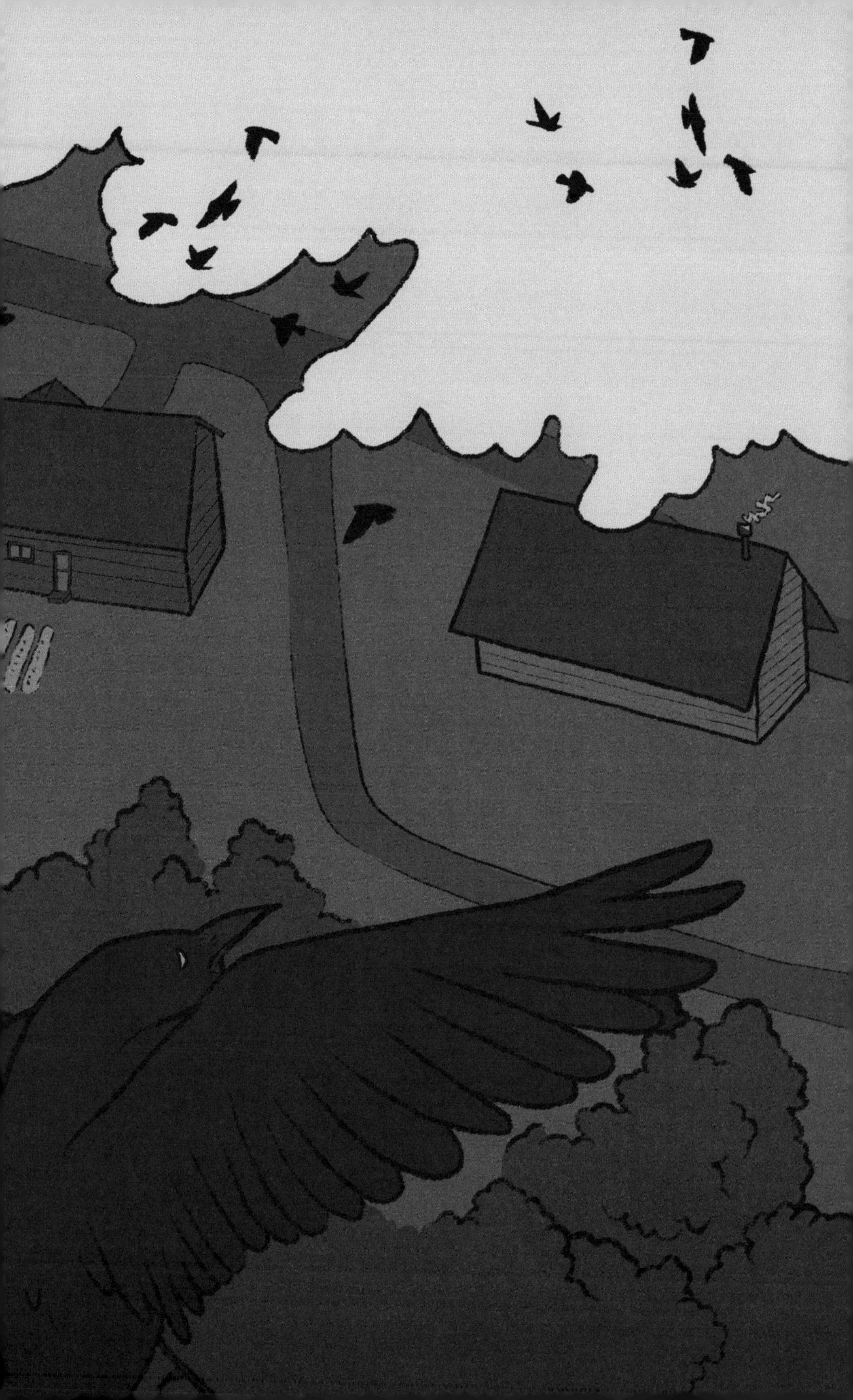

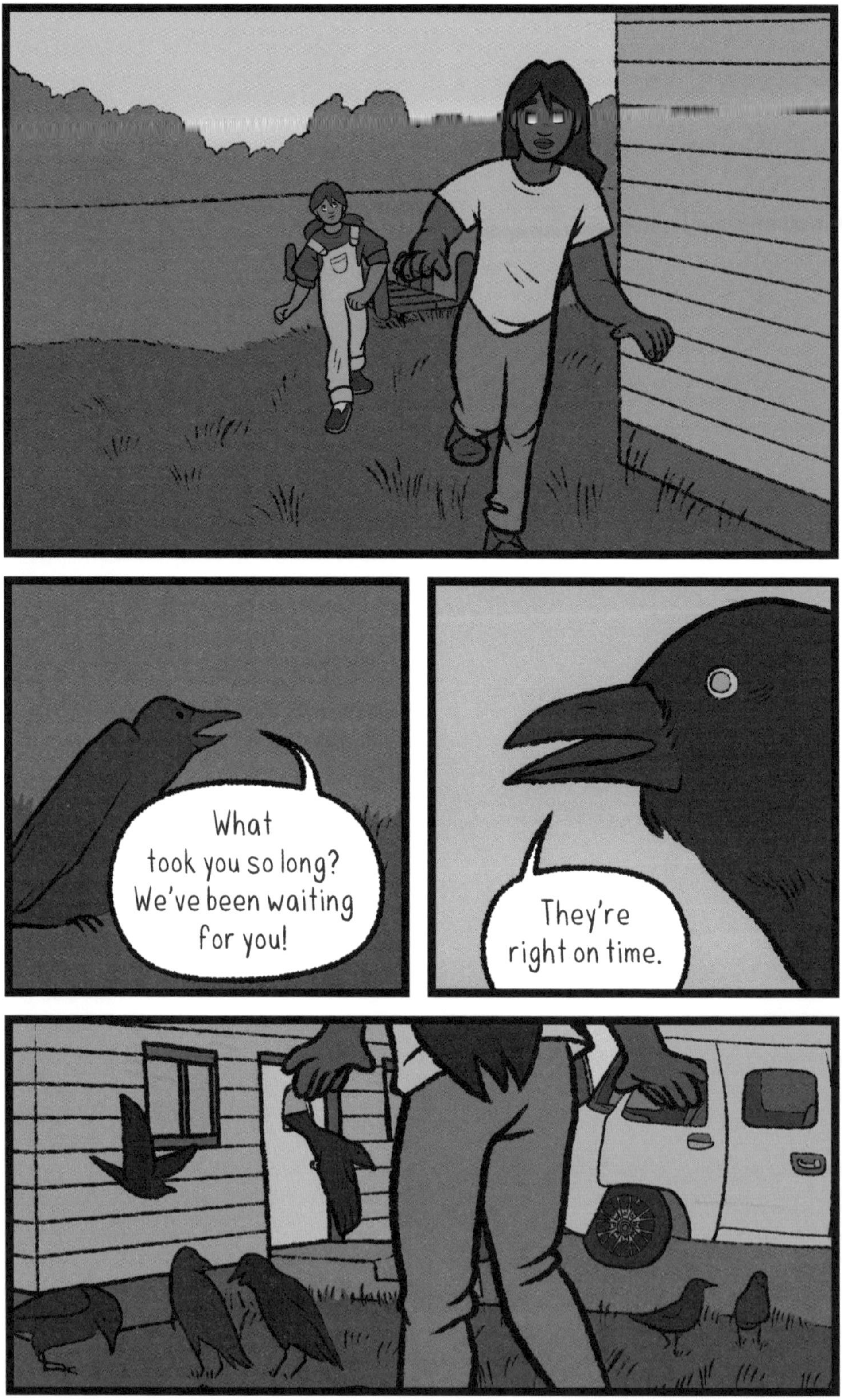
What took you so long? We've been waiting for you!
They're right on time.

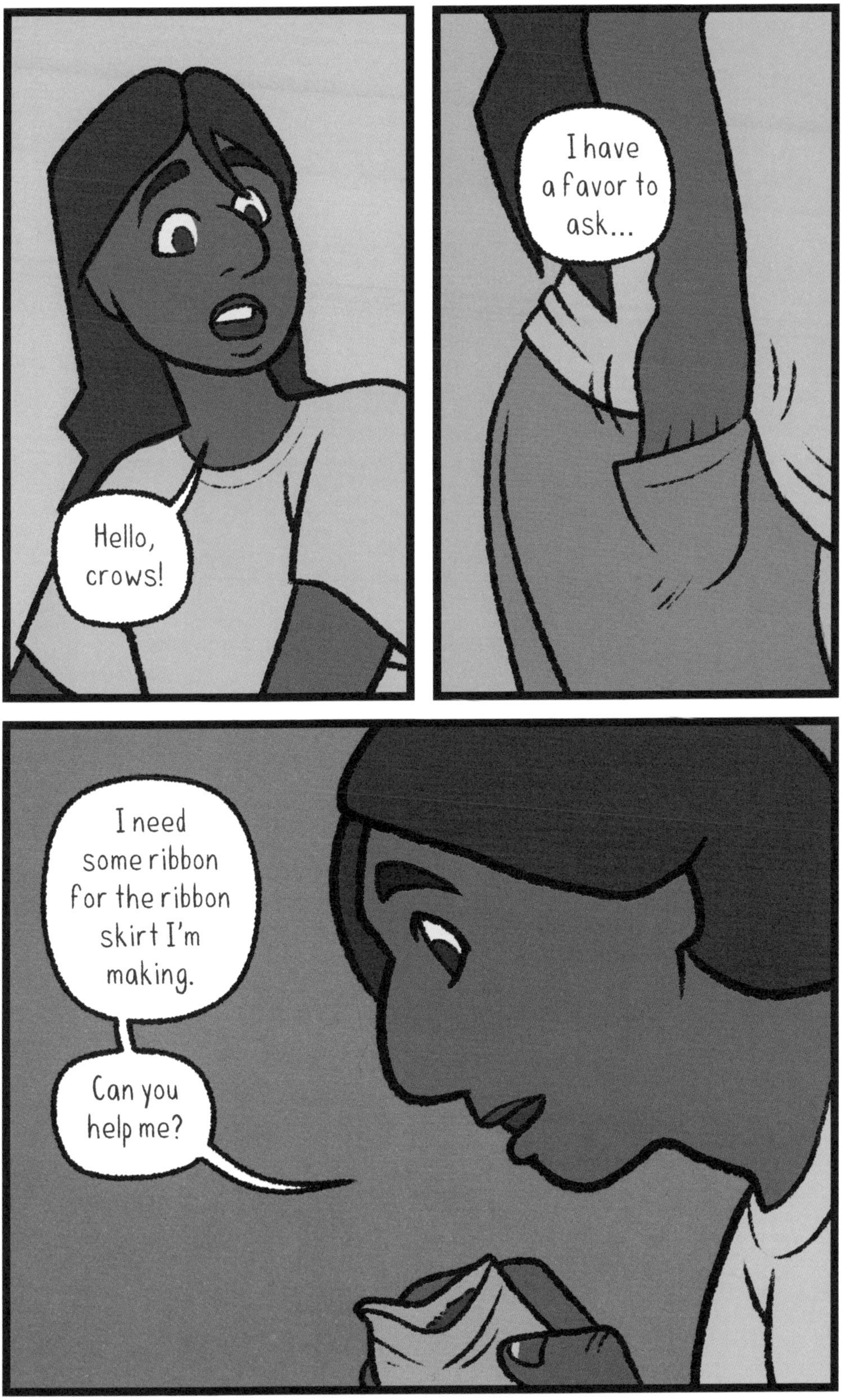
Hello, crows!
I have a favor to ask...
I need some ribbon for the ribbon skirt I'm making.
Can you help me?

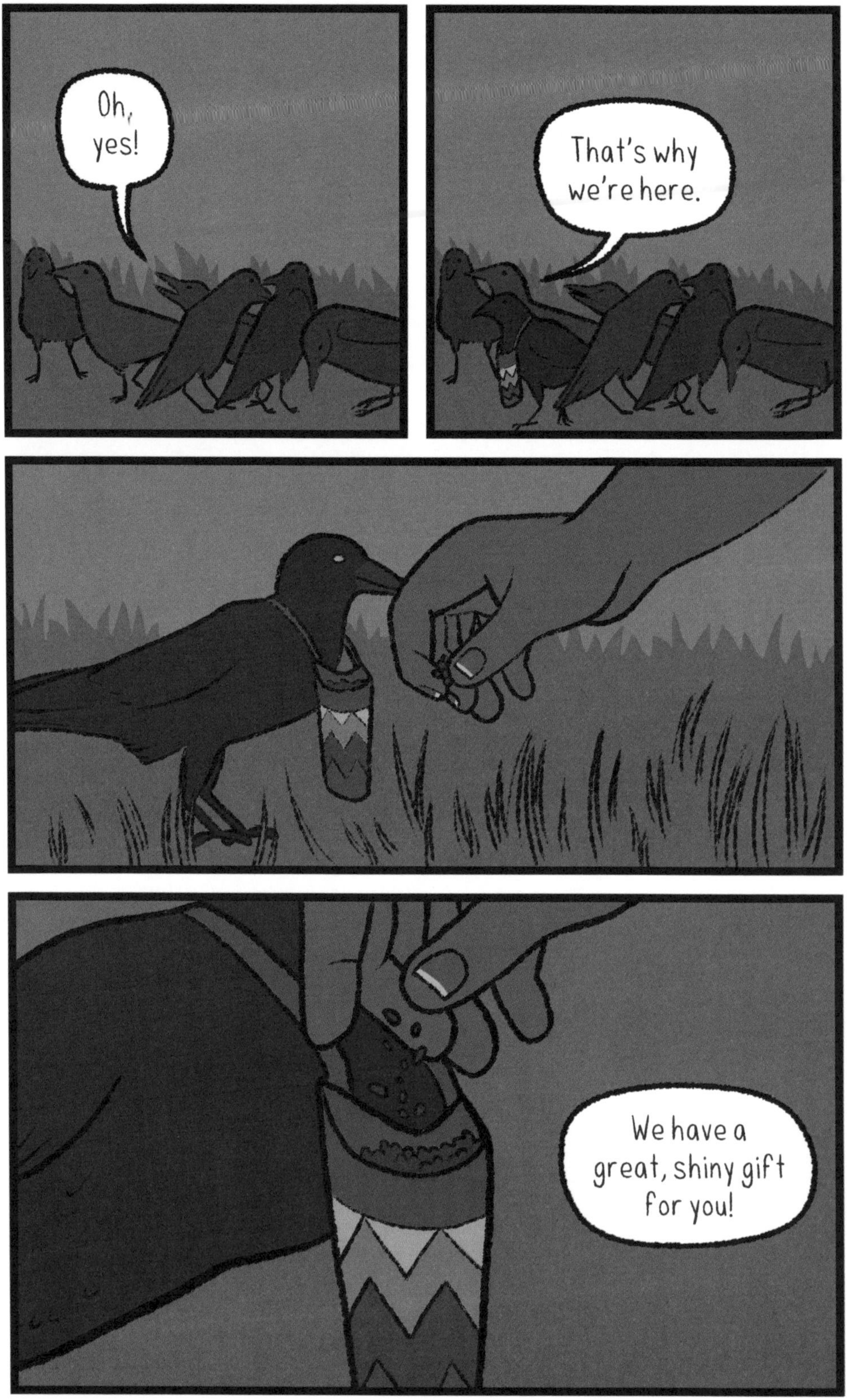
Oh, yes!
That's why we're here.
We have a great, shiny gift for you!

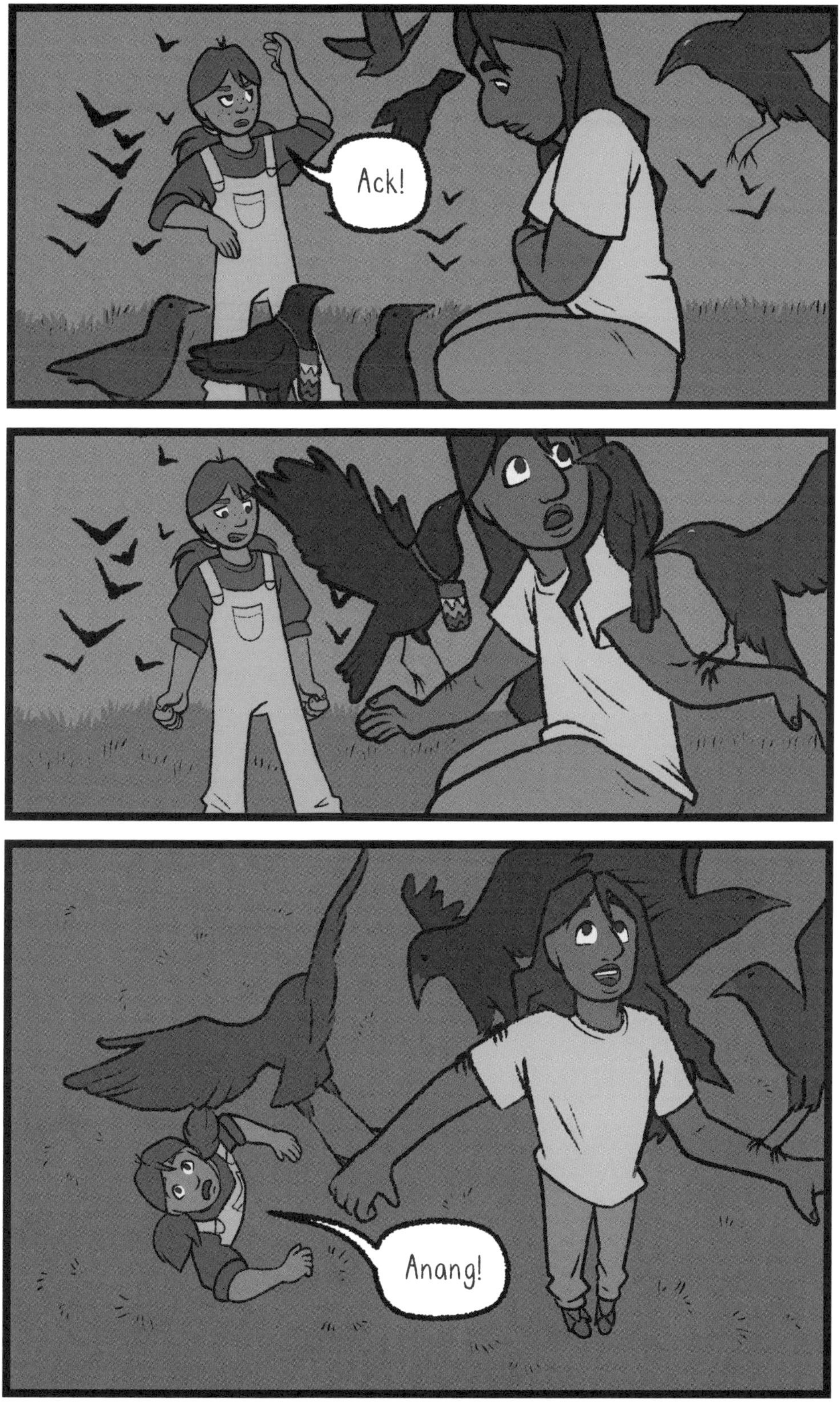
Ack!
Anang!

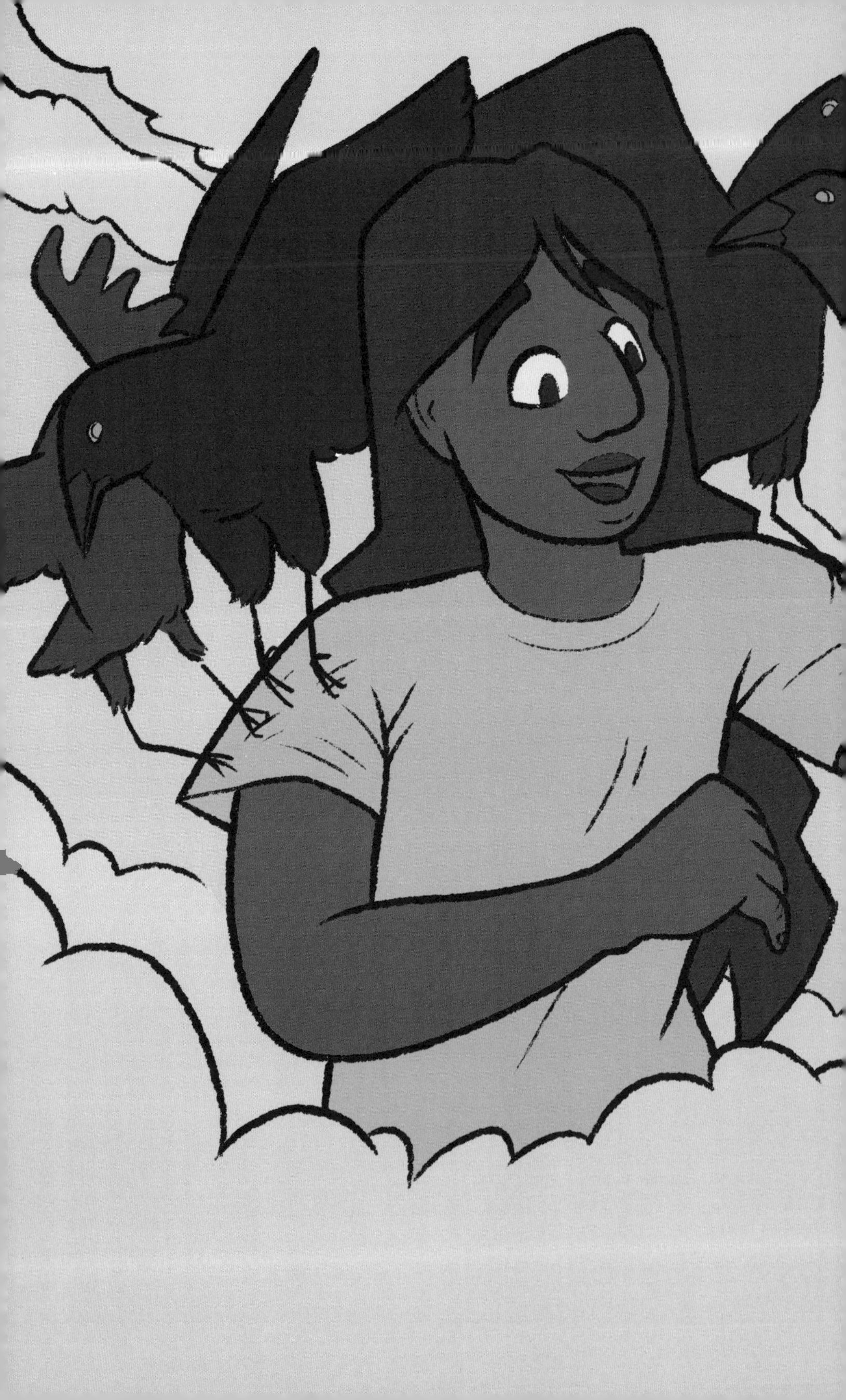

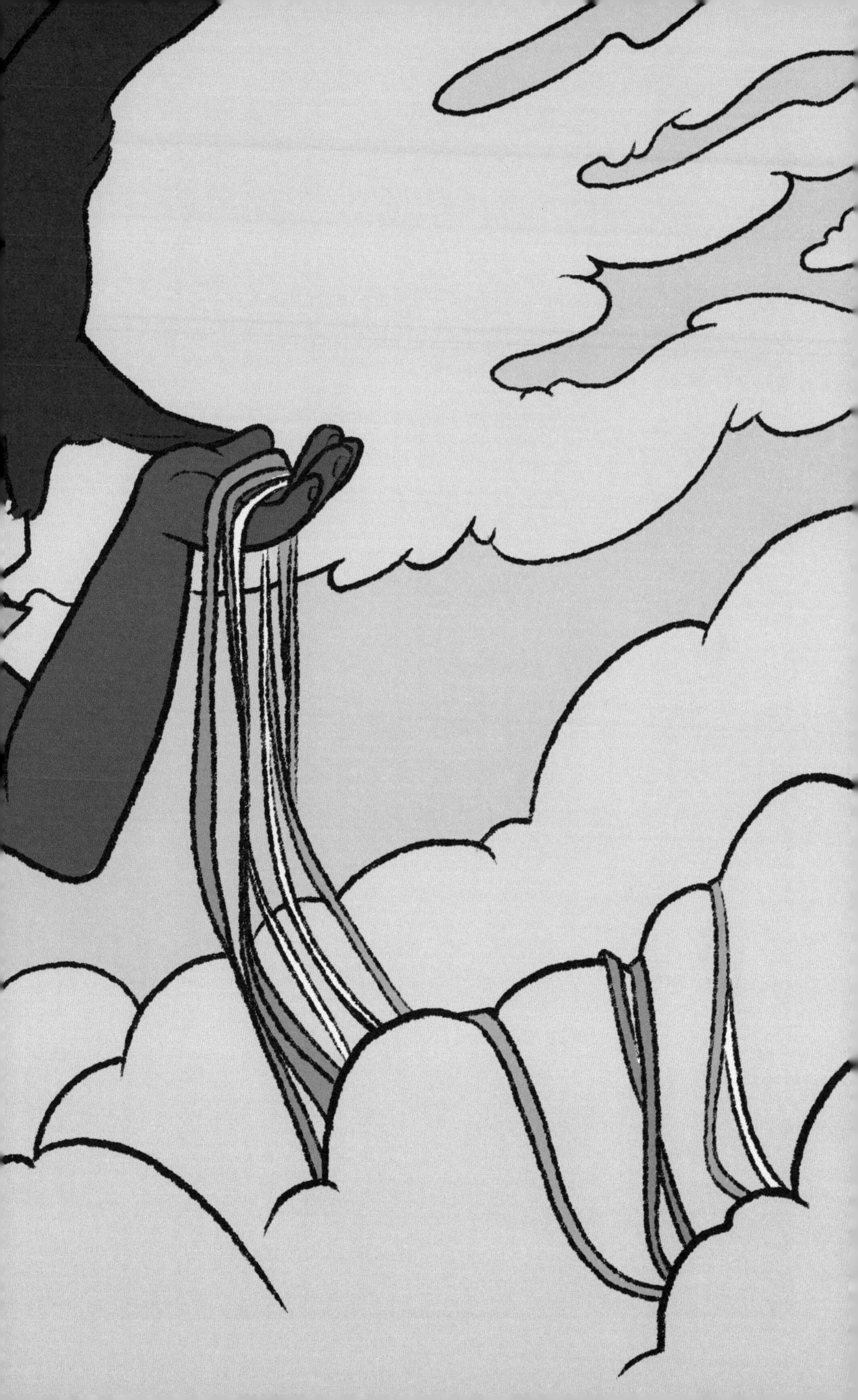

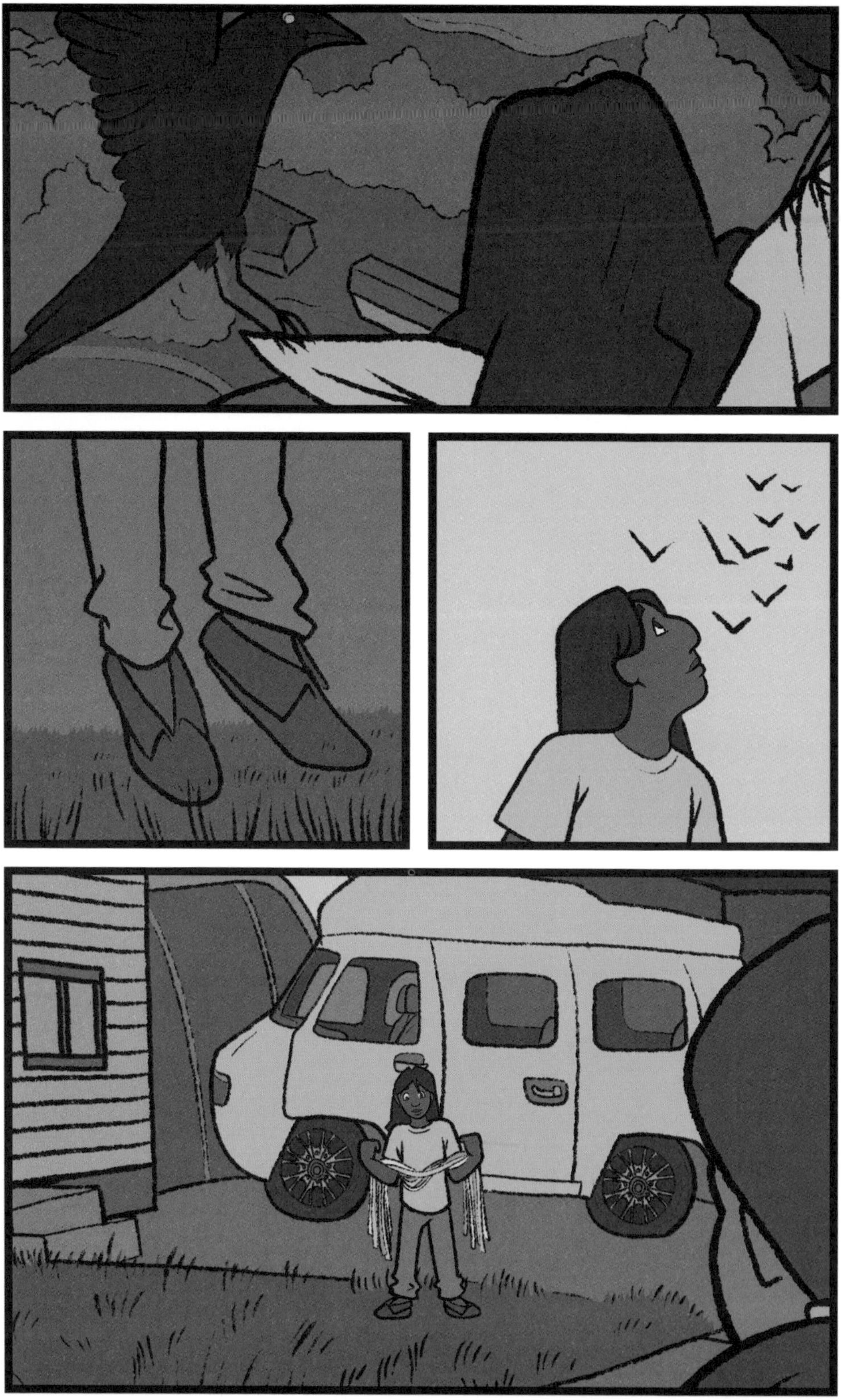

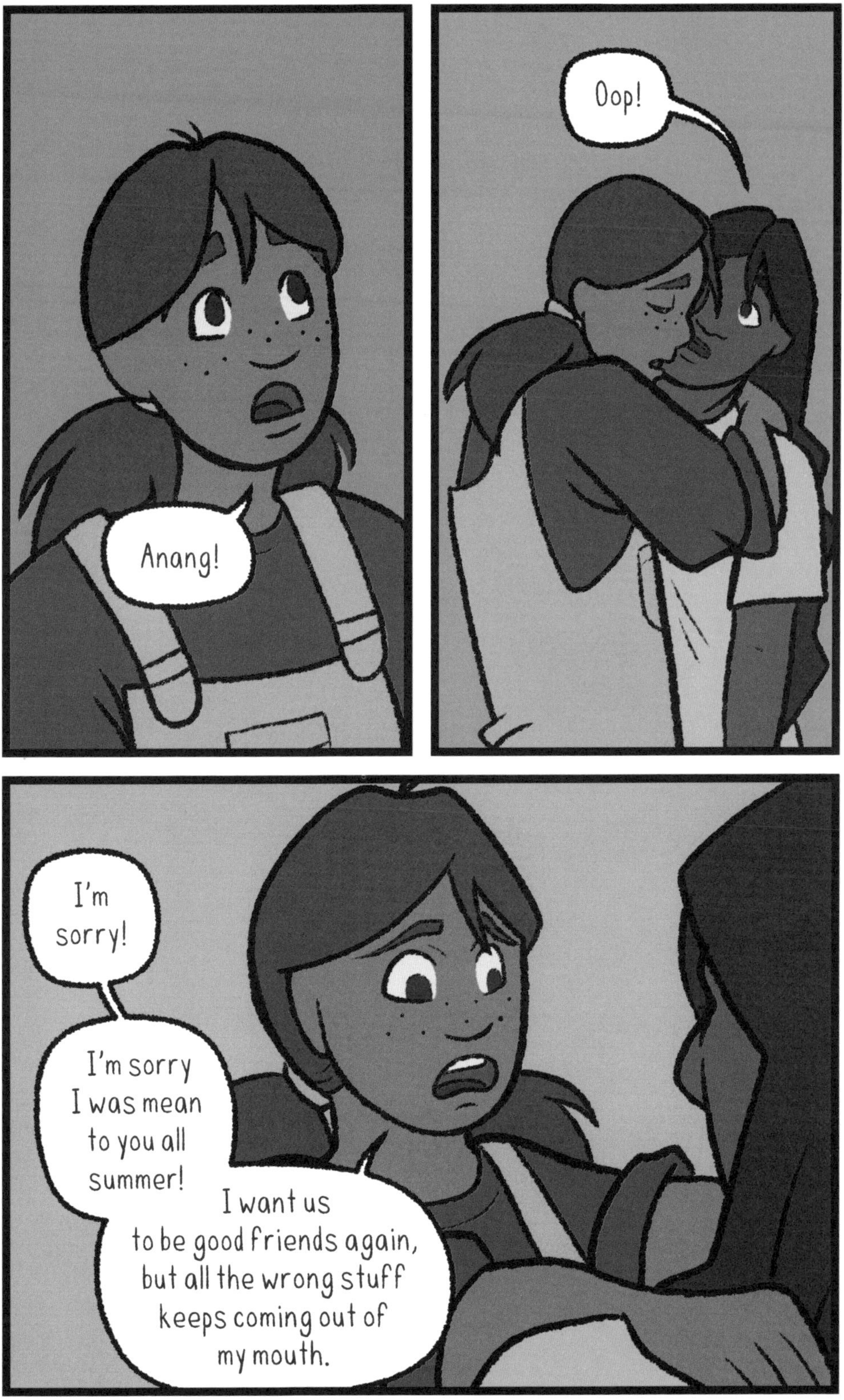
Anang!
Oop!
I'm sorry!
I'm sorry I was mean to you all summer!
I want us to be good friends again, but all the wrong stuff keeps coming out of my mouth.

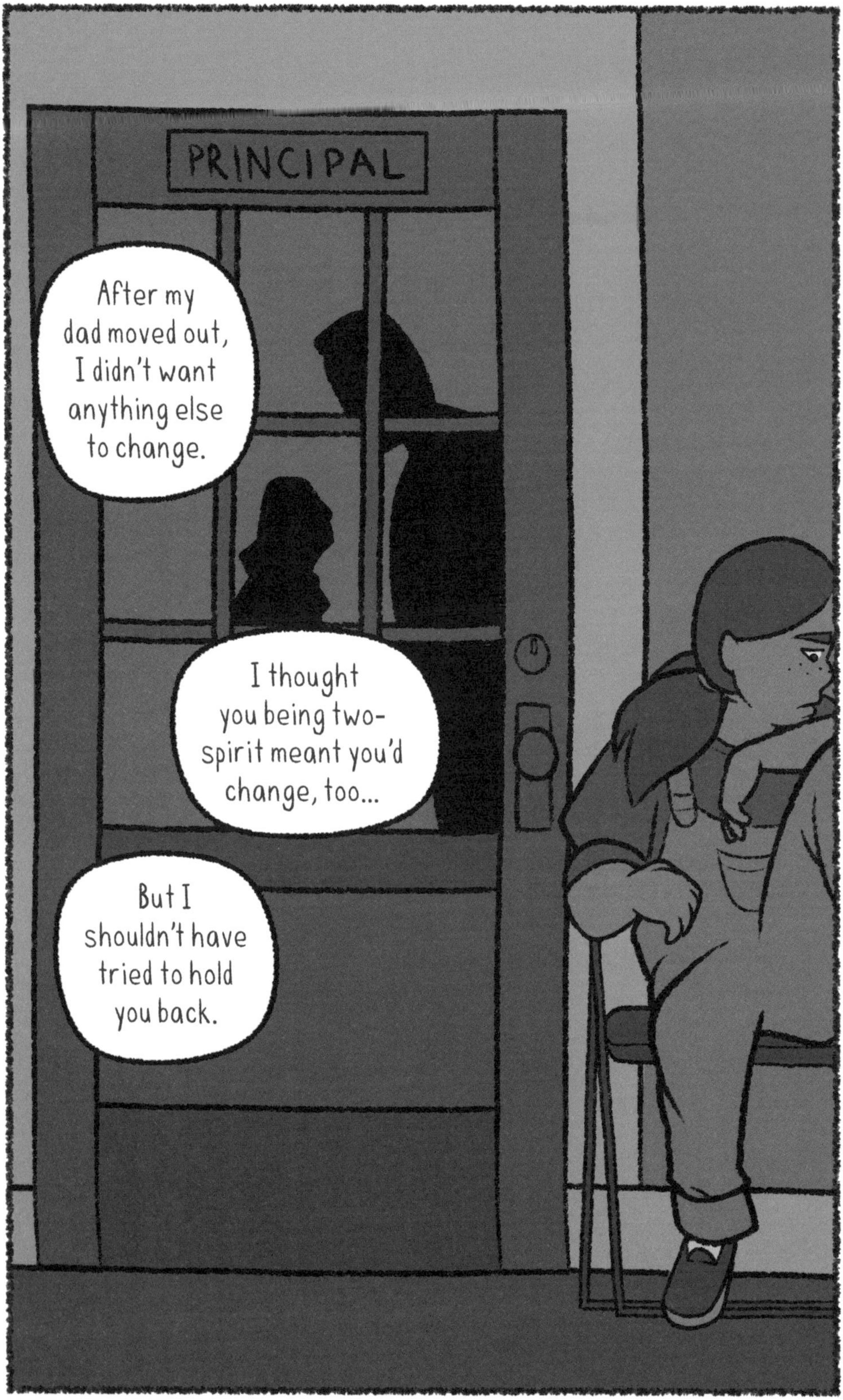
PRINCIPAL
After my dad moved out, I didn't want anything else to change.
I thought you being two-spirit meant you'd change, too...
But I shouldn't have tried to hold you back.

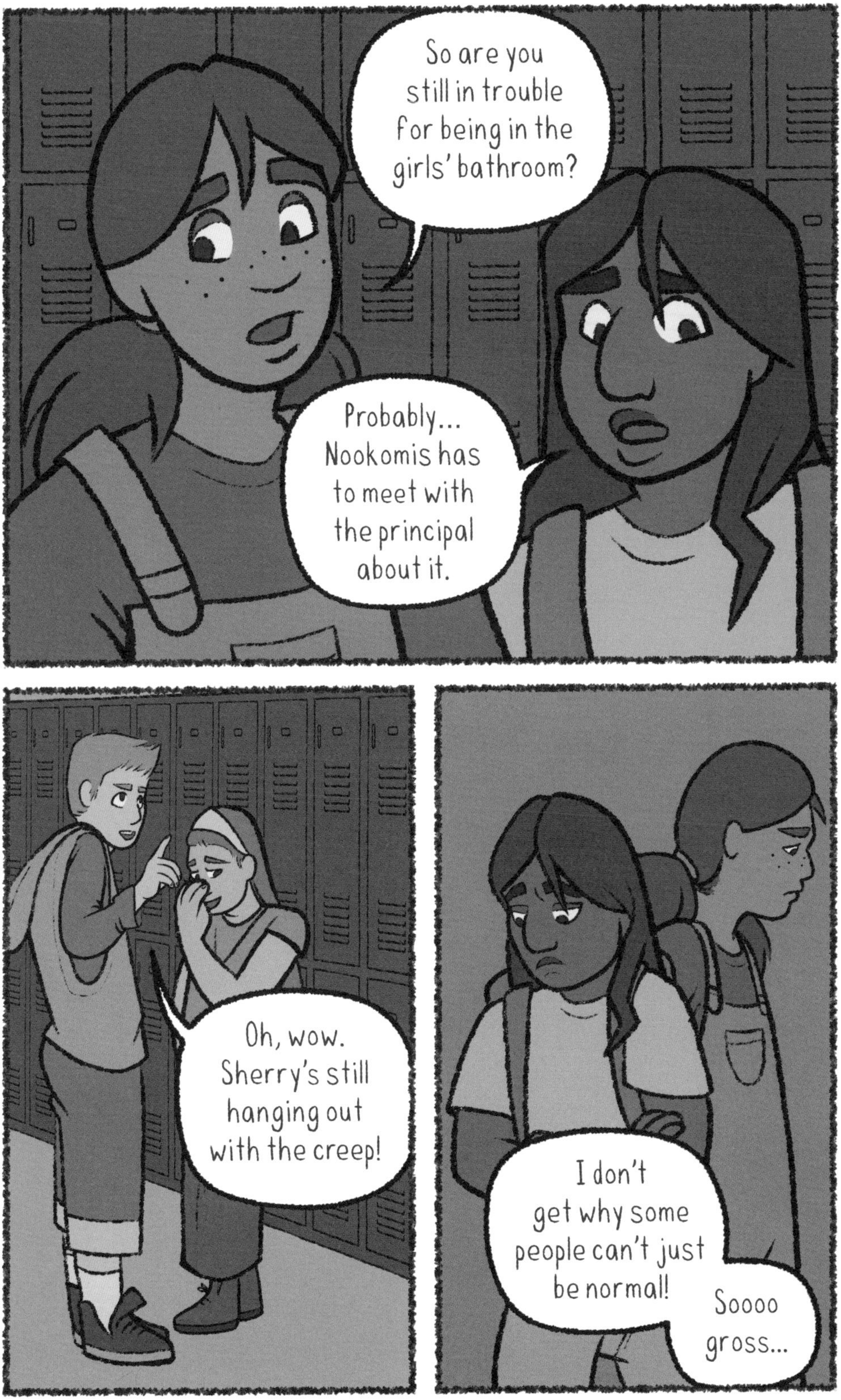
So are you still in trouble for being in the girls' bathroom?
Probably... Nookomis has to meet with the principal about it.
Oh, wow. Sherry's still hanging out with the creep!
I don't get why some people can't just be normal!
Soooo gross...

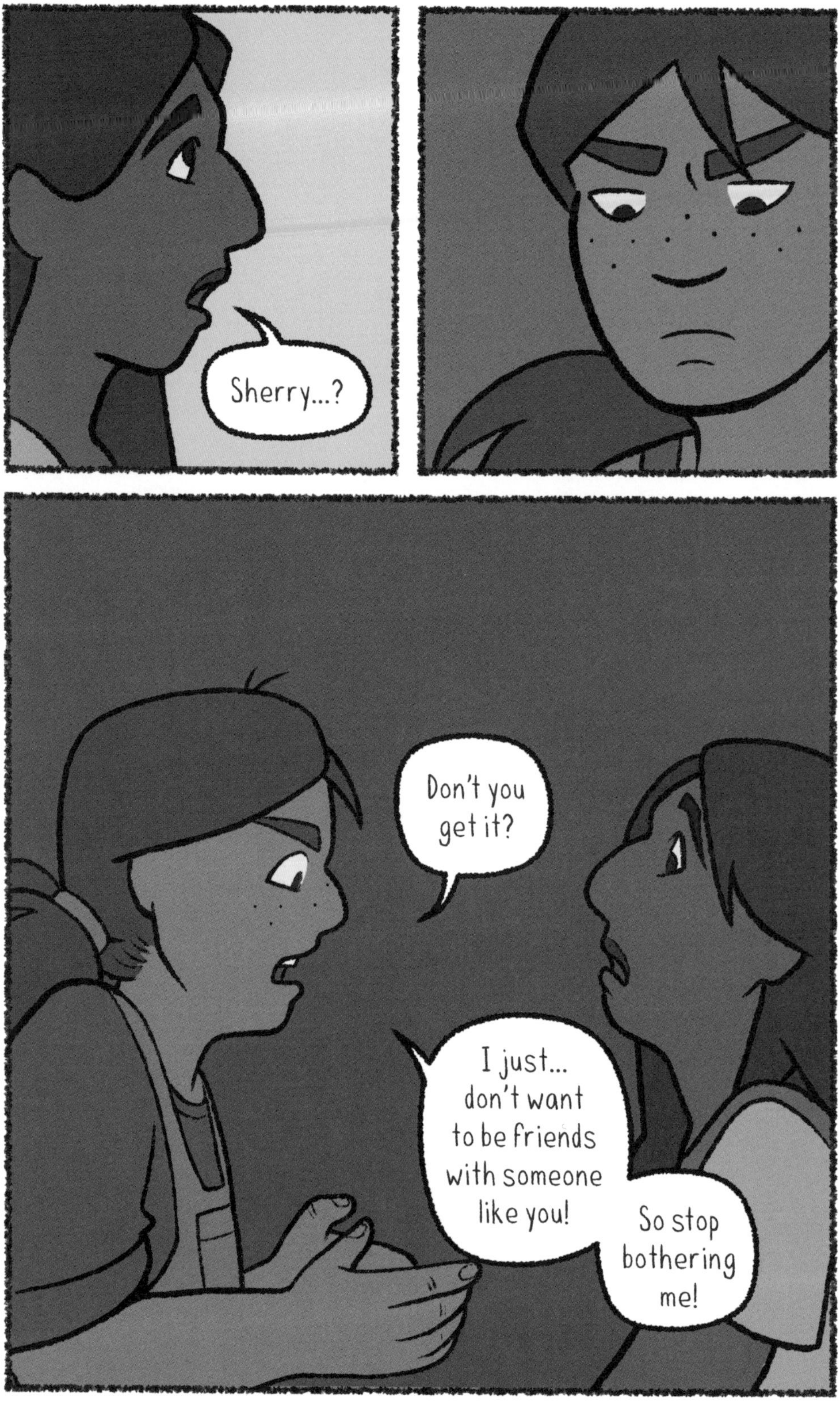
Sherry...?
Don't you get it?
I just... don't want to be friends with someone like you!
So stop bothering me!

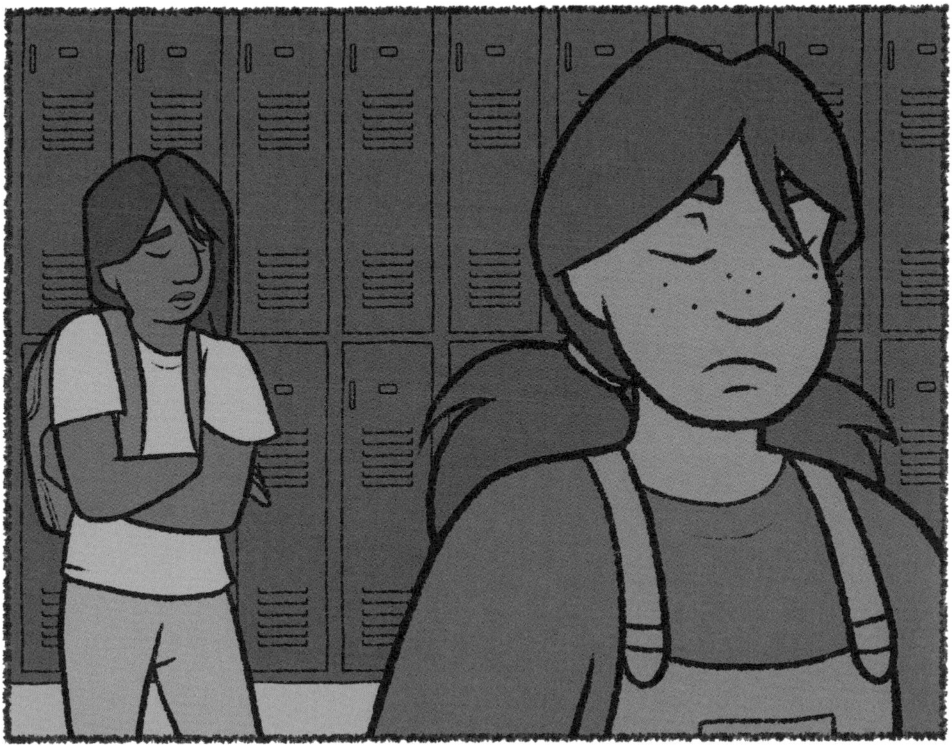

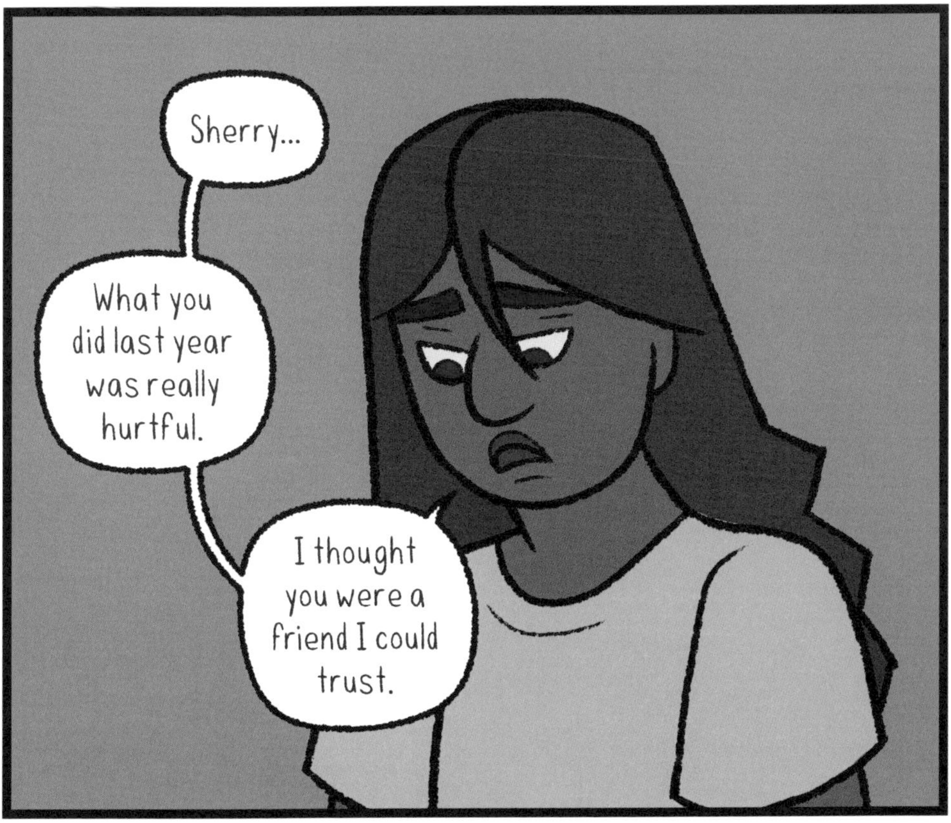
Sherry...
What you did last year was really hurtful.
I thought you were a friend I could trust.

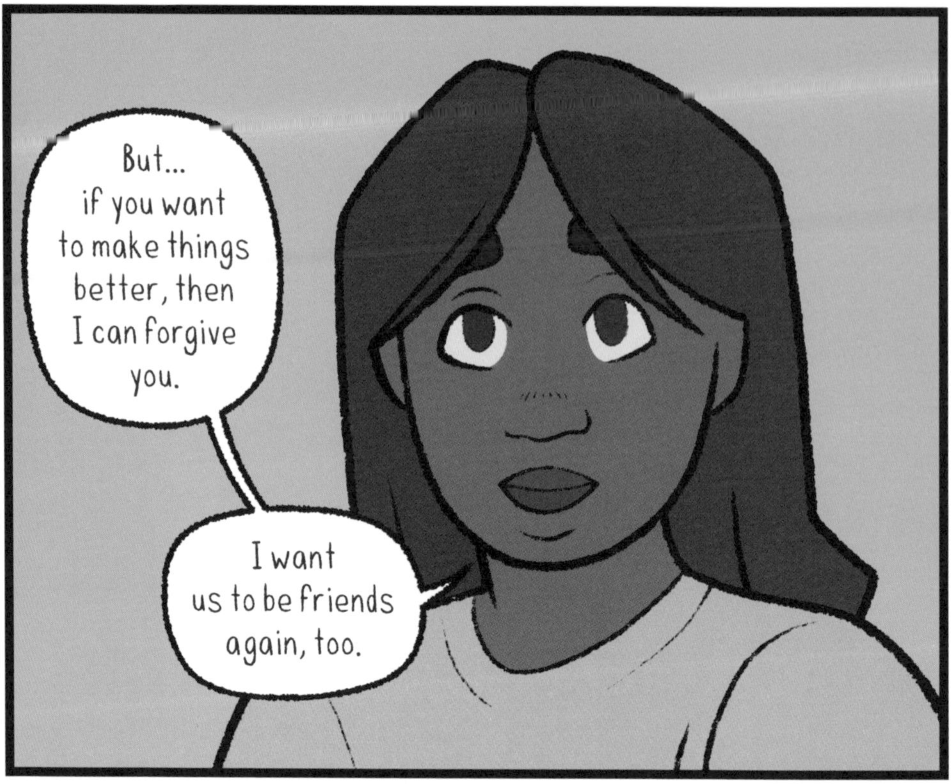
But... if you want to make things better, then I can forgive you.
I want us to be friends again, too.

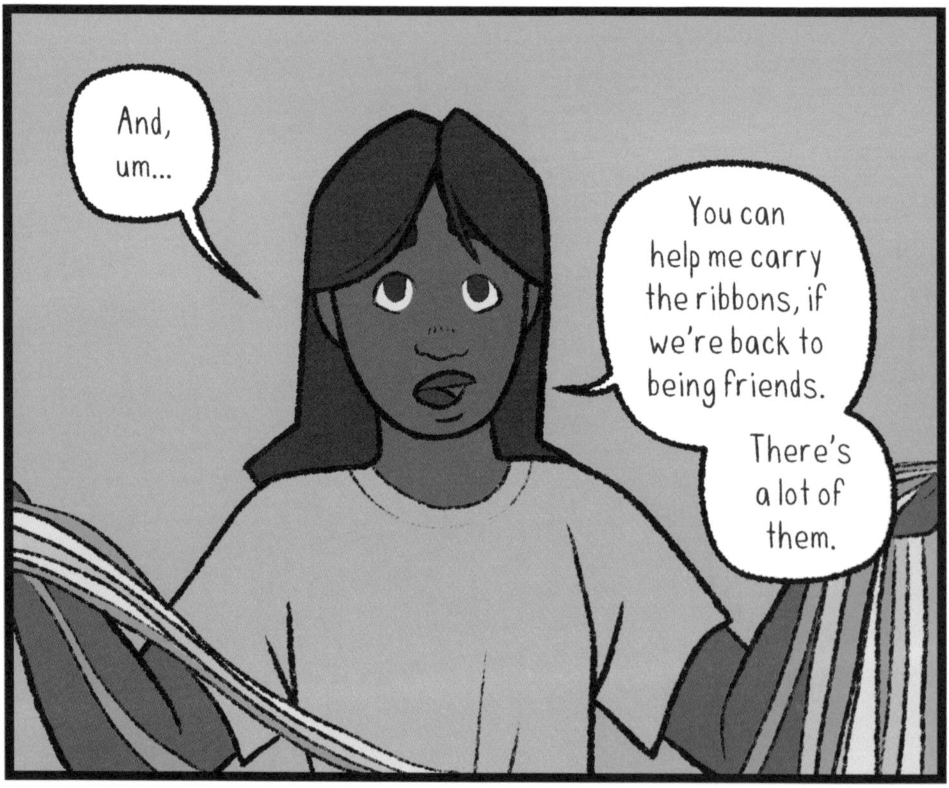
And, um...
You can help me carry the ribbons, if we're back to being friends.
There's a lot of them.

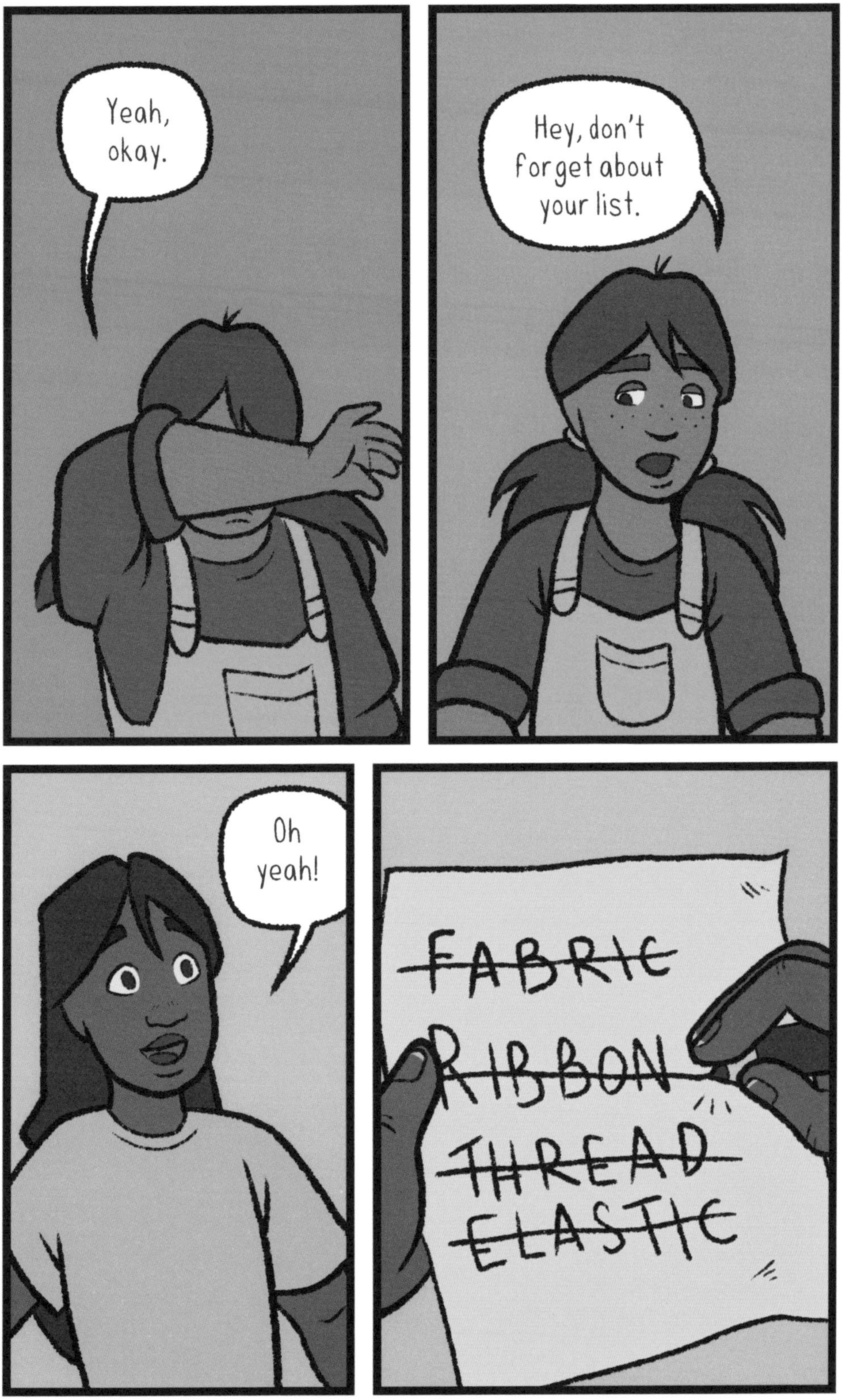
Yeah, okay.
Hey, don't forget about your list.
Oh yeah!
FABRIC
RIBBON
THREAD
ELASTIC

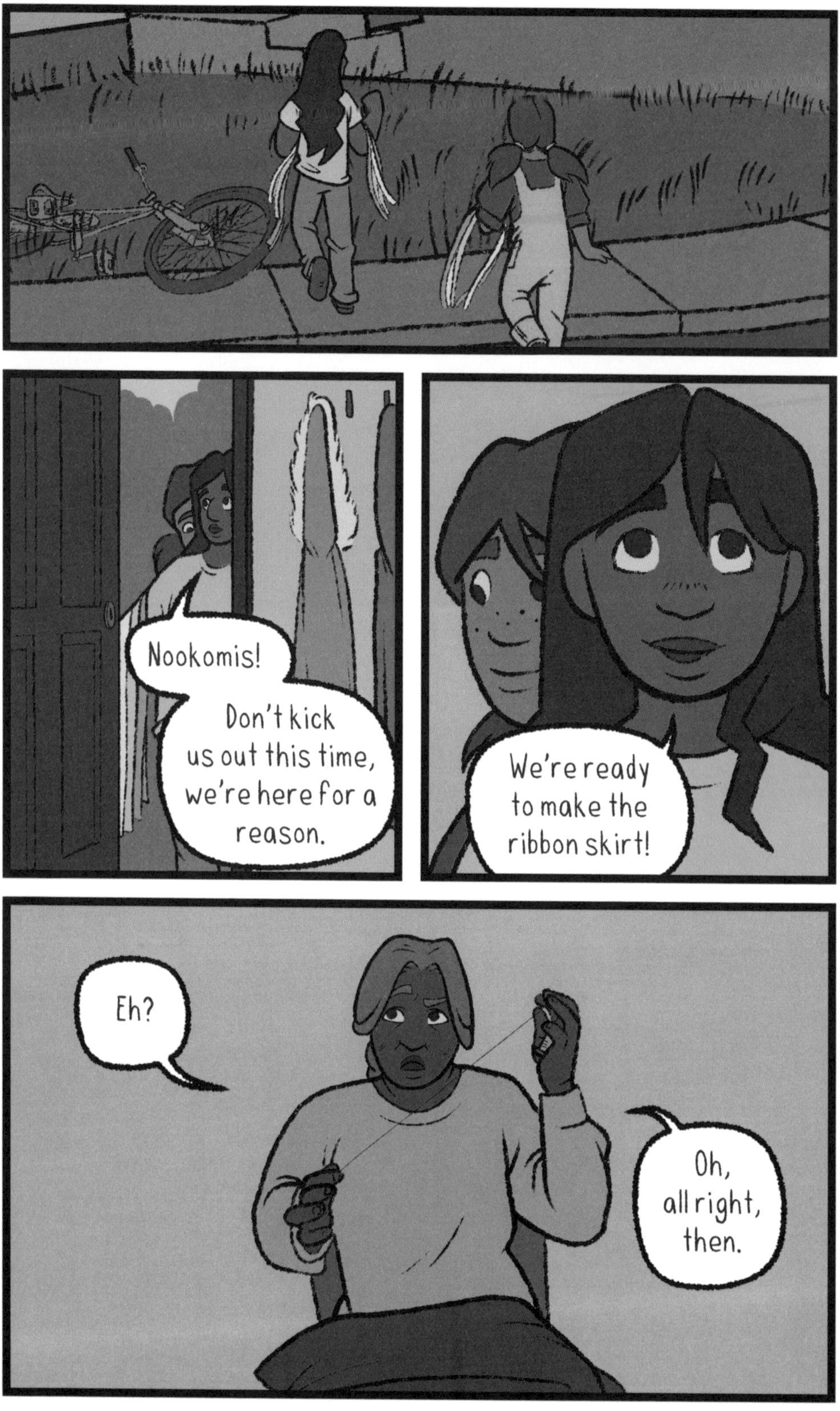
Nookomis!
Don't kick us out this time, we're here for a reason.
We're ready to make the ribbon skirt!
Eh?
Oh, all right, then.

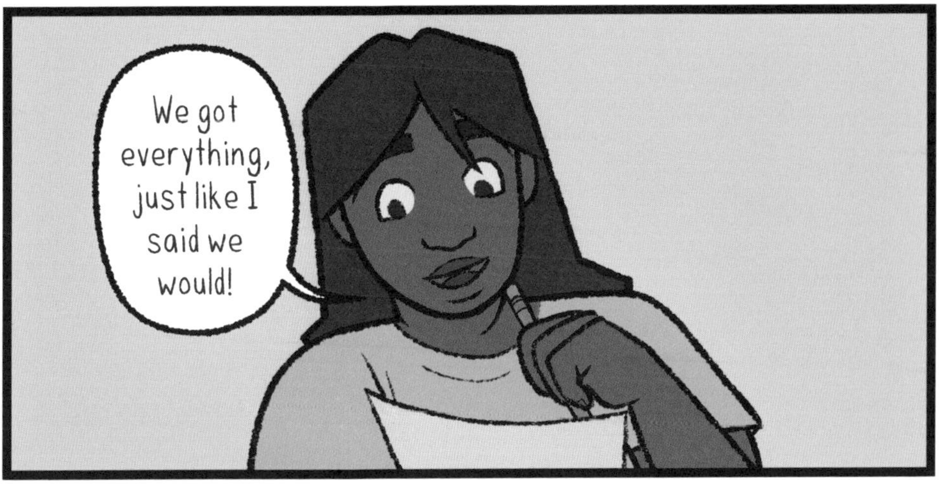
We got everything, just like I said we would!

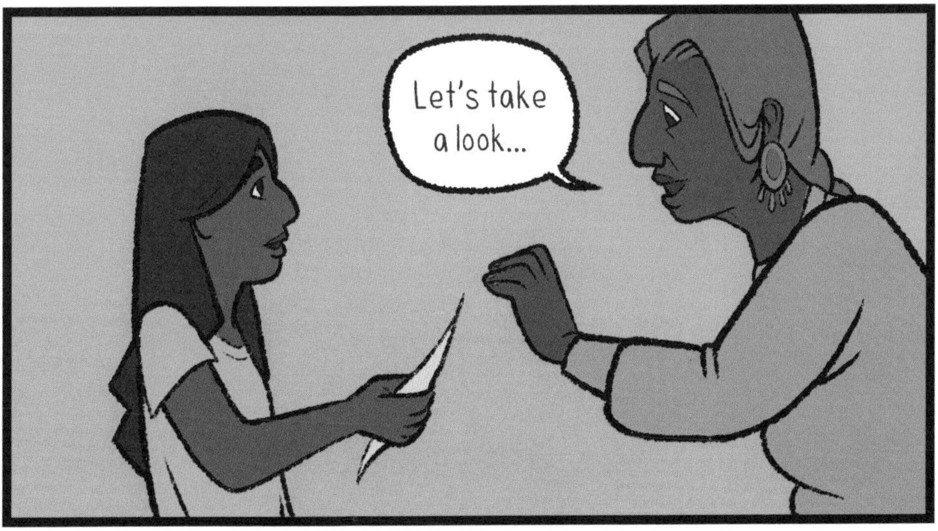
Let's take a look...

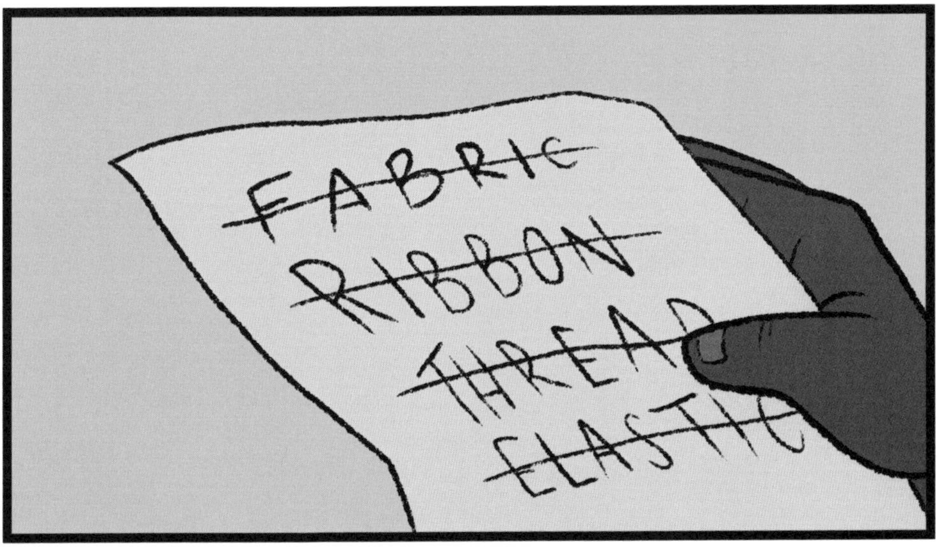
FABRIC
RIBBON
THREAD
ELASTIC

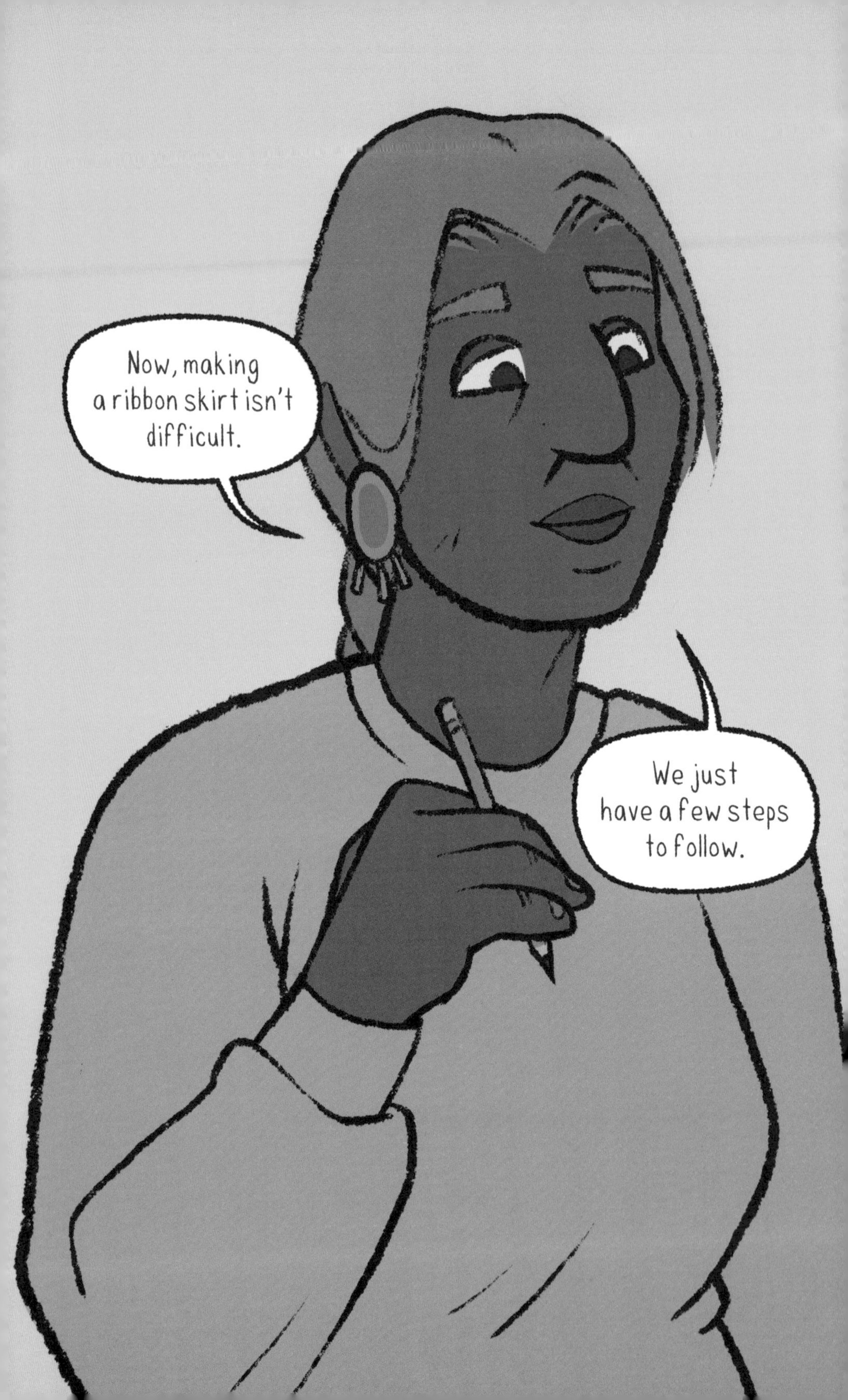
Now, making a ribbon skirt isn't difficult.
We just have a few steps to follow.

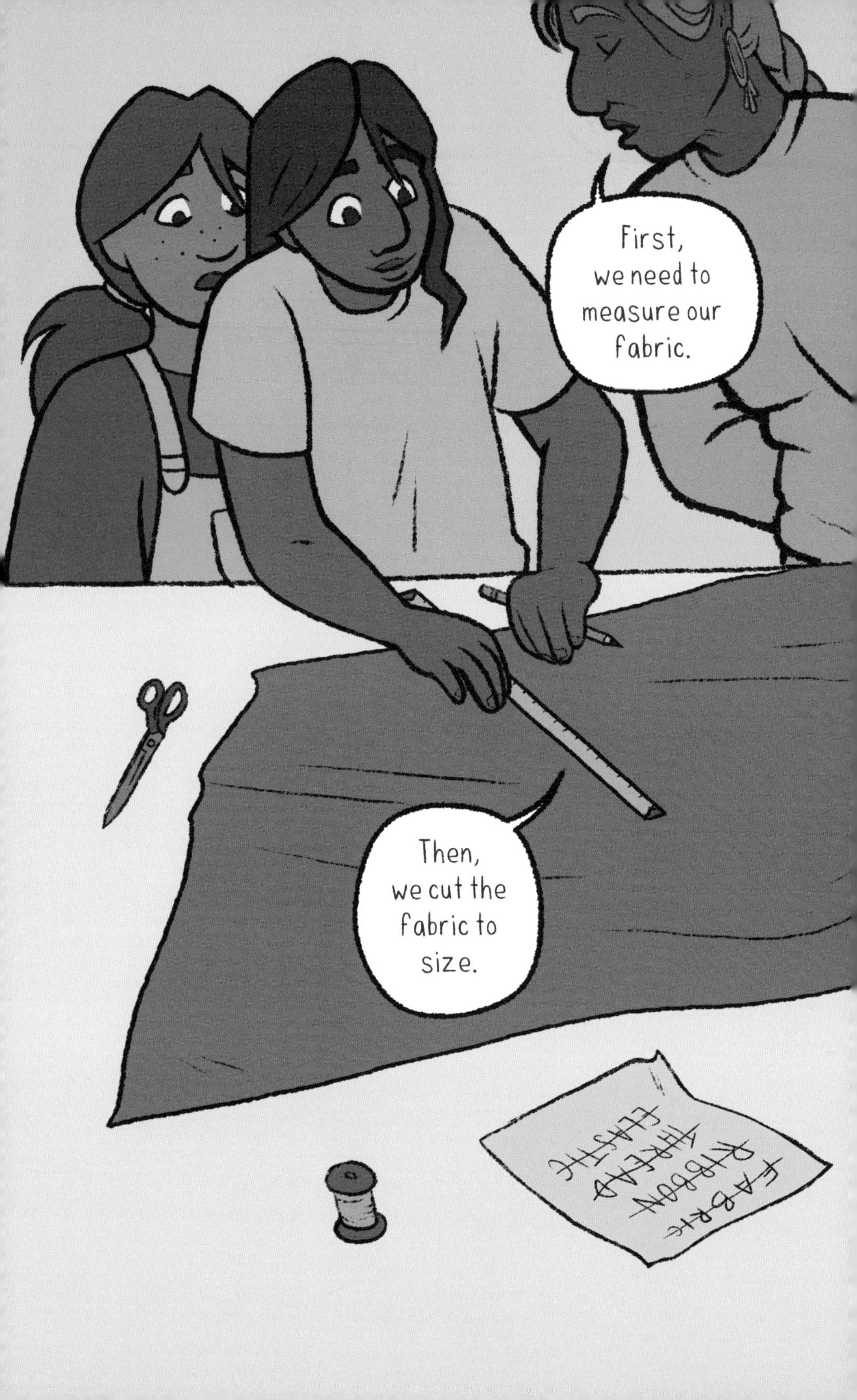
First, we need to measure our fabric.
Then, we cut the fabric to size.
FABRIC
RIBBON
THREAD
ELASTIC

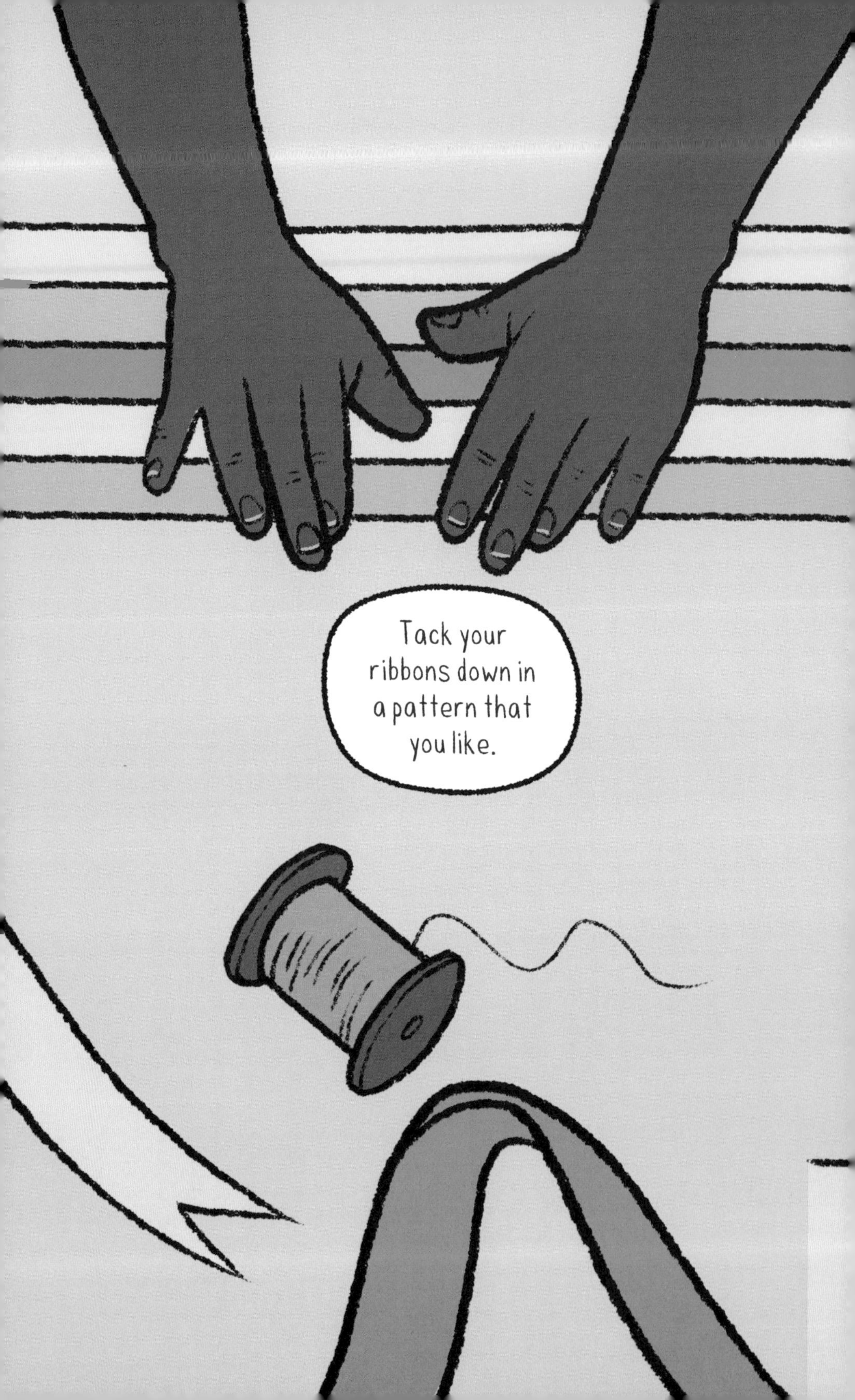
Tack your ribbons down in a pattern that you like.

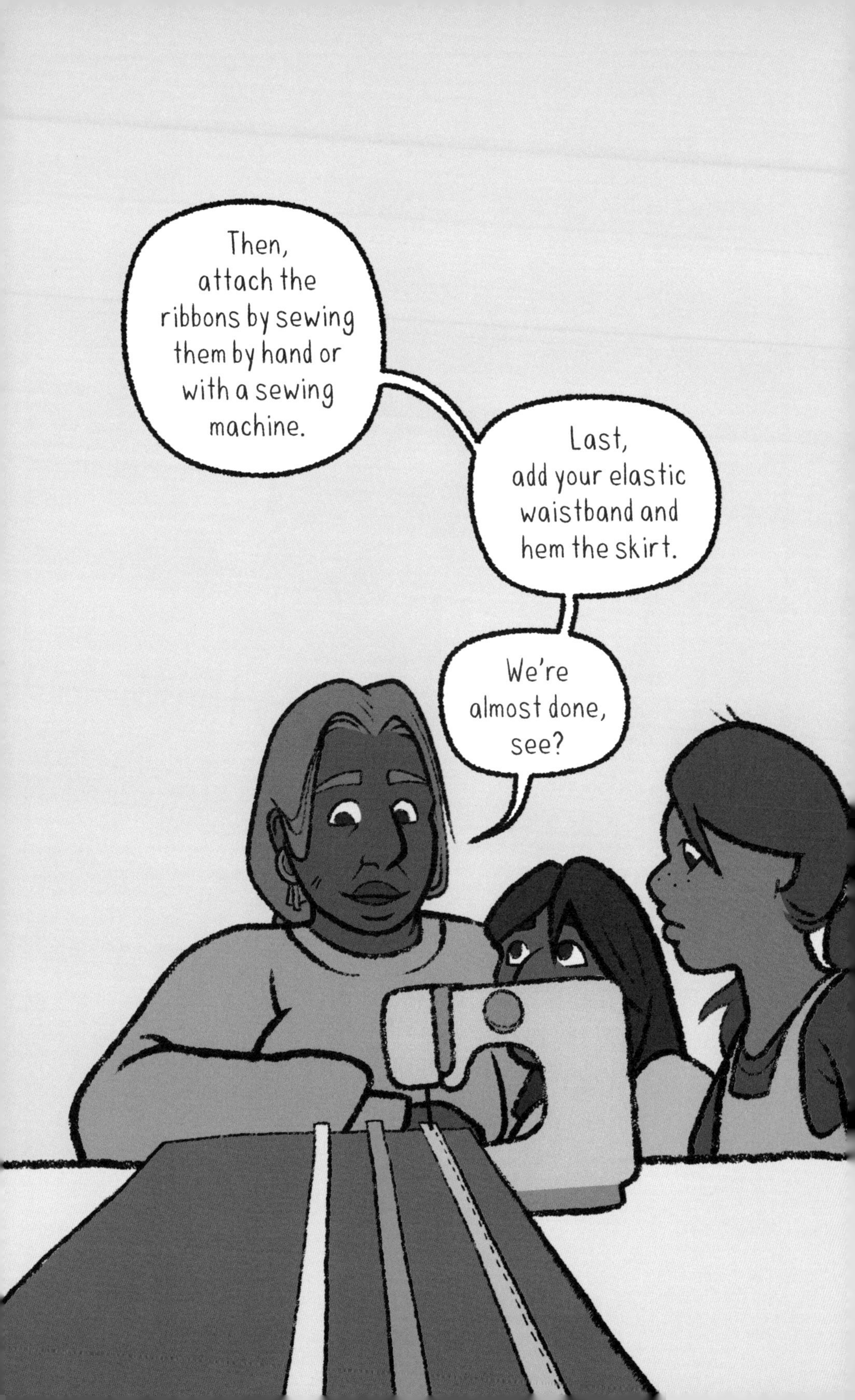
Then, attach the ribbons by sewing them by hand or with a sewing machine.
Last, add your elastic waistband and hem the skirt.
We're almost done, see?

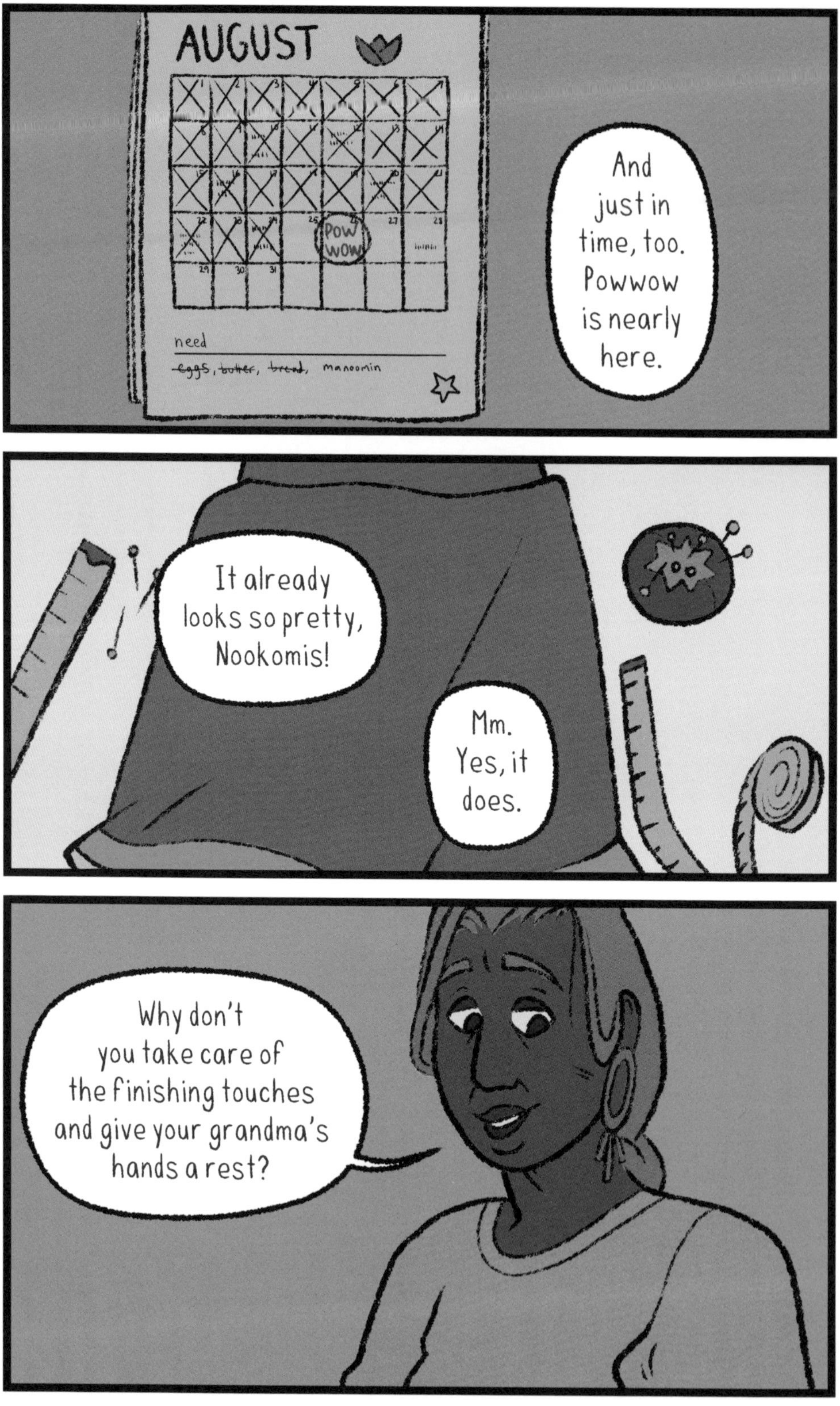
AUGUST
POW WOW
need
eggs, butter, bread, manoomin
And just in time, too. Powwow is nearly here.
It already looks so pretty, Nookomis!
Mm. Yes, it does.
Why don't you take care of the finishing touches and give your grandma's hands a rest?

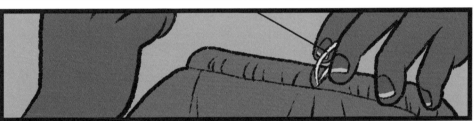

Awesome!

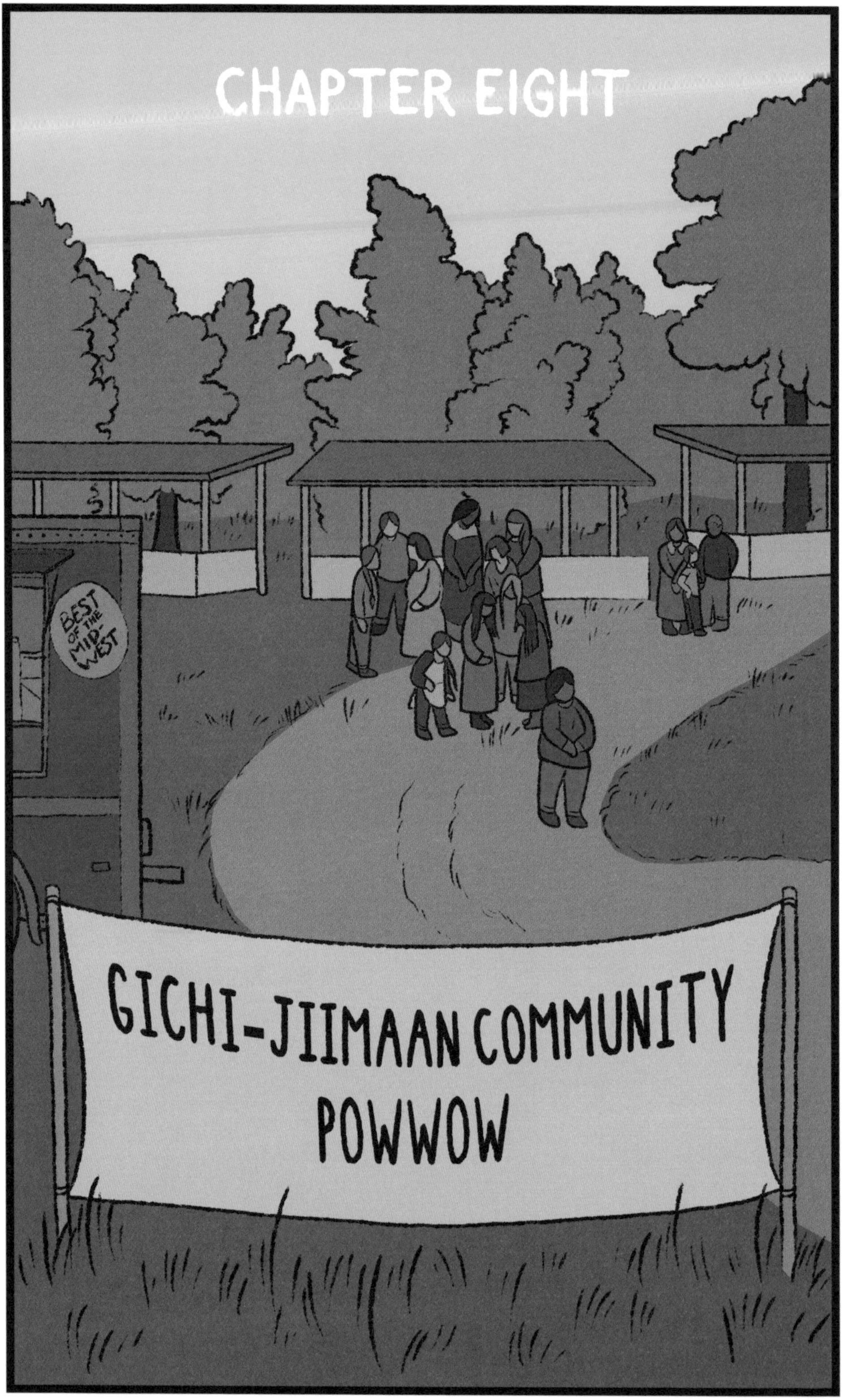
CHAPTER EIGHT
BEST OF THE MID-WEST
GICHI-JIIMAAN COMMUNITY POWWOW

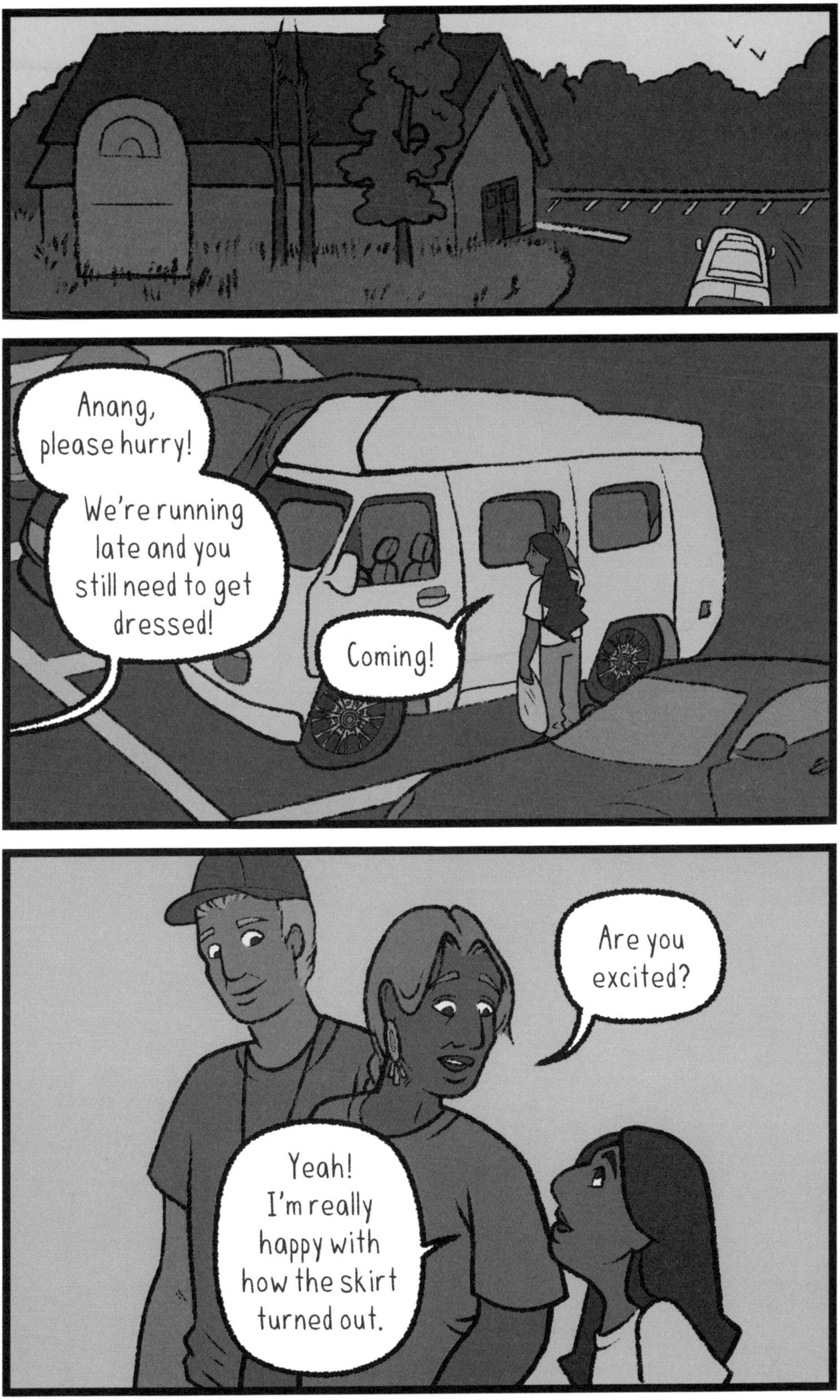
Anang,
please hurry!
We're running late and you still need to get dressed!
Coming!
Are you excited?
Yeah! I'm really happy with how the skirt turned out.

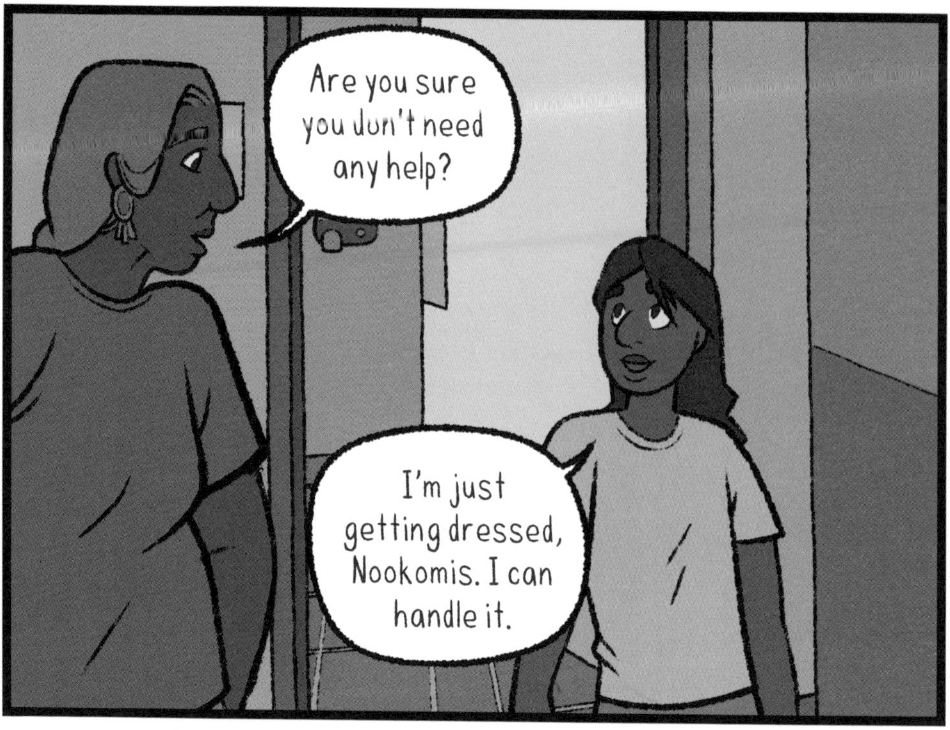
Are you sure you don't need any help?
I'm just getting dressed, Nookomis. I can handle it.

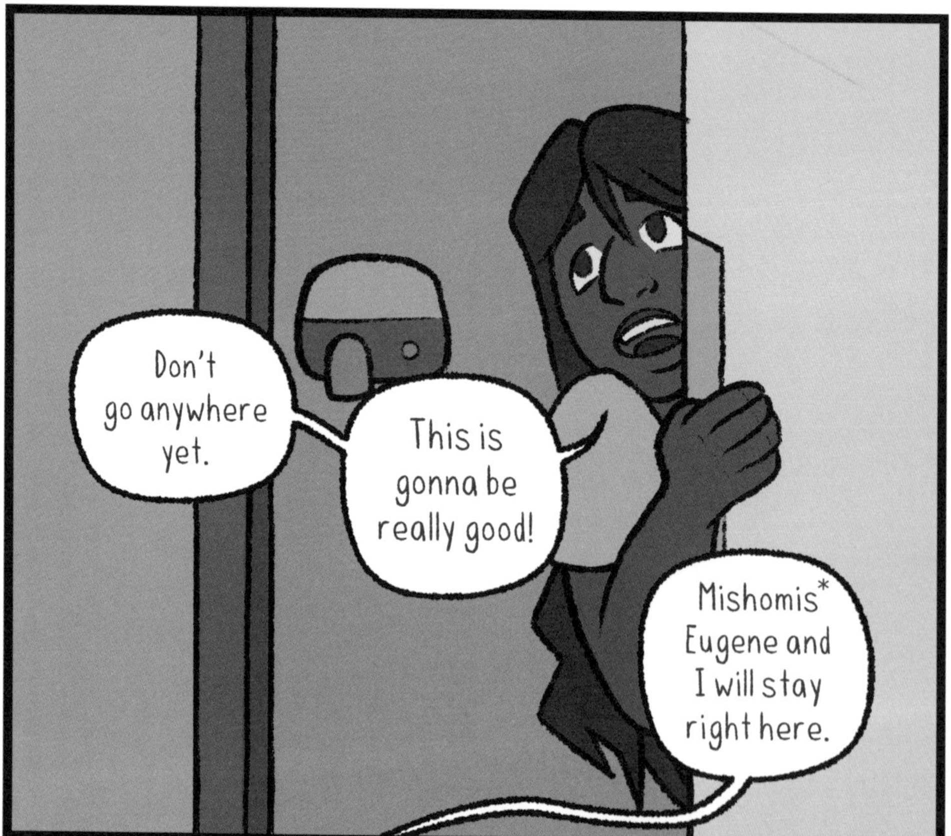
Don't go anywhere yet.
This is gonna be really good!
Mishomis* Eugene and I will stay right here.

* Grandpa

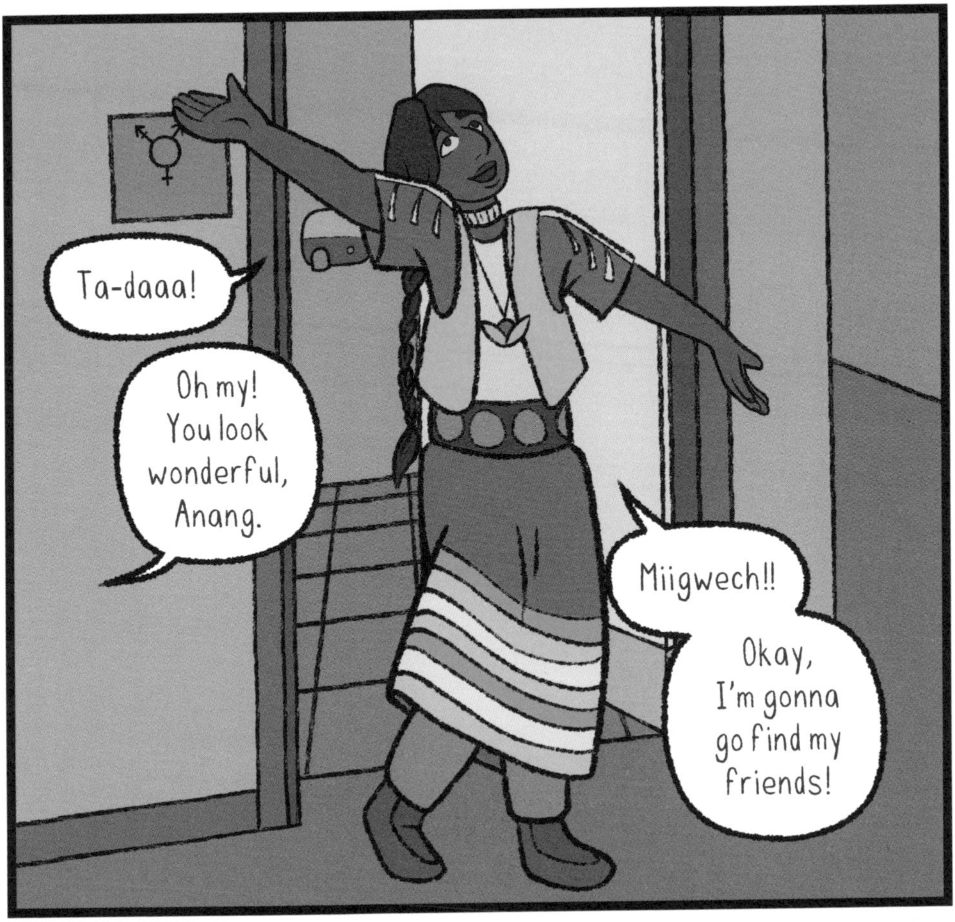
Ta-daaa!
Oh my! You look wonderful, Anang.
Miigwech!!
Okay, I'm gonna go find my friends!

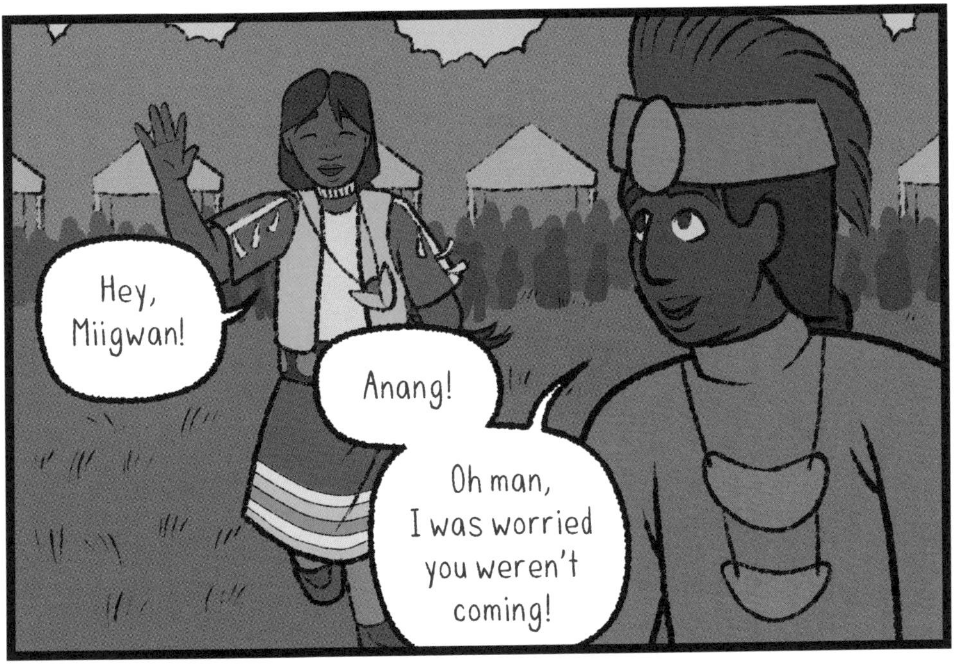
Hey, Miigwan!
Anang!
Oh man, I was worried you weren't coming!

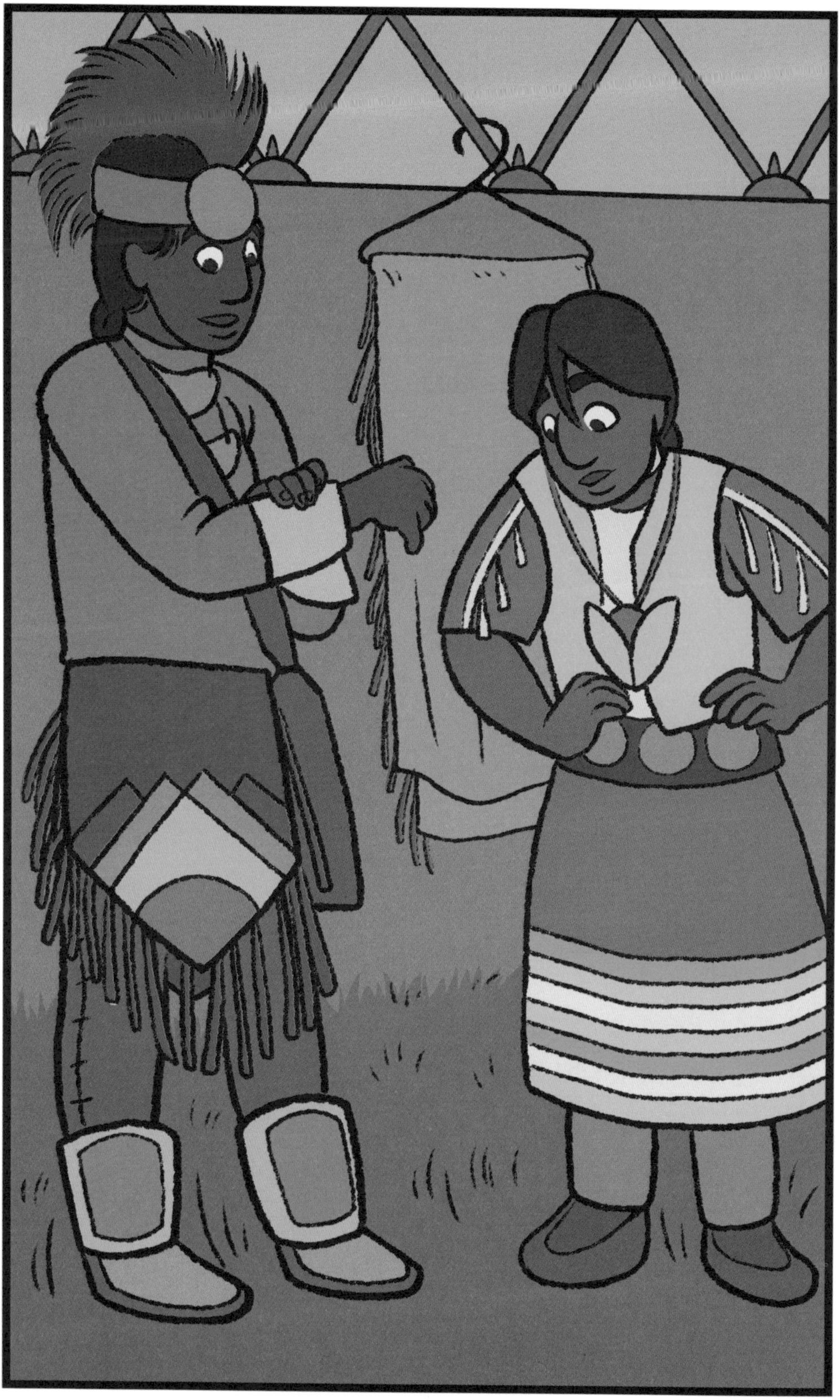

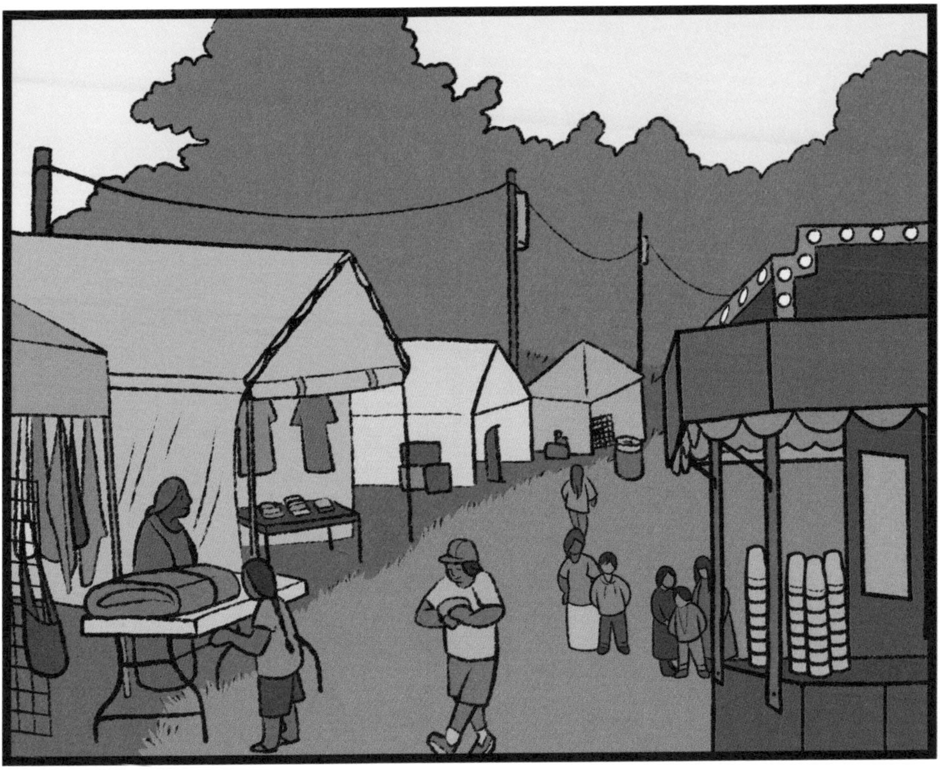

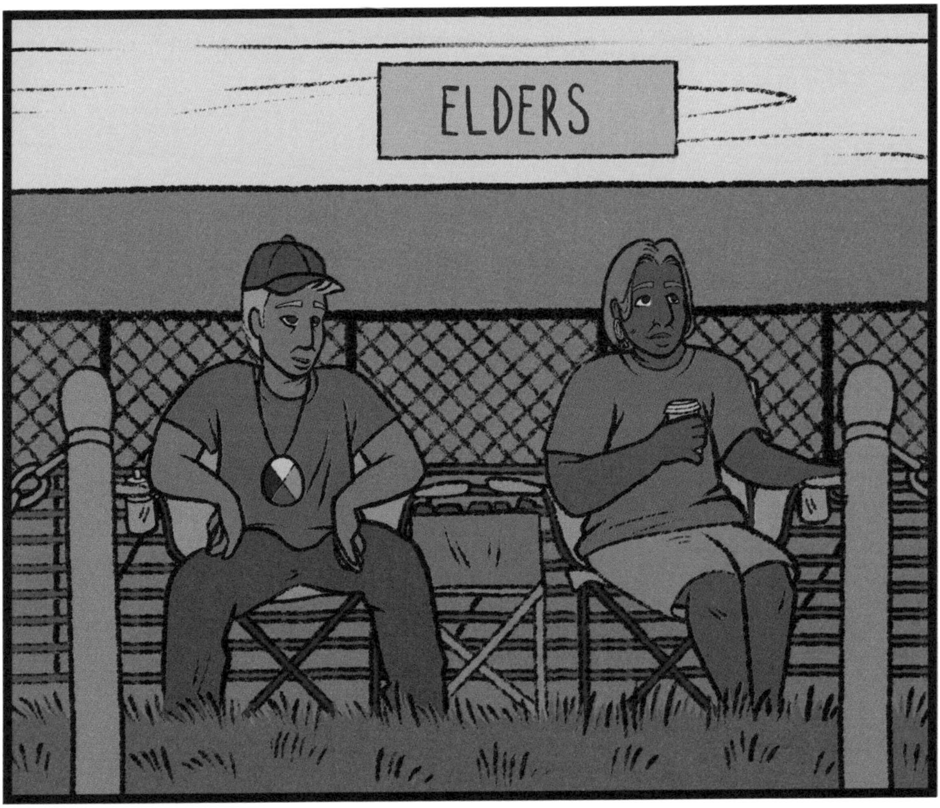
ELDERS

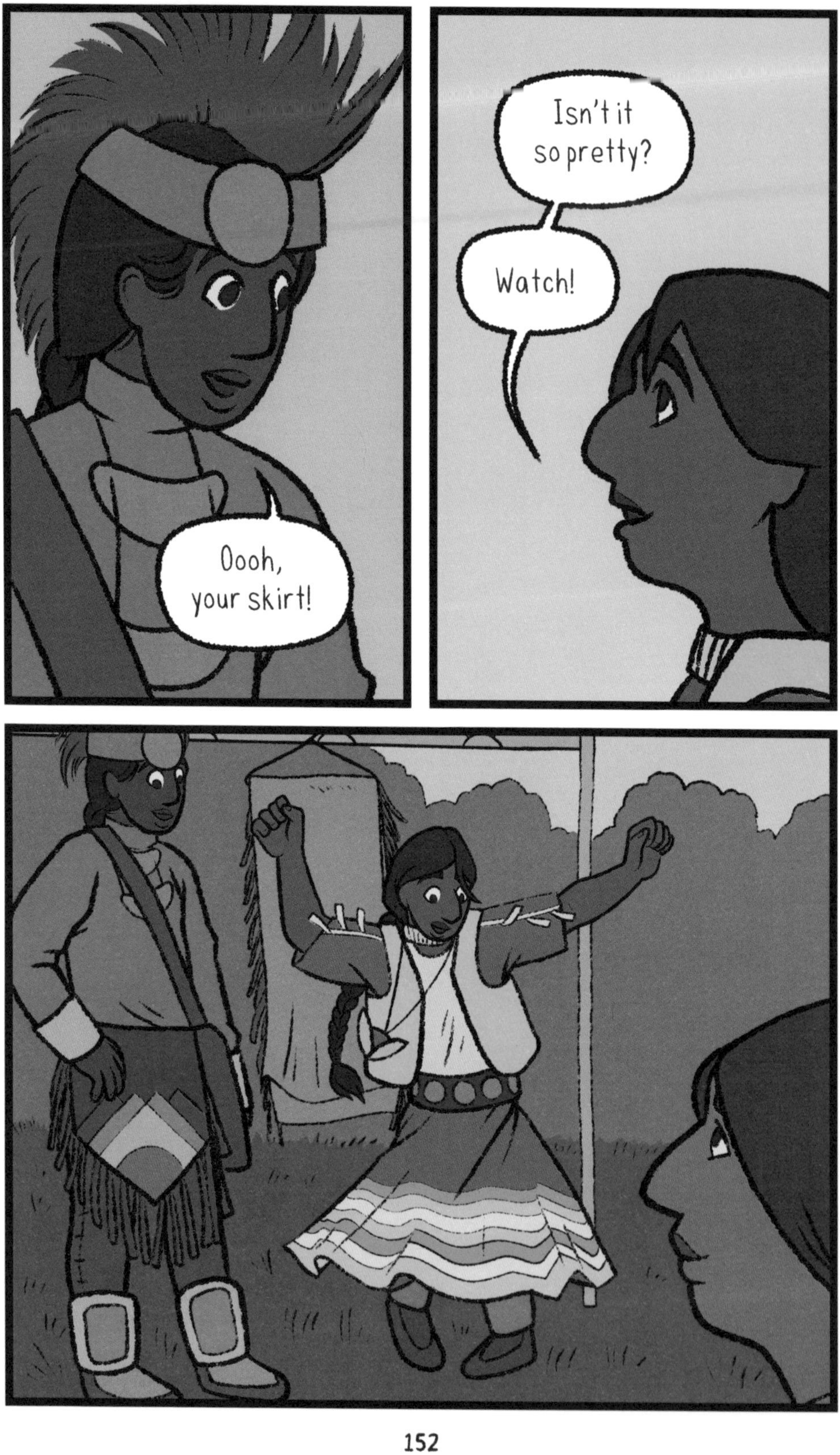
Oooh, your skirt!
Isn't it so pretty?
Watch!

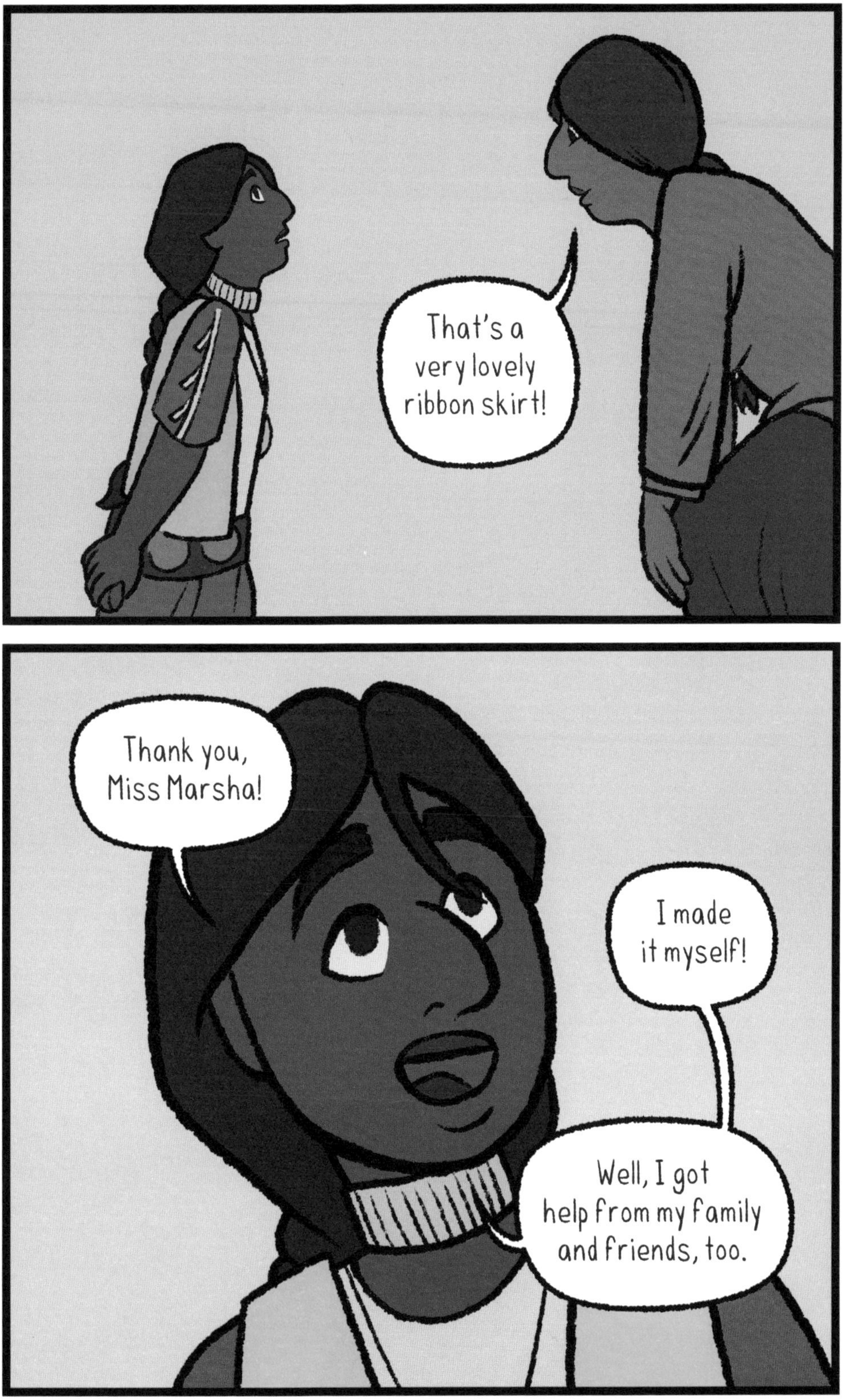
That's a very lovely ribbon skirt!
Thank you, Miss Marsha!
I made it myself!
Well, I got help from my family and friends, too.

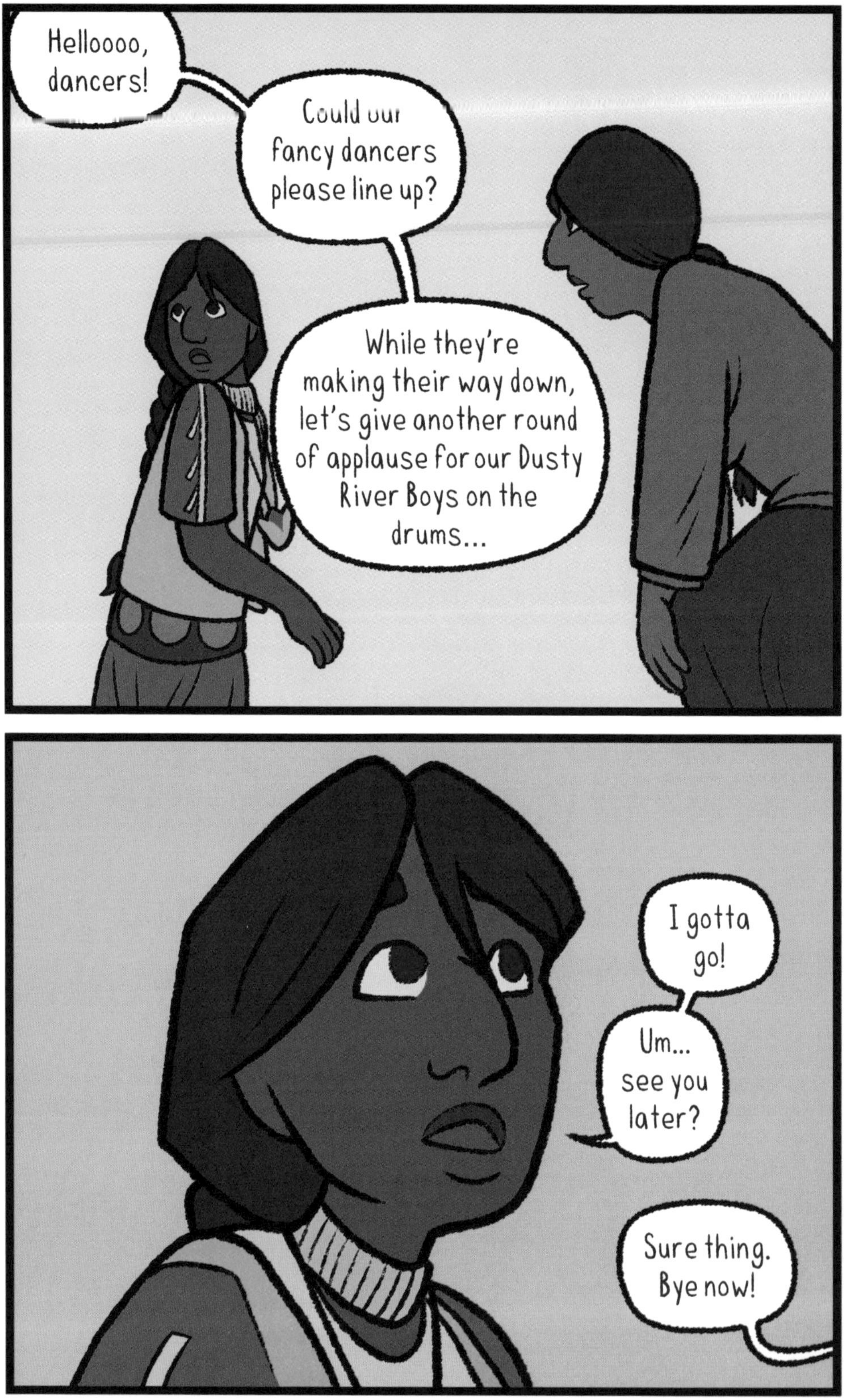
Helloooo, dancers!
Could our fancy dancers please line up?
While they're making their way down, let's give another round of applause for our Dusty River Boys on the drums...
I gotta go!
Um... see you later?
Sure thing. Bye now!

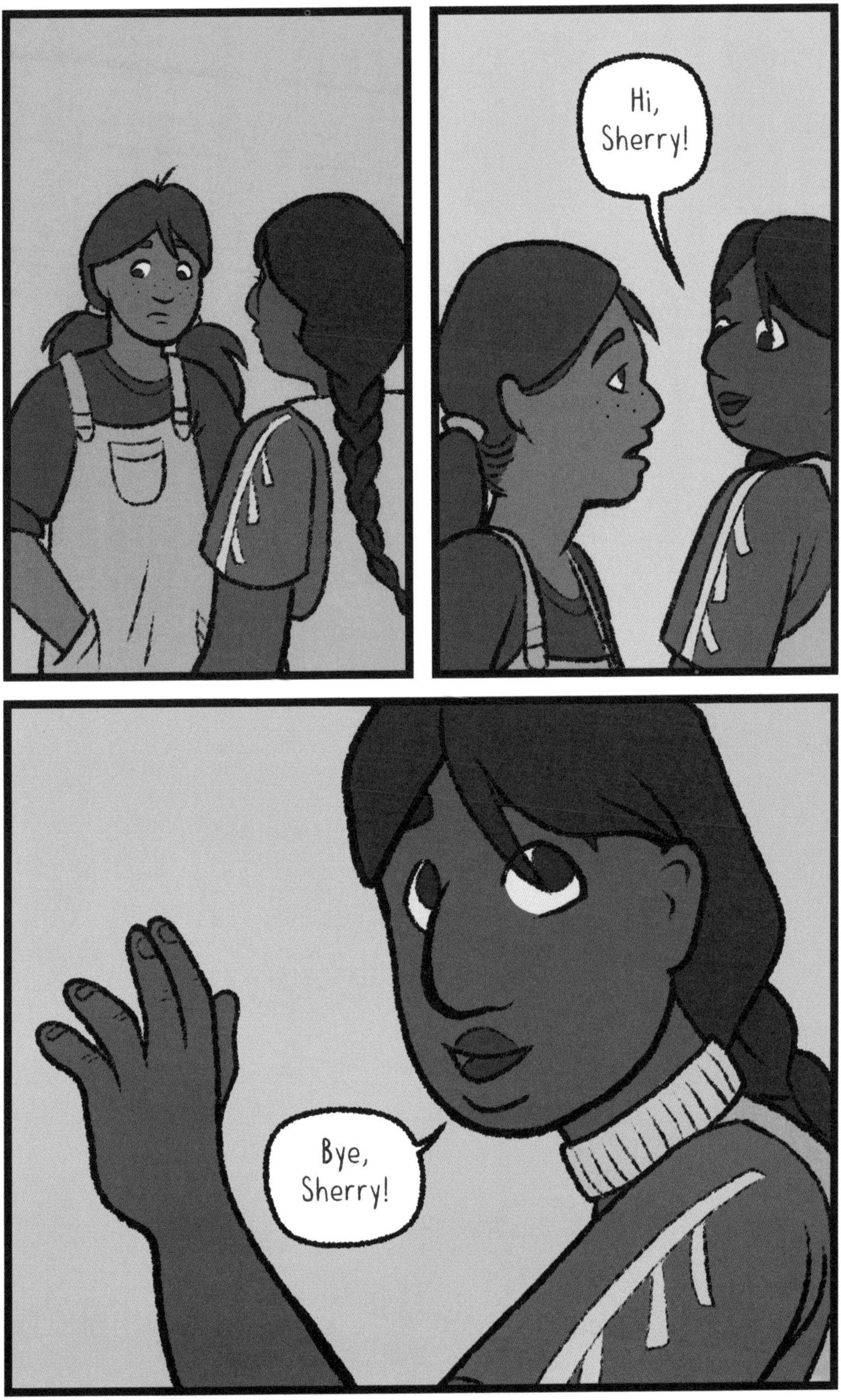
Hi, Sherry!
Bye, Sherry!

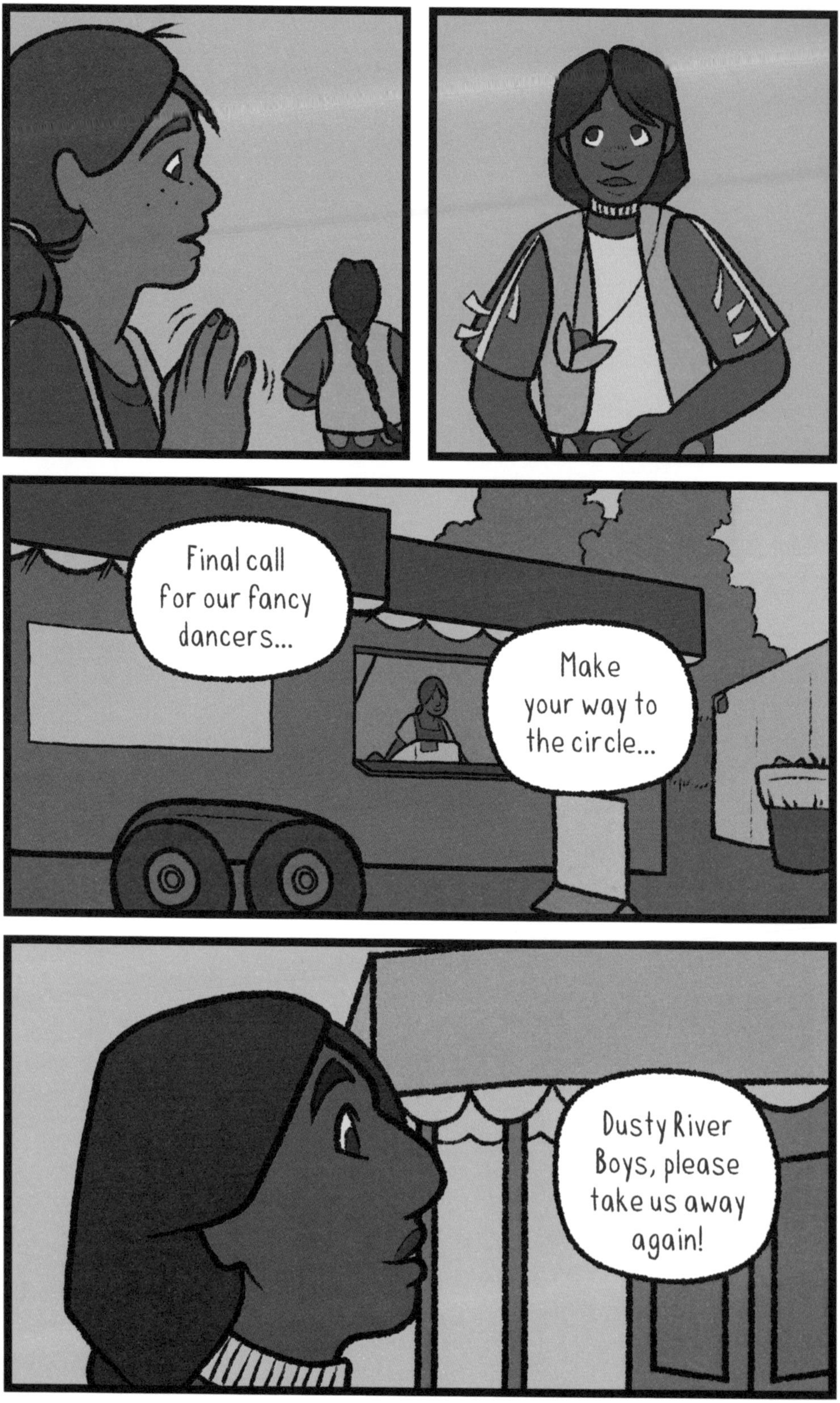
Final call for our fancy dancers...
Make your way to the circle...
Dusty River Boys, please take us away again!

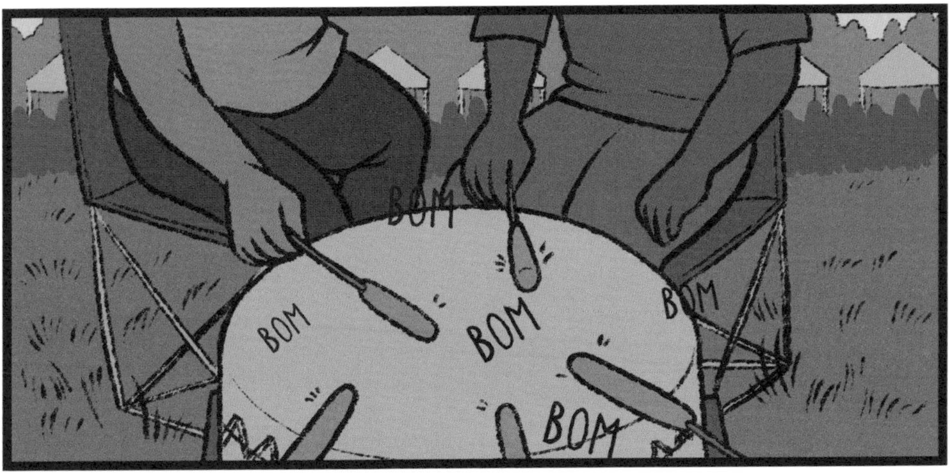
BOM
BOM
BOM
BOM
BOM

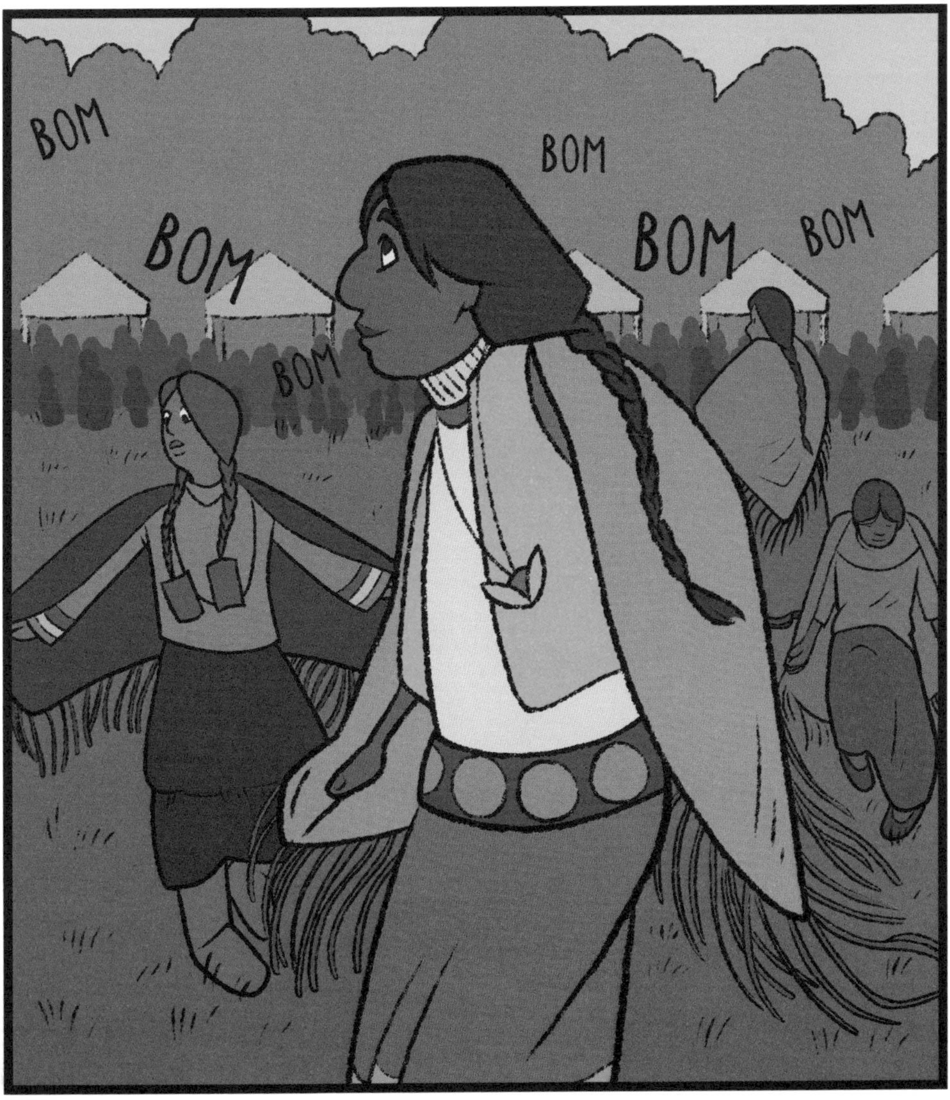
BOM
BOM
BOM
BOM
BOM
BOM

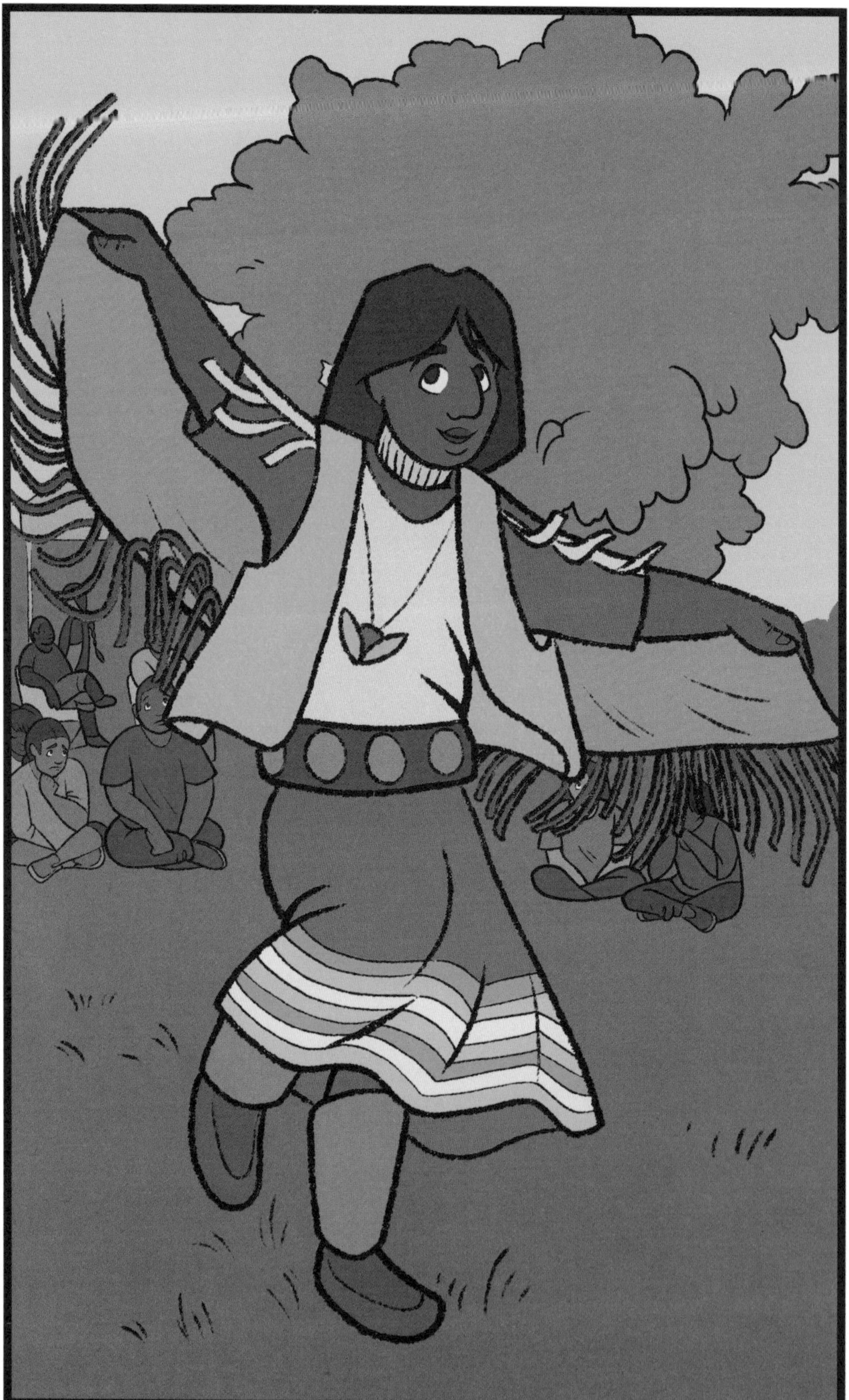

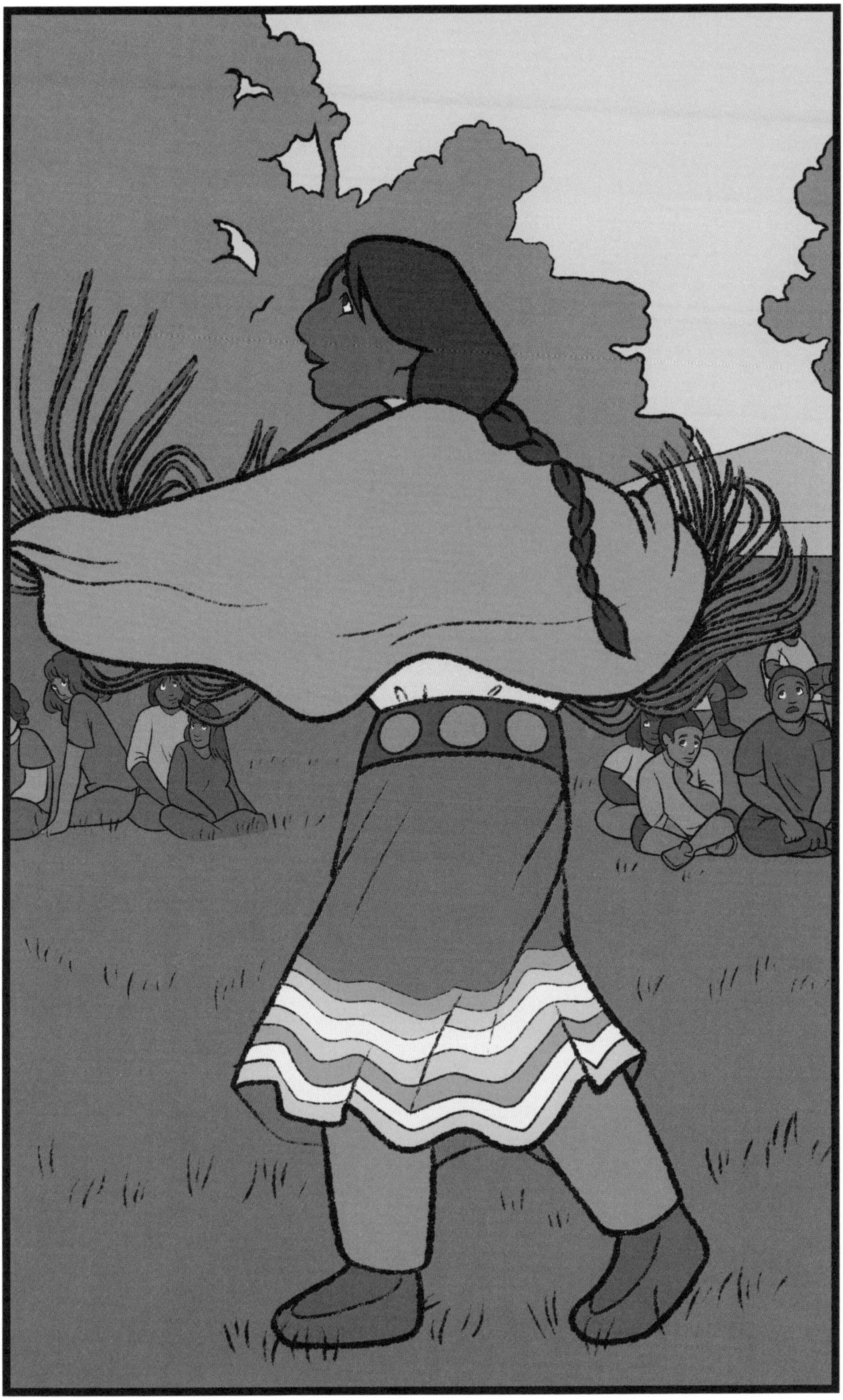

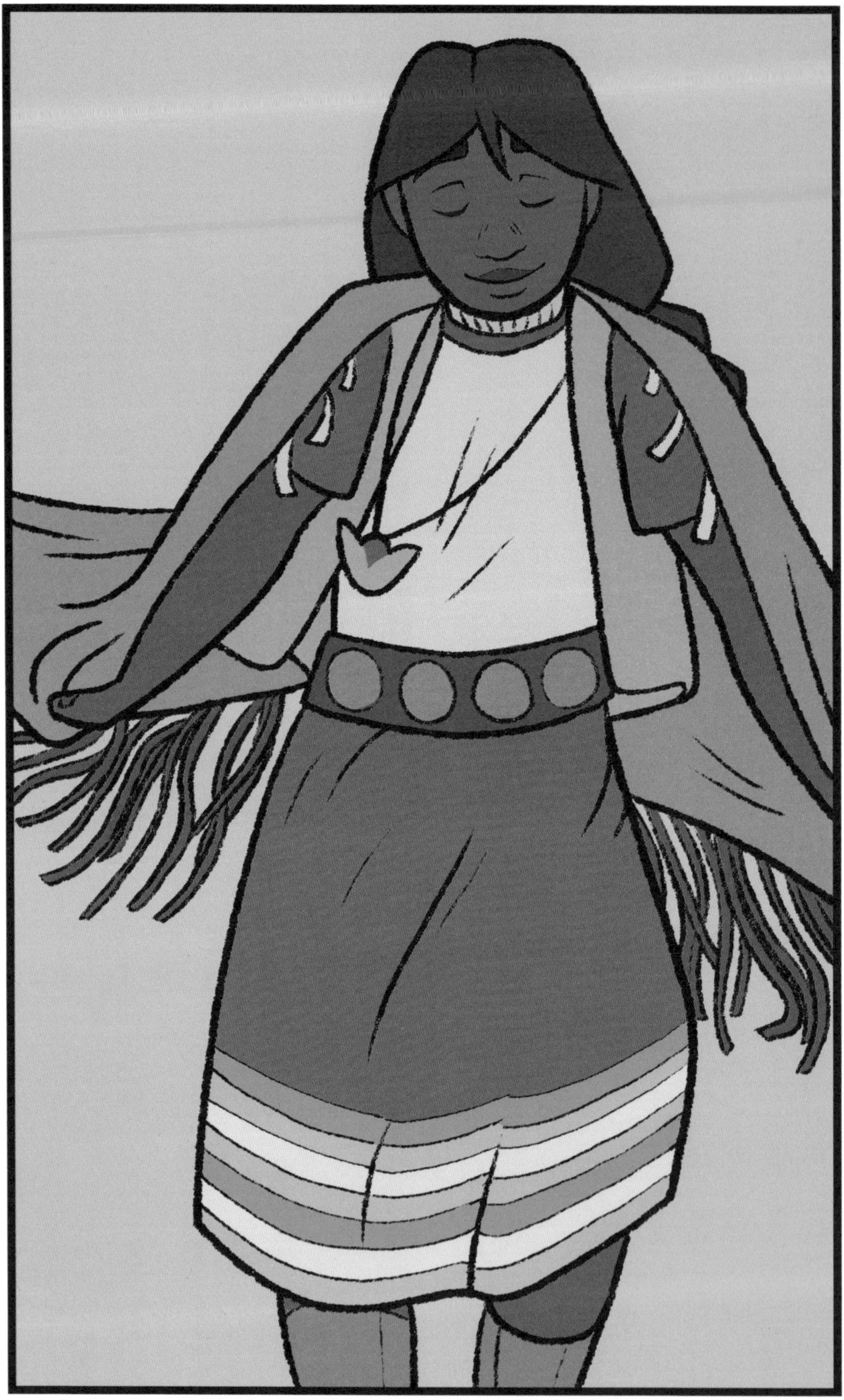

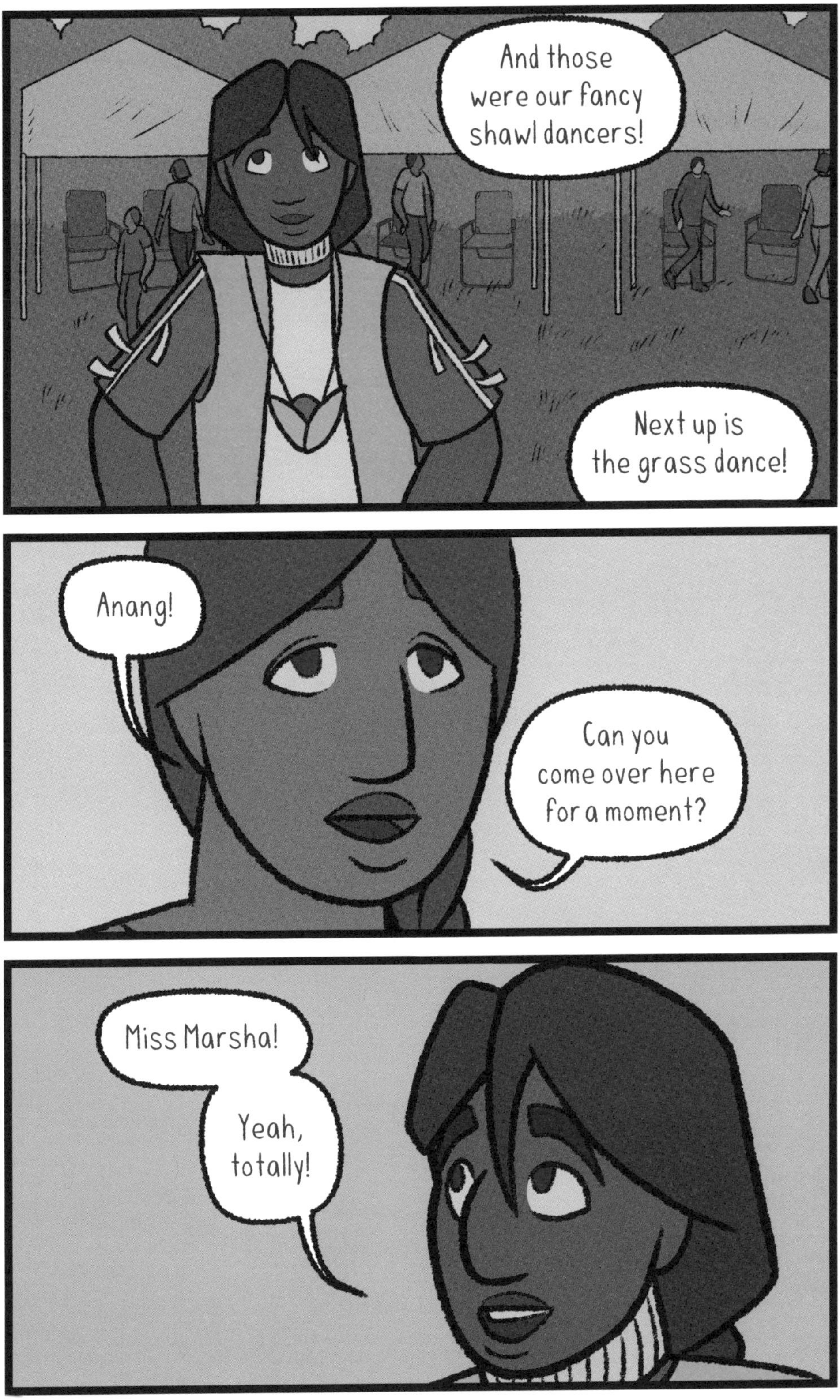
And those were our fancy shawl dancers!
Next up is the grass dance!
Anang!
Can you come over here for a moment?
Miss Marsha!
Yeah, totally!

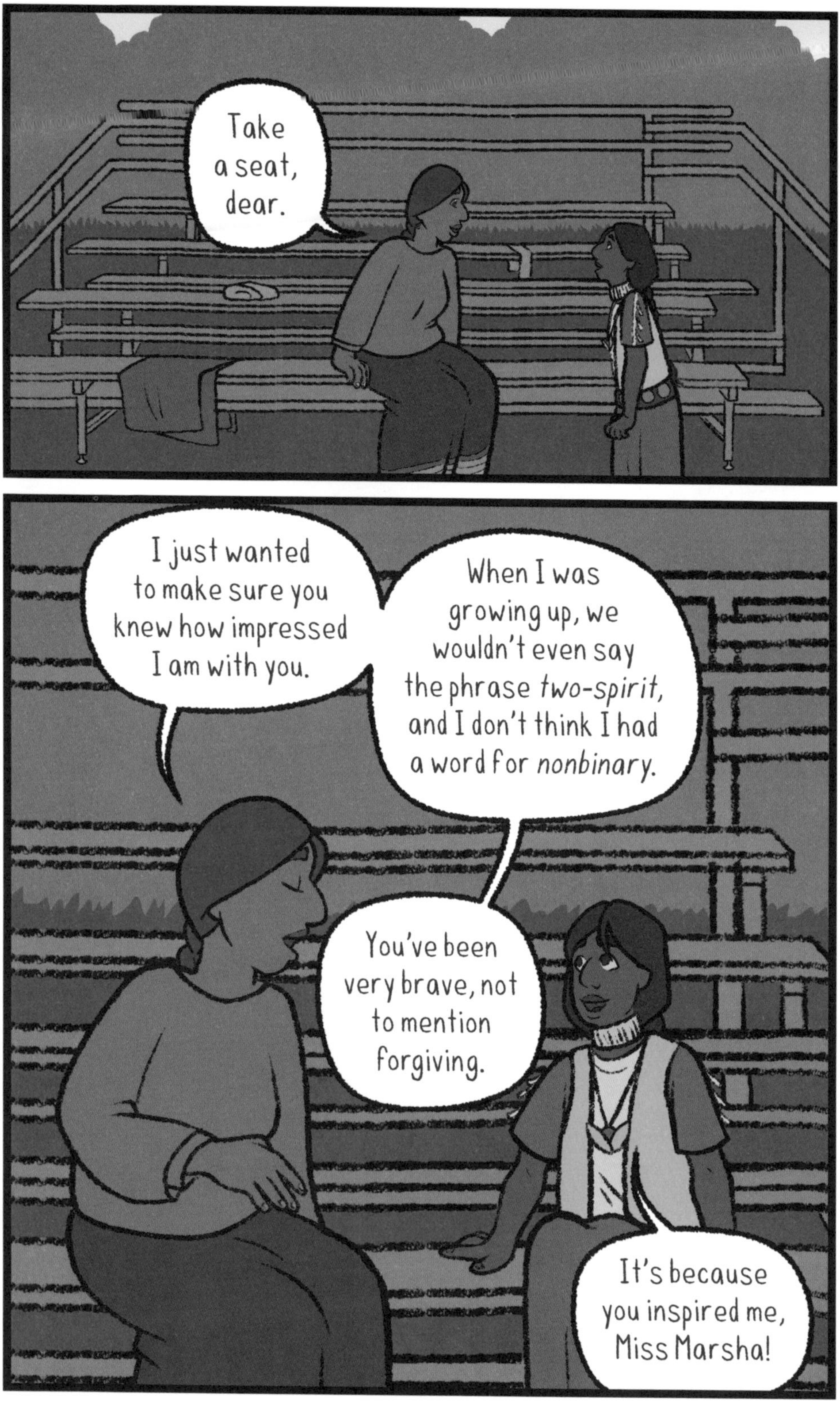
Take a seat, dear.
I just wanted to make sure you knew how impressed I am with you.
When I was growing up, we wouldn't even say the phrase *two-spirit*, and I don't think I had a word for *nonbinary*.
You've been very brave, not to mention forgiving.
It's because you inspired me, Miss Marsha!

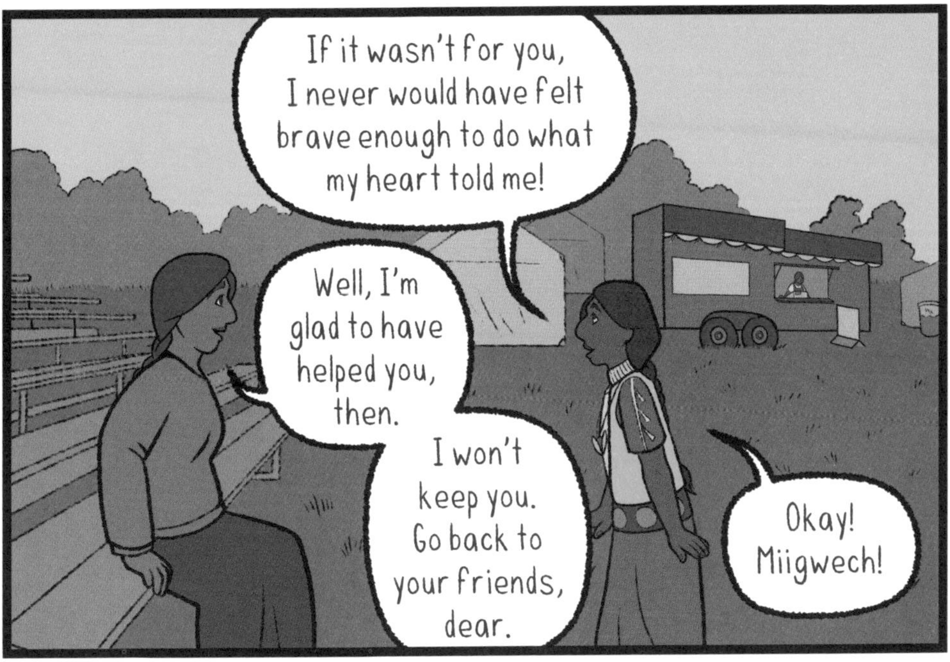
If it wasn't for you, I never would have felt brave enough to do what my heart told me!
Well, I'm glad to have helped you, then.
I won't keep you. Go back to your friends, dear.
Okay! Miigwech!

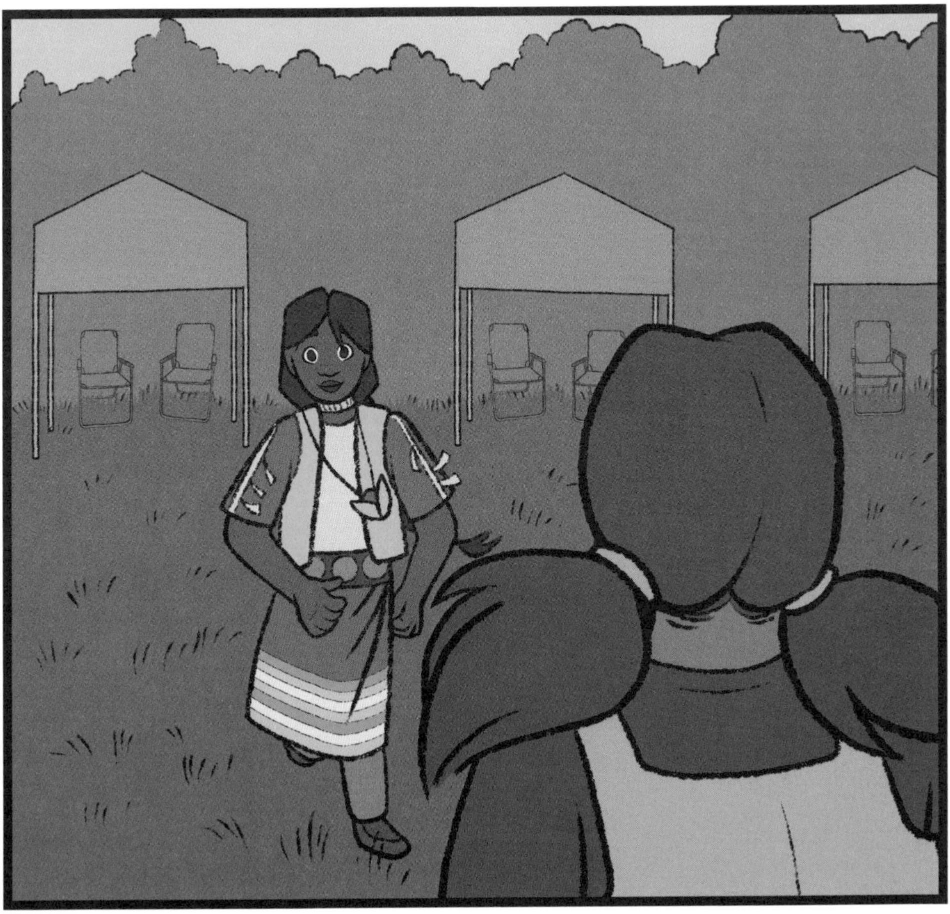

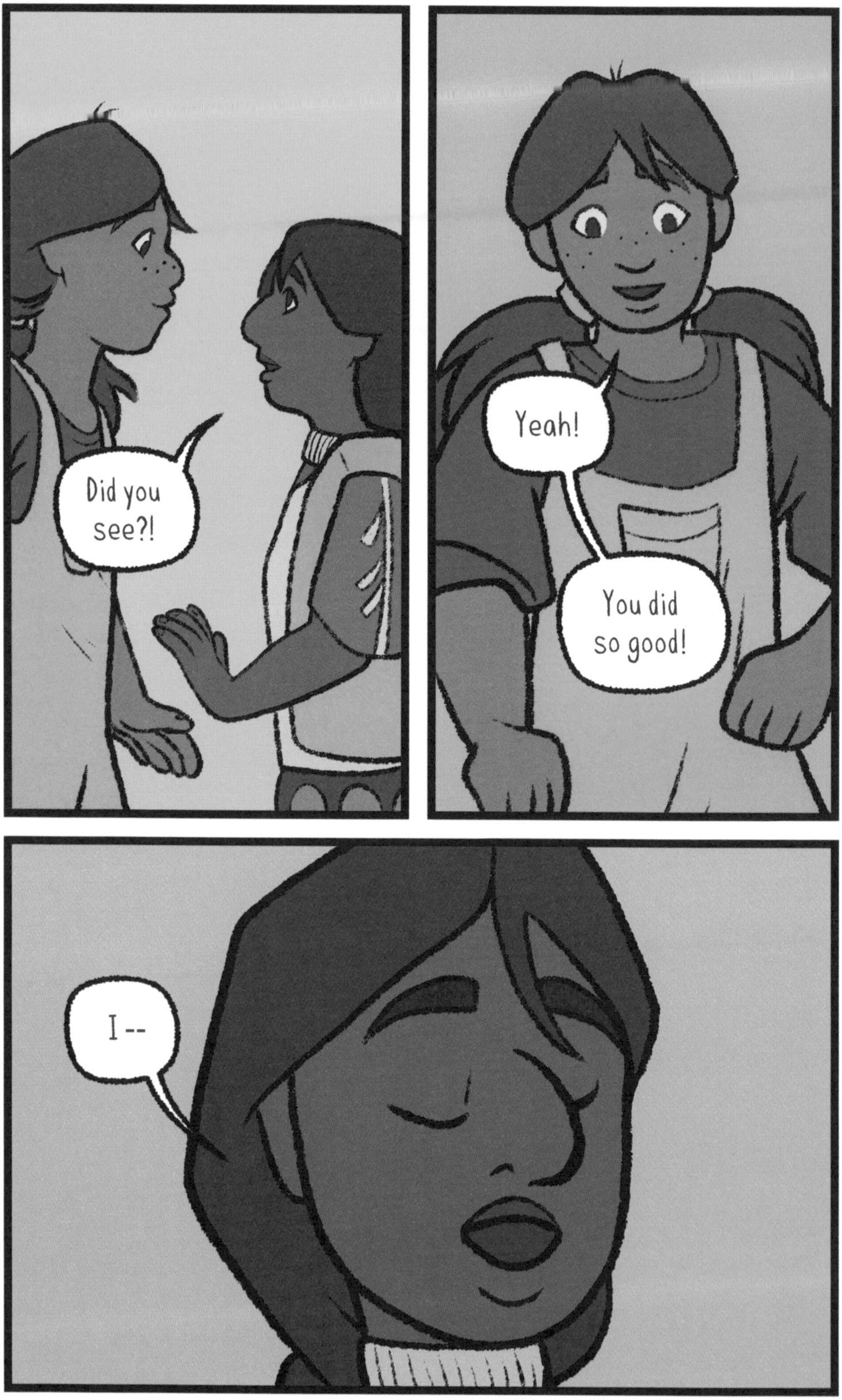
Did you see?!
Yeah!
You did so good!
I --

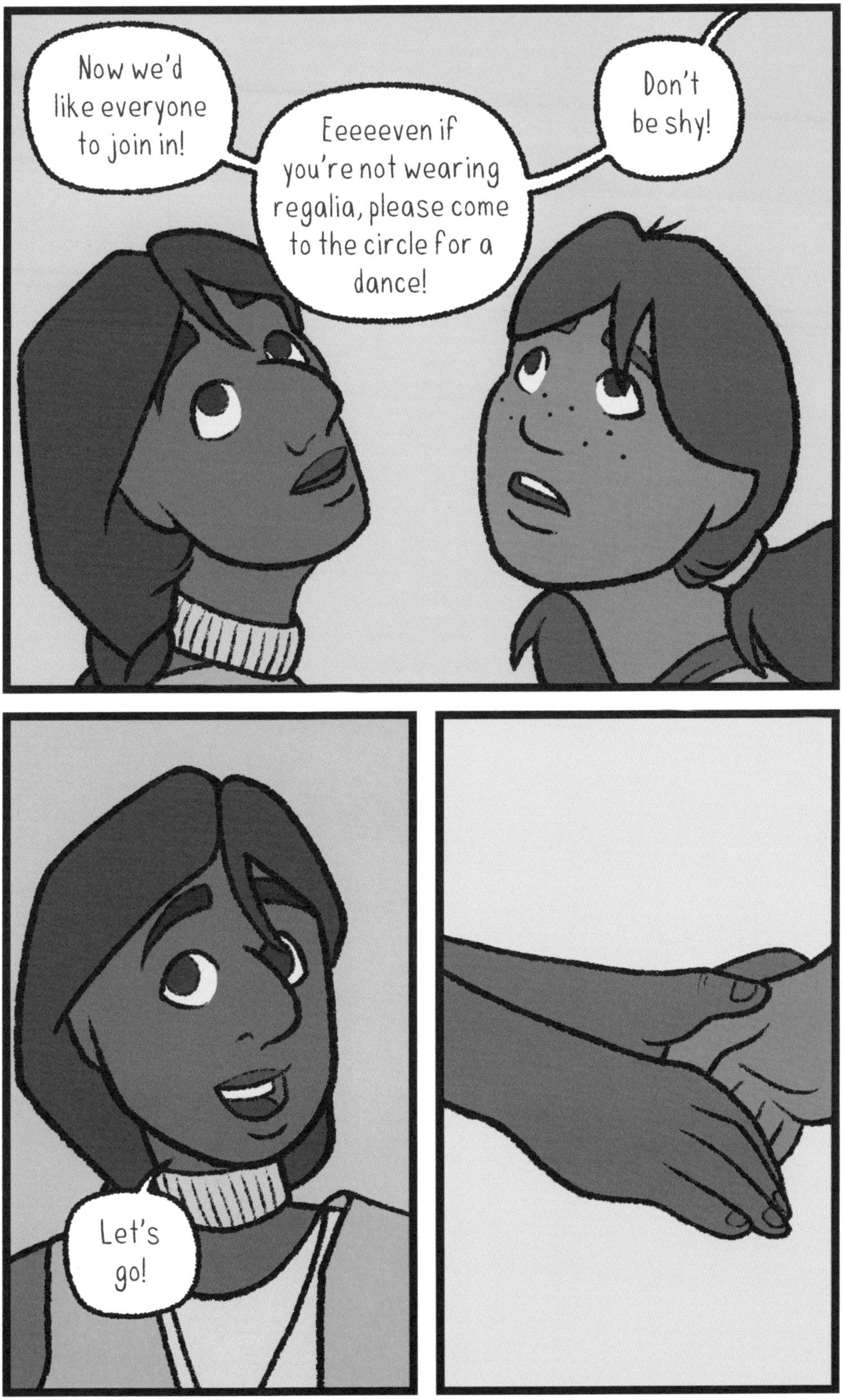
Now we'd like everyone to join in!
Eeeeeven if you're not wearing regalia, please come to the circle for a dance!
Don't be shy!
Let's go!

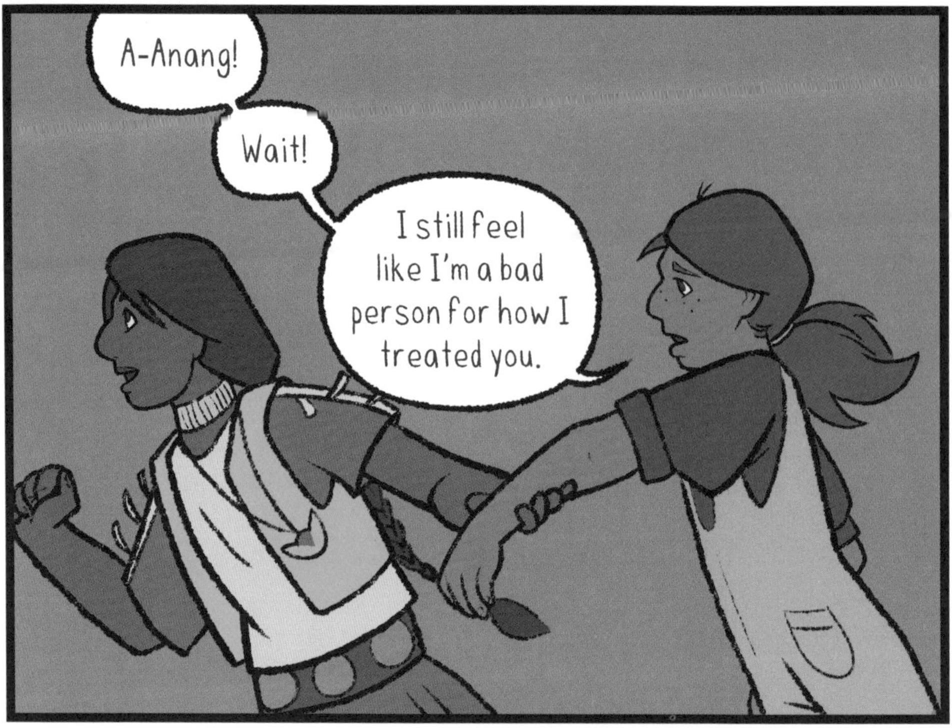
A-Anang!
Wait!
I still feel like I'm a bad person for how I treated you.

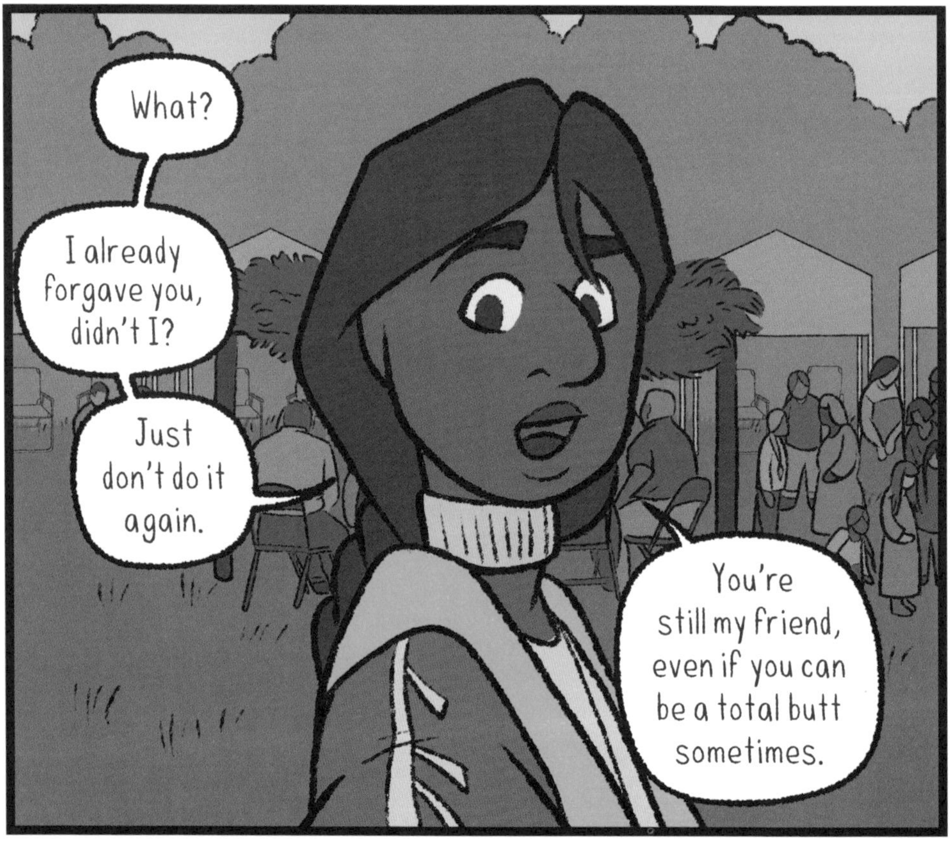
What?
I already forgave you, didn't I?
Just don't do it again.
You're still my friend, even if you can be a total butt sometimes.

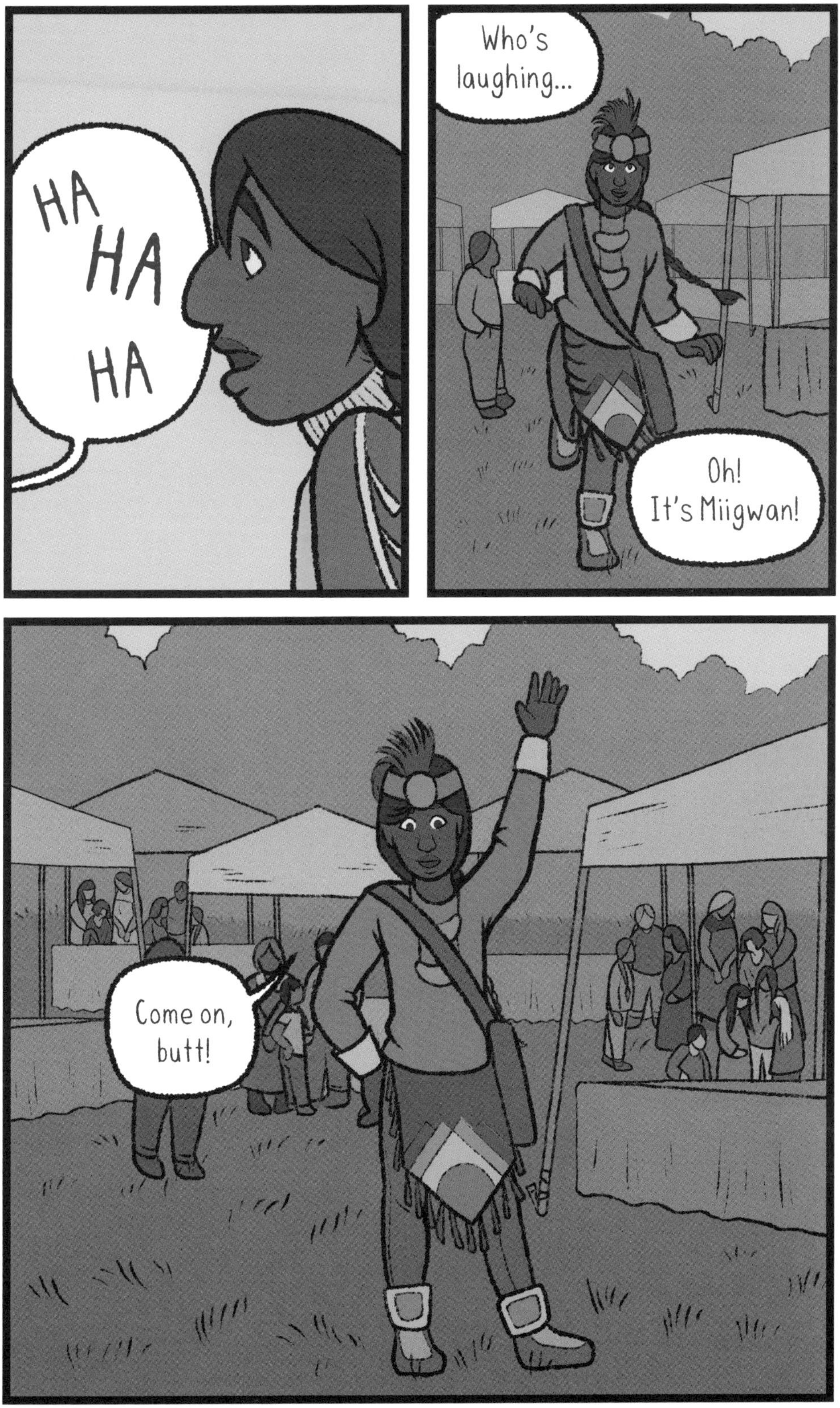
HA HA HA
Who's laughing...
Oh! It's Miigwan!
Come on, butt!

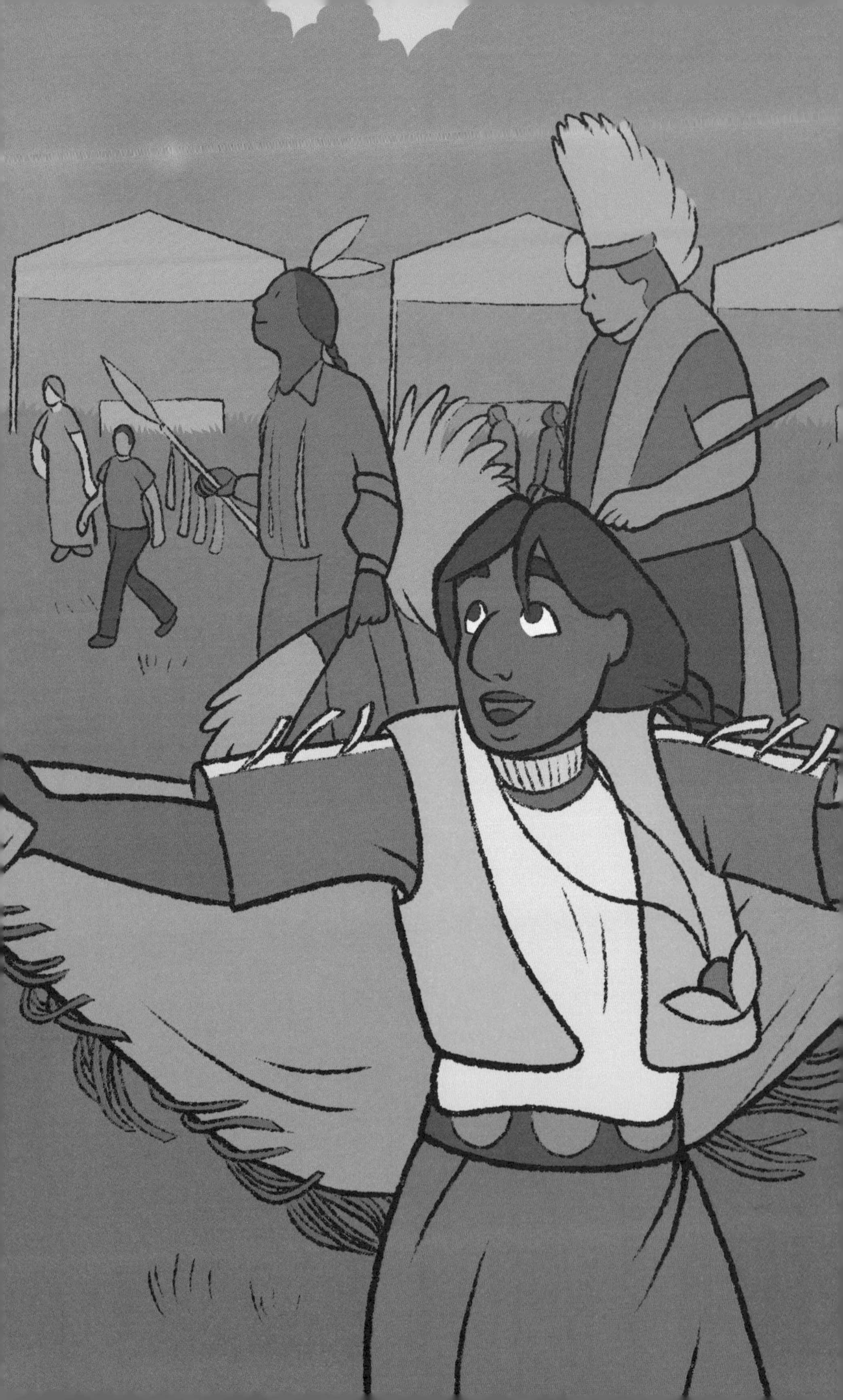

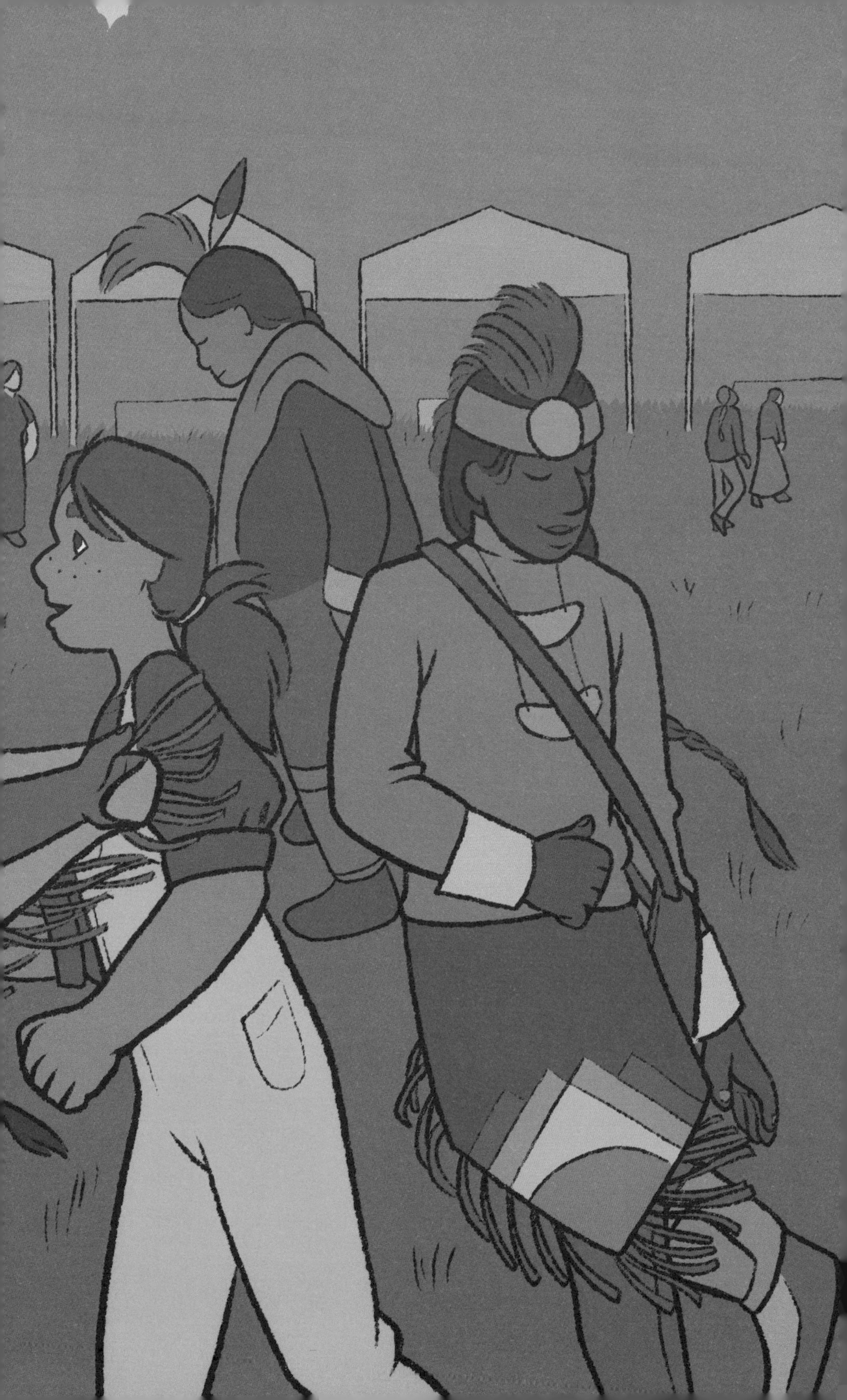

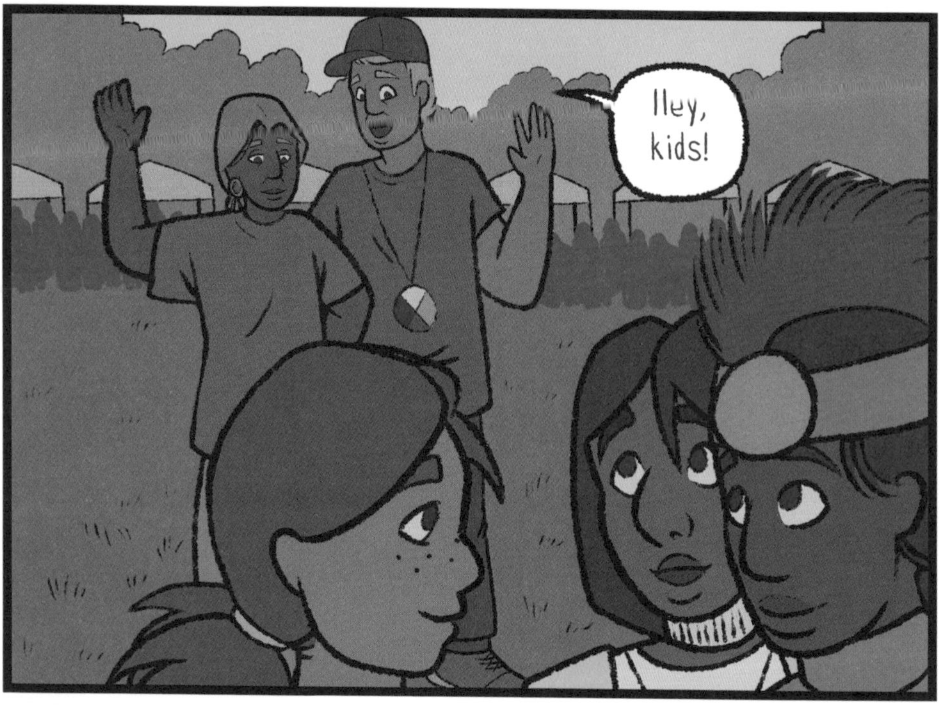
Hey, kids!

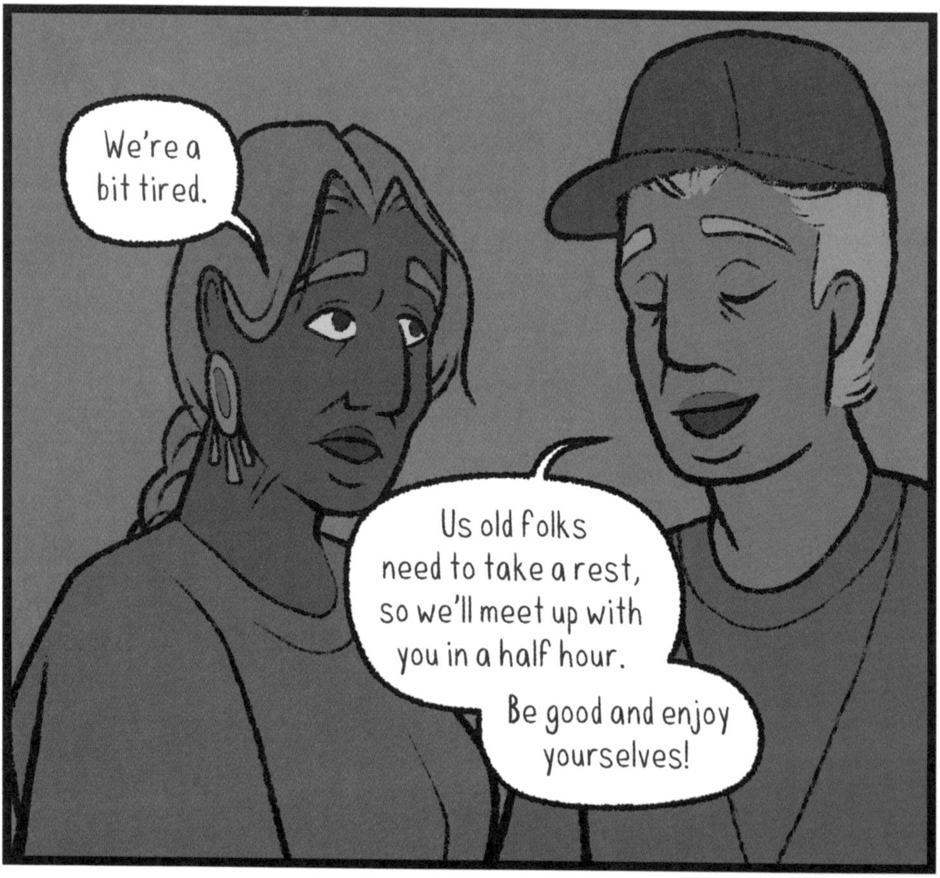
We're a bit tired.
Us old folks need to take a rest, so we'll meet up with you in a half hour.
Be good and enjoy yourselves!

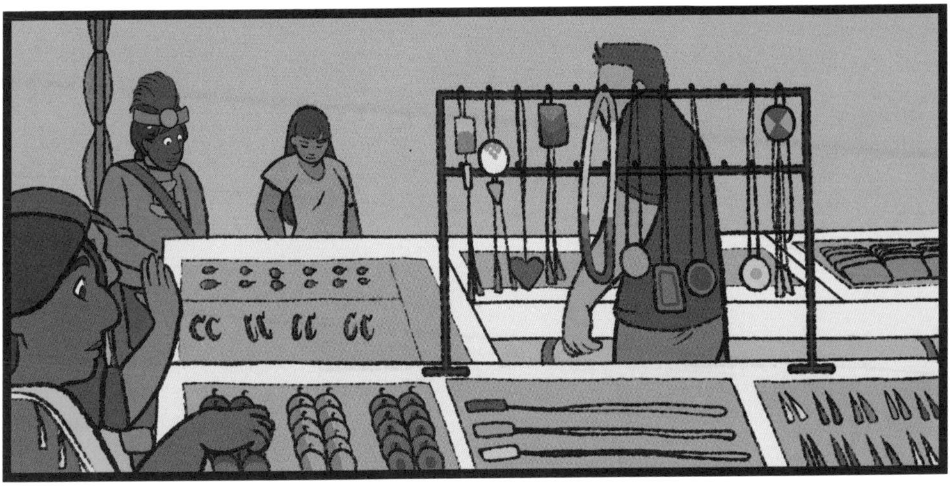

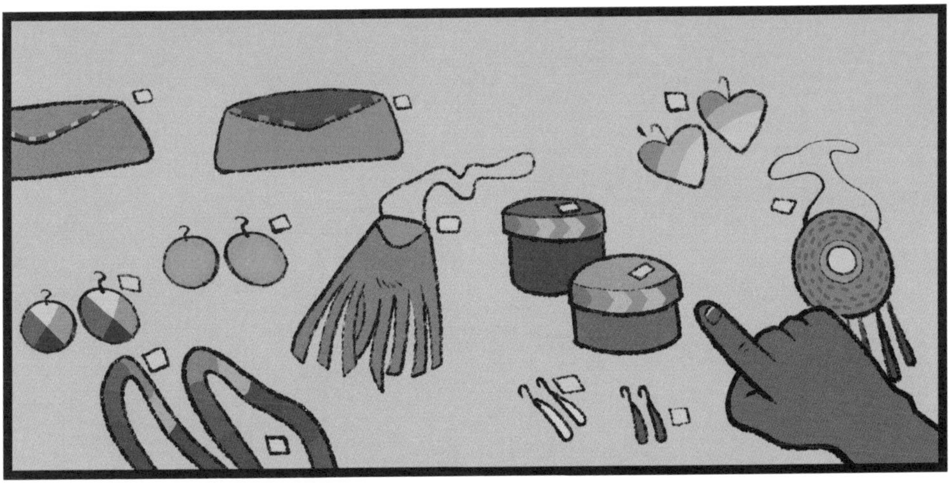

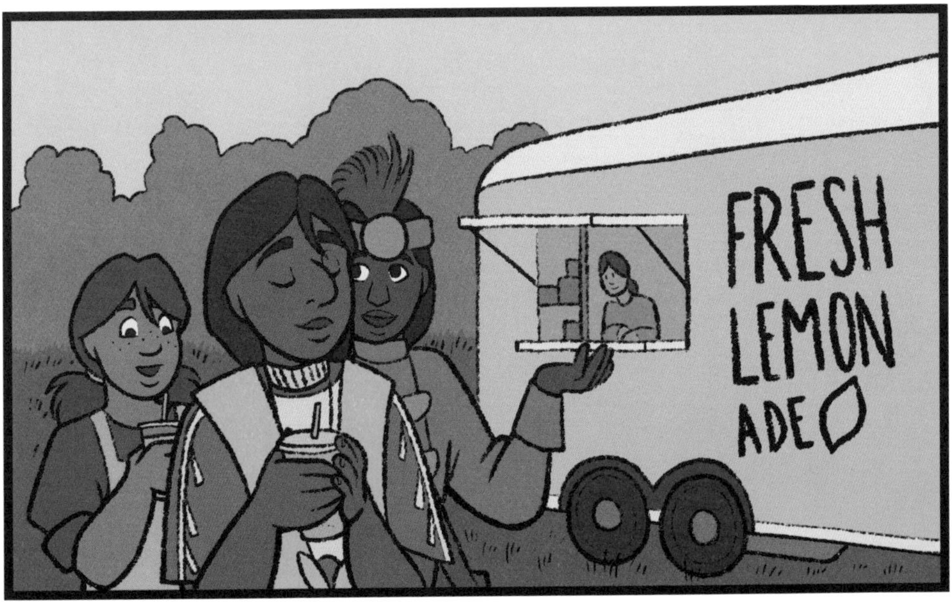
FRESH
LEMON
ADE

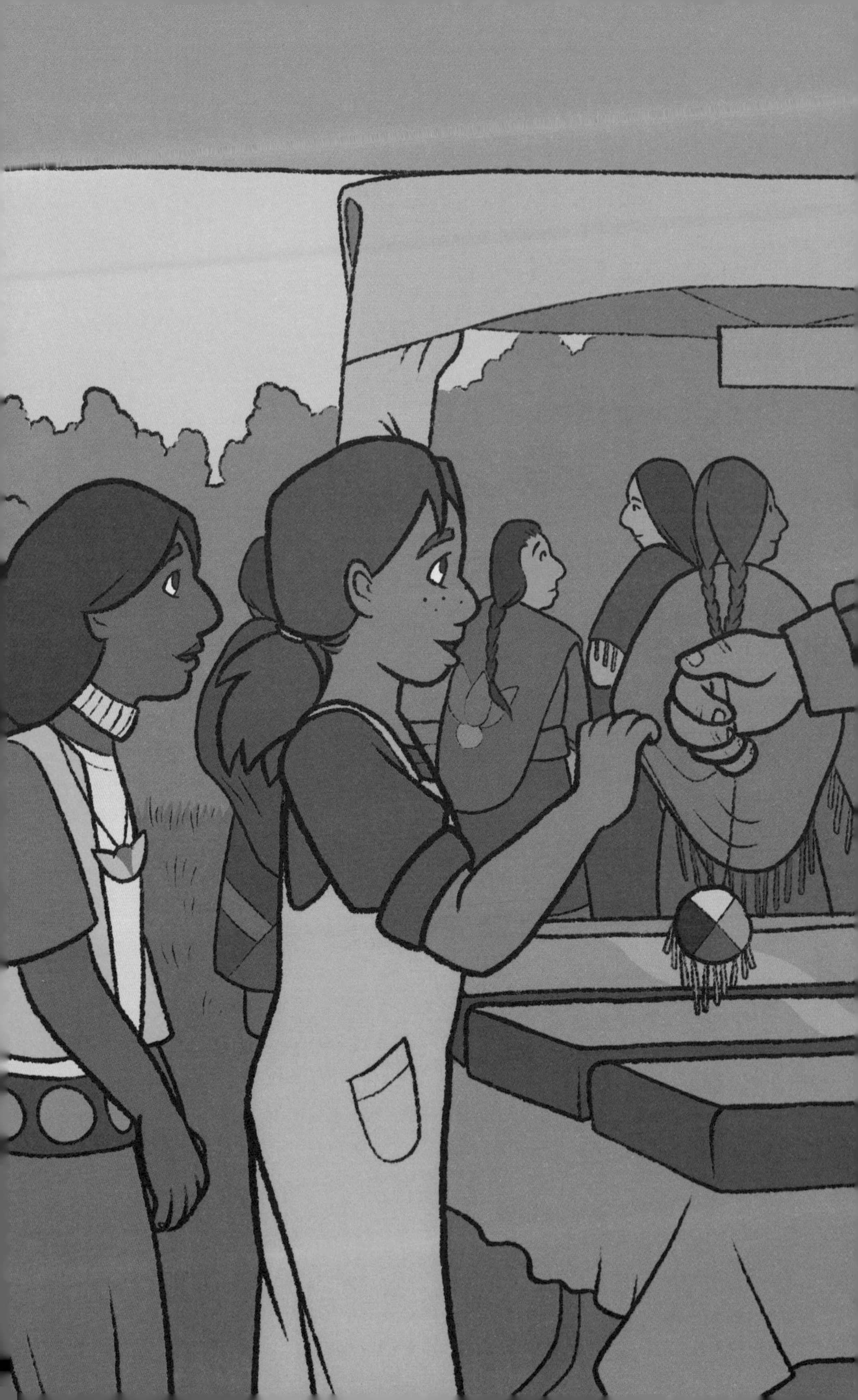

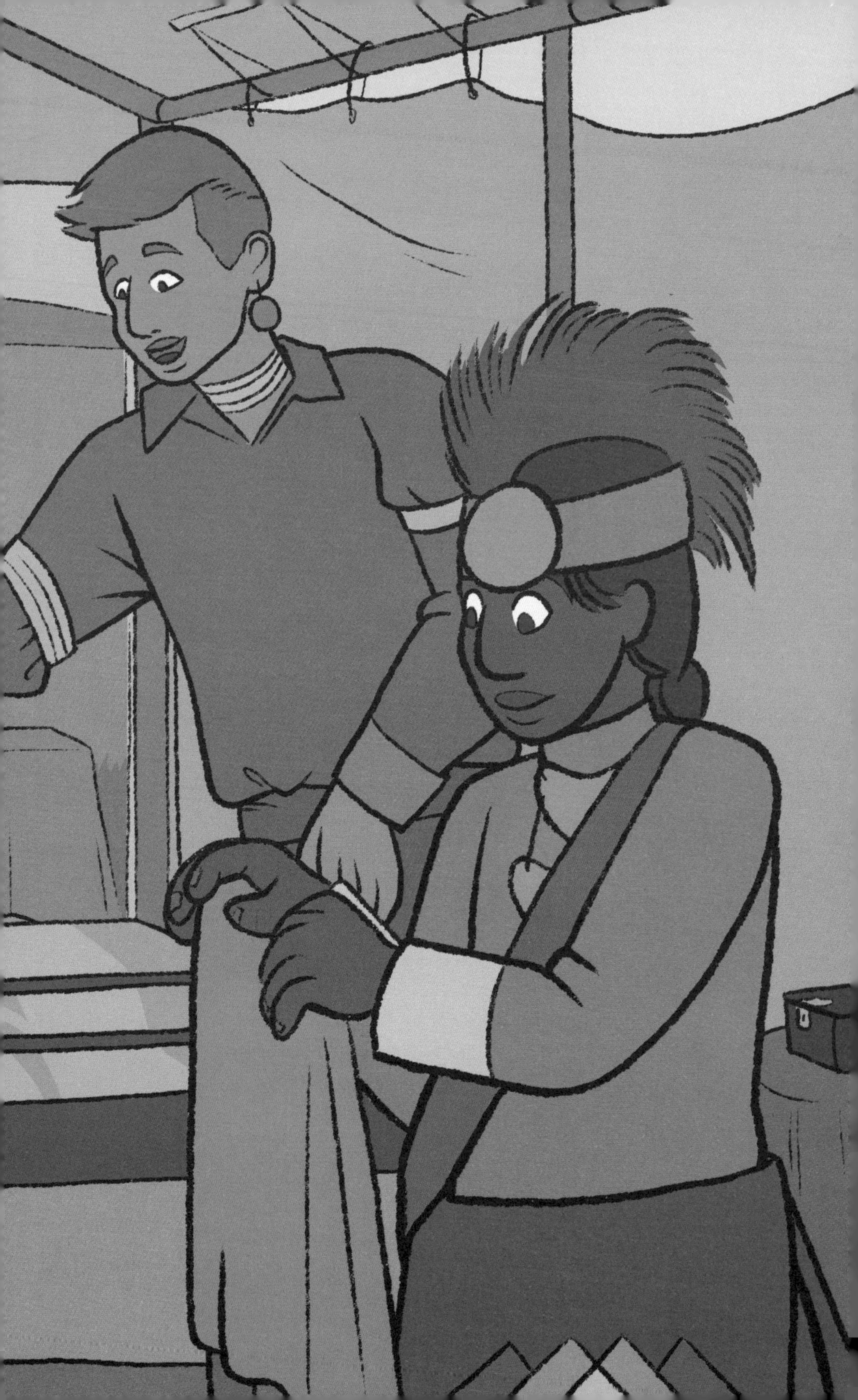

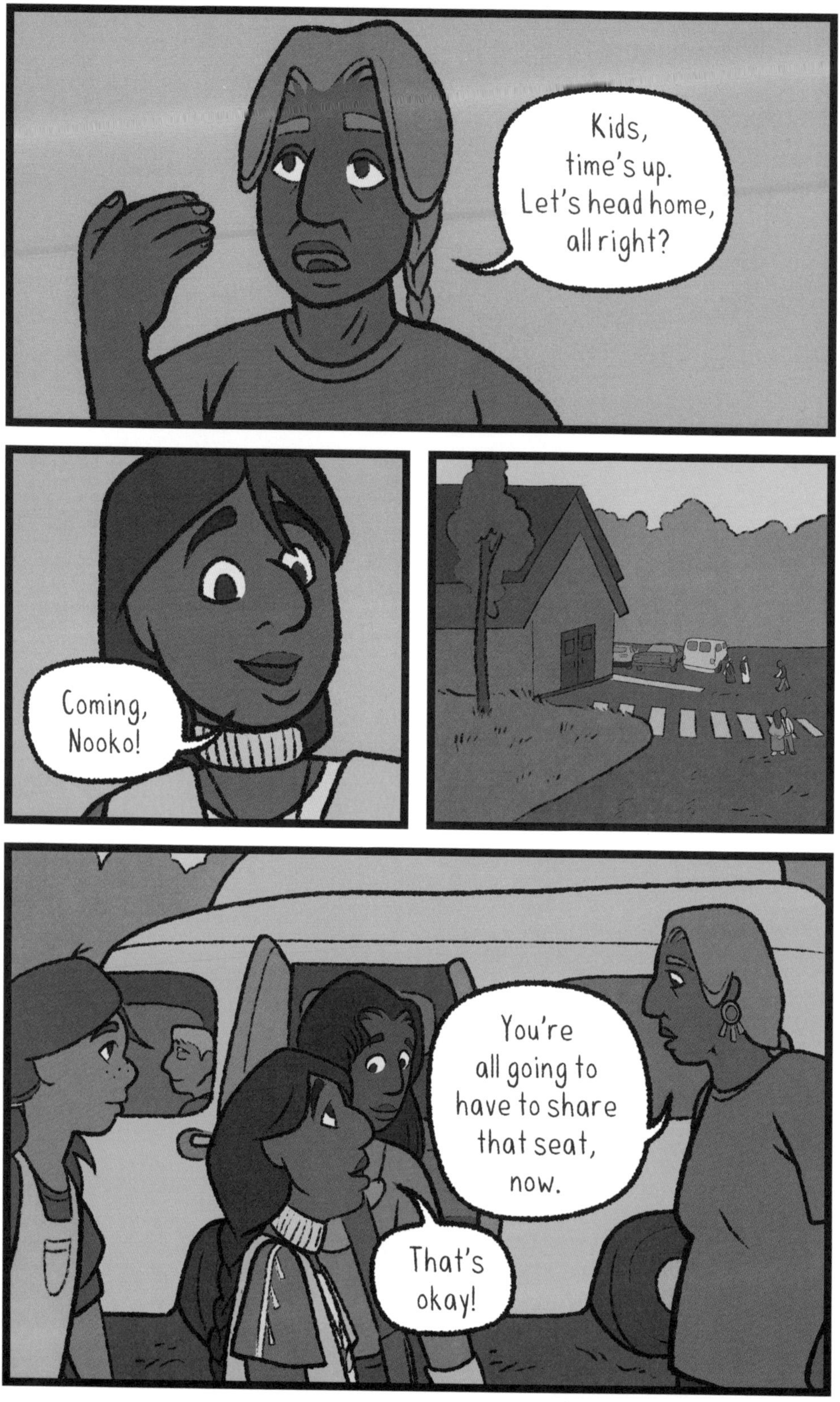
Kids, time's up. Let's head home, all right?
Coming, Nooko!
You're all going to have to share that seat, now.
That's okay!

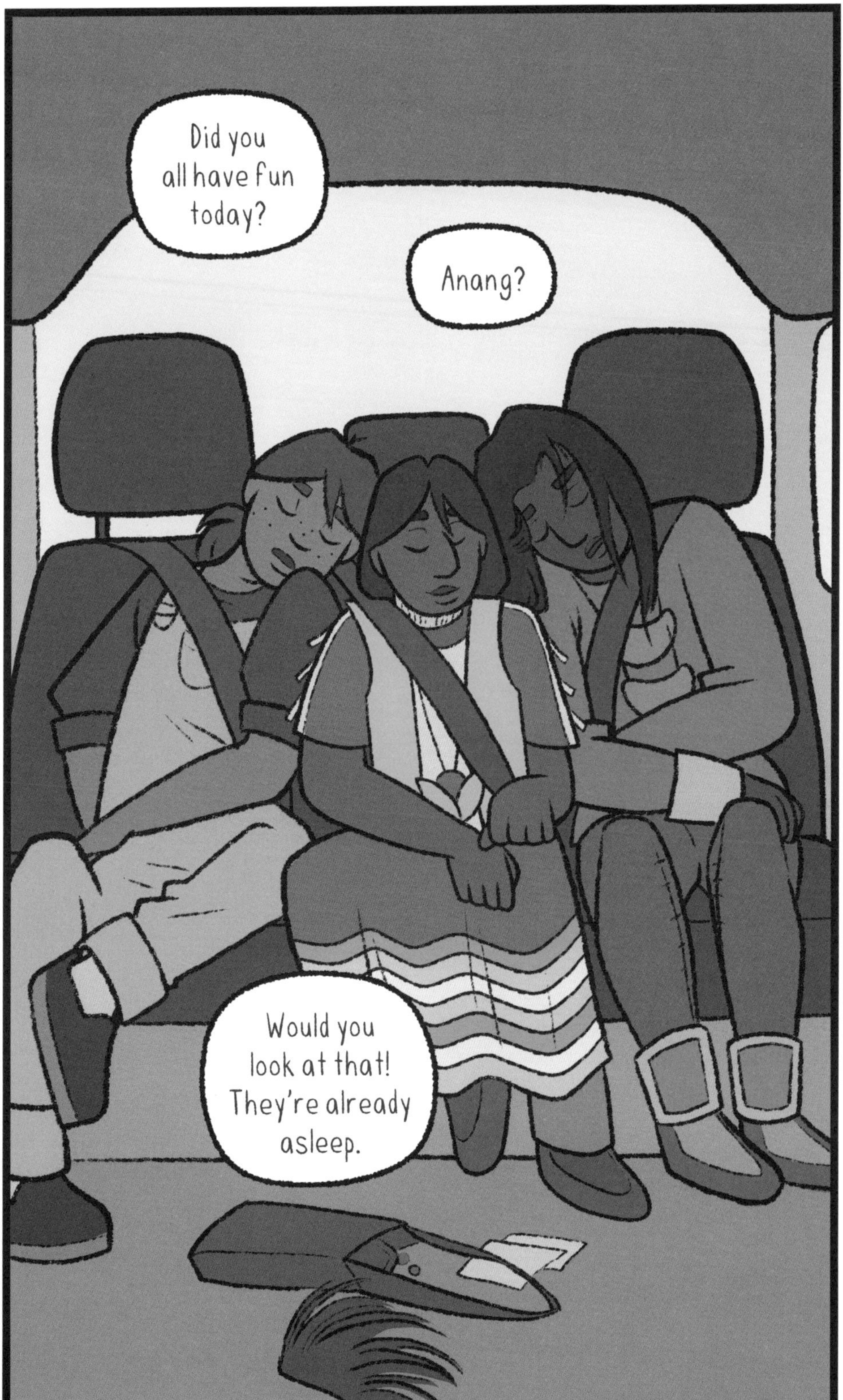
Did you all have fun today?
Anang?
Would you look at that! They're already asleep.

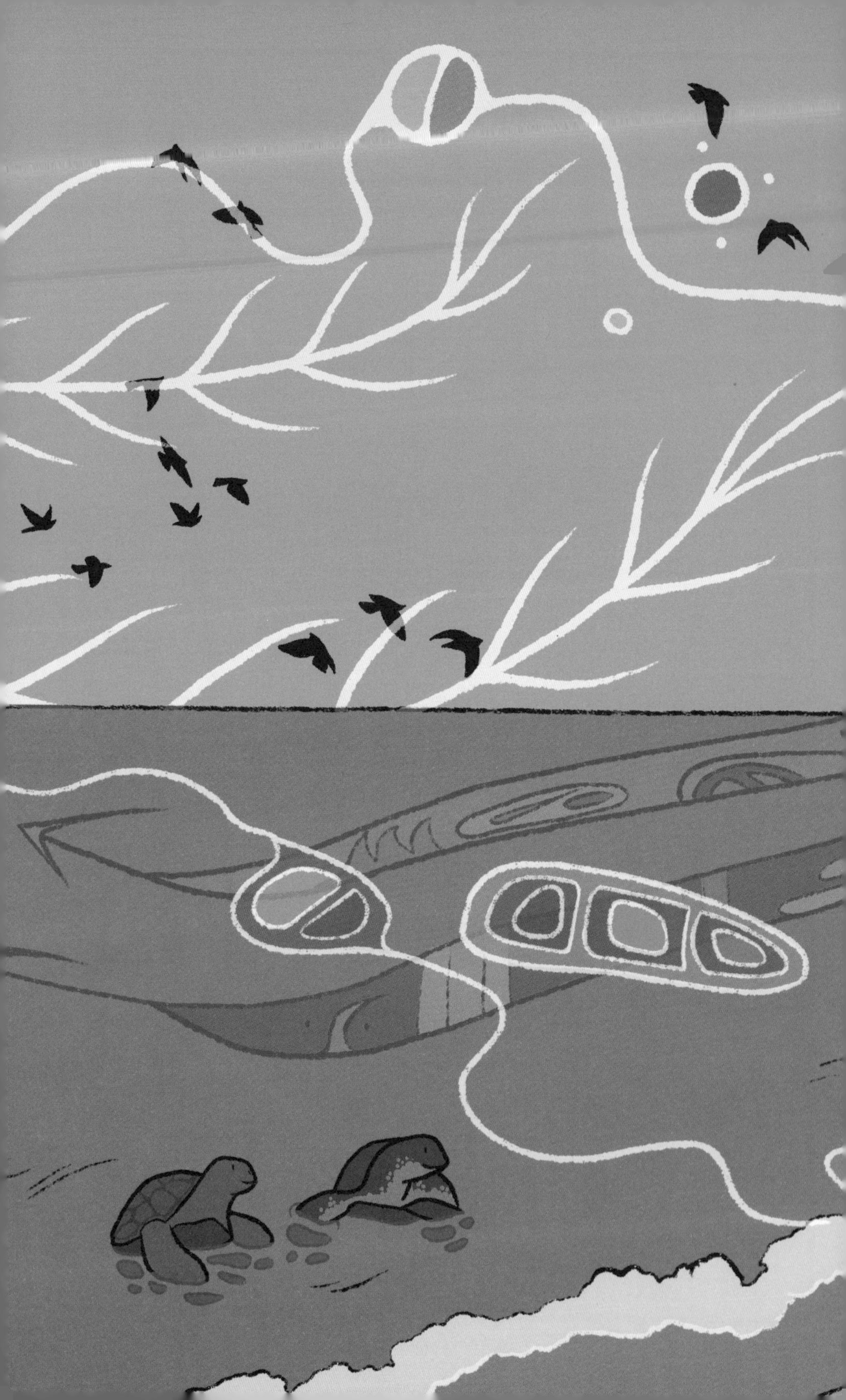

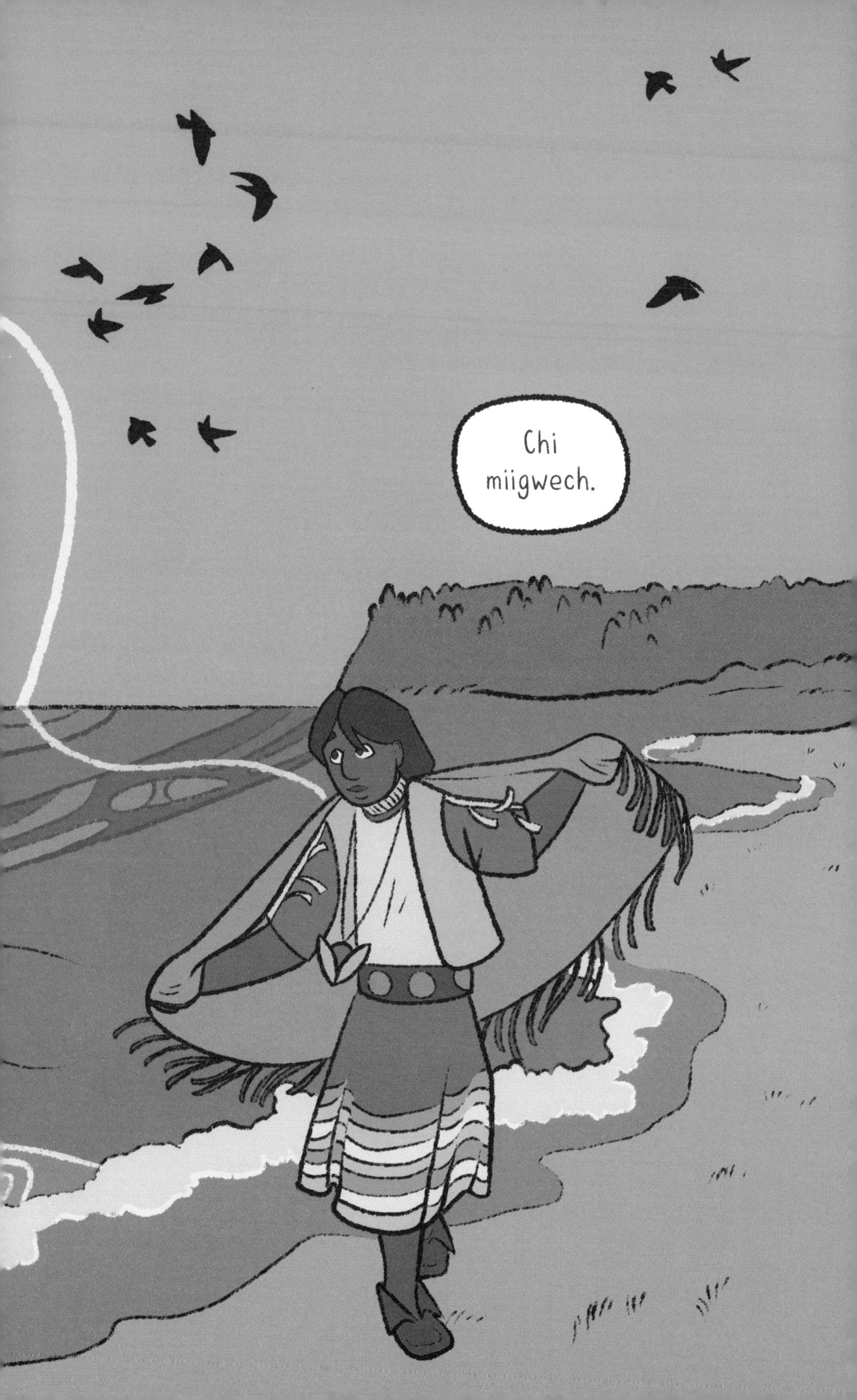
Chi miigwech.

GLOSSARY

All terms are translated from Southwestern Ojibwe, also known as Minnesota Dialect of Anishinaabemowin.

Aanii boozhoo: Hello
(This phrase has a meaning deeper than just being a greeting. It's also a phrase you would say to the Anishinaabe trickster hero, Nanabush. If the person flinches, they could be the trickster in human form.)

Aanii: Shortened form of hello

Anang: Star
(in this case, used as a name)

Chi miigwech: Many thanks
(literally translates to "big thank you")

Gichigami: Big lake

Gichi-jiimaan: Big canoe

Indizhinikaaz: My name is

Indoodem: My clan
(Anishinaabe families are organized by clan, such as beaver, deer, turtle, bear, and many others.)

Miigwan: Feather
(in this case, used as a name)

Miigwech: Thank you

Mino bimaadiziwin: The good life

Mishiikenh: Turtle

Mishomis: Grandfather

Nibi gizaagi'igoo, nimiigwechiwenimigoo, nibi gizhawenimigoo:
Water, we love you, we thank you, we respect you

Niishin: Good
(in this case, used as a name)

Niniijaanis: My child

Nookomis: Grandmother

Nooko: Shortened form of Nookomis, similar to how someone
might say *Granny* instead of *Grandma*

A HISTORY OF THE RIBBON SKIRT

The ribbon skirt is a form of fashion and art with a long history in Indigenous communities. Following early trade with French colonists, silk or taffeta ribbon was used to decorate edging as well as create full skirts as the art form developed. Like all Indigenous art of North America, colonization has disrupted this art form at different points throughout history. The ribbon skirt's resurgence as a form of expressive textile art in Indigenous communities is a testament to the resilience of the people who carry the stories and technologies behind the art. It is worn today by people of all ages and is most often seen at powwows or community events. For this book, the ribbon skirt was chosen as Anang's form of self-expression due to the pressure on two-spirit youth to fit into a gender binary. Ribbon skirts are often seen as women's clothing and are suggested to be worn for important cultural events and ceremonies. Many gender-nonconforming Indigenous people have chosen to reinterpret the ribbon skirt, creating ribbon pants and short skirts, or wearing clothing that does not represent (according to society's general expectations) the gender they were assigned at birth. In Anang's case, rather than choosing to dress in a way that makes certain members of their community comfortable, it is important that they dress in a way that is true to their heart.

A HISTORY OF POWWOWS

A powwow refers to a large gathering of Indigenous people to celebrate culture. These gatherings can be specific to one tribe, or intertribal, and both the length and cultural significance of the powwow depend on who is planning the event. However, dancing, drumming, and art and food vendors are almost always included in the event. The name "powwow" originally comes from the Narrtick term "Pau Wau," which means "medicine man." Over time, this term was incorrectly applied to meetings of Indigenous medicine people, eventually being used to refer to any group of Indigenous people meeting together.

As colonization continued, Indigenous people were generally not allowed to hold traditional cultural gatherings and would have been punished for criminal behavior if they were found to still be following their traditions. In some parts of the country, such as Michigan, powwows were allowed as a tourist event, meant to bring more visitors into the area. Many mainstays of the powwow today come from a period of oppression, where Indigenous people forced from their homes had to move into the lands of other tribes, resulting in intertribal exchange. Anang can be seen participating in the women's fancy shawl dance near the end of this story, which is practiced by Indigenous people across North America today.

In Anang's time, powwows have become a popular event in the summer, and are a way for their tribe and many others to celebrate traditional dances and food. Many artists from Indigenous communities sell their artwork at powwows, such as traditional clothing, ribbon skirts, beadwork, jewelry, and much more. These events are open to people of all backgrounds, unless otherwise mentioned. That means you can go to a powwow, too!

GOING TO YOUR FIRST POWWOW

If you aren't Indigenous and have never been to a powwow before, there are a few things to keep in mind. First, acknowledge that you are a guest. It's important to realize that you may not understand everything happening, and that's okay. This is a celebration of Indigenous culture, which is a beautiful thing! Second, this is not a reenactment. The people you see at a powwow are expressing their modern selves. Whether the dancers are in regalia (a word for traditional clothing, *not* costume) or not, everyone at powwow has gathered to celebrate our continued survival. It's important for guests to remember that a powwow is different from a museum, and not an opportunity to take pictures unless you first check with the person you would like to photograph. There are many reasons to say no, such as religious reasons, privacy, or just not liking photos very much. Always ask! Lastly, remember that the dancers in their regalia are wearing artwork. Please do not touch their clothing or hair, even if it's tempting.

That's a lot of don'ts, but what *can* you do? Well, make sure to support the vendors! Indigenous artists rely on powwows to make money for their families, and buying art is a great way to help. You can't walk through the powwow grounds without smelling delicious frybread and corn soup, so give it a try — you won't be able to get it anywhere else! And of course, make sure you sit in the stands and enjoy the music and dancing, and help celebrate Indigenous resilience.

WHAT IS TWO-SPIRIT?

The phrase "two-spirit" generally refers to people who are both Indigenous and experience a sexuality other than heterosexuality or identify with a different gender than they were assigned at birth. An Indigenous person might use the term two-spirit to describe themselves if they are a man attracted to another man, transgender, or have an experience with gender and/or sexuality that does not match what is considered normal in mainstream American society. Many cultures have their own terms for two-spirit. The words "two-spirit" were originally proposed as a blanket term for Indigenous people who fall on the LGBTQIA+ spectrum during the 1990 Third Annual Intertribal Native American, First Nations, Gay and Lesbian American Conference by elder Myra Laramee. This term is a direct translation from the Anishinaabemowin words "niizh manidoowag," which literally mean "two spirits." While it is commonly understood that being two-spirit means that someone has both a male and female spirit, that is an oversimplification. Each culture has its own understanding of what it means to be two-spirit, as does every individual who identifies as two-spirit. Not all Indigenous LGBTQIA+ people identify as two-spirit, but all two-spirit people are Indigenous.

MANOOMIN (WILD RICE) BERRY SALAD RECIPE

One of the dishes that Nookomis often serves is a manoomin berry salad, which is a very fun and easy meal to make! Manoomin can also be referred to as wild rice, which might sound more familiar to you. This dish can be served hot or cold at any time of year. Make sure to personalize it to your taste!

Ingredients:

- 1 cup manoomin / wild rice, uncooked
- 1 to 1¼ cup fresh berries
  (Use what's in season! Strawberries and blueberries are always great picks, but raspberries also work well in this recipe.)
- ⅓ cup real maple syrup
  (Support Indigenous people who make maple syrup, if possible.)
- Spices
  (You can adjust the flavor to your taste and what berries are in season, but black pepper and cinnamon are a good start.)

Instructions:

Heat a medium-sized pot at medium low. Add 1 cup manoomin and 2½ cups of water to the pot, then cover. Cook for 45 minutes or until the water has been absorbed by the manoomin. The rice should look as if it has "popped" and give off a fragrant aroma. Turn off the heat and then add berries, maple syrup, and spices. Stir the manoomin mixture until combined, tasting and adjusting sweetness or spices as needed. Serve and enjoy!

BIBLIOGRAPHY

"American Indian Powwows: Multiplicity and Authenticity — History." Smithsonian Center for Folklife & Cultural Heritage. Accessed October 17, 2023. https://folklife.si.edu/online-exhibitions/american-indian-powwows/history/smithsonian.

Heitland, Kaija. "What Is a Ribbon Skirt?" The Ribbon Skirt Project — from Indigenous Nouveau, 2022. https://www.theribbonskirtproject.ca/whatisaribbonskirt.

"History of American Indian Ribbonwork." Milwaukee Public Museum. Accessed October 17, 2023. https://www.mpm.edu/research-collections/anthropology/online-collections-research/ribbonwork-woodland-indians/history-an.

"Manoomin Salad." Mill City Farmers Market. Accessed October 17, 2023. https://millcityfarmersmarket.org/recipes/manoomin-salad.

Oxendine, Jamie K. "History of the Powwow — Origin & Background — Native American." PowWows.com, October 3, 2023. https://www.powwows.com/history-of-the-powwow.

"Story of the Ribbon Skirt." Seven Generations Education Institute, March 16, 2023. https://www.7generations.org/story-of-the-ribbon-skirt.

"Two-Spirit." Indian Health Service. Accessed October 17, 2023. https://www.ihs.gov/lgbt/health/twospirit.

"Two-Spirit Community." Researching for LGBTQ2S Health. Accessed October 17, 2023. https://lgbtqhealth.ca/community/two-spirit.php.

Weasel Traveller, Serene. "Ribbon Skirt Tutorial." Galt Museum & Archives, May 19, 2021. https://www.galtmuseum.com/articles/ribbon-skirt-tutorial.

What Does "Two-Spirit" Mean? | InQueery | them. YouTube, 2018. https://www.youtube.com/watch?v=A4IBibGzUnE.

CAMERON MUKWA is a two-spirit
Anishinaabe cartoonist, illustrator, and children's
educator whose portfolio of work is dedicated
to showcasing Indigenous and transgender joy.
The Ribbon Skirt is his first graphic novel. Visit
him online at cameronmukwa.com.